CLAN

CARL WASIELEWSKI

ISBN 979-8-9935127-1-6 (paperback)
ISBN 979-8-9935127-0-9 (ebook)
ISBN 979-8-9935127-2-3 (audiobook)

Library of Congress Control Number: 2025923076

Book Cover by Idilia Copertino

First Edition 2025

For Family

it's all there ever was

PART 1

CHAPTER ONE

There are things that are right, and there are things that are wrong, and sometimes, you do them anyway. Rip thought this as he rolled the rocks in his pocket, his thumb and his forefinger caressing the drugs and feeling their power.

He shouldn't be touching them. This, he knew. It was like picking at a scab: all you get is a finger stained with blood, and maybe, later, a scar.

But it felt so good.

He glanced at Grandma, lifting his head ever so slightly to let her know that, yeah, he knew she was there, and no, he didn't care. But Grandma just stared back. She wasn't the type to be intimidated. Rip wasn't doing right, and she knew it.

Rip knew it wasn't the wrong that bothered her. After all, wrongs just pile up and there isn't much you can do about them. But who was doing the wronging? Yeah, that bothered her. Rip watched her expand. He saw her iron back stiffen with rage, saw the giant rising to smite him. Smite him as the Lord crusheth the Israelites, whom he loved.

"Man, Grandma. Just leave me alone."

Do other people's dead grandmothers haunt them, Rip wondered?

Grandma stared at him when he was in the car with that girl last year. She glowered at him as he smoked out back in the alley. She glared at him when he walked out of the guidance counselor's office, slammed the door, and told the counselor he could go to hell.

But oh Sweet Lord, he had never seen Grandma stare like this. He had never felt the anger radiate off of her like noontime sun on a summer's day. Rip got it: she was angry because she was looking at the biggest goddamn fool the universe had ever seen, her own flesh and blood, and all she could do was stare and call upon her unquenchable righteousness to save him.

And it wasn't going to work.

Rip felt the rocks in his pocket freezing his body to ice. He knew people saw his thin bones and delicate angular face and thought they needed to protect him. But his thin bones were elegant, his muscles stronger than they knew. His eyes only looked around so much because he was seeing more than other people saw. Rip looked around at the moldering old mansions broken into rooming houses, the big apartment buildings halved into smaller ones, the vacant lots a reminder that something once stood there. His family, generations of them, had built those blocks. Now his family was gone. Other people couldn't see them anymore, but Rip could see them, and they were staring at him.

And so he laughed. It was the kind of laugh you use to prove you aren't scared. He laughed even louder when he thought about his brother. Unlike Grandma, who was dead, and whose ghost could only haunt him, his brother was all too real. If Cornelius were here and knew what he was doing, he would beat, kick, punch, knock, and stomp him down. And then, just to make sure he got the picture, he'd pick Rip off the ground, dust him off, and beat him again. That's what Cornelius thought "helping" was.

The only thing worse than what his brother would do to Rip though, was what he would do to the man who put these rocks in his pocket. That man would wish he wasn't alive after Cornelius was through with him, and honestly, he probably wouldn't be.

But Cornelius wasn't there, and neither was his family. His friends and neighbors . . . they weren't there either. Grandma was there, but she was nothing more than an angry ghost, shimmering in the air and hardly even talking anymore. Everyone else was gone. Rip was the only one left.

Rip stayed planted on his corner, his firm young roots straining the potted soil.

The police car startled him. It couldn't be more than a hundred feet away. Where did that thing come from? He didn't like that thing here. He began to walk away, but then he remembered that walking away looked suspicious, so he stopped.

He saw the Corner Boys start giggling out of the corner of his eye:

"Man, you can't be walking away from a police car when they are right on top of you," one of them said.

"You got to walk away before they even hit the block!" another chimed in.

"And if your dumb ass missed them until they got there, well you might as well stand there and stare, cause if you walk away now, they will surely know something dirty about you."

"Them ignorant-ass officers don't know nothing, but they can smell fear, and you walking away stinks as bad as the load of crap you dropped in the toilet last night."

The Corner Boys laughed and laughed and laughed, like they always did.

Rip knew they laughed to drown out the stink of their own fear. He could see through them (literally, they were just ghosts

—shimmering little losers that appeared whenever he least wanted them to). But for some reason, Rip still cared what they thought. Why? How did their nothing somehow square itself by another nothing to turn itself into something?

To relieve his mind, Rip thought about his home. Biggest house on the block. Six bedrooms, a double lot. You could play hide-and-seek in that place and never get found. The old-fashioned wallpaper, the worn out old-lady furnishings, the torn couch and pile of empty Nike boxes holding up the brand new TV. It was the only home he had ever known. He knew his little sister would be sitting there—watching whatever stupid show she was always watching—giggling, drinking juice, and spilling cracker crumbs on the floor.

Part of him wanted to tuck his tail between his legs and go home. But Rip knew that if he went home, he'd be admitting that he had been doing something he wasn't supposed to be doing. And then Grandma would be right. Again. And she'd come chasing after him, telling him how stupid he was and wondering why no one was around to smack him upside the head.

And that floored Rip. That's right, Grandma, he told himself, where were they? Rip imagined Grandma looking around at the empty chairs, the empty bedrooms. The place that was once stuffed with people was now only stuffed with old furniture. And suddenly, picturing this, he knew that, for the first time ever, he might see fear in Grandma's eyes.

At first, Rip thought that imagining Grandma's fear would make him scared too, but it didn't. Her fear made him stronger. So he straightened up, showed the iron in his back and flashed the sharp pointed edges of his gleaming white teeth to anyone who dared to see him.

Rip's confident gaze took in the squad car. This time, he watched it with disdain, waiting for it to show the same lazy nonchalance they always did. But this one didn't. This one was looking for something. Slowly and purposefully, it prowled. The eyes from within scanning back and forth, searching for its meal, its mate, or whatever else it could scrape from the neighborhood.

Rip's neighborhood.

Rip wasn't leaving. Grandma couldn't make him. And hell no would he let this insolent police car change an inch of his lifestyle. Rip stayed where he was. He even stood a little taller.

The cool spring air was bright, and the sunshine warmed his jacket. It felt good to breathe the air and know that it belonged to him. That life itself belonged to him.

So Rip played the game. He knew that when the police are around, you can't ever go wrong taking out your phone and pretending to use it. Everybody knows that. It's the sort of strategy the Corner Boys were always talking about amongst themselves.

Rip reached into his right pocket for his phone. Casual, the way he'd done it a thousand times before. But he'd somehow forgotten about the rocks. All that time caressing them, yet they'd fallen out of his mind. When his fingertips touched them, his hand leapt from his pocket. (Rip remembered when he was little and a bee stung him; everyone pointed and laughed and hollered while he yelped in surprise and pain.

And then Rip pictured himself: a ridiculous Corner Boy stopping and starting and literally patting himself down in the middle of the neighborhood while the policeman sits in his car laughing at him.

He still had time to turn around and walk back into the house. There was still time. They hadn't taken that from him.

But Key was there, and she would see him. His baby sister would hear his heartbeat and know that Rip was hiding something.

And then the rocks in his pocket would swell up like bombs and hollow out his thigh like that poor boy Holler who got shot and paralyzed and stuck in a wheelchair, and then his diabetes flared up and his leg got that big nasty smelly hole in him and you could see right into his bone. His whole crew laughed at him, saying that was where they should hide the stash because ain't no police man going to look inside a man's thigh to find out where the dope is.

Key wouldn't be able to see the rocks, but she would *see the rocks*. She would start yelling at him, "What are you hiding?" His Grandma would be yelling at him too, and their voices, combined with the voices blaring at him from the television would force him to press his hands against his ears and scream.

He would not be walking back into that house.

When he finally found his phone, the text messages were stacked up like cans of soda pop. One, two, three, four, five . . . every single one of them from his girl, Vicki: "Rip? Why aren't you answering? Are you with that girl? Everyone says you were with that girl."

And aw man, he *had* been with that girl, but how did she find out? It was just a little messing around, nothing serious. Why hadn't he answered his phone when she first called? Why was he always missing things, important things?

He was just about to call her back when the solid clunk of a car door closing interrupted him.

Not ten feet from him was the squad car—the car that had fallen out of his mind the moment he saw his phone. A guy with a uniform and a badge was looking at him, a slight tilt to his head and a tight bit of nothingness inadvertently leaking out his eyes.

"What's up, bro? Got anything illegal on you?" the cop said.

Rookie mistake upon rookie mistake.

Rip turned.

He ran.

"Ooooh! Look at him run!" The Corner Boys hooted and hollered with delight.

"*You wasted time thinking about your pretty girlfriend, and now look at you!*"

"*Now you running when they are on top of you and they are going to catch you and beat you and your head's going to swell up like a pumpkin and you'll wish you did drugs cause it's going to hurt so bad!*"

The Corner Boys laughed and laughed as memories of their own beatings (taken and given, given and taken) turned their phantom stomachs to knots.

Rip ran past his front door, through the side yard, and out to the alley. It was too late to go home. His front door was like the papier-mâché Rip remembered from art class. It couldn't stop anyone who wanted in. And once the cops were out of their car, they always chased, they always ran. He wasn't going to let them drag themselves into his house with his sister screaming and his uncle upstairs, just home from prison. He wasn't going to bring any of this on them. He was the one on the corner. He was the one causing the problem. He was the goddamn fool.

So he fled down his gangway, away from his heart, away from his home. Past his momma's car that didn't run anymore, out the tidy square of backyard, down the alley, down the tunnel of his life, the blacktop swift and swirling beneath his feet, the wind rippling through his hair, his arms pumping, his lungs filling. Powerful and scared and scared and powerful.

And confidence came with every breath too. He was free. This was his neighborhood. He knew every vacant lot and broken down pathway there was. And he was fast. Everyone knew he was fast. His speed would set him free.

Rip heard the cop run after him, heard him yelling into his radio, heard the squeal of tires from the squad car. There must have been two cops, and now the other cheating cop was driving after him too. That's fine, Rip thought, he would outrun the car too.

But cars go quick, quicker sometimes even than fear. Sure enough, at the end of the alley, there it was: parallel, watching, holding him in. So Rip broke the other way, through the vacant lot. The running cop was behind him. Closer than Rip thought he'd be. He heard the cop's footsteps and the crackle of his radio. Rip flashed through the lot and into the street, down a gangway and past the abandoned building.

He broke through a different vacant lot and streaked across the street. In his peripheral vision, he could see the squad car stalking him from the end of the block. There was a six-foot wooden fence blocking the next yard, but he scaled it like it wasn't even there. Rip was about to jump over the second fence when he heard screeching tires and saw what had to have been a different cheating squad car pulling into that alley, blocking that path too.

What are the chances another car would be so close? Grandma said that bad chance multiplies like roaches: if you see one, you can be pretty sure that millions more of them are hiding in the walls.

Rip changed directions, running south, hopping over the low fences that separated each small backyard. He could hear the other police cars in the alley so he doubled back. He couldn't keep running. This wasn't working. Nowhere to go but home.

Rip's breath came heavily, raspily, and he regretted quitting the JV basketball team last year because he thought he should have made varsity. The pounding in his head wouldn't go away. He couldn't hear or see the cops. He seemed to have momentarily lost them. His lungs were now desperately dry, so he stopped running, started walking, and tried to act like he didn't have a care in the world. He saw Mrs. Sherman watering her lawn with the hose, looking at him like Grandma used to look at him when she knew he had done wrong. If Grandma were still alive, he would surely get no dinner tonight.

Rip was back at his alley, wondering whether he should try to make it back to his house or whether he should go to Tron's house down the block, where he knew the back door was always open. Tron and his cousins would be playing video games, eating chips, and wishing they had enough money for weed. They would welcome him with open arms, listen to his story, and laugh. Just thinking of their laughter made Rip's chest loosen a little. Sure, they'd call him a dumb idiot for the trouble he'd caused himself, but Rip knew they wouldn't really mean it. These peaceful thoughts rose up in Rip's mind even as he heard the light putter of an idling car cutting across his escape, and his dream.

A government car was parked in the alley, right behind his house.

Rip backed up and hid in the concrete alcove below the back porch of the abandoned building on the other side of the alley. His breath heaved so loudly he wondered if the whole neighborhood could hear it.

Every kid on the block had played in that abandoned house for years. Before their bodies, their smiles, and their minds all became hard. The stoop was filled with the garbage of the recent past: candy wrappers, chip bags, dog poop, rotting leaves. There was a comfort to this filthy place. It was safe, cloistered, familiar.

Gradually, Rip's breathing slowed, and the sounds of the neighborhood started coming up as the sounds of the police radios went down. He felt the breeze again, and it felt good. He was warm inside his jacket, and he began to relax. The sounds of the police cars turning corners, the gunning engines, the voices of men who were not from the neighborhood, the crackle of the CB radios. It was all dying away. Softly fading like the sound of Grandma's television as he drifted off to sleep as a boy.

Then from his pocket, Rip heard the horrifying ring of his phone. Why? Whose phone rings anymore anyway?

But Rip heard it. And the trees heard it. And the neighborhood heard it. Even Grandma, creeping around the back with her head peering around the building and her palms pressed against her ears in surprise, heard it before Rip frantically shut it off. All those noises that had been fading away suddenly roared back to life, like someone had accidentally turned the volume all the way up on the car radio.

Behind. In front. Cars stopping and cops yelling. Mrs. Sherman was gone—probably back to her own house to mind her own problems and her own grandkids. Plenty of problems for everyone, no need to wait on someone else's.

Rip glanced at the text messages, his phone glowing softly in the darkness beneath the porch. He couldn't stop himself.

Vicki: "You are such an idiot. How could you do this? I'm going to make sure your baby knows what a piece of crap you are."

Rip lowered his head in shame. This was how he would learn he was a father? Crawling in wet-kneed jeans to a basement stoop filled with trash?

There was no time for pity. The iron gate to the yard squeaked, and Rip saw a cop standing in the sunlit backyard, not thirty feet from Rip's hiding place. It was light out, but Rip felt like there were searchlights coming from the cop's eyes, swinging from the yard to the darkened porch, a menacing, roving monster.

There was an indifference and intensity to his eyes. Rip saw that he wore violence like a comfortable undershirt, worn two days in a row because it didn't matter anyway.

This was an old-school cop. Rip remembered how his uncles used to talk about the way cops were, how they'd beat you within an inch of your life. And even though it hurt, when you deserved it, you could bear it. Besides, the beating was quicker than a trip to lockup, and it still wasn't as bad as the beating your father would give you if he had to pick you up from jail.

But Rip had never been beaten, and it scared him. He'd seen his cousin Cordero, *The Loudest Bastard on the Planet* (he had those words tattooed in script arching over his chest), talking back to everyone: teachers, cops, gangbangers . . . he wasn't scared of nobody. He fought anyone who dared to disrespect him. He didn't win every fight, but he made sure to hurt everyone enough so the word got out: it wasn't worth it to mess with crazy Cordero. Well, one day, Cordero talked back to the wrong old-school cops and they took him away and he didn't come back for a while, and when he did, it was with a lazy eye that never stayed focused again.

Worse yet, he came back quiet.

Sure, Cordero still talked back to most folks—short of killing him, nobody could actually shut him up—but it was different now, it didn't have the same edge: he saw the line and he never crossed it again. Rip didn't want to see the line, and he sure didn't want to cross it. He didn't want any of this.

Rip wanted to go home.

The cop did the same knowing walk he must have done a thousand times before: moving toward the porch, crouching down, looking at Rip, pointing his gun. Speaking.

"Hey. Kid. Put your hands in the air where I can see them," he said casually, like it didn't matter at all, "or I will blow your head off."

Rip could taste the beating in his mouth. He was caught. Grandma was standing there, hands on hips, shaking a rolling pin at him (where does a ghost get a rolling pin?), saying, *"What have you done, young man, what have you done?"* Rip wondered if he would be killed. If he would be beaten until his brain swelled up. If he would die in a ghetto hospital bed, never knowing his unborn child. He thought of his girlfriend and his friends and his dead relatives and his live relatives all wailing at the hospital. But even over all that noise, the thunderclap of stupidity came upon him so strong and so powerful that it hit him in the head like a hammer.

He had forgotten to get rid of the drugs.

For the last three blocks, through the alleyways and

yards, and hiding right here behind the porch, he had held onto the drugs. He, Richard Washington, the undisputed most intelligent boy at Hawthorne Elementary, winner of the Carver Award for Science (he had a picture of his goofy smile as he shook hands with the mayor to prove it). Richard Washington, fourth-place winner in the National Debate Society Championships in Washington, DC (the highest honor earned by a Freshman that year). Richard Washington, recipient of impossibly perfect SAT scores, pride of Chicago Pastors United, owner of a full-ride academic scholarship to pretty much any college he wanted to attend next fall. Rip—acknowledged wunderkind, computer genius, poet laureate, miracle child—had been hiding in a vacant yard with time to check his cell phone, time to think of his girlfriend, time to be afraid. And yet he had failed to get rid of the felonious crack rocks now exploding in his right pants pocket.

The cop was pointing the gun at him, and Rip—in one smooth motion, all fear annihilated—swept the rocks into his mouth, stuck his hands in the air and, in a last ditch bid to save the next twenty years of his life, swallowed.

The blow was two-toned: first, the crunching blow of the boot catching his jaw, causing his two upper-right teeth to pop off neatly like two sweet kernels of corn; second, the dull, hollow thud of skull meeting concrete with the void that enveloped it all.

WHEN RIP CAME TO, HE'D BEEN DRAGGED FROM THE STOOP TO the backyard, his hands cuffed in front of him. The high wooden fence around the yard and the clear blue sky above him made Rip feel like he was on an island. He could see the drugs that he'd failed to swallow sitting on the ground a few feet away from him, dripping with saliva. The cop was squatting over him, a dark looming object, the sun forming an angry halo around his body.

"Kid, don't you try and swallow no rocks. You hear? A man carries his own weight in this world, you hear me?"

Rip looked up, tasting the salty viscosity from the blood trickling down his throat. "Yeah, yes. Yes sir."

"What's your name, kid?"

"Richard Washington, sir."

"Washington? You Colfax's son?"

Rip narrowed his eyes, surprised. Who was this? How did he know his dad's name? These cops in uniforms don't ever know anybody.

"My father is dead, sir," Rip said.

"Yeah, I know. I heard." The cop rubbed his forehead. He was sweating, his hand was shaking. "Well, kid, I want you to know I'm sorry."

Rip wanted to be able to look at him, to understand him, but he couldn't. The sun behind the cop was too strong. "You ain't got nothing to be sorry for, officer," he said. "You're just doing your job."

"No, kid, I'm not. Nobody knows what the job is anymore. You don't deserve it. None of us do. It's over."

Rip winced as the cop shifted his weight onto Rip's shoulder, pinning his hands. The cop then pulled out a fancy silver pistol—it was almost feminine—and placed it gently into Rip's manacled hand.

"Sir, that ain't my gun. I ain't got no gun."

"I know, kid. I know it's not yours. I'm sorry."

Rip could barely feel his own body. The cop's weight made it hard to breathe, and the cuffs were making his hands go numb. "Sir, please. I ain't got no gun. I've never had no gun. You can't put that gun on me."

"Kid. I ain't putting no gun on you. You leave this gun right where you found it. With a little luck, you'll get away."

"What? What'd you say, sir?"

The cop placed his fingers behind Rip's hand and pushed the gun against his own forehead.

"Don't worry about it, kid. There's no need to worry anymore."

Rip felt his finger being pulled, the barrel of the gun wobbled on the ridges of the cop's forehead. Rip could hear the microscopic sound of metal on metal as the trigger, slowly, grindingly, pressed itself together.

The gun went off.

CHAPTER TWO

The pounding was deep and painful. Neverending. The powerful boat was plunging his body down. The weight of the water constricted his chest. His lungs grew shallow and desperate. His mind raced for the oxygen that wasn't there.

And then, suddenly, it stopped. The dark room, the smell of baby, and his own exhausted body, rejoined him in life.

"Papa!" screamed the delighted baby. "Papa up!"

"That's right, Baby, he's up. Aren't you sweet?" Ginny said. Kasper could hear her trying to keep the edge out of her voice. "You can see he's not the only one with a job, and that Momma's got a job too, but unlike Daddy, Momma's actually got to get up and get going. Momma doesn't get to laze around in bed, not make breakfast, not get the kids to school, not do the laundry. No, not like your wonderful Papa. Not like that big fat pig that won't even get out of bed so I can make it and actually get to work on time for once!"

That last line, Kasper thought to himself, Ginny didn't actually succeed at keeping the edge out of her voice.

Kasper didn't say a word. Why bother? Whatever words he chose wouldn't make a difference. Just the sound of his voice made her angry. He'd always swear he was trying to say it nicely, but she would say he had a "tone," and even if he didn't think he had a tone, that accusation would definitely drive him to one. And then she'd start throwing something (and he might throw something back), the baby would start screaming, and Kasper's blood pressure would shoot up even further than it already had from the pounding dream and the three hours of sleep and the life that seemed to go on forever.

"Are you going to court this morning?" Ginny yelled from the bathroom. "Or are you actually going to spend some time with your child?"

"There's no court this morning. We won the case yesterday," he yelled back.

Ginny stood in the doorway, hands on her hips. She was still a hot little number, especially when she dressed up—though Kasper thought she was dressed a little too sexy for a mom going to work at an office gig.

"Oh great! I'm so HAPPY for you!" she said. "Are they going to give you an award? More money? Or . . . oh my gosh . . . are you actually going to have some time to start helping this family? You can't hide in your job forever, Kasper."

"Jesus, Ginny, I have to go to court. It's a state subpoena for crying out loud. I mean, they can throw me in jail if I don't go. For God's sake, it pays time-and-a-half. And hell, I never asked you to work. You can quit whenever you want. Stay home. Take care of the baby. Quit your complaining all the time and enjoy life for once. And for the record," Kasper was trying to pull the sheets up over his body, they'd inexplicably become so tucked into the bottom of the bed that they barely went past his belly button, "the department did give me an award for that case. It was a darn good arrest, not that you care."

"Oh yeah, sure, great, I'm the one who doesn't care. And aren't you the one that's full of great ideas this morning? Yeah, I'll quit my job and then we can not pay the mortgage and lose the house. Great idea. You're a real smart one, Kasper."

"I never wanted this house, Ginny. I told you it was too big and too new. We could have gotten by on half this house. We don't need four bedrooms, so don't be complaining to me about bills when you're the one making them."

"Well we don't need three kids either, but we've got them, and three kids plus us makes four bedrooms. Not that math, or reality, was ever your strongpoint. And don't pretend you care about my life and this family and me not working when you go out and buy a brand new Jeep without telling anybody."

"I have to get to work! You know that damn piece of crap car I had wasn't running well," Kasper said.

"A fifty-thousand-dollar car! You need a fifty-thousand-dollar Jeep to drive six miles to your job in the ghetto? You are some piece of work, Kasper, some piece of work. And since when do we start swearing in front of the baby? Is that the family we are? Is that the kind of father you are? You want to start swearing in front of the baby? Fine. Try this: Hey Joey, your father is a GODDAMN ASSHOLE!"

Joey was evidently quite pleased with that opinion, as he immediately squealed with delight: "Ass ho! Ass ho!" Joey hurled himself backwards onto the bed and shook his fat little legs in the air, giggling delightedly.

"Oh great, Ginny, some kind of mother you are. Now you've got the baby swearing just like your father. And why does Joey's diaper weigh about ten pounds? His diaper is so full we could use it as a sandbag to hold back the flood. Did you even change the kid this morning? If you don't change his diaper, that rash is going to come back."

"Don't you talk about my father. He warned me to stay away from you and that was about the only good piece of advice he gave anyone in his life. And since you haven't changed a diaper in two weeks, now sounds like the perfect time for you to start."

Ginny slammed the bedroom door. Soon, he heard pots and pans and doors and God knows what else slamming downstairs. He'd give Ginny one thing: that girl was a true Jedi warrior when it came to door slamming. The heavy metal explosions ended and Ginny yelled up, "I've got to stay late at work tonight. You'll have to call your mother to watch the kids. She can pick up Vince and Jeffrey from daycare and you can bring Joey to her whenever you want. But tell her not to feed them all that candy. It's going to make their skin look terrible."

She didn't wait for an answer. Kasper heard the back door slam and knew she was gone.

Kasper sat up in bed and looked at the clock. Six a.m. He looked around the room. It was nice, but so filled with crap and toys you hardly knew it. He caught his reflection in the mirror. Not too bad, he thought. He sat up a little straighter so the folds of fat on his stomach went away and he could see the hard muscles underneath. Those sit-ups were paying off. The shadow of a beard gave him a rough look that he liked. If it weren't for the bags beneath his eyes that were so big you'd think he'd gotten into a fight last night, Kasper had to say he looked pretty darn handsome.

Joey was laughing and crawling dangerously close to the edge of the bed. Kasper caught him by the leg and dragged him back to the middle. What was he going to do with this kid for eight hours when he barely had energy to think?

"So Joey," Kasper said, "got any plans for the day?"

Joey sat up on his haunches on the bed. He put his fingers to his chin like he was pondering the question. Then he broke into laughter, pointed his finger at Kasper, and screamed with glee: "Ass ho! Ass ho! Ass ho!"

Kasper laughed. Guess he'd have to figure it out for himself. Maybe they could watch some TV on the couch or something while Kasper half slept. He hated not having the energy to play with Joey, but he needed to save his energy for work and the gym. He sure wasn't going to drop him off at his mother's like Ginny wanted, at least not right away. He'd take care of his own family. That was his job. And he definitely wouldn't be telling his mom what to do if he did drop Joey off. His Mom had raised him just fine. You can't ask an old lady to watch your kids every night and then complain about how she does it.

But why was his Mom having to watch Joey every night? Ginny should be home. If she was staying late at work, why wasn't she bringing in more money? Any idiot could see it, but between work, court, gym, kids, and (not nearly enough) sleep, Kasper didn't have time to think about it. Thinking was something he couldn't afford.

Kasper wanted to stay in bed, just let the world be for a while so he could rest, but Joey climbed all over his face and made sure to let him know that wasn't going to happen. The day starts when the day starts, Kasper thought, even if the night never ends.

Kasper took the two tiny baby hands into his own, cocked his head sideways at Joey and made a silly face. The baby laughed and laughed.

"Ass ho, huh?" He couldn't help it. Kasper had an idea: he screwed up his eye, made a face like a monster, and got close to Joey like he was a criminal on the street that needed scaring. "You got that right, kid." Joey's eyes got wide. "You got that right."

CHAPTER THREE

Mike sat at the dark bar table. No windows, medium music, medium crowd. It was forever since he'd been here. He had to force himself to sip his drink every now and then just to show the people he knew what he was supposed to do. No one in the bar was who they used to be, and that thought comforted him. It meant he didn't have to talk to anyone, except, of course, the guy he'd come to meet.

But as Mike looked a little closer, he realized he was wrong. The specific faces may have changed, but everyone in the bar looked exactly like they had all those years ago. The same ages, the same socioeconomics, the same aspirations. Interchangeable young professionals and wannabes, sucked up from the vast spaces and small towns of the gray Midwest. They came to this town—the only home Mike had ever known—thinking they were doing something new, something different.

They'd make some money, dream some dreams, and move on. Dump this town like a rich person's summer fling. Mike could return to this bar in another ten years and the only thing that would have changed was himself.

Although Danny was fifty years old now and maybe not quite what he used to be, he still walked through the door like he owned the place. Mike already knew what Danny would do next. He would take one step into the bar, pause, and survey the room. He wanted to see everyone and for everyone to see him. Mike knew he didn't do it consciously, didn't need to. He Was.

And everyone did see him. Danny wasn't that remarkable, objectively speaking. He was handsome and athletic enough, but nothing special. And yet, you couldn't help yourself. You noticed him even if you didn't want to. That was one of his gifts.

Danny and Mike met eyes. Danny walked over. The two men shook hands, embraced.

It had been five years.

Before Danny could even sit down, the waitress came over and exclaimed, "Oh my God, Danny! It's been so long! How have you been doing, hun?"

"Everything is great," Danny said, "but I need a ginger ale with a lime and some ice so I can talk to my friend."

"Oh yeah, of COURSE, but how are you?" said the waitress.

"I'm fine, sweetheart. Good," he said. "Thirsty though."

"Oh, I get it," she frowned. "I'll bring it right over."

"So how does a recovering alcoholic somehow know every barmaid in the city?" Mike said.

Danny smiled. "I don't know all of them, just the ones I care to know. I haven't really got time for this place anymore. Too busy with the overtime and the kids."

"I bet you can still make time for certain types of attractions," Mike said, watching the swing of the waitress's hips as she walked away.

"Nah, really. It's over, it's done. I'm not just saying that, I'm really done. In the end, they're all the same. Only the trouble is different, and I'm tired of trouble. Old tits are a little lower, but once you adjust your aim, they still feel pretty good."

Mike grunted. If Danny thought he could change, that was fine by him, but Mike knew Danny couldn't.

Danny leaned back in his chair, crossing his arms over his chest. He was big enough that you could imagine the chair breaking under his weight. "Except, of course, for your wife. I saw Gloria on the news yesterday. She sure hasn't changed. You tell me: How does a fifty-year-old woman still have the same breasts she had twenty years ago? You're a lucky man, Mike. A lucky man."

"I know it." Mike smiled. "The whole family is great. She's great. The kids are great. It looks like David is going to get a scholarship to University of Pennsylvania, Alex is a Sophomore at Lane and is on track to become the captain of the tennis team, and Jenna will probably be going to Lane next year too. And, of course, you already know how Kasper is doing."

Mike liked talking about his kids. He could present them as he wanted to think about them: young, beautiful, full of hope. Not how he actually felt about them. People sometimes still told Mike he looked young, but he knew it was a lie. He'd seen himself in pictures. The police hat hid the thinning hair, but it didn't hide his sagging neck. For years, he'd felt younger than he looked, but now he felt even older than he looked.

"How's your family?" he asked Danny.

Danny smiled ruefully when he thought about his children. "One, three, and five. They're killing me with the bills, but they're happy and healthy and I won't complain."

"You still in the old neighborhood?" Mike asked.

"Yeah. But I'm tired of it. We're moving out. Jasmine still likes it. Her family is still there, but everyone else we used to know is gone. She likes the barbecues and the get-togethers and all that, but I don't like the influence. Her family is nice enough, but I don't like how they talk and I don't want the kids to grow up sounding like busboys and waitresses at the local taqueria. They're going to do better than me. They're going to do better than her. Jasmine knows where she came from, and it's taking her a minute, but she'll eventually agree with me."

Danny looked up sharply at Mike. "We can't all marry the Queen of the Nile like you did. Some of us have to bring ourselves up, not marry into it."

"That's what you want to say?" Mike asked. "It hasn't even been three minutes."

"Alright. I'm sorry," Danny said. "I shouldn't call her that. She's a great girl, and you're a lucky man." Danny kept talking as the waitress set his drink on the table. "But when Jasmine found out I was meeting you, she got all upset and started screaming about you and Gloria. Man, I gotta tell you, you don't show up for a girl's wedding and she will never forgive you. And that ain't a metaphor, she will seriously never forgive you."

"Aw, come on," Mike said. "It was in the middle of those protests. You know that no one could take off. I had to pull some strings just to make sure *you* could get the days off."

"Yeah, sure. You pulled some strings." Danny's hand clenched slightly while he rubbed his chin. "Do you seriously think I'm going to believe the department would have denied me a day off for my own wedding if it hadn't been for your clout? Even in this day and age, with all the stupid people in charge, you can still get married without the Chicago Police Department falling apart. Not everyone needs you to save them, Mike. I sure don't."

"All I can say is I made sure you got the day off, but I couldn't get the day off myself and I'm sorry I missed it," Mike said.

"Yeah, Mike. I know. You're a big boss and all that. I've

told her that a thousand times, but she won't hear it. Women are like that."

"Yeah," Mike said. "They are."

The two men sat. Drank their drinks.

"You remember Felton?" Mike asked.

"Felton?" Danny snorted. "From the academy? That idiot? I haven't thought about him in years, but yeah, I remember him. He come by begging you for a job or something? I hear he lost his clout."

"Yeah, he did come by. Wanted to talk about stuff—more or less like that. I was wondering if you had run into him," Mike said.

"Nah. Absolutely not. I got nothing to offer him, and if he did see me, I'm pretty sure he would walk the other way. Don't you remember the Serrano incident? When she beat the crap out of him at gym class?" Danny said.

"Hah! I had almost forgotten about that. She broke his jaw, right? Pretty embarrassing to get your jaw broken by a cute little one-hundred-pound firecracker. But that was some of your work, wasn't it?" Mike said.

"Well, I may have had something to do with it, but it was purely from an inspirational point of view." Both men knew it was better to talk about old times than the present. Mike saw that Danny had wrinkles around his eyes too, but they were smaller than Mike's, and they almost made it look like he was laughing. Danny leaned back again as he continued, "Old Felton had a crush on her. Just before that gym session he had tried to ask her out. Now, she happened to be messing around with me at the time. Naturally, I was about all she could handle, so she turned him down."

"Probably looked at him like he was the dumbest beached whale there ever was too," Mike said.

"Yeah. Probably. Felton wasn't the handsomest of guys. And handsome was kind of her thing back then. Later, when we were waiting in line, someone must have told her that she wasn't the only girl I was seeing. That crazy woman pulled me out into the hallway and screamed at me," Danny said.

"Yeah. Shocking. Women have a tendency to do that when you're cheating on them," Mike said.

"I wasn't cheating on her!" Danny wagged his finger like a vaudeville entertainer. "I can assure you, I may have been a whore, but I was an honest whore. Wasn't nothing exclusive about us. If she gets mad at me for something we never even talked about, that's her problem, not mine."

"Turned out to be Felton's problem," Mike laughed.

"Oh it sure was. She stormed back into that gym just as she and Felton got paired up on that baton drill. Felton was the bad guy in the protective equipment and she was the officer with the rubber baton." Danny's shoulders shook as he spoke, and he let out a low whistle. "That girl absolutely annihilated him."

"Oh God, I remember. It was crazy." Mike said. "The sound of that smack when she first laid into him was like a bomb going off in that gym. Nobody else was hitting half that hard—it was just a drill—but she was like a tiger laying into him. Forehand, backhand. Pow! Pow!"

"I know. Hell, even with me she might have got a few licks in before I could have stopped her. With Felton? Poor bastard. I'm sure she was thinking about beating my ass as she whupped all over on him. Felton having just asked her out, everybody knowing he got turned down . . . and then getting his ass kicked by a girl? That's a bad day. Even for a fat piece of crap like Felton. I mean, he couldn't have won. Even if he could have withstood that onslaught, the only way she would have stopped is if he'd actually hurt her. You can't hurt a girl without being an asshole, and if you get beat by one, it's even worse," Danny said.

"I remember those two instructors trying to pull her off

while she was screaming at him and then that weird Russian instructor started swearing at her in Russian, all four of them rolling around on the ground and the Russian dude popping up with that huge black eye he must have gotten on one of her backswings. What was his name again?" Mike asked.

"Kalashnikov!" Danny's eyes lit up. "That's what everyone called him. I think his real name was Khazzi, but nobody called him that. Why would you call a Russian gym instructor Khazzi when you can call him a cool nickname like Kalashnikov instead?"

"Yeah," Mike said, "what a crapshoot that day. What a good goddamn crapshoot of a day."

They laughed. Easy.

It died though.

"So what's with memory lane, Mike? Ain't nobody willing to talk to you down in headquarters? And why'd you want to meet here, anyway? You figure no one here would recognize us?"

"A little privacy never hurt anyone. You know it's best if we don't dredge up the old stuff. Every time they see me with you they think of the old dirty cop nonsense and I have to parade my family in front of media potlucks for three months until they forget. All that attention won't help you any, either," Mike said.

"Screw that. That attention is done. They tried to fire me and they failed. They dumped me down to P.O. and put a brick so heavy on my career that I'll never do anything significant again. I don't care. Once they've dumped you down to the bottom, they can't push you any further. That was their mistake: you can't take everything away from a man if you want to control him. You have to leave him something he still cares about so he knows there's still something you can kill. That's the handle in your skull they can push you around with. Well, those dumbasses took everything, and now they got nothing." Danny was clenching the glass so hard the veins on his forearms flared. Mike pictured them popping, the blood spurting out into their drinks, the ice cubes tinged with red.

"Besides, I like it this way." Danny cracked his neck to the left and the right as he tried to loosen his shoulders. "A career path ain't for me. They want me down in the dumps, no problem. I like it there. I stay in the ghetto. It's where I belong. Be the police, and try and teach the young coppers the right way to do things. The right way, Mike. You hear me?" Danny's voice was rising again. "I know who I am. You not meeting up with me in public isn't about me. It's about you preserving your prestige and your politics. That's fine. I don't care. You worked hard and you earned it. But we're the same guy. So don't be lying to me." The vein on the left side of Danny's neck pulsed. "We're the same damn person, only you are where you are, and I am where I am, and that's that. Don't pretend you're anything other than who I am."

"Yo dude, the only reason you've still got your job is because I looked out for you, and if I hadn't, you'd be lucky to have a job as a security guard right now. You would have drunk yourself to death and taken down half the people who love you at the same time."

"Shut your face." Danny half-rose in his chair.

"Danny, I'm—"

"Shut the hell up." Danny pounded his fist on the table.

Mike started to stand up to meet him, but then he felt the people in the bar looking at them. Strangers. They didn't belong.

The two men sat down. Composed themselves.

"Look, Danny, I'm sorry. I know it could easily have gone the other way, that my son could be dead instead of yours. But things didn't happen that way, and there's nothing we can do about it."

Time goes by slowly sometimes. The two men's words wavered in the air. Mike felt for the thousandth time like a man trapped beneath a heavy boulder. He could lift it off his chest just enough to breathe, but he wasn't strong enough to push it off completely. He was so close. Just a little bit of help and he could do it. Danny could help him.

But it wouldn't matter, not really. The boulders were all around him. Even if he threw this one off, another one would be rolled on top of him.

Danny broke the silence. "He's a good cop, you know."

"What?" Mike said. "Who are you talking about?"

"Your son. He's a good cop," Danny said.

"Kasper? You're damn right he's a good cop. I look up his numbers every week. He's killing it out there. I'm proud of him."

"Are you?" Danny replied. "Because he doesn't seem to think so. He says he hardly ever sees you, and when you do see each other all you do is complain about something he isn't doing very well and then you talk about your other kids as if he isn't one of them. He says you barely even mention the grandkids. And I'll tell you, man, you sure didn't mention any of them when I asked about your family."

"You asked about the kids. Not the family." Mike squared his shoulders against Danny's accusation. "You ask about the family, I'll tell you about the grandkids too. Kasper thinking I don't think about him and the grandkids is all in his imagination. He thinks the world is always out to get him, just like his mother. My grandkids come over every Sunday for dinner and we have a great time. All of us. Together. Even his wife comes—who knew that SHE'D turn out to be the good one? I just wish Kasper would come too. But he doesn't. Says he's working. Just so you know, whatever he tells you, I'm not the one who walked away from him. He walked away from *me*. Someday, he's going to realize it, and he'll come back. You'll see." Mike finished his speech awkwardly. He hated talking about Kasper. He hated knowing his son couldn't stand him and there was nothing he could do about it.

Mike looked at Danny and he saw the same conversations and the same ruts. They were never going to go away.

"Danny, I didn't come here to talk about family," Mike said. I came here to ask you a question. This other stuff . . . nothing we can do about it, right?"

"Nah," Danny said. "Probably not."

"You still working out there?" Mike asked.

"Work? I work every day. Sometimes twice a day when I've got a side job," Danny said.

"No. I don't mean showing up for work and collecting a paycheck, and I don't mean overtime or a sidegig, either. I mean work, real work. Police work," Mike said.

"Police work? What the hell is that? Police work is dead. You killed it, don't you remember? What's it to you anyway, Mike? Numbers are down citywide and you want to talk to me about how to inspire the troops? Well screw that. I work when I want to work, and with the people I want to work with. And you know what, man? I guarantee you already looked up my numbers and know exactly what I do, so stop playing those lawyer tricks where you ask me questions you already know the answers to. Ask whatever it is you really want to know so I can get on with my life. I'm not gonna kiss the ring, so you can stop waiting. I don't give a crap about you, or anybody else, unless you're my family, or the guys I work with on the street. I back them up like I always have. Like we always did. You remember that, Mike? You remember what we once did?" Danny said.

Mike looked at Danny, and remembered a time when they both would have considered each other family without a moment's thought. That time was over now.

"Danny, I need a gun."

"A gun? What are you talking about? So buy a gun. I sold you that Ruger twenty years ago. I haven't got anything else to sell," Danny said.

"Hah. That's funny. I've still got that Ruger. No. I don't

want a clean gun. I want a dirty gun. A ghetto gun," Mike said.

"What the hell? This department destroys thousands of recovered guns every year. Go there and grab one of those if you want a ghetto gun. I'm sure they'll give you one under the table before they melt the whole lot into aluminum cans. No one will know a thing," Danny said.

"No. I want an untraceable gun. Or if it is traceable, I want it traced back to the hood. I need the kind of gun you find on the streets. One of those guns some asshole throws over his shoulder and you can't put it on him cause you never saw him throw it. I don't chase people anymore, and even if I did, there's the media and a thousand people everywhere I go. I can't put it in my pocket and save it for later," Mike said.

Danny grimaced. "You're talking to those damn liberals too much. If cops ever did carry around drop guns, they sure don't do it now. That's some conspiracy theory from a world that died a long time ago. I ain't got no gun."

"I know you don't," Mike said, "but you'll find one. You always do. They drop out of the sky for you. You barely need to look."

"Oh, I look. I always look, ain't nothing lucky about it. But I only work now when I've got a kid who's worth it, and I sure as heck ain't going to get them involved in any of the sort of nonsense you're talking about. Don't get me wrong, I don't mind the nonsense—in fact, I kinda like it. But like you said, my career has smelled like dog crap for so long nobody even remarks about the stench anymore. But those kids," Danny was rubbing his temple where his slightly receding hairline used to be, "they don't need to learn how to live with the stench like I do. Clean, Mike. I keep those kids clean,"

Mike saw Danny pause before asking, "What do you want a gun for anyway, Mike?"

"Just get me what I need," Mike said.

"You in some kind of trouble or something?" Danny asked.

"Danny, there's no such thing as a conspiracy of one. I'm not asking for a therapist, I'm asking for a gun," Mike said.

"If you're in some kind of trouble, I'll help you. Jesus, I've known you for forty years. I'd do anything for you. What's going on?" Mike asked.

"If you're going to help me, then just get me the goddamned gun like I asked," Mike said, "and stop asking questions."

Danny looked at Mike. Rubbed the stubble on his chin. Slowly took a sip of his drink. He remembered the roundness of a real drink in his mouth, the ease and freedom he felt when he drank it. All these years later, the fake stuff still didn't do the job. He longed for the sharp burn on his tongue.

"You know," Danny said, "you should call him. Spend some time with him. Kasper. He needs his father."

"Yeah, I know. I'll call him. I'll try and make it up to him. I'll call him as soon as I get home." Mike was feeling a headache coming. "You know he talks about you all the time? All. The. Time. Jesus, it's annoying. I've had to listen to your stories for thirty years, and now I have to listen to my son tell me those same stories, and he doesn't even realize that I was actually IN most of them."

Danny laughed. "Yeah, I do leave names out of them. Habit, I suppose."

"He doesn't even realize that the person he likes in the story is me. Because when he looks at me, it's like he's looking at the lowest form of life on earth," Mike said.

"He'll come back man. He'll come back," Danny said.

Mike looked at Danny. Still giving advice after all these years. "He's lucky to have you out there on the streets, Danny. Everybody needs someone to talk to." Mike didn't look at Danny while he spoke. "I mean, sometimes I think half the reason he doesn't talk to me is because he's got you. He probably wishes you were his father anyway."

"It ain't like that, Mike."

"But at least he's got someone to talk to. People need someone to talk to. They need it." Mike looked at Danny. "People are talking AT me all the time. I'm the one who's spent thirty years figuring this stuff out, but when I try to explain it to them, they don't even hear me because they decided I was an idiot before I even walked into the room. Oh they're listening, but it's only so they can grab my words, twist them up, and stuff them down my throat."

"You OK?" Danny asked.

"Yeah," Mike said.

"You sure?" Danny asked, "because you're sounding like a whining dick right now."

"Yeah, thanks for the insight, real helpful," Mike said.

"Gotta speak truth to power, man," Danny said. "You know how it is."

Mike saw the wrinkles around Danny's eyes curl up into a smile again. "Yeah, alright, thanks. It's OK. I just do the dumb stuff they tell me to do. It isn't worth it to fight anymore. I know it's not going to work, but since it's their idea, they're the ones who have to take the blame, not me."

"They ain't taking the blame," Danny said.

"Well, they ought to," Mike said.

"Huh." Danny rubbed his chin. "They got the handle on your skull, Mike. They're pushing their thumbs into your brain and moving you wherever they want you to go. Let it go, man. They ain't got nothing on you unless you let them. Just do your job. That's all you got to do. You're the boss, for crying out loud. If you ain't the boss, then who is?"

"Danny—," Mike started to say.

Danny interrupted him before he could go any further. "Well, you're right about one thing, Mike. You do need someone to talk to."

Danny stood up, put his coat on, and placed a five-dollar bill on the table for the soda. "Alright," he said. "I'll give you what you asked for. I'll get the gun. That all you really wanted?"

"Thanks," Mike said.

"Yeah," Danny said.

"Danny, Clean. I want it clean." Mike said.

Danny sniffed, flexed his thick, meaty shoulders, and leaned in. "You don't get to tell me what to do."

CHAPTER FOUR

R ip had no idea how he ended up at Vicki's door. How was it that police were around every corner when he was minding his own business, but now that he was handcuffed and covered in a dead cop's blood, there suddenly wasn't another soul in the world? But there he was, scratching at Vicki's side door like he'd done a thousand times before, praying that she was home.

And there she was: small hips, hair pulled back tight, righteous indignation flaring in her eyes. It occurred to Rip that she looked exactly like Grandma in that old family photo on the piano that no one played anymore. Rip had never had a luckier day than the one that brought Vicki, and her family, into his life.

Her anger was snuffed out almost instantly when she saw Rip. "My God, Rip. What have they done to you? You're covered in blood! Did my father see you? I'll call the ambulance, or he can drive you to the hospital. Good Lord! What happened?"

Vicki ushered him up to her room. The domesticity and intelligence of the surroundings struck him like never before: the desk with her latest writing project arranged neatly on top, the picture of her smiling parents on the dresser, the "Jesus Saves!" cross-stitch above her bed, the webcam she and her sister used to record and post music videos online. It was everything he deserved and didn't deserve. It was everything he wanted and didn't want. And it was all annihilated and she didn't even know it yet.

"Did your brother's friends jump you? When are they going to learn that they aren't going to turn you into one of them? Is this what it's going to take for you to stop hanging out with that crowd? You getting beat up? Can we finally leave this place and get out of here? I'm serious, Rip."

Rip wanted to respond, but he couldn't. The wail of the sirens was getting louder and louder. Vicki was cleaning Rip's face with a cloth when she saw the glint of the handcuffs.

"Rip? What are those?" she asked.

"Vicki—"

"What are you hiding? Let me see." Vicki's concern was getting a harder edge.

"I'm trying to tell you—"

"Rip, are those handcuffs? Why do you have handcuffs on?"

"Let me—"

Vicki grabbed him then, like he was a toddler trying to hide something incriminating. She pulled his bloody shirt over his head, her tone half frantic and half prosecutorial, as she said, "Why weren't you answering my calls? Whose blood is this? Rip?"

The front door slammed downstairs, and then the booming voice of Mr. Harris, Vicki's father, yelled, "Vicki, are you up there?"

"Yes, Papa, I'm here. Why are you yelling? What's going on?"

"They've gone and killed a policeman down on Stewart Street," Mr. Harris's voice filled the house like a living entity." Rip could hear Mr. Harris rummaging around, slamming doors. "Sweet Lord, the police are going to go crazy, absolutely crazy," he continued. "Call up that boyfriend of yours. Tell him to get over here immediately. The police are going to lose their minds and lock up any young man they find on these streets. There are plenty of young men that need to get locked up tonight, but Richard Washington is not one of them. But with his family? Why, they will bring him down to the station and shake him down just because of the name on his driver's license." Mr. Harris continued to stomp around downstairs. "Vicki, do you hear me? Why aren't you answering? Vicki, do you know where Richard is?"

Rip could see the words forming on Vicki's lips. She would call out to her father and Mr. Harris would come upstairs and Rip would tell them everything. He would tell them about the drugs, about all the weed he'd been smoking. He'd tell them about how his brother had gone to jail and how his little sister cried every day and how there was a stack of unopened letters from the gas company piled up so high he didn't even bother opening them anymore. How his uncle, since coming home from prison, was always calling him soft and wondering aloud about how, if Rip was supposedly so smart, how come the family didn't have no money. And how it was a damn shame that Rip wasn't a man like his brother and father. And how he, just home from Stateville, ought to be relaxing but would have to provide for the family, while Rip, who had no record at all and could stand to get arrested a time or two—and besides he was just a juvenile so they'd thrown the cases out anyhow—wasn't doing a damn thing because he was soft, and pathetic, and thought he was better than everyone else. But Rip wasn't better than anyone else, his uncle continued. He was a piece of crap and had been protected too long. He wasn't a real man at all, and soon everyone would know it.

Rip wanted to confess everything to Mr. Harris. He could already feel his chest becoming lighter thinking about it. Mr. Harris believed in him! He loved and trusted Rip, and he knew that Rip would never be involved with something like this. Rip needed Mr. Harris's sweet absolution.

And Mr. Harris knew everybody. He knew the pastors and the aldermen and the state senators and the police commander. He'd even been on TV, and he preached to thousands every Sunday. If Mr. Harris believed in him, then Mr. Harris would fight for him.

He would fight for him like he was the son he never had, because really, he was. Mr. Harris had always made sure Rip went to the best schools and was occupied with activities that exposed him to the world outside the block.

The sirens were getting louder. Rip could feel the vibrations of a firetruck's horn. The firetruck must have been boxed in because it kept blowing and blowing and blowing. He could hear a helicopter somewhere close by. Rip saw the Corner Boys cackling and laughing, slapping their thighs and falling all over themselves like they hadn't heard anything funnier in their entire lives, even though Rip hadn't said a word:

"Oh Rip, you are something!"

"Why Rip, you must be the most hilarious man who ever walked the earth!"

"You think some sonofabitch with a cop's blood on his face and hand-cuffs on his hands is going to get away with it?"

"You must think you're OJ Simpson! Only, if your ass was OJ Simpson, then you damn sure should have been able to outrun that cop. You're a poor bastard from the ghetto, and nothing's gonna change. You just killed that cop and you gonna fry like an egg. Fry like an egg!"

Rip's head was swimming from the cop hitting him, and his stomach was going round in circles. He had to concentrate with all his might not to throw up.

And then when Rip thought about it, he couldn't really remember who had pulled the trigger. Maybe it wasn't the cop after all. Maybe he and the cop had done it together. Maybe they were both guilty, and if they were both guilty, then both of them would probably have to die.

But the cop was already dead, so that just left Rip.

As Vicki's lips opened to call out to her father and to create that path to forgiveness and freedom, Rip got scared. He pulled up his manacled hands, shook them back and forth, and silently mouthed the word "no."

Vicki's eyes hardened as her father called out, "Vicki! Do you hear me? I can't hear a thing with all this noise!"

"Please," Rip whispered.

"WHAT is going on up there?" Mr. Harris said.

Rip held his hands together in supplication.

Vicki decided.

"No, Papa. I don't know where Rip is. I'll call him as soon as I can," she said.

"Stay inside the house and for God's sake, get that boy home! I'm going to make sure your sister gets home."

The front door slammed. Vicki looked at Rip and didn't say a word.

"Let me explain," Rip said.

"You bastard," Vicki said.

"Vicki! Don't talk like that!" Rip said.

"You goddamned bastard! Don't tell me how to speak. You don't get to tell me nothing."

"If you'll only listen to me for one second," Rip said.

"No!" She pushed him in the chest with open palms. Hard. Her sharp wrist bones sunk into him like dulled spears. It staggered Rip.

"No!" she repeated and pushed him again. Rip held his hands in front of him as he fell into the wall to protect himself as Vicki rained down on him with her fists: blow after blow to the side of his head, to the top of his head, to his arms, to his shoulders, to his heart, to his heart, to his heart, to his heart.

"Everything this world has given you. Everything the Lord has given you, all the gifts he has blessed you with. Everything my family has given you. Even your family—full of sneaks and cheats and OG gangsters—even they protected you and worked to make sure you had the best of opportunities. And then you just throw it away. You throw it away like some two-bit corner hustler."

"Let me explain," Rip said again.

"Oh, explain! Oh please explain, Rip the Great Philosopher. Please explain why you are in my room wearing handcuffs with blood all over you."

"They started chasing me and I just ran, and then—"

"Whose blood is that? Whose blood?" Vicki asked.

"I'm trying to tell you!" Rip said.

"Is it your blood? Don't lie to me. I know it isn't your blood. Your face is all swelled up and you're missing two teeth. You look like the Lord put the mark of Cain upon you, only it isn't even the mark of Cain—it's just the mark of a stupid dumb wannabe corner player who is too ignorant not to befoul himself. Whose blood is that?"

"If you would just give me a minute to explain . . ."

"Is it a cop? Is it a police officer's blood? Did you hear my father say that a cop is dead, and you got scared because you are the one who did it? Do you even know that my father is on the board of the Pastors Benevolent Police Officer Association, and he has raised hundreds of thousands of dollars to help police officers' families? To save them from people like you?"

"Vicki, I'll tell you that cop sure wasn't trying to help me."

"You self-centered bastard. Why can't you just do anything like anyone else? Why do you have to be so great and so wonderful that you can't just sell small-time weed on the corner, or gangbang, or rob people? Oh no, that's not enough. You have to go right to murder. Right to capital crime police murderer."

With that, Vicki closed her eyes and the anger whooshed out of her like a popped balloon. She sat down on her neatly made bed and began to cry. She cried as the police sirens wailed intermittently and the sound of the helicopter gradually faded into softness. Rip put his bound hands on her shoulder as best he could.

Her body stiffened at his touch and she flung his arm from her shoulder like it belonged to a monster.

"Our baby's father is a murderer," Vicki said.

"Vicki, why didn't you tell me about that earlier? I would have liked to have known. And it's not like that. It's not murder or anything like that."

"Say it then, Rip. What is it? What do you call that blood on your face and those shackles on your hands?"

"I can't say anything now. I have to think before I say anything." Rip avoided looking at Vicki as he spoke.

"I suppose you'd tell everything to that other girl you were with," Vicki said.

"No, of course not. That's not real either. I just have to be careful what I say. I'm not even sure what happened. I don't want to get you involved."

Rip knew he'd said it wrong. He'd been stopping her from being involved for the longest time. It was the last thing he should have said.

"Get out of my house," Vicki said softly.

"What? No. Why?" he said.

"You're no good, Rip. Momma was right. She was always right."

"What does your mom have to do with any of this?" Rip asked.

"Just go. You'll never understand my family," Vicki said.

"Vicki, I can't. I can't leave the house like this."

"Get out of my family's house," Vicki said.

"There are cops everywhere. I won't stand a chance," Rip said.

Vicki stood up. How did she get so tall? Wasn't she way shorter than him?

"You think I care?" She turned on him, ominously. "You just made me lie to my father to protect a murderer. I gave everything to you. EVERYTHING. I took the Lord's most precious gift, the most beautiful thing I can give, and I gave it to a murderer. Get out of my house."

"Vicki, I can't. They'll kill me." Rip stood up, trying to establish his own height. "I won't."

Vicki's eyes flashed. She didn't back down an inch as she looked him up and down.

"You scared of the police, Rip? You think they're going to hurt you? Well how about this then, Sweetheart: if you don't get out, I'll call the police and you can just wait here while they come and get you."

"Please don't say that," Rip said.

"You think I won't? You think I'm like the rest of these people and won't turn you in? You're not my baby's father anymore. You're nothing. You've never been anyone. I just didn't figure it out until now. I'll call the police, and I hope they do kill you." She grabbed her phone off the desk, and Rip instinctively snatched it from her.

"Oh, so that's the kind of man you are? Wrestling a phone from a girl? You going to kill me too? You going to kill your girlfriend? Because that's what you're going to have to do. You're going to have to kill me if you want to stay in this house. You can stack my body right next to that police officer's. Vicki strode toward him. "Get out of this house or murder me. Those are your options. Get out of this house, Richard Washington. Get out of this house!"

"Vicki, please." Rip held up his hands in a prayer.

Vicki's face filled with revulsion. "Oh you little man." She spat on his clasped hands. "Fine, then. You can go to the garage and sit in there like a dog and call your miserable family so they can rescue you and be proud that you're finally one of them. Finally one of those horrible people you always were and always will be. But get out of my house."

"I'm sorry. I'm so sorry," Rip said.

Vicki stood, her eyes glowing with righteousness, the gates of paradise gleaming behind her. This woman, flaming sword in hand, she would never let him pass.

Rip scuttled to the garage. He dialed Tron's number. Tron would help anyone out. He was the friend that was always there. In the garage, Rip felt lonelier than he had in his entire life. He looked around. Something was missing, but he couldn't put his finger on what it was. And then it hit him: he was alone. For the first time in five years, mercifully, painfully, horrifyingly: Grandma's ghost was gone.

CHAPTER FIVE

K asper had been a screw-up his whole life. "Fails to meet expectations" had been pretty much stamped on his report card ever since Miss Suzy (the almost-a-nun preschool teacher) had told his parents: "Kasper is a . . . difficult boy. Most children like to *please* adults more than Kasper does."

Kasper's dad had glowered at this. His dad had spent a lifetime mastering the art of the glower. Many grown men would have saved their mean mugging for someone other than a preschool teacher, but not his dad. His dad expected the same level of gravity from a three-year-old that he expected from a judge sitting on the bench. He saw weakness as a flaw. Kasper's dad taught him to stand up straight, hold his shoulders proper, walk the narrow line.

Only Kasper wouldn't.

It hadn't started out as defiance, just baffled ignorance. He didn't toe the line because he didn't see a line. Instead, he saw curves, polka dots, sparkles. His dad made him see it. He pointed it out again and again until, one day, Kasper could see it too. But just because he could see it didn't mean he had to follow it. Everyday he mocked the line, and made his father catch him at it. Now who was the winner? Sure the prisoner had to stay in jail, but so did the warden.

So Kasper stayed near the line, but never on it. Not so far off that you could say he wasn't listening, but far enough off of it that they both knew he was being disrespectful. No capitulation, only withdrawal and the will to fight another day. The guerilla war continuing long after the armistice was signed.

In school, Kasper made sure to mess things up with Bs and Cs, occasional Ds, but never As. He was the best athlete on the schoolyard while the most disappointing one in every organized league his dad ever put him in.

Half the time his dad was the coach. Kasper remembered all the single moms standing close to his dad, touching him on the shoulder, smiling. Those moms were always extra nice to Kasper. They invited him over to play with their kids and make him snacks and ask about his dad.

He hated those moms. He had his own mom and she loved him. A hot mess of a mom is better than someone else's mom.

So Kasper told those moms that he didn't live with his dad, and because he didn't live with his dad, he didn't know anything about him. This was only partially true. The moms would always act surprised because Kasper and his dad were always together.

Kasper's earliest memories were of walking around the neighborhood holding his dad's hand. He liked how strong his dad's grip was, and how it made him feel. But later, Kasper found out that holding his dad's hand wasn't optional. His dad would hit him if he didn't hold his hand and stand up straight and nod politely to the neighbors.

He remembered his parents' last argument so clearly.

"Why do you treat him like that? Can't you talk to him? You can talk to everybody else, why can't you talk to your own son?" his mother said.

"I do talk to him, but he doesn't listen. If he doesn't listen, you have to step it up or he won't respect you. And then he'll end up treating everyone else the way he treats you. You're sitting here criticizing me, but you should be asking yourself: Why do you let yourself get walked all over by a four-year-old?" his dad said.

"Because he's a FOUR-YEAR-OLD! He's learning, for crying out loud. It's not an affront to my personal dignity that a four-year-old doesn't always listen. That's life. And once I've repeated myself enough times, he understands," his mother said.

"No, you repeat yourself until you forget and he wins," his dad said.

"Wins what? A little freedom? A little love? A little affection? What's he ever gotten from you? You act like you're some dignified immigrant from the old country with your old-school ways and your stick-up-the-ass mannerisms, but for God's sake, you were born here. There's nothing exotic about you, yet you give him this fancy name like you're hoping he'll become Chopin or something, and instead he's just a regular old American kid who plays video games and thinks for himself. And you can't stand it," she said.

"I'm not going to have a four-year-old child disrespect me in my own house," he said.

"Oh for crying out loud, Mike, I know your parents, remember? I know who you are. Your parents were sweet, wonderful people who worked hard and liked to watch TV on Friday nights. You can fool all those other idiots with this charade of yours, but you can't fool me."

"Yeah, just like you can't fool me coming home awfully late from that bar job of yours," he said, "and I'm pretty sure they aren't having you stay late to do the dishes."

"Oh shut up. As if you ever gave me or this boy anything. You wouldn't even marry me. I'm surprised you even consented to giving Kasper your last name," she said.

"I tried to marry you, remember? You didn't want me.

Besides, both of you get money, a house, stability. Don't say I don't give you anything," he said.

"Oh you wanted to marry me like you wanted to take the garbage out last night. You offered to marry me as a duty, not something you actually wanted. I'm not going to marry a man who doesn't love me. And I don't need you for anything anyway. My dad gave us a great deal on the house. It wasn't something you got for us, so why don't you just pick up and leave like you've always wanted to?" she said.

"That's exactly right. You don't need me. You've made that abundantly clear. And after six years, congratulations—you've finally won the argument," he said.

And then he was gone. Even though he no longer lived in the house, he would come pick Kasper up to spend time with him and make everyone believe he was the world's best dad. He always waited out in the car, stone-faced, and angry. "I'm here," the only communication his parents ever had.

And then, when his dad married his new perfect wife and had his new perfect children, it was as if the man Kasper knew disappeared and was replaced by a man who looked like his dad but was a completely different person. Suddenly, he was this wonderful, caring father who adored his children, read the latest books, went to the theater and to art galleries, talked philosophy, organized and empowered "the community," and gave speeches.

Kasper visited this new person who replaced his dad and his wonderful children and his wonderful wife every week. They all smiled so much and smelled so good and were so loving and accepting of Kasper. But Kasper never asked for this love, and he didn't want it. He knew this dad was a lie, and so, logically, he knew that his new family must be a lie too. So Kasper was there, but he wasn't, and the stamp on his report card remained triumphantly the same: "Failure to meet expectations."

Kasper spent a lot of time at his friend Ryan's house.

Ryan's mom was a hoot with her tiny bohemian two flat filled with her old jazz records, scholarly books, and vegan cooking that always made the apartment smell like an oriental rug shop. She was always pushing that crazy food on Ryan and Kasper, while all they wanted was a goddamn pizza. One time, the two of them turned the oven up to 500 degrees when Ryan's mom wasn't looking, and her bean casserole caught on fire. The house smelled like burned beans for three months, but they got carryout pizza that night, and they considered it one of the greatest triumphs of their young lives.

Kasper's dad and Ryan's dad were partners on the job and always had been. Their moms lived across the street from each other and, depending on what shifts their dads were on, that pretty much dictated who was sleeping over at whose house. Still, Kasper and Ryan could not have been more different. Ryan was thin boned, book smart, and hyper-responsible; Kasper was, well, everything else.

One night, when Kasper was about ten, their dads and their work buddies were playing poker in Ryan's basement. Ryan had fallen asleep hours earlier, but Kasper was still awake, lying on the lower bunk of the enclosed back porch, lazily listening to the men talk. He liked their stories, their swearing, the clink of their glasses, and the smell of their cigars. Uncle Charlie—who wasn't actually anyone's uncle and whose real name wasn't even Charlie—was talking about how Ryan and Kasper were so different.

"Hey, you guys ever notice that Mike's kid looks like Danny, and Danny's kid looks like Mike? Maybe the two of you were swinging back in the day at the wrong time of the month, or maybe you guys got so drunk that you went to the wrong house and screwed the wrong girl, or maybe it was like some weird porno and your wives blindfolded the two of you and switched places and never told you because they always wanted the other guy inside of them."

Uncle Charlie was a loud mouth, even a kid could hear

that. Wouldn't shut up, and spoke so loud he couldn't hear anyone else. Through the vent in the floor, Kasper could hear the men telling Charlie to shut up, that he was out of line, that he shouldn't drink so much. Then the men started yelling, and Kasper could hear bottles breaking and chairs scraping and the shuffle and hue and cry of large men fighting in a small room.

He guessed that Ryan's dad was beating up Uncle Charlie. Ryan's dad did that. One time, Kasper was with Ryan and Ryan's dad at the drugstore when the store manager came running down an aisle chasing a big homeless-looking guy who had half a dozen liquor bottles stuffed into his sweatshirt. The manager was a little guy with a prim tie and a pencil-thin mustache, and when he grabbed the big guy from behind, the big guy just pushed him down like a rag doll and kept stumbling along. The manager screamed, "Call the police! Call the police!" to the girl behind the counter.

When the big guy ran past, Ryan's dad threw his shoulder at him, and the big guy went sailing by—a slow-motion look of surprise on his face, as if the physics of his flight was too much for his brain to handle—and went crashing into a toothpaste display. The toothpaste and the liquor bottles and the big dude all crashed and exploded in a heap on the floor. As the big guy was on his hands and knees trying to gather up the bottles he'd dropped, Ryan's dad strolled over and kicked him squarely in the stomach like he was kicking a field goal. You could hear the whoosh of the air exiting the big guy's lungs as he collapsed onto the floor. But instead of stopping there, Ryan's dad rolled the guy over and straddled him MMA style. Ryan's dad never said, "Stop! Police!" He never took out his gun and told the guy to get on the ground. He never put handcuffs on him. Instead, he hit him again and again, wailing lefts and rights in big, windmilling arcs across the guy's face while the guy just lay curled up on the ground trying to block the blows with his hands and mumbling, "You don't have to hit me like that. You don't have to hit me like that."

Later, the beat cops came and laughed and laughed as they reviewed the security tape footage of the big guy hitting the display case and all the stuff shooting out like a cartoon explosion. The beating was just out of view of the security camera, so Ryan's dad told the whole story in dramatic fashion while everyone stood around and listened. The biggest laughs came when he told them that the only reason he stopped beating the guy was because he got winded that he could barely breathe, and he better get back in shape because it was embarrassing to huff and puff like an old man while you kicked someone's ass.

The manager was so happy, he just kept shaking Ryan's dad's hand and saying "thank you!" again and again. Evidently, the guy had been stealing several hundred dollars' worth of liquor every day for the last month and was practically putting him out of business. The manager told Kasper and Ryan that they could have as much candy as they could fit in their sweatshirts since candy was a lot cheaper than liquor. He and Ryan stuffed their pockets as full as they could and carried it all home. But that's not what would stick with Kasper.

What he would remember from that evening, and for the rest of his life, was the look of pure exultant joy on Ryan's dad's face as he beat that man. When he was older, Kasper would also remember that Ryan never ate any of the candy. He gave it all to Kasper. Said he didn't want it, didn't like how it tasted. Ryan pretty much never ate candy again.

So as Kasper listened through the vent, he knew that Ryan's dad was beating the smithereens out of Uncle Charlie. After twenty or thirty seconds of grunting and groaning and furniture getting knocked about, Kasper heard the back door bang as two men hurled out into the backyard.

Kasper ran to the window and watched as *his* dad, not

Ryan's, pushed Uncle Charlie's face down in the snow with one hand while hitting him on the side of the head with the other. He got in four or five blows before the other men pulled his dad off of Uncle Charlie and pushed him back into the house. Uncle Charlie and Ryan's dad remained in the yard, Uncle Charlie holding his bleeding nose in a drunken stupor as Ryan's dad calmly squatted down next to him smoking a cigar and sipping from a plastic cup.

"Jesus, Danny! What'd he do that for? Mike ain't even with that girl no more. There's no reason for him to have done that. It's no fair fighting a man as drunk as I am when you're as sober as that asshole. I ain't playing cards with him no more. You can't trust a man who doesn't drink when he plays cards."

Ryan's dad just nodded and listened. When Uncle Charlie was done sniffling and complaining, he wrapped his arm around Uncle Charlie's back and helped him up.

"Come on, Charlie. I'll give you a ride back home."

"I don't need no ride. I'll give myself a ride back home."

"I know you don't need no ride, Charlie, but I'm giving you one anyway."

"Screw you. I ain't taking a ride from you or that damned sober partner of yours."

"Charlie," Danny said, the kindness in his voice growing a sharp edge, "I'm giving you a ride home."

"Fine. Yeah, whatever. I've already had one too many arguments with you assholes." They disappeared into the garage.

Ryan had joined Kasper at the back window, rubbing the sleep from his eyes. "What the heck was that all about, Kasper?"

"Uncle Charlie was talking crap about our moms. There was a big fight and my dad beat the snot out of Uncle Charlie."

"There's no way Uncle Charlie would have talked about

our moms that way, and your dad wouldn't never beat nobody up. He doesn't do that."

"Whatever, Ryan. I don't even know why you got out of bed then. You should just go back to sleep. You must be dreaming."

Ryan cocked his head "You're right," he said, confused. "I was dreaming."

CHAPTER SIX

C ornelius assumed the relaxed and lethal lean of a napping cobra. It wasn't easy. A lot of people could look dangerous, and a lot of people could look relaxed, but it was the rare prince of darkness that could pull them both off at the same time, particularly here, in County Jail.

Fury and menace surrounded Cornelius. Tight corridors, metal doors, dirty concrete floors. And the noise. Oh, the noise: clanging, banging, shouts bouncing off the walls so you couldn't even tell who yelled them. These weren't the sounds of people. They were the sounds of the slaughterhouse, and animals who knew their friends kept disappearing. Back in the neighborhood, with his family serving as a buffer between himself and the world, it was easy. He could be both strong and loose in his own skin. But here, he was running with a broken leg.

Some men ached for the past. But Cornelius was not one of them. He dealt with the world he lived in, and where he lived was now.

At least Cornelius was top dog here. A five-star general among boys. Those poor fools at the bottom couldn't hardly move without bowing and scraping at every puffed-up thug that came by. Not Cornelius. Hell no. He was the one they were bowing and scraping to.

It wasn't because he was bigger. There were plenty of guys with bigger muscles, though Cornelius knew his were wrapped harder and smoother than most. And it wasn't because he was handsome, either, though that didn't hurt. He was average height—if anything an inch shorter—but his glowing skin and jarring bright eyes had always drawn attention.

But he had not earned those things, so they did not matter. What he *had* earned was the industrial spring coiled within him that wound tighter and tighter each day, generating tension and power. Cornelius enjoyed the feeling of power and the way that power made people around him take notice. He sensed them leaning in, even though they knew they shouldn't, and he was glad that anytime he felt like it, he could unleash that power on them, and if he felt like it, break their goddamned skulls.

CORNELIUS LOOKED AROUND AT THE YAPPING, BELCHING FOOLS around him and he spat on the floor. The whole scene reminded him of a nature documentary he'd seen about these crazy-looking elephant seals. They were as big as cars—no, bigger—and they had these huge noses that made them look freakish and alien, like something out of *Star Wars*. Every year, hundreds of them came from all over the world to battle it out on the ice and see who was the strongest. Charging, attacking, bloodying things up all savage like. At the end, the strongest son of a bitch emerged, with all the lady seals lined up to worship him, and declared himself king of the world.

It was awesome.

The documentary started out with Small Seal, the poor bastard, swimming around all cute and happy. But that didn't last. From the moment he got onto the ice, all the other seals just started beating his ass to nothing. You'd think Small Seal would get tired of getting his ass kicked, but he didn't. He just kept trying. Little dude must have truly loved himself some females to go through all that.

It went on like that for weeks. Little Seal would try to slip past those other seals, but they always found him and beat him down. Even though they were all twice his size, the whole gang was fixated on Small Seal, and if one of the other seals spotted him, the whole crew would come flopping over to get a piece of the action. Cornelius wanted to yell at Small Seal: stay down, little dude! You aren't going to win. But Little Seal just kept at it. Cornelius supposed it had to be that way. If you don't try, you cease to exist, evolutionary speaking and all. And besides, if Small Seal dies, that just means some other seal has to take his place. World always needs someone to get their ass kicked.

Now on the other hand, you had Big Seal. That dude was the man. He had everything. All the women, all the space at the center of the herd. Everywhere he looked, he was the king. But then, of course, there was Medium Seal. He wanted to be Big Seal, so he'd be smacking his flippers together, running and flopping around trying to get attention. But Big Seal didn't pay him no mind. Big Seal just sat there, roaring every once in while just to show Medium Seal that he could.

But Cornelius knew it was all an act. Whatever it might look like to an outsider, Big Seal wasn't relaxing. He couldn't. He didn't actually have any friends. This wasn't a team game where a bunch of seals worked together to control the place. This was a one-seal job, and at any moment, Medium Seal could rise up and challenge Big Seal, take what was his. Big Seal had to prepare for that. Big Seal beat Medium Seal down again and again, but Cornelius knew what it took out of you to give a beating. He knew that every time Big Seal beat somebody, he lost a bit of himself. Eventually, Big Seal wouldn't have anything left to give.

And really, even when Big Seal was winning, Cornelius knew it wasn't as great as it seemed. Hell, Big Seal was starving to death (the documentary didn't even mention that until three quarters of the way through)! All the other seals got to go out fishing, but not Big Seal. For months at a time, Big Seal had to hold his kingdom together, keep all the women satisfied, and fend off the final battle that would one day kill them all.

Honestly, when Cornelius thought about it, Medium Seal was in the best spot. First of all, just knowing that Small Seal had it worse than him seemed to give Medium Seal some satisfaction. And then he didn't have all of Big Seal's responsibilities. Goddamn if Medium Seal didn't almost seem happy when you looked at him.

After all, his days were all right: First he'd get up and pound on Small Seal for a while. Then, maybe he'd go out and get himself some fish. After that, he'd be chatting and woofing it up with his medium seal buddies (no doubt telling stories about how he'd just pounded Small Seal), and then, if he got bored or whatever, he could always try inching closer to those ladies.

Now, inching close to the ladies risked getting his ass kicked by Big Seal (the documentary showed it a couple of times, Medium Seal would start yucking it up with the ladies and then faster than you can say, "Goddamn! Medium Seal's about to get his ass kicked!" Big Seal would come roaring and flopping and messing and moving, and just knock the snot out Medium Seal) (Small Seal would be watching and you could tell he wanted to laugh, but you could also tell that he didn't want to be the next seal to get his ass kicked . . . so Small Seal just laughed a little on the inside so no one would much notice). But even though Big Seal tried to protect all his ladies, he couldn't, and every once in a while, it would be a lady seal who inched over to Medium Seal. She'd sidle up to him, he'd sidle up to her, and then, bam! They'd hit it fast and hard and in like two seconds, the deed was done. Wow. Big Seal would turn around and even though you could tell he was sure one of his girls had just been screwed by some scrawny seal thirty feet away, there wasn't a thing he could do. Medium Seal had got him some.

Good job little dude.

Oh that Medium Seal: food, friends, ladies . . . really not too shabby at all. And even more important: Medium Seal, he got to relax.

Medium Seal didn't have to get his ass kicked or be tough all the time. He could take a break, chill, hang out with the ladies, even dream. Every single day of his life, Medium Seal got to dream about being Big Seal.

One day, Medium Seal could gather his courage, summon his strength, rise up against Big Seal, and strike him down. And the worst thing was that Big Seal probably wouldn't even die. He might want to die, but he wouldn't. Instead, he'd be forced from the herd, hungry, beaten, starved. The only thing left for him to do would be to wander the ocean, a lone Israelite left in the cold.

The Israelites. Why the hell was Cornelius thinking about them? Wasn't that religious nonsense part of his life finally over after all these years?

There was only one explanation: Grandma. That goddamn biblical language was returning with her. How in the world did a seventy-year-old dead lady get her ass into County Jail anyway? Cornelius laughed under his breath and snuck a glance at Grandma.

She didn't think it was funny.

~

Grandma hadn't been with him in years. Cornelius figured his dominance had scared her away. There had always been that great schism in the family: generations of church people and crime people battling it out in one big barbecue of life. When Cornelius became the head of the family, it had finally broken one way. The church people were all worn out, and the crime people were all that was left. The syndicate wasn't exactly thriving, but it had all the manpower, and Cornelius was running it. He didn't need Grandma telling him what to do. Her ghost died just as quickly as her body had ten years before. Cornelius had buried her.

Turns out her ghost hadn't died though, she just went somewhere else. It had been almost a year since he'd seen Grandma's ghost when little twelve-year-old Rip asked him why he'd never mentioned that Grandma had visited him.

"What are you talking about, Rip?"

"Grandma's been talking to me. She says she'd been talking to you ever since she died, but that you didn't never listen to her no more, so she wasn't going to waste anymore breath on you."

"Ghosts ain't real, Rip. They can't talk. They can't help you neither," Cornelius warned. "Ain't no ghost ever talked to me, and ain't no ghost talking to you now. You hear?"

Sweet little Rip just laughed. Cornelius could see his shiny, brilliant brain running through all the numbers, all the possibilities. He knew that Cornelius was lying to protect Rip just like he always did. Rip had known no real pain or suffering since Grandma died because of Cornelius. He looked out for Rip, made sure Rip could grow into the safest, most intelligent boy in the ghetto because his brother was the biggest, most powerful badass in the ghetto. No one could touch Rip because no one could run away from Cornelius.

But now Cornelius was angry. Grandma had never comforted him. Why was everyone so eager to love and protect Rip, while all Cornelius got was their wrath and punishment? Time for Rip to grow up a little, Cornelius thought. Rip needed some pain too.

There would be no crazy in this family. That was through. Cornelius had killed Grandma's ghost, and he wasn't letting her come back.

Cornelius pushed Rip hard in the chest.

"What'd you do that for?" Rip said. "You're lying. I know you're lying. I can see it in you. I know Grandma was talking to you all these years just like she's talking to me now."

Cornelius slapped Rip then. Slapped him hard. Rip fell to the ground but popped right back up again. A little bit of blood was trickling off his lower lip.

"Grandma's just helping me," Rip said. "She's helping me just like she helped you. You didn't ever have to feel lonely. You had Grandma. Cornelius, she'll help you! It doesn't have to be this way. She'll help all of us. I swear!"

Cornelius hit Rip hard in the face. When he fell to the ground, Cornelius climbed on top of him.

"If Grandma is helping you, how come she's letting you get your ass beat?"

Cornelius hit Rip to the rhythm of his breathing: inhale, hit; exhale, hit. Cornelius was going to beat the crazy out of Rip. Beat the crazy out of the whole family.

"Now tell me Grandma isn't talking to you," Cornelius said.

"She is!" Rip yelled.

Cornelius hit him again.

"Say she ain't talking to you!" Cornelius shook Rip's delicate shoulders.

"She's talking to me just like she talked to you," Rip screamed, writhing on the floor.

Cornelius hit him again.

"She ain't real. She ain't gonna help. No one's going to help, so say she ain't real or I will murder you right here and now."

Cornelius won, like he always did. Rip swore he'd never seen Grandma since she died.

Neither one of them ever mentioned Grandma again.

Cornelius could see the defiance in Rip's eyes, but token fealty was all he required. After all, Cornelius knew perfectly well that he was lying, so he could hardly mind if Rip was lying too. Besides, Cornelius hadn't totally lied because, while it was true that Grandma had visited him all those years, she never spoke to him like she did to Rip. She just stared—no words of comfort or counsel. Righteous indignation was all Grandma had ever given him, and learning how Grandma was kinder with Rip than she had ever been with him made Cornelius seethe with jealousy. For the first time ever, within the garden of love that existed in Cornelius's heart for his brother was planted a dark and bitter seed.

THAT WAS FOUR YEARS AGO.

Looking at Grandma now, in the corner of the prison hallway, she looked smaller than Cornelius remembered. She was still in her church dress and pumps and hat, but her iron back didn't look quite as rigid as it had in the past. Her laser eyes were still strong, but somehow the fire in them didn't burn quite as brightly as before.

"What's wrong, Grandma? Four years go by and you suddenly want me in your life again? You want to talk to me now that your golden boy went and murdered a cop? Now I'm the good son again? Boy, what a sorry state this family must be in if I'm the good son now."

Cornelius wanted Grandma to look away, to feel the shame she had always made him feel. But Grandma just stared at him, pursing her lips. In the end, it was Cornelius who had to look away. Twenty-six years old, and he still couldn't win a staring contest with a seventy-year-old ghost.

When Cornelius was finally forced to look away from Grandma, he was annoyed to see Anthony sauntering over. Strutting, really, Cornelius thought, as if he owned the place. Cornelius curled his lip, noting that Anthony was about the sorriest Medium Seal he'd ever seen. Looking awfully damned happy too.

"Yo, Cornelius, what up, man?"

Cornelius wouldn't condescend to this insolent provocation, given without the proper respect he was owed. But he could tell that Anthony knew something. He had cousins on every block in the neighborhood. He always had information nobody else had, and now he was lording it over Cornelius. Cornelius decided that a mean-looking nod was all Anthony would get.

Anthony was undeterred. He said, "Man, Cornelius, what's a fine piece of work like you doing sitting around here? Ain't you got bail money? I would have thought that high-priced lawyer of yours would have popped you out of here in the first week. Instead, I'm going home and you're still here. How'd that happen?"

How *did* that happen? Cornelius knew one thing: it all started with his heart getting in the way of his head. His stupid girl had gotten into a fight with her brother, who had pushed her down and bruised her pride (and her ass). Cornelius should have just let it go, but his girl was begging and crying for him to do something. Now, his girl was probably at fault—she usually was—but he had to be careful. Her complaints could affect his reputation. You can't allow nobody to mess with your girl. Once you let them mess with your girl, they'll start thinking they can mess with you too, and soon, you'll be fighting everyone.

So he'd gone over to the brother's house with a gun and a couple of guys to demand an apology. Everything had gone just fine. Perfectly, in fact. Once the dude finally stopped whining and crying, he apologized, and Cornelius thought that was that.

What he hadn't counted on was that the dude's aunty had a webcam going the whole time. She didn't appreciate Cornelius and the guys breaking her door down to get to her no-good nephew. I mean, sure, she minded her nephew getting beat, but what really steamed her was the broken door —her landlord would make her pay for that. But before Cornelius could get over there and smooth things over, she'd already turned the footage of him committing some fake-ass, domestic Class X aggravated home invasion over to the cops.

Next thing Cornelius knew, the detectives were kicking down his door, shoving a gun in his face, and dragging him to the station on a warrant.

And then there was that damn female judge. Cornelius's girl, her brother, her aunty, they all did the right thing and said it had all been a misunderstanding (Cornelius had paid for the door), but the judge watched the video and said she wasn't allowing them to drop the case until they'd all gone through some domestic abuse counseling. Domestic abuse counseling for a family that thought throwing an empty liquor bottle at someone was an act of love—yeah, that was gonna go well. The lawyer had managed to get Cornelius out on bond, but it was one of those bonds where, if even one thing went wrong, the judge would revoke the bond and Cornelius would have to sit.

Well, one thing did go wrong. Not one week after being let out on bond, Cornelius was taking that skanky girl home from the club to screw her when the cops pulled him over. That whore had apparently left an eighth of an ounce of blow in his car, and the cops pinned it on him instead of that stupid, drugged-up female. Rip had been there too. He even offered to carry it for Cornelius, saying it wouldn't matter if a juvenile got a drug case, but Rip was Baby Obama in the neighborhood, and Cornelius was not going to let his perfect little brother get in trouble for anything, let alone something he didn't do. Rip would carry no weight for nobody—unless it involved some algebra equations. Cornelius would make sure of it.

He owed Grandma that much.

Besides, he was half afraid the old bat would materialize out of thin air and cut his throat if he didn't do right by Rip. There was no telling what a crazy ghost could do if you really pissed her off. So there Cornelius was, caught up in this double ridiculousness that wouldn't go away until he completed a thirty-day counseling course in the jail led by a therapist who, once he and Cornelius came to the mutual understanding that neither of them gave a crap, spent their sessions reading the newspaper.

Anthony was still flapping his Medium Seal flippers. "Man, your brother sure don't play around. That guy goes from squarest dude in the city to cop killer overnight. Who knew? I figured you guys must not be true blood, but turns out he really is part of your family."

"Shut up. Rip didn't kill nobody," Cornelius said. "That's just some neighborhood foolishness."

"Well I guess since you already know everything, you don't need to know what I know. Man, I don't even know why I'm talking to you." Anthony brushed his hand through the air like he was knocking crumbs off a table. "I'm going to be out of here tomorrow, and you'll still be sitting."

Cornelius smiled a little. He had seen it from a mile away: Medium Seal wanted to play.

"I've been talking to Kingman," Anthony said. "He says he can get me some nice product. He says you were running the spot fine while you were out there, but it runs like crap now that you're in here, and the people you got out there now are lazy. So I told Kingman—since you're here indefinitely and all—that I'd do him and you a favor and take over the spot. You know, just until you get out. I'll hold it for you. Nice and proper. It'll be a good thing. You can relax."

Oh Anthony, Cornelius thought, don't you know that Big Seal can't never relax? And here you are foolish enough to tell Big Seal something you're about to do? Bold, son. Stupid. You can't approach Big Seal unless you're ready to fight. Cornelius looked Anthony up and down, saw his eyes glancing away from him.

Anthony was not prepared.

Hell, Cornelius thought, Anthony's so dumb he doesn't even realize he's Medium Seal. His lack of self-knowledge made Cornelius pity him.

"So what you're telling me," Cornelius said, "is that you and Kingman been talking without my permission."

"Damn, Cornelius. It's a free country. I can talk to whoever I want," Anthony said.

"A free country? Here? Your dumb ass is sitting in the county jail and you think it's a free country?"

"I told you." Anthony's voice cracked a little. "I'm helping you. I'm not pushing you out or anything like that. I'd just be holding it for you, like I said. I'll keep your family involved and everything."

"My family? You think you're going to talk about my family while you're stealing food off our table?"

"Naw, Naw. It ain't like that."

"You know what? Maybe I should call Kingman over here and see if he'd even back your story. You think he's gonna come over and tell me that you and him was talking? Or do you think he's gonna say you're crazy, and he would never dream of talking to you?"

"Man, how am I supposed to know what Kingman would say?" Anthony's fingers were twitching now.

Cornelius moved in closer and whispered into Anthony's ear, "If you don't know what Kingman's going to say, you shouldn't have come over." Cornelius had to restrain himself from biting off Anthony's ear and then smashing his earless skull into the concrete floor. "Don't you know that, unlike you, Kingman doesn't have just one night left in this joint? He's sitting on conspiracy to murder, and his trial ain't starting for two years, minimum. Sure, he's got some nice product out there, but how many soldiers does he have in here? How many nights you think he wants to stay up in his cell wondering if the door will open and he'll get beat to a bloody pulp by people who don't like the way he does business?"

"Cornelius, I'm telling you, it's not like that."

"In fact, now that I think about it, you still got one more night up in here. You want to stay up all night? How well does your cell door lock? You think Sleepy the Guard is gonna come running when you start screaming? Or you think he'll just turn up the TV volume because he got told there was some jail discipline that had to get taken care of. How about that child molester cellmate of yours? You think he's gonna remember a thing when the guards come and pick your bloody body off the floor and ask him what happened?"

Cornelius watched as Anthony looked over his shoulder. Looking for more medium seals, no doubt. But they weren't there. They never were. Those medium seals only showed up when it was time to pick on Small Seal. When it's Big Seal, well, you're on your own.

"I'm sorry, man," Anthony stuttered. "I didn't mean nothing by it. I'm just talking, you know how I am. Like I said, I was only thinking of you. I thought of how messed up this thing with your brother is, and I thought you might like a little help. That's it. Nothing at all like what you're talking about. I shouldn't have been talking to Kingman like that. You're right. That's my fault for talking out of turn. Look, let me tell you what I heard. It's a messed up story—"

"Well you don't know nothing about my brother I don't already know myself, so don't be telling me no foolish rumors. The neighborhood talks more than it ought to."

"Naw man, this ain't no rumor. I heard it straight from my cousin, Tron. And anyone can talk bad about Tron, but he's about as straight and honest as a dude can be. When that cop got killed, Tron got a call from your little bro. He said he needed help. Said he was at Vicki's house and they needed to pick him up and hide him because nobody could see him how he was."

"What was Rip doing in Vicki's garage? And if he really was there, why the hell would he want to leave? Ain't no police been in that reverend's house without taking their hat off in twenty years. There couldn't be a safer place in the world than that girl's house."

"That's the thing!" Anthony exclaimed. "She wouldn't let Rip stay. Normally, Tron would have just rolled over there and threw Rip in the trunk or something until they got him home, but Tron ain't got no valid license—I don't think he even knows what a license is—and with a cop getting killed, there ain't no person looking like Tron going outside without getting stopped by the police. The police would definitely impound their car, and I don't know anybody who'd be able to explain away a bloody-ass handcuffed little teenager popping up from inside a trunk once they got back to the station."

"Bloody? Who hurt Rip?" Cornelius asked.

"That's what I'm trying to tell you. Ain't nobody hurt him. It was the cop's blood," Anthony said.

"Shut the hell up." Cornelius looked around. A lot of people in this jail. They naturally gave Cornelius plenty of room, being Big Seal and all, but still. "You don't know that. Even a softy like Rip knows better than to tell anybody something like that."

"No doubt." Anthony lowered his voice. "But why else would he be hiding in the garage and not want the police to see him? You and me both know what's going on. Tron may be one of the dumbest people that ever walked this planet, but every once in a while that doped-up mind of his strikes upon some genius. He had the brilliant idea of having Tin Can go get him."

"What the hell is Tin Can?" Cornelius asked.

"Not *what* the hell, *who* the hell. You know that homeless dude with a grocery cart full of tin cans? Tron figured Tin Can has been up and down every alley that ever was and draws about as much attention as a garbage can. They threw Rip into the cart, piled all the cans on top of him, and rolled him back to the house. Smooth as silk, that operation. I mean, they still got stopped by the police twice, but got let go on account that two smelly-ass dudes pushing a shopping cart in a ghetto alley is about as common as sand in the desert."

"So you're telling me that your people threw my brother into a homeless man's grocery cart and rolled him over to your dumbass cousin's basement . . . and you expect me to be happy about that? Damn, my brother's so straight you could measure out houses with him," Cornelius said. "He probably got a parking ticket and got nervous about it, that's all."

"Yo man, I hear you, but that ain't what happened. Tron says when he got to Vicki's garage, Rip was covered in blood. I mean absolutely filthy with it. And he was handcuffed, man. Handcuffed and bloody with a dead cop one block away." Anthony shook his head mournfully, like a bad actor pretending to be sad. "I don't know what to tell you, but your brother lost his mind and killed himself a cop."

Cornelius took a moment to contemplate the situation. He wasn't sure exactly what was going on, but he knew one thing was definitely true: if Anthony and Tron are revealing intimate things about your family that you don't know anything about, then something has definitely done gone wrong.

Cornelius waved Anthony off, advising him to think about where he wanted to sleep that night, but Cornelius was the one who couldn't stop thinking. He stole a sideways glance at Grandma. Her lips were pursed like she'd been holding in a fart all day. Jesus Christ. He ain't never seen Grandma like that before. She looked at him and nodded. So, it was true then.

"Hell of a job, Grandma!" Cornelius said. "You sure did raise yourself some fine-ass grandchildren!"

Cornelius chuckled. Now wasn't this a spot. He'd have to think long and hard on this one. This wasn't no simple problem, and it'd have to be done right. Now Anthony and Kingman, he could handle them. He'd just have to decide who was going to get their ass kicked tonight. He ought to break into both their cells, beat both their asses, and then have them beat each other while he watched. But he didn't have the energy to do them both. One beating would have to do, and he hoped the other would get the message by reason of example.

Anthony and Kingman were right about one thing: the people he had on the outside were lazy fools. But who could he put there? All the good ones were dead or in jail, and the customers kept dying or moving away. Can't run no operation like that.

Cornelius sighed long and low so no one would notice. Big Seal was tired. He just needed to close his eyes, even for a moment. He couldn't afford to, but he had to. Cornelius looked around and spotted a place where he could take a quick nap.

It was a risk, but it had to be taken. If Cornelius had any luck at all none of the medium seals would notice. Hopefully, they'd be too busy with their dreams.

CHAPTER SEVEN

Danny never knew how he and Mike became partners. Honestly, it was probably because they were the two youngest guys in the district—both of them made twenty-one just weeks before getting hired—and they were both so ignorant that neither one of them knew how intolerable the other's youthful enthusiasms actually were. But God, had it been fun.

Every cop in the hood is a superstar. Every idiot with a badge becomes a hero. As far as Danny was concerned, you ain't never really lived until you've driven down a ghetto summer street and seen a hundred people all turn and stare at you as you round the corner. Why? Because you're the police and they ain't, that's why. Sure, 95 percent of them hate you, but that doesn't really matter. Because they're the ones looking at *you*. Hell, it ain't even about the individuals, it's about the mob, the seething, heaving mass of humanity. That mob is the only thing you'll see, at least at first.

The anonymity of the mob is great for the assholes trying to make the place miserable. It's like a school of fish all swimming together so the shark can't see the little fishes. If you can't concentrate on one, you miss out on everything. Only later, when you get good, can you see beyond the mob, see into the dark holes in people's minds, see their fear. Fear is the tell. Like a lightning bug hanging out with the mosquitos. Just wait it out, keep watching, and sooner or later, that lightning bug's ass is going to light up. The lightning bug—that's the guy you want to stop.

He and Mike learned quick. Within a couple of months, they were hopping out of the car left and right. They got into so many foot chases that some of the guys on the watch bought them old-school track uniforms with the local gang colors and polyester shorts that were so high you could practically see their ass cheeks. He and Mike even wore them once while working a plain clothes car. Everybody laughed and took pictures. Even the guys on the corner broke into smiles when they spotted them, saying, "You know, for a couple of goofy-looking cops, you dudes are fast."

The watch commander didn't see their outfits until everyone was getting ready to go home. He about exploded, yelling, "Goddamn you assholes. Don't you take anything serious? This is a job, damn it! People are getting killed out there, and you guys are running around like a bunch of queens. You make me sick." They were in the doghouse with the captain for a whole year because of those outfits, but it was worth it. People still talked about it decades later: "Weren't you the two who worked in those tight-ass shorts and jerseys back in the '90s?"

Sure were.

Who needed a plain clothes car anyway? They made more arrests than anybody after the captain dumped them back to uniform. Working in jeans was for guys who needed to show off. Loser cops need plain clothes to show they're tough. He and Mike didn't. If you gotta prove you're tough, then you ain't. What you look like don't mean nothing. What you do shows who you are.

Danny wondered what life would have been like if they

hadn't messed it all up. If they hadn't started out too young and turned mistakes into problems and problems into families. But there it was.

Mike fell in love with Sara, but then Danny went and married her. Then lovesick Mike knocked up the strip club owner's daughter. Three years on the job, only twenty-four years old, and the two of them already had babies at home and wrinkles around their eyes.

At least it gave them something in common with the guys on the corner. They had babies coming out of their ears too.

They'd met Sara on the job. They'd gotten into the habit of going to a little coffee shop near the university (even though the hippies behind the counter probably considered them to be a bunch of fascists). But they had that pathetic liberal-guilt thing going on that compelled them to give Mike and Danny free cups of coffee and hibiscus tea. It was nice—sitting at a table next to the potted plants for a minute; saying please and thank you, holding the door open for the stroller set. People over there thought that ideas actually mattered, and that those ideas would make the world different. Crazy.

It wasn't long before they started chatting up Sara. She was sexy as hell, with glasses and a long, thick black braid running down her back. She said she taught English at the university every Thursday, once at 3:30 p.m. and again at 7:00 p.m., which gave her two hours in between to sit in the coffee shop and read. She said she had to distract herself because teaching the exact same class twice always made her feel like her life was literally going nowhere. She'd laughed at her misuse of the word "literally,' but Danny told her that, as far as he could tell, she was using the word exactly right. She literally wasn't going anywhere. It's the same damn place.

Mike immediately fell head-over-heels in love with her, and they'd go to the coffee shop every week so he could get his fix. Those two would talk about books, or politics, or why race relations hadn't improved (Danny kept his mouth shut on that one). After three months, Mike still hadn't asked her out. God knows why. Danny was sure she'd have said yes. One Thursday, Mike had to miss the first three hours of his shift, and Danny had ended up at the coffee shop by himself out of habit. Sara was there.

"What happened to your partner? You guys break up?" she asked Danny.

"Nah," he laughed, "Mike's just running a little late. I'll pick him up from the station soon and we'll get to work. I'm just killing time right now."

"How come you never talk? Mike's a regular chatterbox, but you just stare out the window like you'd rather be somewhere else," she said.

"I would rather be somewhere else. I'd rather be locking people up. This neighborhood ain't for working. And besides, I'm pretty sure you wouldn't like what I have to say," Mike said.

"And why would you think that?"

"Because I live in the real world. Not this academic ridiculousness you live in. I know that unicorns aren't real, and if they were real, they wouldn't be prancing around making magic. Nah, they'd probably be goring you in the stomach and then stealing your purse to buy something nice for their girlfriends."

"Haha. So tough guys make unicorn metaphors, huh?" She played with the end of her braid. "Is this unicorn a lovely shade of pink, or is it more of a manly gray?" Her laugh was like magical bells tinkling in the distance. He'd never noticed it before. "Don't worry, macho man, you don't scare me. I can smell a liar when I see one, someone pretending to be something they aren't. That'll give us plenty to talk about when you take me out."

"Who says I'm going to take you out?" Mike asked.

"Oh, you'd rather not go out and just come straight over to my house? That's fine too. Here's my number."

And that's how it began. What a mess. It was the best sex of his life, and he got his son Ryan out of it. But it began with a betrayal, and nothing turns out right when it starts like that. And sure, Sara and Mike hadn't even gone out, let alone become a couple, but Danny knew Mike loved her, even if Sara never claimed to have noticed—so the betrayal was there in Danny's heart, the only place where betrayal ever truly lies.

Hell, he couldn't even get up the nerve to tell Mike they were going out. For weeks, Mike kept showing up at the coffee shop every Thursday, wondering where his professor girl was. It was pathetic. He'd ask the staff if they had seen her, and they didn't even know who he was talking about. After about a month, it got to the point where Mike was about to go to the university police and illegally look up her personal information on the computer. That's when Danny finally told him.

"Jesus, you've been seeing her every day for the last month?" Mike asked. "Why didn't you say anything while you watched me make a fool out of myself wondering where she was?"

"Yo, man. I'm wrong. In so many ways I'm wrong. I just didn't have the courage to tell you. I totally messed up. I don't mess with other guys' girls. Least of all my partner's," Danny said.

"Well, she wasn't my girl, so you're clear on that one. Man, do you even like her? Like, really like her? Or is it just about the physical stuff?"

"Naw man, I like her. I like her a lot. I don't know why I never saw it before. All those times we went there and I never noticed a thing."

"Yeah," Mike said. "All those times we went there, and you never noticed a thing. The two of you never see a thing and somehow I'm the one who ends up looking like a blind man. What a world."

What a world indeed: seeing her, knocking her up, marrying her, loving her (in that order). And then buying that crap-hole two-flat and fixing it up, watching her get fat, having a baby. Which all led to getting other girls' phone numbers and all the lies, complications, and inevitable nonsense that came with it.

When Danny's marriage really got bad, there wasn't anybody for him to talk to. He spent eight hours every day in the car with his partner, and then eight more hours at home with his wife and baby. Sixteen hours a day of people you love silently hating you. That really messes with a man. In the eight hours of the day that were left over, he could either get some sleep or go mess around and have an entirely different life.

Danny chose the latter. Sleep would have to wait. As long as he drank enough alcohol and coffee, he hardly missed it.

The job was still good. Just a little less sparkle in the daily grind. He and Mike still did their thing and laughed at the world and moved around the department—joining teams, writing warrants, tapping phones. It was fun. Cops and robbers in real life.

When they went to narcotics, that was the best. Once a month, they would let Mike try to buy on the street. It was hilarious. Those street thugs would see his wholesome-ass self coming from a mile away. He would dress as a gangbanger, a street person, a plumber working from a van. Nothing worked. They wouldn't sell him a dime bag for a dollar.

One day, couldn't nobody buy nothing so they sent in their big strikeout artist, Mike, to see if he could break the drought. Man, Mike went all out: he shaved his head, got a gown and slippers from the mental hospital, practiced a speech impediment in front of the mirror for about an hour, and then put eight dollars in loose change and a couple of one-dollar winners from instant lotto together for his impressive ten-dollar buy.

And wouldn't you know, it actually worked. Mike bought. He was so happy. He had succeeded where everyone else had failed.

But it was way better than that. When they brought the dude who sold to him back to the station, the dude said he knew Mike was a cop, but he bought from him anyway. He explained that he knowingly bought from a cop because his girl had just found out he cheated on her, and he figured he was safer spending twenty-one days in jail than going home to her. Mike was outraged, said that was total BS. That dummy was in jail, and he had put him there, and whatever ridiculous story he made up didn't change that. But the dude said to look on his phone, and sure enough, he'd texted a friend, "Man, police been trying to buy from me all day. Sharon about to kill me, so I'm figuring, screw it. I'll just sell this last one to the police and call it protective custody. Stop by and get the money before I take myself to jail. This cop's gonna buy my love dope."

"Love dope!" They laughed and laughed about that. Mike could hardly speak his face was so red. They called Mike "Love Dope" for years after that. It was the best nickname ever.

Danny and Sara's marriage died a little bit more with every new woman Danny saw. But somehow—who knows how—they stayed together. For years. Sometimes, Danny thought, love keeps a thing going that should have rightfully died long ago. The only good news was that once Sara finally left him, Danny and Mike could actually talk again. In the end, a wife for a partner is a pretty decent trade.

If only that trade had lasted. But it couldn't. The betrayal remained. Danny had planted it in that coffee shop with Sara and, like a fungus, it grew. Poisoning the air, overwhelming the biosphere, killing the only thing he couldn't stand to lose.

CHAPTER EIGHT

They started calling Rip Baby Obama when he was twelve years old. The whole class had been assigned to write a speech on a famous Black American for Black History Month. Rip had totally forgotten about the speech until that morning, when Cornelius went through his backpack and found the assignment.

Cornelius was furious. "What do you think you're doing, Rip? You think you can just not turn in assignments?"

"Aw, come one, I'll turn it in a day late. She only takes 10 percent off your grade if you turn it in a day late. I've got the highest grade in the class, so it won't make a difference. The game is on tonight," Rip said.

"The game? Basketball? Grandma won't be having you watching basketball instead of turning in your homework, especially for Black History Month. You know she'd go up a wall if she heard that. Turn that thing off," Cornelius commanded.

"Damn, Cornelius! Look at the TV—the whole screen is filled with Black people!" Rip had to duck to miss Cornelius's swat to the head. "This is living, breathing Black history taking place right in front of us. Grandma would be thrilled!"

"Grandma wants the man on TV to be wearing a suit, not sneakers. You know that. So start writing that report now before I break your hand. You won't be dribbling nothing after I'm through with you."

"Cornelius, if you break my hand, I can't do no writing. Make some sense, man!" Rip could see that Cornelius was about to get really angry, so he switched tactics, "I'll do it tomorrow morning. I'll wake up before breakfast and get it done. I promise."

"Promises are for yesterdays, not todays. I'm not going to have Grandma's sighs and lamentations keeping me up all night. Do your work."

"Fine. I suppose I can write a few paragraphs about my favorite player. He's about the swiftest Black man I know."

"Rip! Shut it. No sports. Grandma wants Black history, not chitlin history. Write something proper."

"Now I know Grandma wouldn't want you disrespecting cultural history with that culturally insensitive metaphor, so I advise you to apologize right away and think about what you've said." Cornelius looked at him darkly, but Rip continued, "Now, look here. I'll watch the game, and when you're finished thinking about what you've said, let me know and I'll start writing." And with that, he propped his foot up on the sofa and leaned back. Rip was never more pleased with himself than when he outsmarted his brother.

But cleverness didn't run the family. Cornelius grabbed Rip's head with two hands, looked right into his eyes, and said, "I'm done thinking." Then he hit Rip squarely in the nose with a spatula that seemed to come out of nowhere. Then Cornelius tipped the whole couch over, dumping Rip onto the floor. After Rip's eyes stopped tearing up from the spatula, he found his eyes flitting back and forth between the angry face of Cornelius and Grandma's old-fashioned clock hanging over the kitchen table, with a quote by Dr. Martin Luther King, Jr., spiraled around the clock's face: "The time is always right to do what is right."

Clock, Cornelius. Cornelius, clock.

Rip decided.

"Alright. I'll do it." The twinkle returned to Rip's eyes when he added, "But you shouldn't be hitting me when I'm about to write a paper about nonviolent resistance!"

Cornelius smacked him again with the spatula, playfully this time. "Smart boy. Write your paper and don't be talking about hypocrisy in this family."

"You can't even spell hypocrisy!" But even as he said it, he was sprinting away to grab his backpack and pencil. Cornelius grunted and let him get away with it.

In a few minutes, Rip had scrawled out some words about how Martin Luther King, Jr., would want young people to be making a difference right now, not later, and that's what Black History Month is all about. Rip handed the paper to Cornelius and watched him count the number of words. Cornelius sniffed, then nodded toward the TV. Rip had permission to watch.

The next day at school when everyone gave their speeches, he was the only boy who hadn't written about sports. Rip won the class contest.

To his surprise, the winners had to give their speeches in front of the principal the next day. Since the speech had gone over so well in class, that night he did some revisions and tacked on about five minutes more. Rip was feeling good about his speech and, although he wouldn't admit it out loud, he was glad that Cornelius had made him write it. The next day, after Rip gave his speech, the principal announced that Rip had been chosen to represent the school at a chamber of commerce meeting, where kids from all over the city would be presenting.

Three weeks later, there he was, giving the speech at a downtown hotel in front of a thousand people wearing suits.

The whole family got dressed up in their Sunday clothes—even Cornelius, who hadn't gone to church since Grandma died.

Mo-Ma was somehow nominated as the appropriate person to drive the family downtown for this momentous occasion.

Mo-Ma was Rip's church mom. Ever since Grandma had died, Mo-Ma had put herself in charge of Rip and his sister's religious edification every Sunday from 8:00 a.m. to 6:00 p.m. Those ten hours belonged, inviolate, to Mo-Ma and the church, just as the other 158 hours of the week belonged to Cornelius and the neighborhood. Near as Rip could tell, there had never been any discussion on this matter. It just came to the family like night came to the moon.

Every Sunday morning for the last eight years, Mo-Ma and her husband, Mr. Wilson, had picked Rip and his sister up for church in their ancient Lincoln Town Car. They had never heard Mr. Wilson utter one word, not one word, in all those years. Given that Mo-Ma had never allowed a minute of silence, this was fairly understandable. But still, it was weird to see a grown man acting like a mute funeral director.

But that was it. Just those ten hours. For the rest of the week, Mo-Ma and Mr. Wilson, though they lived only four blocks away from Rip, buried themselves in some wormhole of their own creation and were never seen. Rip had only seen them outside of Sunday one time. When they'd spotted each other on the street, Mo-Ma's head had bobbed up and down like a nervous ostrich, and she had walked straight past Rip as if he wasn't there. She just kept on chatting to the silently nodding Mr. Wilson. Only the glint of recognition in the corners of Mo-Ma's eyes revealed that she really had seen him.

The church and the neighborhood were not supposed to overlap. As far as Rip was concerned, they were two parallel worlds, and if they came into contact with one another, they would surely annihilate themselves like matter and antimatter, disappearing in a puff of nothingness.

So having Mo-Ma drive Rip to the speech was an unprecedented colliding of worlds. That Thursday evening, when Mo-Ma and Mr. Wilson rolled up in their town car, Rip and Key looked at each other in shock. They would have been less shocked if they had shown up at elementary school to find that the entire Chicago Bulls squad had replaced their lunch ladies and were ladling out frozen vegetables to the adoring children.

Mo-Ma had bought a suit for Rip to wear.

"Mo-Ma, ain't no way I'm wearing that suit," Rip said.

"Richard, this suit was purchased for you on your day of glory and it will be worn," Mo-Ma replied.

"Mo-Ma, it's got a BOW TIE," Rip said.

The suit was a double-breasted, pinstriped monstrosity, complete with a shiny red bow tie (Mo-Ma had apparently conflated her storefront church with the downtown club).

"Mo-Ma, I dress up nice for church every Sunday," Rip said. "You ain't never had no cause to complain about the way I look, and I am dressed perfectly nice today, even though it isn't Sunday. That's enough. This isn't your day; this isn't the Lord's day; this is my day. I'm the one that got invited. Not you, not the family. Me. I ain't wearing that suit."

Mo-Ma stood there with her white heels and matching church hat, holding the suit in its plastic bag in one hand and a pair of shiny black shoes in the other. Mo-Ma held firm. Her eyes narrowed, and the iron will of Grandma seemed to possess her soul.

Mo-Ma won. Cornelius said, "Put the suit on, Rip. I'll be in the car."

Rip seethed in the backseat, the bow tie cutting into his neck every time he swallowed. When they hit a stoplight, Mr. Wilson turned around and spoke for the first time ever: "Cornelius, we have always believed your soul contained nothing but evil, and we have prayed for you. But knowing that you have done right by your brother and loved him as Abel loved Cain, we know that our prayers have been answered and the garden will be reborn. The garden will be reborn." Mo-Ma wrung her hands nervously in the front seat, muttering, "Such a fine young man; such a fine young man."

Despite the suit, Rip's speech went off like sodapop, and after it was over, everyone lined up to talk to him. Besides his own family, Mo-Ma, and Mr. Wilson, the only people in the audience who were from the neighborhood were Mr. Harris and his daughter. Rip knew Mr. Harris as the big-shot local pastor, but he never knew he had a daughter. Rip wished he had known, because he had never seen a more beautiful girl in his life. After asking around, he found out that her name was Victoria.

Mr. Harris shook his hand and said, "Son, those were some mighty fine words you were saying up there. But you need to learn to speak up in your own neighborhood. The community needs your words far more than the people in this audience—though I will admit, you are unlikely to get a standing ovation from your own block like you did here."

As Mr. Harris continued to shake Rip's hand, he added, "One thing you can learn from these people is how to shake hands. At least learn that." Rip looked down and noticed the way his limp hand was swallowed up in Hr. Harris's. He tried to squeeze a little harder. "The men around here don't shake your hand because they have to," Mr. Harris continued. "They shake your hand to see if they need to respect you or not. That's part of the code. Do you want them to respect you, son?"

"Yes, sir. I do."

The pastor dropped Rip's hand and turned toward Cornelius. "Your brother is going to have to learn the way of the world, Cornelius."

Cornelius spoke carefully, in slow, measured words that

somehow managed to be both respectful and menacing: "My job is to protect my brother. I promised that to my grandmother."

"I see." Mr. Harris looked at Cornelius appraisingly. "Your grandmother was a fine woman. Very strong in her faith— though we disagreed on many spiritual matters. She always spoke very fondly of you, Cornelius. She said you would lead the family wherever it needed to go. But how can you lead if you do not know where you are going? Of course, you and your family are always welcome at St. James, though I'm sure your grandmother would be quite pleased to know you're still attending the Great Redeemer Church. You *are* attending, aren't you, Cornelius? A man cannot lead his family if he cannot lead his church."

Cornelius didn't say a word. He turned and walked away.

The next day when Rip walked into class, everyone started sniggering, saying, "Nice suit, Rip. You gonna wear that for Halloween too?" His teacher had bought half a dozen copies of the newspaper and spread them around the room. On one of the inside pages was a big picture of Rip with his enormous double-breasted suit ballooning around him, the red bow tie sticking out from his neck like a clown's. Rip's hand in the photo was raised up in the air like he was a pastor blessing the people. One of the girls in the back yelled, "He looks like Barack Obama in that photo!" Another kid yelled out above the snickers, "Like a little Baby Obama." The whole class started chanting then: "Baby Obama! Baby Obama!" The chant was a mixture of laughter and pride, but Rip only heard the mockery and it tore his insides out.

It wasn't fair. That was his day. If he'd just been wearing normal clothes, that picture would have been awesome. I mean, sure, it would have been better if he'd been on TV— most of these kids didn't even know what a newspaper was— but fame was fame and nobody else had their picture in the paper.

Cornelius had broken the rules. When he'd made Rip wear the suit, he'd connected the two carefully crafted worlds that were supposed to stay separate. As the mocking chants rose up around Rip, he thought of the ways he would make his brother suffer. The anger comforted him. The bile and shame that surged in his stomach were gradually tempered by honeyed thoughts of revenge.

CHAPTER NINE

Ryan didn't know why he let Kasper drag him out. He didn't like it. Driving around the city, trying to meet up with girls from Madonna High. The windows down, the radio up. It was all so noisy you couldn't think, let alone talk. What was the point in going out to meet people if you couldn't even have a conversation with them? Kasper normally went with the other guys, but every once in a while, he would try and get Ryan to go.

Ryan figured Kasper felt sorry for him. Honestly, he couldn't blame him. It was pretty lame to stay home and do nothing on Friday night besides listening to ball games on the radio. He knew that other kids didn't have to turn the radio up to block out the sound of their moms talking to their girlfriends on the phone about whatever loser man they were, or were not, dating. Or heck, maybe they did. Ryan wouldn't know. How would he know anything about what other people did?

Still, home was safe, peaceful. Outside wasn't like that. He had his books at home, and sometimes, his mom would ask if he wanted a sandwich. Turns out, you can't feel like a loser when someone's making you a sandwich. It's just not physically possible. And even though the sandwich was lousy, and he frequently wasn't hungry, he never turned her down. He would say, "Yes, please,"and the sandwiches somehow tasted good, even when they weren't.

WHEN THEY WERE BOYS, HE AND KASPER WOULD HANG OUT every night. Didn't even have to ask. It just happened. They would walk around with the other guys from grade school, and someone would always have a couple of bucks so they could buy some candy from the store or from one of the old guys pushing carts.

When they were really young, they always ended up at Kasper's dad's house. He had a huge house on three lots with a basement and a big-screen TV and a refrigerator filled with every kind of pop and sweet imaginable. Kasper's dad had even built a basketball court out back where they could play as loud and as long as they wanted. They had the place to themselves since Kasper's dad worked afternoons.

They played there uninterrupted for years, until Kasper's dad got promoted. He got switched to midnights, and suddenly, he was always there. That's when Kasper stopped inviting everyone over and they lost the nicest spot in the neighborhood.

It never made any sense to the rest of them. Kasper's dad was nice. He'd put frozen pizzas in the oven for them, ask if they wanted any new video games. All of Kasper's little baby half-siblings were there, but they had some nanny to take care of them so there wasn't anything for Kasper's Dad to do but hang out. Sometimes he would take them to the park and hit long, sky-high baseballs into the air—farther than any little kid could dream of hitting them. The balls would arc through the sky, getting smaller and smaller before suddenly plummeting. The boys would be left wondering what would happen when the ball finally came down. Would it slam into the center of their mitt and make their palm hurt so bad they'd have to shake out the pain? Or would it plop with a satisfying kerplunk into the webbing of the glove. And you would swear you could do it all day again and again, and that you wanted it to last until the end of the world.

Sometimes when the ball was at its highest point, they'd remember that it could miss the mitt completely. It could slam into their mouths, knock a tooth out, make their gums bleed. They could taste the salt and blood just thinking about it. The fear was there, but the ball was coming and it would arrive. The kids would gather together, reach their arms up, believe.

Except for Kasper. He didn't even bother trying to catch it. He'd kick at the dirt, whine, complain it was too hot. Eventually, his dad would get mad and start to swear at him. It didn't matter how nice Kasper's dad was to them; Kasper didn't want anything to do with him. Family ain't like any other kind of relationship. Nice doesn't matter with family. Nice doesn't affect how you feel about them. Something else makes you love them—or hate them.

So that was it. Kasper stopped inviting them over. But that's alright. The neighborhood was still theirs. Hanging out with Kasper was all Ryan ever wanted anyway.

Kasper pulled up in his dad's silver Mercedes.

"Whoa! There's no way your dad let you use that car," Ryan said.

"What he doesn't know won't hurt him." Kasper ran his hands through his hair, like he was some sort of fancy male model. "Besides, if you don't drive it around every once in a while, all kinds of sediment builds up in the engine. I'm doing that jerk a favor. Anyways, he's at work driving that stupid-ass, rusted-out Honda, so he'll never find out."

"The only time I've ever see him driving this car is when he takes you to church."

"He drives the Honda so the cheapskates think he's sensible, and he drives the Mercedes so the showoffs think he ain't. What a fake my Dad is. He's so worried about impressing everybody that he doesn't even know who he is."

Ryan had nothing to say to that. Kasper's dad had never shown him anything but kindness. Just last night, he'd run into him at the Walgreens and they'd had a long talk. He said that he had a colleague who was on the board of trustees at Brown University and that they were looking for kids with potential from the "inner city" (evidently, government workers' kids from the Northwest Side were "inner city" enough). He said Ryan should look into going there. Said he'd put in a good word with his friend.

Kasper's dad said the neighborhood wasn't always great for kids like Ryan—kids with talent. It was like a lazy girlfriend who sapped all your strength. Before you knew it, your hair was falling out, and you were still working the same government job you'd started twenty years ago with nothing to show for it but a boat that needs maintenance and a girlfriend who ain't so pretty anymore.

Ryan had never heard of Brown, but he looked it up online when he got home. Turned out it was one of the best universities out on the East Coast. Ryan wondered what it would be like to live in a place where everyone didn't know what parish you went to.

"Where are the rest of them at, Kasper?" Ryan asked. "Nick and Luke and all those guys?"

"Screw them. I've been spending too much time with them. It's a race to the median with those idiots. Every hour I spend with them I can feel my IQ getting dragged down." Kasper rolled his shoulders back. "I'm hungry. We're going to El Taco."

"Come on, Kasper. We can't go there in this car. Some

gangbanger is sure to start something over there. They always do."

"I like starting things. Plus, the tacos are fantastic."

El Taco wasn't the real name of the place, but their families always called it El Taco. It had been their favorite place since they were kids. It was a one-room countertop place with peeling linoleum tiles and yellow walls that turned beige in the sunlight. But the food was delicious. None of those silly, muckety-muck beans in the burritos. All meat. The pale juices ran down your arms and made you smell like charred beef for at least a week after you ate one.

Neither one of them lived in the old neighborhood anymore. Kasper's mom had finally moved out only a couple of years earlier, when some harmless kid on the block got shot by someone who was aiming at someone else. But Kasper still liked the old neighborhood, and he wished he still lived there. Ryan figured it was because the old neighborhood gave him some street cred. Better still, it aggravated his father. But Kasper insisted he just liked it. Nothing more to it than that.

Ryan had to admit, it did have a way of getting into your blood: the chock-a-block housing, the garbage smells wafting through the alleys, the gangbangers hanging on every other corner, the possibility of anything happening anywhere. It was alive. Kasper dragged them to the old neighborhood even though he wasn't allowed. Meanwhile, Ryan didn't like going there but was permitted to go whenever he wanted. Like Kasper, Ryan's dad had a soft spot for the old neighborhood. He probably figured it was good for Ryan too, and that Ryan needed some toughening up.

It sure did feel good driving down the avenue with your best friend in a fancy car with the windows down. The avenue was four lanes, full like the United Nations, only everybody had the same accent. Then you added the smell of hairspray, Drakkar Noir, testosterone, and gasoline. The game was simple: accelerate, slow down, burn out, look at the cops in your rearview mirror, feel the pretty girls looking at you, too scared to stare back but too ashamed to look away.

That is, if you were Ryan. Kasper wasn't afraid to look at anyone, certainly not the girls. Ryan always liked that about him, even though it frightened him too.

They found a parking spot two blocks away from El Taco. They were munching away on their burritos when Ryan noticed a pretty girl and her friends looking at them from the booth across the way.

Kasper noticed too. "Hey baby," he said to the pretty one, "this ain't just window shopping. You can touch too."

The girl rolled her eyes at her friends and then shot back, "Is that how you talk to people in that uptight new neighborhood of yours, Kasper? I would have thought they would have taught you different."

Ryan looked more closely. The girl did look familiar, but he couldn't place her.

Kasper could though. "Oh, I remember you!" he said. "You guys lived down the block from us."

"Lived?" she said. "I still live down the block. You guys are the ones who moved away, not me."

And then Ryan connected the dots. Yup. She was part of that family from the middle of the block. There were so many uncles and cousins coming out of that bungalow that he was never sure which of them actually lived there. But in the morning, they would see four kids in backpacks walking to the public school down the block, looking like little baby ducks all in a row, biggest to smallest—only the momma duck was nowhere to be found.

This girl had to be about two years younger than Ryan and Kasper. She had an older sister who was about their age, but that sister knew better than to talk to two fancy Catholic school boys. Her dad would never allow it. There was also an older brother who ran with the local gang and used to shoot them dirty looks on the playground when they were kids.

But this little girl sure didn't look like a little girl anymore.

The group of them kept talking back and forth, flirting. Kasper loved to talk. Even when he knew he was being an asshole, he just kept going, pushing right through, past any reasonable point of return, until you finally figured that anyone who kept acting like such an asshole couldn't possibly actually be one. "Whoa, I didn't even know you talked English," Kasper said. "You can't blame me for not recognizing you."

"'Talk English,' huh? Nice grammar," she said. "You recognize me enough to talk smack, but you probably don't even remember my name."

She was right. Ryan could see it in Kasper's eyes. She'd caught him. But Ryan remembered her name. He spoke up for the first time, "Come on, Melanie, take it easy on Kasper. He doesn't know any better. He was raised proper, but he's an asshole, so his parents' lessons never really took. Don't worry, though. I promise to remind him of your name for as long as it takes."

Melanie smiled at Ryan then, and Ryan beamed back. The world was good, better than it had ever been before.

And so it went. They joined booths and chatted. Kasper talked too loud, but the girls seemed to like it. Ryan even inserted a few soft jokes and they laughed at those as well. And when Kasper asked the girls if they would go on a drive with them, they looked at each other and giggled. Ryan was pretty sure they were about to say yes when a familiar voice broke in from behind them.

"You in the wrong neighborhood, boys. This one don't belong to you. Why don't you run back to whatever little suburb you came from and leave this block to those that know it?"

They turned around and saw Melanie's older brother standing there like a peacock with a brand-new set of feathers. But Ryan could see he was still the same doofus he'd always been. Even with his puffed-up confidence, he couldn't shake the look of a little twerp gangbanger who didn't get enough vitamin D. Why were they all like that? Every one of the guys he ran with was two inches too short with an unhealthy pallor.

But the two gangbangers he came in with weren't the usual mopes. Must be there was some sort of high-class gangbangers Ryan hadn't been familiar with before. What were they doing with that loser brother of Melanie's? They were sitting at the booth Ryan and Kasper had just moved from. The one looked strong and healthy as a horse. He had a thick chest, a shaved head, and a low beard all over. The other one was a quiet dude with careful eyes that looked like he could pull a knife out of nowhere at the slightest provocation.

But the brother was the one doing the talking. "And who gave you permission to talk to my sister?"

Melanie answered before anyone else could. "Shut up, Julian. I'll talk to who I want. I don't need permission from a little nobody who didn't finish school and can't hold down a job."

Ryan and Kasper laughed a little then. Even some random dude two booths down gave a slight snort and a shake of his shoulders.

It made Ryan smile to hear Melanie stick up for herself and take down her brother. Plus, the more she stuck up for herself, the less Kasper would feel compelled to do it for her. Kasper wouldn't hold back from anything, and definitely not from looking tough in front of a pretty girl. Kasper would win any fight he had to, and even if he lost, he would consider it a pleasure to see out of one swollen eye for the next week. But the old neighborhood wasn't like that. You didn't just fight; you warred.

A fight around here would roar up on you like a lit fuse on a bomb. The guy would call his block, so then you'd have to call yours. It wouldn't even matter who won the first fight because three days later your friend who wasn't even there when it happened would get jumped in an alley. They'd beat him with bats and hammers, and his brain would swell up, and his momma would cry over him in the hospital. Before you knew it, shots would ring out and your living room would be filled with shattered glass, and the only thing left for you to do—logically, inevitably, irrefutably—was to kill a man you barely knew for a reason no one could even remember.

Ryan didn't want that. Not tonight. Not with the beautiful girl across from him, and the neighborhood glowing from the setting sun, and the room so filled with oxygen he could hardly breathe.

But Kasper had to talk like some people have to sing. Ryan watched as Kasper and Julian raised their voices and their body language became more and more belligerent. But Ryan remembered what his dad had told him: "The people talking loud, Ryan. They're not going to do anything. Talking is all they got, and their yapping proves it. So even though they might tell you a hundred times they are going to kick your ass, they won't do anything unless you make them, so don't make them. They're barely worth looking at, let alone wasting your time on. Now, the silent guy," his dad continued, "the one who is looking but not speaking? Well he's not saying anything because he's thinking. The thinkers are the dangerous ones. He is making plans, and he is not going to tell you those plans. Pay attention to that man, Ryan. He's the snake that's going to bite." Ryan had to give it to his dad sometimes. He was a loud-ass troglodyte most of the time, but every once in a while he would come out with some serious Sun-Tzu-Jedi-Warrior kinda stuff.

So while Julian was strutting around and woofing like he owned the place, Ryan noticed that the big dude was exchanging the occasional underhanded word with the quiet man. The big dude was clearly annoyed. He obviously didn't want all this attention. But he also couldn't let Kasper make his boy look like a fool, because everybody knows that foolishness is a communicable disease that the whole group can catch if you don't snuff it out quick.

Kasper was getting smarter, leaning back all easy and proud with his arms folded lightly across his chest. Like Ryan, he had clearly figured out that Julian was all talk. "When the schools got rid of the special education teachers," Kasper said, "did you figure you couldn't make it no more so you might as well just drop out? I mean, Jesus, surely your dad would let you ride in the back of the pickup truck with the mowers at least."

"You're nothing but a punk," Julian said. "You guys think you're tough because your dads are cops, but if you're so tough, how come you left the neighborhood? I know why you left. It's because your mommies and daddies were scared their sweet little baby boys would get the crap beat out of them by people like me."

"Oh, that's funny," Kasper replied. "You know, I was thinking of getting out of here, but it'd be a shame to leave you all alone in here. I think it'd be more fun to hear you keep talking about something you are never going to do. In fact, I think I'm going to order some more food. You want anything, Julian? Let's order you something that will help you build some muscle. Looks like you need it. And of course, I know you ain't got no money or nothing, so out of respect for your little sister, I'll buy you a taco so you don't go hungry."

Right then, the big dude motioned to the quiet man. The quiet man pulled out his phone. Ryan knew what was going on. They were calling their people.

He and Kasper should leave. This was getting out of hand. The smell of blood was rousing the sleeping wolf.

"Kasper," Ryan said quietly, "they're making calls. There's going to be more of them here in three minutes. Let's go. We didn't come here for trouble. This was supposed to be fun, and you know if your dad finds out that you took the Mercedes and got into a fight, he won't let you leave the house for a month."

Kasper looked over at the big dude and the quiet guy for the first time. "Alright, fine," he mumbled. "I'm tired of this place anyway. Damn shame. That chick was cool. Too bad about her family."

Ryan said loudly, so everyone could hear them, "Come on, Kasper. Let's get out of here. I'm tired of this place."

Kasper stood up then, and Ryan felt good. Kasper never listened to him. He wondered why Kasper was listening now, and what that said about their relationship. Maybe he was becoming a man like his father. Maybe it was the confidence that was swelling in him as he felt the soft edges of the rolled-up piece of paper in his hand. The piece of paper that he had written his phone number on and decided to give to Melanie.

Heck, it didn't even mean anything—they'd already exchanged numbers on their phones—but Ryan wanted everyone to see him plop that piece of paper onto the table. He wanted to make sure they heard him say, "Hey, Melanie, when you're done with these losers, give me a call and we'll get together. It'll be fun." Ryan could feel Kasper's silent chuckle behind him as they turned to walk away, out into the exultant night air, and the life beyond.

But as they reached the door, Julian screamed at Melanie, "Bitch, don't you touch that thing." Then Ryan watched in horror as he shoved Melanie's face against the wall with his open palm.

Ryan saw the fear in Melanie's face, the way the power drained out of it. While he didn't know what was going on back at her house, he could pretty much imagine that Julian's come-up in the gang had coincided with a come-up in the house, and that maybe the confidence he had seen in her a few minutes earlier had started dying before he even got there. Ryan couldn't stand it, no, *wouldn't* stand it. All the loud voices in the restaurant dimmed to white noise as he took four strides over to Julian and threw a wild punch to the side of his face. When his fist struck Julian's face, it was like Julian's face wasn't there at all. He didn't even feel the contact, but he saw Julian's head snap sideways like a paper doll, saw the way his eyes glassed up and disappeared into his body, saw the way his body slumped over the four-top table and the way the chairs skittered to the ground like a deck of fallen cards.

"Well, goddamn!" Kasper whispered.

Ryan stood there breathing heavily, as the bell on the door tinkled and four more gangbangers slunk in.

It was like a scene from a Western as the four other people in the restaurant scooted to the insides of their booths and tried to make themselves invisible. A mother walked through the front door with her child and took one look at the scene before grabbing the child by the elbow and spinning her little body around 180 degrees. They were back out the door before it had even closed all the way.

The big dude stood up casually and broke the silence: "You've had your fun." He brushed his hand towards the door. "And you're leaving now."

"No they ain't," Julian whined from the floor as he rubbed his jaw. "They can't hit me and not get the crap beat out of them."

"Naw. They're leaving now, and they're never coming back." The big dude looked at Kasper. "You hear that, tough guy?" He nodded at one of the four gangbangers who had come into El Taco. The guy lifted up his shirt to reveal the black butt end of a handgun sticking out of his pants.

"No way," Julian said. "They're interfering with my family. They gotta pay."

"And you're making noise when you shouldn't be," the big dude replied, turning on Julian. "We're on nation business right now. I'll teach you to take care of your family, but that's a lesson for later." He looked at Melanie and the other girls at the table one by one. He seemed to have the ability to put people in their places with his eyes. "This is bigger than your family right now," he said. "We'll take care of her later."

The big dude turned once again to Kasper: "You're leaving right now and you're never coming back, or you're never leaving at all. I ain't going to say it again."

Ryan looked at Kasper too and for the first time since the whole night had turned to crap, Ryan didn't want to leave. He wanted to stay and fight. He couldn't just let Melanie sit there and have her life dominated.

But Kasper was reading the odds—just like Ryan had told him to before—and he knew this wasn't a fight with a pretty ending. It was time to leave the neighborhood. "Come on, Ryan. Let's go."

And God did Ryan want to fight, to kill someone, but without Kasper, Ryan couldn't do it. You can't shrug off history in an instant. You can't raise yourself from the position the years have put you in, whether you want to or not.

"Kasper," Ryan said, almost pleading, "come on, we can't do this. We can't leave right now. It isn't right." But Kasper walked out, and Ryan couldn't stop himself from following.

The cool night hit Ryan as he walked outside. He screamed, long and loud, but the sound was drowned out by the highway and the vehicles on their way to anywhere but here.

Kasper walked on, calm and collected. "Screw them, Ryan. You've been right all along. This place ain't worth it. Those losers aren't doing anything. They don't know anything about life. They're going to ruin everything they touch. Look at that car. I guarantee that's their ridiculous car with the damn rims costing more than the rest of the vehicle put together. Their values are so messed up they haven't got a clue what anything's worth."

And sure enough, right there, two-hundred feet from the restaurant, was a sharp-looking box Chevy. It was painted a flat gray that made it look like a battleship and fitted with twenty-two-inch rims that glinted under the streetlights.

"Go get the car, Kasper. I got an idea."

"Ryan—"

"Kasper, just bring the car."

Kasper raised an eyebrow. He couldn't believe how tough Ryan was talking. "What are you thinking about? You'd be better off messing with a gangbanger's momma than with their car."

"Screw you. And their Moms. Bring the car around or I'll do it right now and half the restaurant will have time to come out and see us running away."

Kasper chuckled a little, "Damn, Ryan, I seriously think you've lost your mind. But sure, I'll bring the car around? I'll be back in two." Kasper jogged off toward the Mercedes.

Ryan looked through the windows of the Chevy. It was clean inside, with a custom interior. There wasn't a thing in it. This wasn't a work car. No, this car was made for showing out on Friday. As Ryan leaned against the building trying to stay out of sight, he noticed a dark green Ford Expedition parked behind the Chevy with a heavy, broken winch hanging off its front bumper. He knew immediately that the two cars were a pair: one was for show and the other for work. The Ford had a rammer in front so they could crash into whatever they wanted.

Ryan cupped his hands against the Ford's tinted glass and pressed his face against his hands to see in. He could see the outline of two black duffel bags in the back seat. He remembered what the big dude had said back in El Taco: "We're on nation business." Ryan wasn't sure what nation business was going on that day, but he'd bet a fair chunk of change that it involved those two black bags.

Ryan tried lifting the handle on the door, and it opened just as easily as can be. He could feel the heat from the engine and could see the cigarette smoke still lingering in the air.

Those four jerks who came into the restaurant had been sitting here the whole time. Ryan looked toward the restaurant to make sure no one was coming and then grabbed the bags out of the Ford just as Kasper was pulling up in the Mercedes. Those idiots. They were so eager to run to the aid of their precious boss that they forgot to lock the car doors.

Ryan lifted the two bags above his head to show Kasper and tossed them into the open passenger window. "Hit the trunk, Kasper."

"What's all that?"

"I don't know, man, but they're ours now. The nation can go to hell." Kasper shook his head and laughed, but he popped the trunk. Inside, just where he knew it would be, Ryan saw Kasper's dad's little emergency pack in the trunk. It was everything Kasper's dad needed to go to work, all in a neat little bundle tied up in the corner. He spotted Kasper's dad's expandable baton sitting in a holster like a lightsaber. Screw those guys, Ryan thought as he grabbed it.

Ryan slid over to that beautiful Chevy and extended the baton. He raised it up and brought it down on the front passenger window, shattering it in one glorious motion. God it felt good. Next, he smashed the rear passenger window. Incredible. Then he walked to the front of the car. He could hear Kasper yelling as he struck the passenger window. He was losing a little steam now, and it took three tries before he managed to break it.

"Ryan, Jesus. Get in the car!" Kasper hissed.

Ryan thought about busting out the last window, but he figured the car (and he) had enough. Kasper had stopped so close to the Chevy that Ryan could barely open the door enough to squeeze in. Ryan slammed the door shut and roared with satisfaction. Kasper hit the gas and the car thundered off.

Ryan looked behind him and saw Melanie standing there holding her purse. Her face was sad, defeated. Kasper took a hard right onto a side street to get out of view of the restaurant. Ryan was positive no one had seen them except for Melanie.

Ryan was haunted by the look he had seen on her tear-stained face. He knew that he hadn't saved her. That he hadn't done anything for her. Her brother couldn't just let time wear her down now. They'd have to break her.

Ryan was sure Melanie had nowhere to go but home. Maybe, without all the attention he had just flung at her, she could have laid low, escaped the house, and started her own identity as an adult. But now—because of him—they'd get to her when she was still just a kid. Melanie was left with those losers, and there was nothing Ryan could do about it. Whatever was going to happen to her, it was going to happen to her right now.

"What's in the bags?" Kasper asked.

Ryan opened them up. They were heavier than he had expected, like the bags at the boxing gym. Inside were neat, brick-sized rectangles wrapped in duct tape. One of them wasn't covered in duct tape, it was covered in clear plastic wrap, and he could see through it to the white contents.

"Oh my God," Ryan said.

"What is it?" Kasper asked.

"Jesus, Kasper. It's cocaine."

"What?"

"Bricks of it. There's dozens of them. There must be millions of dollars of cocaine here," Ryan said.

"Damn, Ryan."

This wasn't some neighborhood nonsense. It was the cartel. Only the cartel could get ahold of this amount of drugs. Both Ryan and Kasper had seen the news stories about Mexico. They'd heard their dads talk about the bodies stuffed in the backs of the trunks: tied up with their fingernails ripped off and their bones broken and their dead elbows and joints all turned out the wrong way.

The neighborhood rarely touched the cartel, but that doesn't mean it wasn't there. It was there in every tiny blunt and Ziploc bag of coke, in all the little syringes littering the playground. And in these two bags.

These weren't the kind of bags the cartel would let go.

"Ryan, did anybody see us drive off in this car?" Kasper asked.

"Yeah, Melanie did. Nobody else. I looked the whole time. Nobody else came out. But Melanie saw us," Ryan said.

"Melanie. Damn. Do you think she'll tell? She wouldn't tell them what our car looks like, would she?"

Ryan had seen her face, her broken spirit. As the street-lights passed by, faster and faster, like lasers blazing across his retinas, the silence spoke all the words Ryan couldn't say. They both knew. Melanie would tell. She'd have to. And then the cartel would come for them.

CHAPTER TEN

Vicki sat up and imagined herself in front of the congregation, she felt the fullness in her chest and allowed the sweet breath of the Lord to swell into her soul—or, at least, that's what she hoped she was doing.

Sister Mary had told her many times how she *should* feel: that it would be as though precious oils were filling her fifteen-year-old vessel. The oils would enter through her heart, then splash down to her feet to fill the rest of her: her legs, then her hips, then upwards toward her breasts. That was when the tightness would begin, almost like drowning. "Plunge in," Sister Mary said. "Let it fill your lungs." And to Vicki's amazement, as she breathed in the oil, something even sweeter than air flowed over her, through her fingertips, and toward the body of the church. The congregation would feel it too, the way you feel the sun on a cool spring day when the breeze makes you think you probably ought to have a jacket, but the sun is on your face and your body and it glows to bursting such that you will never need anything to warm you ever again.

Vicki was pretty sure that feeling—the one she was now

experiencing—was awfully close to what Sister Mary wanted her to feel, but not quite. Because mingled with the proper and correct feelings that Sister Mary wanted her to experience, there were also some improper and incorrect feelings—and most particularly, pride.

Sister Mary was not a fan of pride.

Of course, what did Sister Mary have to be proud of? She was one of the most shriveled-up old raisins Vicki had ever seen. "Oh shoot, there I go again." Vicki shook her head. This wasn't right. This was beneath her. Sister Mary was a beautiful woman, and Vicki could surely be a better woman herself, if she only tried.

Still, she was close to what Sister Mary wanted, and sometimes, that's good enough. It felt good to have the eyes of the church on her back and on the beautiful curve of her neck that she had previously been admiring in the mirror. And Vicki could see that her presence made the congregation feel good too, to see her so beautiful and clean next to the altar. And what could be wrong with that?

Vicki stepped up to the pulpit for her reading. The great heavy book was before her, but she didn't need it. She had already memorized the words. It wasn't hard. It'd only taken her a few minutes to practice, including the cadence and the pauses in which she would rest her eyes on someone she thought might need it most. The words were locked in and ready for whoever needed to hear them.

Years back, she had told her father, who was known to the congregation as Pastor Harris, that it felt wrong to practice the reading. It felt like acting. She felt she ought to be able to let the spirit come out of her naturally. To do it beforehand felt calculated, like a bit of a lie. But Papa told her that was part of being human, that part of church was performing and that the best performances were always planned out a little bit. Besides, Papa said, the way you act is the way you are and the more you practice it the right way, the more the right way will become the only way, until, eventually, the act will become actuality, the falsehood will become real. And—Papa summed it up quite nicely, as he always did—Jesus will make all falsehoods true in the end, so you might as well start it out here on earth trying to do the same yourself.

So Vicki trusted Jesus and she trusted her parents and she acted the right way and Jesus had—for the most part—made it all come true in her heart as well as her mind.

As she paused to take a breath, she looked at Rip, who was still sitting in the same spot he had first slipped into three years earlier. Before Rip showed up, she'd never known a boy to come to church by himself.

THREE YEARS EARLIER, AFTER THE SERVICE HAD ALREADY started, young Rip had tried to slip into the pew undetected. But no one—*no one*—can slip into St. James Hope Community Church without being greeted personally with the love and embrace of Jesus Christ Our Savior as exemplified on earth through the loving form of a duly appointed deacon.

Vicki stifled a laugh thinking about poor Brother Farley and thirteen-year-old Rip. Brother Farley was charged with welcoming God's flock every Sunday. He was stationed in the back, ready to fulfill his duty for latecomers like Rip. When Rip had entered, like a toddler too scared to look beyond his mother's shirt, Brother Farley had foolishly assumed that his timidity indicated inaction, and he arose, languidly, to greet the frail young man. However, Rip later revealed to Vicki, Brother Farley was not the only one who had made a pledge that day. Rip's pledge was simpler and was backed by speed, audacity, youth, and planning. That morning, Rip had pledged to the Lord that he would sneak into church without anyone noticing him, or he would die trying.

Rip had frozen when he saw the finely dressed forty-year-old man approaching him with a smile and an upturned hand. Rip had scouted out all of the church's entries and exits on previous Sundays of lurking, but he had not anticipated that there would be more defenses beyond the doors.

When the two men, young and old, saw each other, an Olympian competition commenced.

Poor, poor Brother Farley. He came to this war believing he was coming to afternoon tea. Vicki had seen the boy's face and knew this was no tea. The rest of the congregation (who, one by one, began cautiously side-eying the struggle) had also noticed it. And though the only noise the two men made was the soft swoosh of their feet on the burgundy carpet, the whole church felt the silent pantomime and wondered where the battle would end.

Rip's opening move was speed: he feinted left, moved right, and then ducked underneath the outstretched arm of Brother Farley, squeezed past the folds of Sister Smith's skirt, and slid swiftly into the farthest, deepest pew he could find. Rip: one point. Brother Farley: zero.

Brother Farley's whispered welcome died with a whimper as his hand, previously sent forth in gracious greeting, now dangled empty in the air. Brother Farley was nonplussed. Never before had he been forced to chase down a parishioner in order to greet them, but his duty remained clear. This was Brother Farley's church. He had underestimated his opponent (and indeed, initially had not even recognized he had an opponent), but that would not happen again. He would not fail in the Lord's work.

All Brother Farley had to do was walk down Rip's pew, a pew that was nestled between the aisle and the wall. Rip was trapped. By now, the entire congregation was watching. Even the most cataracted among them could clearly see it was Rip's intention to flee from Brother Farley's advance by either crawling beneath the pew or flinging himself against the man in attack to save himself from the terrors Brother Farley wrought (those terrors being warmth, attention, and human love).

Who would win this war? Where would this battle end?

The congregation silently leaned in.

Vicki, having just read about World War II in school, could see that the Switzerland of this conflict—the Maginot line that must be breached—was Sister Smith, who was stationed at the end of the pew Brother Farley intended to traverse. That boy had flashed by her before she knew what was happening. This aggrieved her greatly. But now she was prepared. Her pew would not be violated a second time. Brother Farley pled with Sister Smith with his eyes to let him through; Sister Smith informed him with her frown—in no uncertain terms—that she had just rearranged the pleats of her dress after the initial effrontery, and she would never— ever—let a second passage disarrange them.

Brother Farley briefly contemplated planting his hand on Sister Smith's head and vaulting over her (Brother Farley's name still hung on the high school gym as the record holder in the 110-meter hurdles) but the formal taboo of ever touching a sister's Sunday hair restrained him, as did the sight of her meaty hand clutching a very heavy-looking purse.

Brother Farley retreated to his station with the sad knowledge that he had been defeated by a scrawny, silent thirteen-- year-old. When his eyes met those of his rival deacon, he knew this would be a topic of laughter for his fellow deacons at Wednesday Prayer. Ruefully, Brother Farley knew that this story would continue to be told, at his own expense, for many more years than he cared to count.

The congregation was simultaneously bemused and annoyed by Rip's unusual entry into the church, but that was not how Vicki remembered feeling. Vicki was impressed. Later, she wished she could say she fell in love with Rip the moment he appeared so fearfully courageous in her church, but in all honesty, she could not. She recognized him immediately from the speech at City Hall that Papa had brought her to the previous month and, while she respected Rip's independence, she did not love him immediately. Her love for Rip grew only after a prophetic warning and an unholy challenge from her parents, and it would grow in the same way her love for Christ had grown: acting growing into truth, flowers springing from unknown soil, fire upon the mountain.

Her mother spoke first.

It was that evening, after the long church day was over and everyone who had eyes that could see had noticed that Rip had not come to the church because he was interested in Jesus.

"Victoria," her mother spoke, "did you notice that young man who visited the church this morning?"

"Why, of course, Momma. You've always taught me to take careful notice of any young people who should find their way into the church, and I certainly noticed him. I mean, really, how could anyone *not* notice that spectacle he caused?" Vicki giggled.

"And did you speak to this young man, Victoria?" Her mother spoke firmly. There was no laughter in her voice.

"Why, yes, I did," Vicki lowered her eyes from her mother's anger. "He came right up to me as I was fixing a plate for Papa during the picnic. He was ridiculous. And, yes, I know I shouldn't say that about people. He seemed like he wanted to talk to me, but hardly a word came out. If I hadn't seen him speak at the Civic Dinner downtown, I honestly would have thought he had a speech impediment!"

"Your father did not bring you to that event downtown to listen to boys from the neighborhood." Her mother's voice was sharp. She spoke in the unnatural phrasing of the women of the church. Vicki did not know why they spoke like that, but she found her own voice adopting that strange formality whenever she was in their company. "He brought you down there so you could see what wealth and power look like."

"I know that, Momma, but the boy was there. I remember him," Vicki said.

"The boy may have been there, Victoria, but that was not your role there, to look at boys. Your job was to see the levers of power and learn how to move them."

"Papa and I spoke about that, Momma. You don't need to worry about what I am learning."

"Oh, I do child. The fact that you think I do not need to worry about your learning only indicates how much I do indeed have to fear." Her mother gathered herself and looked off into the distance. "I did not have the opportunities growing up in this world that you have, and I don't want you to lose them. Women—and especially women like us—had no visions of wielding power when I was young. I felt blessed enough just to be able to grow up and get an education and become a nurse. The idea that I would one day sit on boards and raise capital at the tables of industry was beyond my comprehension."

Her mother turned and looked at her piercingly. "Such things are not unfathomable to you, are they Victoria?"

"No. They are not. I certainly think—"

"Nor should they be." Her mother's voice was rising, and Vicki did not understand why. "Your father and I, as well as Christ Jesus, have given you that possibility. I hope you appreciate it."

"I do, Momma! You know I appreciate it. I work hard and have done everything you and Papa have ever asked of me."

Vicki was annoyed and wanted to defend herself, but she couldn't think of a single thing she had done that needed defending. Her mother, now that Vicki truly looked at her, seemed unbearably sad.

"Did I do something wrong, Momma? Have I done something to disappoint you?"

"No, child. No, of course not. It's just that I saw the way that boy was looking at you and the way you were looking back at him—even if you do not yet know it yourself—and I don't want you to think that just because Papa took you to a dinner where that boy spoke means that boy has received his approval."

"Why Momma, what is there to approve or disapprove of in that boy? He can hardly even talk!"

Her mother's voice rose again: "Men in this world do not need to speak to have power. That is their gift and their curse. They remain silent and still inherit everything. But this boy has nothing to offer you. Nothing. Do you understand me, Victoria?"

"Of course this boy has nothing to offer me, Momma. He just looks fine and handsome standing in front of a crowd, and I don't see why Papa would disapprove of that."

"Oh, your papa," her mother snorted, "of course he wouldn't disapprove. He would never disapprove of anything indigenous to this damned infernal neighborhood. He still believes that any stone can be polished into a pearl if the love of the Lord wills it, that no one can resist the power of God's love when it works on them."

Her mother was standing up, gripping the back of a chair. Vicki couldn't tell if she was holding it as a cane or as a weapon.

"But I am no longer so sure, and you shouldn't be either," her mother continued. "This world has a cancer in it, and dead oysters make no pearls. Do you hear me?"

"Momma, I hear you, but I don't understand."

"That boy," her mother banged the chair against the ground, "will remain a stone. You can crack open that shell and murder that oyster, and still that stone will remain a stone. Your love, your long abiding prayer—they mean nothing. Nothing will have changed except your throat will be hoarse. And the stone won't even be as smooth and clean as it was before because it will be covered in the sick festering rot of dead oyster."

Vicki saw Momma lick her lips. They were white. Speckles of dry flesh clung to them. Her mother sat down abruptly and looked at her beautiful child, embarrassed by her own anger.

"Momma! I do not know what you are saying, or why you are saying it, but I am not sure it is entirely proper. These don't seem like the sort of things you and Papa have always taught me, and I'm not even sure that what you are saying is entirely Christian."

"No, child. You are right." Her mother turned towards her. The fervor was lifting. "My thoughts are indeed not very Christ-like. But you are getting to be grown. You may someday find that not every question can be answered through faith."

"Momma, is something wrong?"

"Yes, Love, something is wrong." Her mother patted her hand, suddenly gentle. "I am tired. I have worked. I have built churches. I have raised women's groups and read the scripture and leaned into prayer chains and hosted services. And for what? For what purpose?"

"Momma—"

"More vacant houses. More lost neighbors. More dead-souled children, like that boy Richard Washington and his family. Is that all the purpose we have for being here?" She spoke that last line to the room, not to her daughter.

"He told me his name was Rip, not Richard," Vicki said.

"Richard Washington is the name his family gave him. Named after his grandfather who was one of our many strong men who are now no more. His grandfather was one of the first of our people to come to this neighborhood. And if things had gone a little better for him, I might have ended up marrying him and not your father. But thank God I didn't. I foolishly believed, when I was your age, that I could change that family. Now his grandfather is dead and Rip is the last true inheritance of his family. But it won't last. They never last. He will turn into rot and despair and evilness like all the rest."

"Momma! That little boy? Evil? I am quite sure you have been reading the wrong parts of the Bible if you are seeing evil in that small skinny thing!"

"Victoria." Momma was fiery again. She half-stood and leaned against the back of her chair, rocking it back and forth. "There are no wrong parts of the Bible. None. The Bible is filled with comfort, but it is also filled with despair. Despair necessitates hope, and without despair there cannot be hope. If you do not understand that, then you understand nothing."

"Momma, what I understand—and what you have taught me—is that Jesus found the good in all places, in all people, and that he spent time with sinners and wasn't afraid to go anywhere. Jesus isn't afraid of this neighborhood or this boy. Neither is Papa, and I certainly don't see why you or I should be either."

"Victoria, as I said, there are NO wrong parts of the Bible. Jesus may not have been afraid of anyone, but he certainly did not try to save everyone. That is a falsehood and a misunderstanding of the Lord's word. Do you remember what Jesus said to Satan in the desert? He said, 'Begone, Satan!' BEGONE! Jesus did not try to save Satan. He cast him out. Jesus was tempted by Satan, but that was only to prove himself, not to save Satan."

"But what if Jesus wanted to save him but simply didn't have time in that moment?"

Vicki's mother put her hands on her hips. She wasn't really angry anymore. She was teaching, and teaching calmed her. "Even if that was Jesus's desire—and even if the Lord did send him out into the desert to be tempted in order to save Satan—that does not mean you should send yourself there. It is not your job to be tempted. Do not think you can save this boy. You cannot. No one can. This place is rotting and dying, and you must cast them out and leave."

Her voice was rising again, and she was shaking. "Save yourself. Save the goodness. Leave Richard Washington and his family alone. I know that family, Victoria. They will either whither and die or flourish and kill. They cannot be saved!"

"Momma, if you truly believed that, why did you offer that boy some juice? You think I didn't see that, hear the kindness in your voice as you spoke to him? I trust you and I love you and I will give you everything I can, but don't tell me stories with your mouth while your body is saying something different."

Vicki's mother sighed and smiled. Her daughter was so smart and loving. She did not deserve her, probably no one did. Because Victoria was correct. She *had* welcomed the boy. Whether out of habit or foolishness, she had offered that boy the warmth of her friendship and food from her table. For who was she to deny anyone the food of the table? It was not her table. It was the Lord's table (though she and her husband had been the ones to physically build it). All were welcome.

"Child, I have said my words. But as you say, the heart sometimes says truth even when the mouth lies. We are a small plot of rich soil here. I do hope we have nourished you well, though sometimes, I lose faith."

"Momma, you have given me everything. Know that I will grow in the soil you have given me. Do you hear me, Momma? Let me finish my homework and then let's do something fun. Pick out some music and let's dance in the living room. Don't you worry. No thirteen-year-old boy is going to hurt us!"

Her mother watched as Vicki skipped up the stairs, watched the small bit of little girl left in the woman that was her daughter.

Her hand went involuntarily to the hard knot on her breast. It had been growing. Becoming painful, more sensitive, harder. She did not know whether the bitterness came from her fear of this boy and what he represented, or if the true source was this evil lump growing inside her body.

She had not told anyone. She wasn't sure why. Maybe it was the fatigue of it all. She was tired of holding back the waters. She related to how weary Moses must have felt, constantly rallying his miserable flock who never did right no matter how many times they had been shown the way. She longed for the Lord to take her to the mountain and show her the promised land. She didn't need to live there, but could she at least see it? See it in her daughter as Moses had seen it from the mount? Had she not earned at least that much?

As Vicki's mother began to prepare dinner, she thought to herself: mysteries are not always solved, but they always end. The Lord never gives people burdens they cannot bear, and the Lord had finally given her this gift of the hardness in her breast to take her burdens away. She would forgive the snake. Maybe that boy would actually grow to love her girl. Isn't that enough? Shouldn't love be enough? She sighed and shook her head. And even if things went wrong and they could not serve in heaven, perhaps they could rule in hell. Maybe that would be enough.

Later that evening, Vicki's father came in while she was reading in bed. "How was church today? Did you and the other young people have a good time? I noticed you were speaking with that new boy?"

"Why Papa, are you going to talk about that nonsense like Momma did? She's already warned me. Don't worry—I'll leave that boy alone. I won't be the one bringing you any trouble. Though, honestly, I don't see what the big deal is."

Her father chuckled. "Big deals frequently come in small packages . . . but no, I will not warn you away from him. I believe he is a fine young man—though far from perfect for he has grown up in a far-from-perfect family. But that family and the circumstances he has grown up in are exactly what could make him such a force for good in this community. Pay attention to your mother in all the important ways, but in this particular instance, I must say that she is mistaken. Not only will I not warn you away from that boy—I believe it is your Christian duty to bring him to us."

Vicki sighed in exasperation. "Bring him to us? What are you talking about? I don't even know where he lives, let alone a way to bring him here."

"My child, I am blessed to have such a wonderful daughter as you, a daughter who doesn't know the power she has. You do not need to worry about where he lives. I am perfectly sure he already knows exactly where you live. He will come to you as an animal comes to a spring of water. Just . . . don't turn him away. Talk to him. For thousands of years people have come to the church for all sorts of reasons, and not all of those reasons need to be in the spirit of the true faith. Someday even the devil himself might be lured to church, and when he does, I hope we have the courage to welcome him. You are bright and good and beautiful, and this boy will surely come. That is a good enough reason for the Lord's work here on earth."

Vicki blushed. Her father had never made her blush before and it did not feel right.

Her father continued, "This community needs that family. It needs all its strong families to work together. Look around you. Look at this neighborhood. It doesn't have to be like this. We can make a difference. You, me, your mother—we can turn this neighborhood around and bring back all the goodness that has always been here. The goodness never left. I know it."

Vicki's father was almost pleading with her. He had never done that before. He had always given, never taken. Now, he was asking her to do something that he couldn't do himself. Her mother warning her, her father begging her—it felt wrong, and it was all over a foolish, skinny, beautiful boy.

Wrenching herself back to her reading, Vicki saw the congregation looking at her expectantly. Her childhood seemed so far away in this moment.

Rip, too, seemed far away, with his brother in jail and all the bills piling up. Vicki wanted to help, but she hated the way his uncle looked at her ever since he came home from jail, so she had stopped going over there as much. But she could see the stress in Rip's eyes and knew he was in trouble.

She thought back to her mother calling him a snake and saying that her father loved the neighborhood a little too much. Vicki wondered whether it's OK to use people, even if it is for all the right reasons.

Oh Lord did Vicki miss her mother. It wasn't fair that a thing that was so beautiful could die. Her mother would know what to do. She tried to channel her mother. Would she still say that Vicki should let Rip go? Would she say it's alright to use people as long as it was for the right reasons? Or would Momma simply tell her to stop listening to these foolish men and get busy saving the world herself?

Did Jesus use people? Did Jesus use his disciples? Vicki wondered. They all died, that's for sure. They were all murdered. Her father always said that no one can resist Jesus, but if Jesus is irresistible, are you really *choosing* to follow him? Don't they always say you don't choose Jesus; he chooses you? Jesus chose to die so that others could be saved, but did his disciples make that choice, or did Jesus do it for them?

At the pause in her reading, Vicki reached out to Rip. She reached out to the snake, the lover, the father of the child she was pretty sure existed but had spoken about to no one. She reached out to him with all the power that welled up in her body and was spilling out of her, all the oil that overflowed her cup, all the love that her family and her church had given her.

Sitting there all alone in his pew, Rip looked distracted. He was somewhere else. But his eyes found hers in that moment, and he smiled. Vicki knew she had touched Rip's heart. That was what she was here to do. But she also felt his mind slipping away. Would she follow him in order to bring him back as her father wanted, or would she let him slip away as her mother had admonished?

And if she did follow him, would she find the boy or the snake?

CHAPTER ELEVEN

R ip wondered how long a person could subsist on Flamin' Hots, orange soda pop, and chocolate peanut butter cups before they collapsed into a heap of malnourished flesh.

"Dude, what is wrong with you? Rip asked. "Have you ever noticed that every single thing you eat is orange?"

"No it ain't," Tron said, crinkling his tawny eyes and looking at the corner of the ceiling thinkingly. "Like, peanut butter cups aren't orange. They're sweet, like me." At this proclamation, Tron beamed.

"Tron, the inside's orange, and the packaging they come in is about as orange as could be. I figured it was some kind of special diet you were on or something."

Tron surveyed the ruin of candy wrappers, chip packages, and crumpled-up pop cans littering the dark basement Rip had been living in for the last three days with a bewildered expression on his face. It was true. All of it was orange. You could have lit the room by the color of it.

"You know, you're right!" Tron placed his awkwardly large head in his hand and drummed his fingers on his cheek. "I'm going to try to find some more orange things to eat. I bet they'll taste good too. That was super helpful. You're so smart, Rip!"

"Jesus, Tron. Here's an idea: maybe you could try some ACTUAL ORANGES. You know, the fruit? Those things that come from a tree, not a factory? That would be an improvement. And maybe then I wouldn't be getting scurvy down in this basement. Yo, and another thing: What's all this old laundry doing down here? You ain't even got no laundry machine down here. It doesn't make sense."

"We used to have a laundry machine, but then Jordan sold it to get a Christmas present for his girlfriend. It sucked at first, but then I bought some new clothes and I haven't needed it for a while," Tron said. "And what the hell is scurvy, anyway?"

"Jordan broke up with his girlfriend two years ago! Are you telling me these clothes have been sitting down here for over two years waiting for a laundry machine that ain't never coming back?" Rip asked.

"I wouldn't say it's never coming back. They might get back together," Tron said.

"Tron, that wouldn't even matter! Even if they get back together, that won't make the laundry machine get un-sold. It'll still be gone, along with the nonsense jewelry or dope or whatever Jordan spent that money on."

Tron sat down on the dusty old couch that had been ripped apart by a dog that had died even longer ago than Jordan's relationship. He looked at Rip. "Yeah, you're right. I guess I should clean this stuff up. Maybe some of it still fits." Tron paused. "You know, for a boy who ain't left the house in three days, you sure are complaining a lot. You got any plans?"

Man, Rip thought, just when you thought Tron was dumber than a box of rocks he comes out with something smart. When *was* he leaving? Truth was, Rip had no idea.

After he'd arrived, Rip was scared to go anywhere. He was sure the cops would be tracking him, so he'd turned off his phone and didn't tell anyone where he was. He'd made Tron swear he wouldn't tell any of his family or friends. Tron was trustworthy, but the rest of Tron's family would sell him out even quicker than they'd steal the family washing machine.

Tron had kept his word, but he was convinced that Rip was overreacting. As far as Tron was concerned, if the cops didn't find any evidence on you, they couldn't make no case. "Rip," he said, "if they didn't arrest you with the dope right away, you're good. Why are you worried?" Of course, Rip hadn't told him what had happened with the cop, but he was pretty sure Tron knew. Tron wasn't *that* dumb.

Although Tron was a pretty chill dude and was happy to go along with whatever Rip said, all this pretending was beginning to wear on Rip. He felt like Ichabod Crane, carrying his head around in his hand while Tron just acted like it was totally normal for him to have a pumpkin perched on his neck where his head used to be. A lot of people wouldn't be able to pull off ignoring something so obvious like that, but Tron? He was good people. He was doing his best.

Tron had pointed out that the whole dope thing didn't make too much sense either. "Rip, you had five rocks on you. That ain't nothing. Even as an adult, you'd just hang out at Cook County until you made bail. You so clean you'd have made bail on nothing but a signature. And even if they made you post some money, your brother would have got you the money in no time. Worse comes to worse, they'd have a hearing and then toss your case out in no time. You'd sit in county jail for three weeks tops. It ain't possible to have probable cause for only five rocks. You gotta have ten for that. Besides, you're a juvy. Juvies can't get cases. Your momma could have picked you up from the station about three hours after they brought you in. You probably wouldn't have gone to court or anything and it would have just been drug school at the worst. Why didn't you just take the hit? I thought you was smart, Rip."

Now, Tron's logic had a couple of flaws in it. First of all, Rip wasn't so sure his brother would have been able to come up with bail. Nobody in the neighborhood knew how low the funds in their family were running. Cornelius still lived large to keep up appearances—you had to, you could never let your guard down and show weakness —but they'd been scraping the bottom of the barrel for months and Cornelius being in jail had really laid them low. Second of all, how would he even find his mother to come get him? She'd been bouncing back and forth between halfway houses and hospitals for years, and if you couldn't get a parent to pick you up, a lot of times they'd put you in the juvy home regardless of your case. And most importantly—and Tron would never understand this— Rip couldn't get caught because he was Richard Washington, the Great Hope. He'd be disappointing three quarters of civic leadership if he went to jail.

"I am smart, Tron. That's why I've got full-ride scholarships all over the place. You don't understand. I can't get caught with drugs. Too many people believe in me. I had to run."

"Ha, you funny, Rip. Scholarship? You ain't even that good at basketball! How would you get a scholarship?" Tron laughed and laughed. The Corner Boys laughed too, rolling on the ground, slapping their thighs, and wiping tears from their eyes.

Rip hated the Corner boys so much. Everyone had left him but those damn fools. Why were they always lurking about, fading into his life when he least wanted them? Even in this basement, where there was nothing to do, they lurked: bored, sullen, listless, occasionally shuffling back and forth with confused expressions on their faces. They were waiting. Waiting for something to laugh at, something to do, anything. But anything never came.

Tron and Rip had a hell of a time getting the cuffs off. Fortunately, Tron had some tools sitting around, and they were able to use a chisel to break the chain between the cuffs. That gave Rip a lot more freedom, but they couldn't get the bracelets off to save their lives. Tron thought he could shoot them off with his older brother's 45 and had even brought it down to try. Tron said he'd seen one of the McAllister twins do it and it had worked perfectly, but Rip had never heard that story and was doubtful of it being true. He was even more doubtful as Tron aimed the gun at one of the bracelets. But it was when Rip saw Tron take a deep breath and close his eyes right before pulling the trigger that he decided he'd had enough.

"Jesus, Tron! You're closing your eyes! What's wrong with you?"

"I wasn't closing my eyes! What are you talking about?" Tron lied, lowering the gun.

"Yes you were. Gimme that. You were probably closing your eyes because you didn't want to see yourself peeing your pants. Did the McAllisters actually do this? Or are you making that up?" Rip asked.

"Well, they didn't exactly do it, but they saw it on YouTube, and that's practically the same. It'll work, Rip, I know it will."

Still, Rip could see the relief wash over Tron's face when he said they would have to think of something else. And besides, he told Tron, the bracelets weren't hurting his wrists that much. It looked a lot worse than it actually was.

That was a lie. The bracelets were actually even worse than they looked. When they were breaking the chain with the chisel, Rip had pulled back as hard as he could and both cuffs had clicked together tight as a trap. Rip's wrists had swollen up and half the metal became buried in his flesh. Blood and puss had been oozing up from the left one for the last day or so. Meanwhile, his right hand had been numb and tingling for at least two days. It had gotten so bad that he could barely move it, and when he did move it, it was like the hand of a ghost: he could see it move, but he felt nothing. It was as if a stranger's hand was grafted onto his body. The night before, Rip had woken up in a sweat after dreaming that his hand had been choking him out like in some late-night, black-and-white horror movie. Remembering the dream made Rip shiver as he imagined his hand twisting around and winking at him like a sock puppet.

Tron had been nagging him for days to contact Cornelius, saying that Cornelius would know what to do. Tron was probably right, but Rip didn't want to call him, not when he could still feel the cop's body heavy on his chest, the way he had to wriggle like an eel to get out of it, and the salty sweetness of blood lingering on his lips.

Blood begets blood, violence begets violence.

Rip didn't want his family here.

He closed his eyes. The image of his throbbing hand hung just behind his eyelids, desiring to choke him out. It wasn't worth it. "Hey Tron, you think you can get a hold of my brother?"

Of course he could. Tron knew how to get in touch with everyone. A few hours later, Rip was talking to Cornelius on a phone that'd been smuggled into the jail.

"Don't tell me what happened, Rip. I don't want to know what happened. Just tell me this: Is what I've been hearing what I should be hearing?"

"Well, how would I know what you're hearing? I've been holed up in this basement for the last three days, remember?" Rip could hear himself whining and was annoyed with himself. This wasn't how he wanted to sound to his brother.

"Don't be smart." Cornelius's voice loomed large, even over the phone. "Cause you ain't right now. The rumor I heard is that some dumb fool went and killed a cop. And then you're telling me that, coincidentally, you and Tron have been laying low ever since then. That about cover it?"

"Yeah, it's something like that, but it's more complicated," Rip said.

"There's always complications, Rip. But complications don't play. Look. I know what's going to happen. I'll take care of this. Just tell Tron everything that happened. The truth. All the details. I want him to know everything."

"What's the point of telling him, Cornelius? I'd rather tell you. Let's keep this in the family. I messed up. I should be the one to take care of this, not you."

"No, Rip. I take care of you, not the other way around. That's the way Grandma wants it."

"Grandma. Come on, Cornelius. I know you're not going to like it, but I have to tell someone, someone who understands."

Rip felt his heart beating faster. You're not supposed to admit crazy. Especially to Cornelius.

"You've always understood, even though you say you don't. But it's just—Cornelius, she left me. Grandma's gone. Everyone left me, and I'm all alone."

Rip could hear the soft breathing on the other end of the line. He could hear the noise in Cornelius's mind.

"Cornelius? You there? You hear me?"

"I hear you," Cornelius said.

"So you gonna say something?"

"Yeah."

"So . . . what are you gonna say?" Rip asked. He was tentative, hopeful.

"Say something. Damn. Sure, I'll say something." But he didn't for a long time. Then he took a gulp of air and said, finally, "Rip, I am going to beat you senseless the next time I see you. Ghosts ain't real. I've told you that."

Over the phone, Rip heard a deep breath of air, like a man about to plunge into a cold, dark, bottomless pit, looking for something he had lost a long time ago. "But Rip, I don't know. All I can say is that she ain't gone. She ain't never going to go. Our family ain't going to go until we're all dead, and even then, I don't know."

"She's with you, Cornelius? She went back to you?"

"Shut up, Rip. Just do what I told you. Tell Tron what happened and lay low. Don't go anywhere. I'm taking care of you."

"Cornelius, I know she's with you. Just tell me. I'm scared. I have to know."

More silence on the line. Finally, Cornelius said, "Rip, I'm not going to tell you what you want to hear, but you can imagine whatever you want. What you think is yours, what you imagine belongs to you. Ain't nobody can change that."

"Alright, alright. I hear you. Thank you. That's good enough for me. But Cornelius? One last thing. We can't get these handcuffs off me. We've tried everything—cutting them, crushing them. Hell, we almost shot them off. Cornelius, they hurt so bad I think my hands are going to fall off. Seriously, Cornelius, I think I'm going to die."

"What, the lock don't work?" Cornelius asked.

"The lock? What do you mean?" Rip said.

"The lock, you idiot. The little hole in the side? You stick a key in and they pop off."

"We don't have the key, Cornelius. I didn't take it."

Rip heard the exasperated sigh on the other end of the line.

"You and that dumbass friend of yours. How dumb can two idiots get? Rip, they're all the same. Every single set of handcuffs in the whole wide world has the exact same key. Jesus, Rip. Tell that idiot to go into his sister's room. She's got handcuffs all over in there. That girl may be fat, but she is dirty as hell. Get those cuffs off, tell Tron everything, and stop feeling sorry for yourself. You better start thinking, because you're going to live, goddammit. You have to."

Rip heard a click, and then he was alone, holding the dead phone in his unfeeling hand. Tron had been right. Cornelius could help him. If he hadn't been so dumb and had listened to Tron, he could have gotten these cuffs off days ago.

But Mr. Harris would have helped him too, and Rip would have felt good about the blood returning to his hands the way Mr. Harris would have done it.

Mr. Harris and Cornelius had always helped him, and Rip knew they would help him now. But the longer he waited, the harder it would be for both of them to help him at the same time. He didn't want to choose, and he didn't want to tell Tron the truth. He wanted to tell Mr. Harris the truth.

After all, once he and Vicki were married, Cornelius wouldn't be his only family. Mr. Harris would be his family too. It would be OK to tell Mr. Harris what had happened because he was family, unlike Tron. Rip tried to swallow, but his mouth was too dry.

Rip was beginning to think that Cornelius knew where he'd gotten those rocks, even though he hadn't said anything about it. Why oh why had Tron made him call Cornelius? Now he'd have to listen to him. Rip had come to the end of his own ideas, and at the end was family. Cornelius always said that family stays together. Always. But they don't always stay together for the right reasons.

Rip looked at Tron, saw his gangly scarecrow limbs bouncing around as he laughed at some stupid video on his phone. He had to get out of here. Rip looked at his wrists. The puss was oozing out and mixing with the blood, forming a sickly orange liquid. He watched, transfixed, as he imagined how it would taste if Tron drank it.

CHAPTER TWELVE

The engine and the wind were the only sounds they could hear inside the Mercedes. Kasper was pissed, but talking wouldn't make it better. Besides, his tongue was dry, and he didn't want Ryan to think he was scared.

Kasper looked at Ryan and knew he was thinking about what Melanie would say, but all Kasper could think about was what a lousy drunk Ryan was. Plus, ya know, trying to figure out how they would get home without being killed.

For now, Kasper's only plan was to drive as fast as possible without looking like a jagoff. Jagoffs get noticed and, sometimes, killed. They also get pulled over. His dad would blow a gasket if he found out Kasper was driving the car, and if he got pulled over while speeding away from a bunch of gangbangers with a duffel bag full of cocaine in the back seat, the big vein in his dad's forehead might get so swole it'd burst. Damn, Kasper thought, even El Taco's food wasn't good enough to justify all this.

And how the hell were they going to get rid of all that cocaine? Ryan had been arguing that they should just throw it out the window and call it a day, but Kasper didn't think that was a good idea. What if someone saw and got their license plate? He could see the headline in the newspaper now: "Cops' Kids Caught with Cocaine."

Dear Old Dad sure would be thrilled with that.

Kasper figured there was another problem with just throwing the drugs out the window: if those assholes managed to find them, they'd have a hell of a lot better chance of not getting killed if they had some drugs they could leverage.

Eventually, they settled on heading over to the old rail yard where Uncle Charlie drove trucks for a living. When they were little, they would go visit Uncle Charlie there all the time. He'd put them in the dump truck and raise the hydraulics as high as they could go. They kept going up and up until it felt like they were higher than any amusement ride they'd ever gone on. Uncle Charlie would always pretend to forget about them and start walking away while they screamed so loud from the back of the truck that they almost peed their pants.

It was super fun.

Back then, the place was bustling with activity: tons of people, weird little tugboat trains, big trucks, everything. A few days a week, a real train would come off the spur and these monstrous-looking cranes would go to work loading the trucks, which would then be driven by people like Uncle Charlie to tiny little factories throughout the city.

But then they terminated that rail spur and it went from a twenty-four-hour operation to a nine-to-five-type thing. Now the place felt empty. It was so different that Kasper and Ryan could hardly even trust their memories of the place. After 6:00, there wasn't a living soul around.

Back in the day, the old rail yard felt jammed full of people. Once they left, you suddenly realized the place was just an empty industrial wasteland, complete with tumble-weeds in the form of plastic grocery bags. All the young guys who used to work there had been let go via seniority. Uncle Charlie was the youngest guy left because his dad had been a union boss and was able to get Charlie in there when he was only seventeen. Jesus Christ, Kasper remembered thinking, if Uncle Charlie is your youth movement, then you really are just waiting to die.

Out by where the train tracks used to be, the grass had grown at least six feet high. Uncle Charlie always joked that you could hide a body back there and nobody would ever know. Even the vultures avoided it because all the heavy metals in the soil would kill them.

That's why Kasper and Ryan decided this would be the perfect spot to dump the drugs. The grass would grow up around them like some horror-movie monster swallowing its own, but if they marked the spot somehow—using the buildings or the telephone poles as grid landmarks or something—they could find it again if they had to. Heck, they could even make a map. A treasure map leading to the only kind of treasure the ghetto had made in years.

The closer they got to the old rail yard, the better Kasper felt. They were going to get away with it. It was going to be OK. If nothing went wrong, this would become a funny story he and Ryan would tell at the bar someday. The first of many, as far as Kasper was concerned.

Kasper had been driving exclusively on the residential streets, figuring it would be harder for anyone to find them, but they hadn't seen any of those thugs from El Taco since they left, so he started easing onto the commercial streets. It was a twenty-minute drive to Uncle Charlie's work, and they couldn't stay off the main streets the entire way.

It felt particularly weird since Kasper knew that Ryan's dad was working that area tonight. If Ryan's dad spotted his old partner's Mercedes, he would definitely pull them over. They hoped that wouldn't happen, but even if it did, it wouldn't be the worst thing. Definitely better than his own dad finding them. Je-sus Christ. He couldn't even imagine the drama that would ensue. Kasper wished his dad would just beat him, but physical punishment wasn't his style. No, he'd yell, and his eyes would bug out, and his skull would puff up out of his skin like it was a virus trying to explode out of an infected cell. He'd keep screaming and glaring at Kasper for at least a month. It didn't seem so bad when he described it, but it was the worst thing Kasper could imagine. His palms started sweating just thinking about it.

But Ryan's dad was different. He wouldn't yell. For him, wrongs have natural consequences—no need for judgment or lectures. Besides, he'd know what to do about the drugs. He always knew exactly what to do. Hell, now that Kasper thought about it, maybe they should just call Ryan's dad. He could picture telling him about all the cocaine. Ryan's dad would raise his eyebrow, say, "Kid," he might even say, "You guys might have one hell of a pinch here." All they'd have to tell him was that they saw it in Julian's unlocked car after overhearing him talking about it in the restaurant, and they decided to make a difference in their community by taking it out of there and delivering it to the police. "What kind of car did you say they were driving?" Ryan's dad would say. Then they'd be the ones chasing those idiots, not the other way around. It felt so good just thinking about it, he wondered, why weren't they doing it? Heck, he and Ryan weren't drunken idiots, they were drunken heroes!

Kasper started shaking his head. When you get into the old neighborhood, you get caught up thinking that everything is your fault and you have to do everything yourself. You forgot there is a whole society out there that thinks there is a right thing to do and a wrong thing to do, and as long as you do the right thing—at least most of the time—it'll all work out. Why shouldn't they just do the right thing and turn the cocaine over to the cops? That's what people are supposed to do.

"Ryan, listen up: call your dad and tell him what happened. He'll be able to fix it."

"Call my dad and tell him we busted out a bunch of gang-bangers' windows and stole their drugs?" Ryan exclaimed, briefly lifting his head from where it had been plastered against the passenger window. "Are you out of your mind?"

"Naw, I ain't out of my mind. Why *not* call the cops, call your dad? We haven't done anything wrong. Taking drugs from gangbangers is what we're supposed to do when we become cops," Kasper said.

"When *you* become a cop, not me. That's your thing. I want nothing to do with it." Ryan turned to him then, his face looking pitifully thin in the pale glow of the streetlights. "If it's such a good idea, why don't you call *your* dad? Why should I be the one who is left explaining this to my family for the rest of my life?"

"Call my dad? Now you're the one talking crazy. First, he'd insult me, then he'd probably figure he wasn't being thorough enough, so he'd plant the drugs on my body and give himself an award at work. I can hear him now: "Evil must be stomped out of this earth, even if it is found in a man's very own home." Kasper imitated his father's lyrical, pompous tone.

"Sheesh, Kasper. He's not that bad. Other than telling you you're a screwup from time to time—and you gotta admit, that can be pretty accurate from time to time—I've never seen him do anything but nice things for you."

"Yeah. Like you'd know. I ain't asking that jerk for anything, I'll tell you that much. Living with that asshole is like getting waterboarded for fun every night. His sanctimonious, holier-than-thou routine drives me up the wall. He's got you fooled too, but the thing to remember about him is that he only does things when he wants something from you. Don't forget that," Kasper said.

It was a cold night. The exhaust from the cars billowed in the air like steam, and the streets were white with salt. It was too cold for anyone to be out walking, but not too cold to drive. It seemed like everyone was out and about in their little lands of freedom on wheels, with the heat and the radio turned up. Kasper was almost feeling comfortable again when he peered into the rearview mirror and thought he could see the outline of dumbass Julian in the driver's seat of a Lexus a couple of cars behind them.

"Ryan, now don't be jumping up and down and making a commotion or anything, but look in your mirror. Is that idiot Julian two cars back in the right lane?" Kasper asked.

Ryan slunk down in his seat and leaned forward to peer through his side-view mirror. The mirror was spidered over with frost, and it was hard to be sure about what you were seeing.

"I don't know, man. I can't tell," Ryan said.

"How the heck did he find us? We've gotta be at least five miles from El Taco," Kasper said.

"I don't know. Maybe he's heading to our neighborhood. We told Melanie where we live, and it wouldn't be that hard to find out even if she didn't tell him. We're still on the route home until we turn south toward Uncle Charlie's work. There are any number of reasons why he could be out here," Ryan said. "No need to panic."

"Yeah, but what are the chances he ends up on this corner, at this stoplight, at the exact same time as us? And look at that Lexus he's driving. No way that loser has a car like that. It's got the antenna for the car phone and everything. Well, the good news is that he got my heart pumping again. I was so drunk before that I could barely see, but this adrenaline is turning me sober real fast."

"Kasper! How much did you drink? I barely had a sip. I can't believe I've been listening to a drunk this whole time. We should have just thrown that stuff out the window when we had the chance."

"I just told you: I ain't drunk now!" Kasper was almost laughing.

"That's an urban legend. Alcohol stays in your system for as long as it stays in your system. There's not an I'm-so-scared regulator that sobers you up when you're in trouble," Ryan said.

"Oh shut up, Dr. Science. The light's changing. Just lay low and tell me if he follows us," Kasper said.

Traffic started moving, and Kasper and Ryan kept their eyes on the Lexus as it drifted a little farther and then a little closer to them in an almost-hypnotic fashion. It was impossible to tell how many people were in the car. The Lexus didn't seem to be following them necessarily, but they had no way of knowing how long it had been there. It could have just appeared, or it could have been following them for miles.

"I don't know, Ryan. I don't think he's following us."

"Well, we gotta figure it out fast," Ryan said.

"I know, idiot," Kasper said. "I'm not even sure it's Julian anyway, maybe I'm seeing ghosts. When the next light turns green, I'm going to take a last-minute left. Hopefully, that car will keep going straight, but if it comes after us, we'll know."

The light turned green and Kasper whipped a quick left in front of the oncoming traffic. Sure enough, the Lexus jutted out and bullied its way into the turn lane, and they could clearly see Julian's scowling face. He was alone.

Just like at El Taco, Julian's presence seemed to pop the top off Ryan, turning him into a different sort of person.

"Yeah, Kasper, it's him. That dumbass somehow managed to find us."

"Jesus."

"Naw, naw. Kasper, don't worry about it. It's just him! He's all alone over there. Screw that asshole. We aren't running from him. Slow down. I wanna talk with that prick."

"Talk with him? Are you crazy? You were right—just throw the drugs out the window. He'll have to stop for them, and once he does, we can lose him. Let's go home, Ryan. It's over. Throw the duffel bag out the window."

Ryan hit the sunroof button, grabbed one of the duffel bags, and stood up. But instead of throwing the bag, he started screaming at Julian like a total lunatic.

"Hey assface! You looking for this? Were you scared your ass was gonna get violated by your own gang and you wouldn't be able to push around your sister anymore? Well, I hope you die. You don't deserve your family, and you don't deserve these drugs either."

"Ryan!" Kasper yelled. "What are you doing? He probably can't even hear you over all the street noise."

But Julian must have heard him because Kasper could see his ugly face contort in rage as he talked into his phone.

"Ryan, throw that duffel out and sit down. You know he's calling his people right now. He won't be alone for long. Once you get rid of it, we'll lose him, and then we'll be done with this."

But Ryan wouldn't stop. Something had snapped, and he just kept yelling at Julian and dangling one of the duffel bags above the sunroof as if he was about to drop it before pulling it close to his chest again and laughing maniacally.

As Kasper tried to pull on Ryan's leg to try and get him to sit down, he felt for the first time the wildness of the car on the bumpy road. He saw the speedometer creep up past sixty. Sixty was too fast for this road, too fast for this cold, too fast for these icy conditions.

But it was too late. It's always too late to think of the smart things when you're doing something dumb. Suddenly the other gangbangers' SUV was pulling in front of them. Julian wasn't alone anymore

Kasper tried to swerve to avoid them, but they were going too fast and Kasper felt the rear wheels of the Mercedes fishtail into the SUV's rammer. The SUV struck the passenger side where Ryan had been sitting before he stood up in the sunroof.

Kasper tried to regain control, but he couldn't. The

Mercedes was pushed into oncoming traffic. Kasper clearly saw the frizzy-haired, forty-something woman in front of them throw her arms up to shield her face as her car smashed headlong into theirs.

The Mercedes, the universe, the beautiful soft skull of his best friend in the entire world—they exploded.

CHAPTER THIRTEEN

D anny was bored out of his mind. That was the problem with working in a decent neighborhood with the regular police. Especially on a cold, rainy day like this. There just wasn't anything going on. The gang-bangers around here were like fair-weather sports fans—gang-banging was a lifestyle, not a real job. They'd only come out for the big things: weekends, gang holidays, summer days . . . you know, times when they could be sure all the other assholes were there so they'd have an audience. They only came when the times were hot, and they sure as heck weren't hot now.

Danny had already done all his paperwork, driven by the rougher (emptier) parts of the district, and checked on each of the squad cars working for him three times. He was only supposed to check on them twice, and he could tell from the looks on the officers' faces that they were getting annoyed at being constantly monitored. He remembered how insulting it had been when he was a police officer and he felt like the sergeants were watching him all the time. But looking back on it now, he wondered if his sergeants were even monitoring him at all. Maybe they had just been lonely and bored out of their minds, like he was now.

Six years as a sergeant and he still wasn't used to it. He thought of himself as an officer, not a boss, just one of the guys. And, at first, he had been. He still went to the watch parties, still flirted with the cute girls, still made arrests. The guys loved him. He was easily the favorite supervisor on every watch he worked on, and he was proud of how hard everyone worked for him. Harder than for any other sergeant, that was for sure—maybe too hard.

And that was the problem. Some of the young guys paid too much attention. Danny would make some off-color joke, or pressure some street guy into giving up some info—pressure that was just shy of the constitutional line—and it was cool, it worked. He'd done it a thousand times before, and he knew what he was doing. But these young guys, they saw what he was doing, and they tried to do the same thing. Only they weren't smart enough and they went too far. What the heck was wrong with them? He hadn't known what he was doing at first either, but he had learned. He learned how to make sure the right guy went to jail, regardless of the reason for the arrest. But these guys did stupid stuff for ridiculous reasons and Danny had to clean up their messes afterwards. Why couldn't they learn? Gradually, Danny had realized that when he had learned, he'd learned from other guys. Veteran guys. Not a supervisor. Never a supervisor.

When you learn something from a guy who's the same rank as you, you're a little suspicious. You aren't sure it will really work, so you approach the idea cautiously. You think for yourself and construct the building from the ground up, the way it's supposed to be. You don't just hang that thing out in the middle of the air because you thought a supervisor told you to.

Eventually, Danny decided that bosses like him weren't there to teach; that was someone else's job. Danny's job was to keep the monster at bay. Danny thought back to this one time when he met a teacher in a bar, and the teacher told him a story that sounded like the same thing. You see, Teach gave the exact same exam every year at his high school. He never changed it, not a word. All the students had to do to ace the exam was get a copy of it from last year and memorize the answers.

Teach knew the kids were doing this, but he also knew that, even with the exam in their hands, they still had to memorize it. And that was the thing: they *did* memorize it. Over the years, he found that if he just gave them the test straight, as a list of vocab words to learn, half the kids wouldn't do it. But if that exact same list of vocab words came from a stolen list of answers from last year, they memorized every word like it was manna from the gods.

But the funny thing was, not every class figured it out. The kids in those classes would take it straight, without cheating, and they'd bomb. Those poor honest children never learned the material.

Teach felt bad for those kids, so he decided to tell everyone about the identical tests from years past. But somehow, when he did that, everything went wrong. It was like one of those old-school sociological experiments where the green eyed kids start torturing the brown-eyed kids for no other reason than that the sociologists set it up that way, and they're forced to stop the experiment halfway through, because otherwise, a bunch of sweet kids from Harvard are going to end up killing each other in a windowless research laboratory when they ought to be out getting drunk at the beach like their richer classmates who don't need the $20 in cash they get for getting experimented on.

That's the kind of thing that would happen in Teach's class when he told them he wanted them to cheat. The kids went bad. They'd start messing around in class, get all rowdy, skip school altogether. One time, some little Christian kid refused to cheat and ended up getting beat up pretty bad. Another one of his students hanged himself in the school bathroom. Obviously this kid must have had all kinds of other problems, but when they found him, the answers to the test were tucked into his back pocket. It ate at Teach when he found out about that. Nothing like that had ever happened when he didn't tell his protégés to cheat on his exams. It turns out you have to lie to them to make them cheat good.

And that's what it felt like to Danny after he made sergeant. Friendship had to go. The guys who worked for him needed something else. So about two years in, Danny stopped making friends and started supervising. He did it because it was the only way he could think of to keep the train on the tracks and the monster under the bed.

And it worked. The guys still tried hard, and Danny made sure to hook the young guys up with a veteran who knew what was going on, so their paperwork ended up tight too. A lot fewer stupid things went down, Danny slept better at night, and the right guys were still going to jail.

But man was it lonely. Heck, there's not even anyone to go to lunch with when you're a supervisor. As a police officer, you've always got your partner, and if you're tired of him, you can go to lunch with any of the other cars working that night. But no one wants to have lunch with their boss, and if they do, they're the suckass kind of folks who are no fun to eat with anyway.

So Danny drove around, talked to the citizens, ate lunch alone in his car while listening to the police radio, waiting for it to tell him what needed to happen so he could make the world a better place, or at least have a good laugh along the way.

It was a little better once he went to narcotics. There, you're a part of a team, and even though you're the supervisor of that team, you're also a little closer to being just one of the guys again.

But the hours were killer. The overtime might make you rich, but it'd send you to an early grave too. You're pretty much working all the time. And even when you're not, you can't get those long-term investigations out of your head. They stay with you. In his dreams, Danny would be doing surveillance in some abandoned building. Only, instead of watching out for him, his team forgot about him and went out drinking instead. Danny'd wake up not knowing where he was, and he could feel his gun in his hand even when it wasn't, and his heart going 180, the sheets soaked with sweat.

Ironically, Danny craved the nightmares because they meant he was sleeping. He barely slept. Working nights didn't help. He'd drive home just as the sun was coming up and it was nearly impossible to sleep with the bright light peeking through the curtains. On the days he went to court, or when Ryan was over, it hardly seemed worth it to try for an hour or two of sleep before heading out, but skipping out on any amount of sleep was always a mistake because, by the time he got back home in the afternoon, it was almost time for his night shift.

One guy told him that the secret to sleeping during the day was to cover all your windows with aluminum foil. So, like a crazy person, he duct taped his windows with foil until it looked like the temple of Sun Ra. And wouldn't you know it, that dude was right. The foil blocked the light out so well that he couldn't see his own hand in front of his face.

But it turns out there's more to day than light, and more to night than darkness. Danny had darkness, but the world kept pushing in. The birds kept chirping, the garbage trucks kept banging down the alleys, and those malevolent goddamned lawnmowers just kept mowing and mowing, trying to keep life as neat and trim as people imagine.

But Danny wouldn't give up. He put extra dense insulation in the walls and mounted pink foam board over the aluminum-foiled windows. (Great, Danny thought, on the odd chance that the aluminum foil doesn't scare away any real woman from his life, the boarded up pink foam windows definitely will.) And still he couldn't sleep. If anything, it made it worse. The inside of his room now felt like an echo chamber for his own thoughts. In the summer, his A/C couldn't keep up and, nightmares or not, he'd wake up in his dark coffined bedroom sopping with sweat.

Prescription pills helped for a while. He even tried some roofies he picked up on a street stop. Those things sure knocked him out, but Danny couldn't tolerate the embarrassment of a divorced guy date-rape drugging himself just so he could go to bed. Particularly when, half the time, there actually was some random woman next to him. And he sure didn't need date-rape drugs to get her there, even though she probably wasn't the type he'd be bringing to see Mom.

The women. They were definitely part of the problem. They were just distractions from life. Same with all the booze he drank at the bars waiting for closing time when those same girls would want to know where he was heading and whether they could come too. Danny was dying; he felt it. Stress, some crazy random girl next to him, blackness, booze, twenty-four hours bleeding into thirty-six or forty-seven or fifty-three or whatever crazy hours he ended up working. He could see the waters of his life running down the drain and wondered how many years he had left. The way he was living now was taking years off his life. The only question was how many and whether he even cared.

IT WAS SARA THAT SAVED HIM. FOUR MONTHS EARLIER, THEY'D both sat in on Ryan's parent-teacher conferences—needless to say, the little brainiac got straight As and glowing reviews. Afterwards, out in the hallway, Ryan asked if, instead of going home, he could go to a play the school was putting on. Danny and Sara practically fell over themselves giving him permission. Ryan sauntered off with a group of girls, leaving his parents alone together with good feelings in their hearts for the first time in years.

It didn't last.

"Wow, would you look at that," Danny said. "Those theater girls look pretty good. Maybe he's finally taking after his old man and he'll get some action backstage tonight."

"Oh Jesus, Danny. Must you ruin every moment? You better hope his good looks are the only thing he inherited from you, because if he inherited your alcoholism, there's going to be trouble."

"What are you talking about? I'm not an alcoholic. You're just jealous because someone probably told you how many women I've been bringing home while you're staying up late reading books or whatever."

"Nobody is talking about you," Sara scoffed. "You smell like a distillery. And if you smell like this now, God knows how you smelled last night. Didn't you notice the way the AP History teacher wrinkled up her nose when you walked in? I don't know if you spilled some liquor on your clothes, or if you're sweating off last night's alcohol, but you stink."

"Aw, come on now, Sara, there's no reason to be mean about it." Danny cocked his head and smiled. "If you think I smell sexy and want to go out with me, just say so. I'd consider it, don't worry. You still look better than most of the girls I know."

"Oh God, Danny. I wouldn't touch you with a ten-foot pole. Do you even realize how bad you look? Your face is so puffed up from the drinking it looks like you've put on thirty pounds. And you're all red. My God, I almost asked if you had gotten a sunburn. But then I figured it out. You're not sunburned; you're just a drunk. You're not half the man you used to be."

"Hey, half the man I used to be is still twice as much man as everybody else." Danny's arms were folded across his chest to hide the shaking he'd recently noticed in his right hand. "I just haven't been sleeping well recently. That's all. The job's hard, and I've been working a ton of hours. That's all."

"Yeah, you've probably been working a ton of hours so you can afford to go out every night." Sara looked at Danny and, for once, the overly confident bastard looked away. "Look, Danny. I need you to be a man. Not for me, for your son. Have you noticed that he and Kasper don't hang out anymore? He just hangs out at the house all the time by himself." She shook her head. "Don't get me wrong—I love having him around, but something's wrong. If you can't pull it together for yourself, at least do it for your son. He needs you."

"Ha! See, you still care about me after all these years! I like that."

"Jesus, Danny, stop."

"OK, alright. I'm sorry. I'll start behaving now." Danny gathered himself. "Look, I know it might not look like it, but I actually have been making some changes. Or at least, ya know, thinking about making some changes. Jesus, I'm getting old. How about I take you out and we talk about Ryan? I promise I'll be a gentleman. Now we can go out and we won't even need a babysitter. We could never do that when we were younger, right? That's gotta be worth something."

"Be serious here, Danny. I don't want that. Besides, you wouldn't be able to stop drinking for the three hours necessary to take a girl out somewhere other than a bar."

"Three hours? Hell, I could do three weeks. I don't need this stuff. I don't need any of it. How about this: if I don't touch alcohol for three weeks, you agree to go out with me to talk about Ryan." The mischievous look in Danny's eyes returned. "Hell, don't do it for me. Do it for him. Doesn't Ryan deserve a sober father?"

"Oh for crying out loud, Danny. Can't you do anything without negotiating something in return?"

"Come on, baby, you know the world ain't like that."

Danny reached out to her. "Just give me a chance. I'll stay sober for three weeks and then we can go out to," Danny grinned, "that wine bar you like so much!"

"Oh shut up!" She pushed his hands away, lightly. "Fine. But to punish you for making a joke about a serious disease like alcoholism, you're going to have to talk to a shrink too. Show me a receipt for the shrink and stop drinking for three weeks, and I'll go out with you. For coffee. To talk about Ryan. Nothing else."

"Aw, come on, baby. There ain't nothing wrong with me that a little loving from you wouldn't fix up. I don't need no shrink." Danny tried to wrap an arm around Sara's waist, but she maneuvered away.

"I'm serious, Danny. You say you want to make changes? Prove it."

Danny looked at her, considering, and then stuck out his hand. "It's a deal." When she placed her warm hand in his to shake on it, he held it for a while and pulled her in closer. When he went in for a kiss, she almost let him, but then she put her free hand over his lips and said, "Fine. Deal. Now let go of me. I've got work to do tonight."

As she walked away, Danny yelled out, "Wait! How am I going to prove to you that I haven't drank for three weeks?"

"Danny, it won't be hard. I'll be able to look at you and see whether a tiny bit of the man I used to think was handsome has replaced the drunken hobo I'm looking at right now."

"Hey! You know I'm the most handsome drunken hobo you've ever seen!"

As she walked away, she was laughing. That laugh, Danny thought, was still the most beautiful sound in the world.

DANNY KEPT HIS PROMISE. HE HADN'T HAD A DRINK, AND HE'D even seen a shrink. (He only saw the shrink one time, but after giving Danny a hard glare, Sara reluctantly admitted that he had technically upheld his end of the bargain.) The first time they met up for coffee went well, and the next few times went even better. Within a few weeks, they had progressed to dinner and a movie. Danny started to believe that maybe he *did* deserve happiness, and a life with a woman he loved.

Now, they didn't tell a soul—not Ryan, not Mike—nobody. Their secret relationship had the thrill of an affair, but it was the most wholesome secret relationship that had ever existed: two formerly married people going out on dates like they were sixteen years old. They even had a curfew. Heck, she wouldn't even have sex with him—not until he left narcotics and went back to patrol where he could have an almost-regular life.

So he did. And here he was. He was pretty sure he'd even be able to make the bid for days in a few months and then, other than the weekends, his life would be about as regular as could be.

REGULAR NEVER LASTS IN THE GHETTO.

Danny heard two explosions rip through the cold night air.

"Squad," Danny said into his radio. "It sounds like there was a big car accident one block over. I'm going to go check it out, but I guarantee you're going to need to start rolling an ambulance over here. I'll let you know the extent of the injuries in a second."

Danny had heard a thousand traffic crashes in his life. They normally started with the sound of screeching tires, followed closely by the crush of glass and metal and pain. But those weren't the worst ones. With the worst ones, you never heard the screeching tires because the drivers never even tapped the brakes. They were too drunk or too dumb, and their cars became pure kinetic energy that ripped through vehicles and buildings and street poles like bullets careening through flesh. This sounded like one of those.

Danny sped toward the scene. He saw a green SUV rolled upside down on the sidewalk. Three gangbangers were trying to climb out the windows, but the roof was caved in, and they were having a hard time. The car didn't seem to be at risk of catching on fire or anything, so Danny quickly handcuffed the driver's wrists to the window frame he was trying to scramble out of.

"You're not going anywhere, asshole," Danny said. The piece of crap started swearing at him, but what the hell did Danny care? He could tell this gangbanger was an asshole just by looking at him.

The other two passengers had collapsed back into the car and were moaning. Danny reached inside and cuffed them together. He figured there was no way they'd be able to climb out of that crumpled car, injured and hooked together like a three-legged racer.

Across the street from them was a little blue Honda that looked like a crushed aluminum can, but, amazingly, a lady climbed out. She was rubbing her head and looking around dazed, but other than that, she looked like she would be OK. She looked fairly square—a license-and-insurance type—so Danny decided he'd deal with her last.

There was a third car up on the sidewalk, a small silver Mercedes.

He knew this car.

As Danny gazed at his partner's smashed-up car, a shiver ran down his spine. The rear end of the Mercedes had smashed through the front of a small grocery store. Danny figured it must have spun out somehow, probably from the first impact that must have crumpled the front end that was facing him.

He saw the body next. A thin adolescent, flopped three-quarters out of the sunroof, dangling headfirst over the smashed windshield like a limp scarecrow.

Danny wondered how, when he first saw the scene, he could have noticed the car but not the body. How could anybody see the car without seeing the body? Even now, he knew it was the body, not the car, that he would continue to picture for the rest of his life.

He'd bathed that body in the kitchen sink. He'd carried that body up the stairs, tucked it into bed, stroked its beautiful blond hair that he could now see was now matted with blood.

He picked up the radio. "Squad. I got a three-car accident. One car is overturned in the middle of the street. We'll need three ambulances rolling out here to start, and let the fire department know they're going to need to cut some people out. Give me four squad cars to block off the intersection. And you might as well notify Major Accidents. I don't think everyone out here is going to make it." The notifications were done, nobody was running away, and nobody seemed to need his help.

Danny walked slowly toward the lifeless body on the sunroof. There was no need to run. For the rest of his life, he would never have to hurry to his son again.

The top of Ryan's skull was totally caved in. The windshield hadn't broken all the way through, but the crushed outline of his skull spidered across the glass like a papier-mâché death mask.

He imagined his son's head whirling 120 degrees around his hips like a whip before crashing into the windshield. The thing Danny didn't understand was how the windshield could have crushed Ryan's skull, glass isn't that strong. But then he saw the dent in the part of the hood that curls over the windshield, and he realized that his son's head must have struck the hood of the car before landing on the windshield. That was the real blow. But maybe that wasn't it either. Maybe the real scenario was that his baby's face had hit the hood, and then he'd swept back 180 degrees like a character in a horror film getting swept around like a rag doll. his head had hit back there, and then the recoil had sent him tumbling forward onto the windshield. But when Danny examined the top of the car, he couldn't see any dents, so he knew that wasn't it. Maybe Ryan's head hit the windshield on the spin out or when the car hit the curb or the building.

Jesus, Danny said to himself, stop thinking about it; stop trying to figure it out. Why in the world did he possibly need to figure it out?

For the first time, Danny noticed Kasper on the driver's side, gasping and heaving. He knelt down next to Kasper, afraid something might have been driven down Kasper's throat. Now he was going to have to watch his best friend's son die in the same car that had already killed his son.

"Kasper!" he said, shaking him, "Kasper! Breathe, deep, say something." Danny put his ear near Kasper's throat to see if any air was coming out, and as he did, he heard the low sound of weeping and noticed the smell of tequila. In that moment, his concern alchemized into rage like water boiling into steam. "There's nothing wrong with you, is there?" Danny stood up. It was all he could do not to kick Kasper's face in. "You're just drunk. You're drunk and you killed my son."

Kasper continued to heave, tears filling his eyes.

"Quit your crying," Danny snarled. "The hell is wrong with you? You killed my son and now you're sitting here crying like a baby instead of saving my boy?"

"Danny," gasped Kasper. "We were driving, and I swerved out of the way of those guys. Ryan was yelling at them. We hit that lady. I don't know what happened. It was so loud."

"How much have you been drinking?" Danny asked.

"What?" Kasper answered blankly, like he didn't understand the question.

"Goddammit." He grasped Kasper by the shoulders and

shook them. "I'm not messing around. Tell me how much you've been drinking."

"I don't know. Maybe a fifth?"

"Of tequila? You idiot. And Ryan? How much had he been drinking? Take your seatbelt off. Let's get you out of here."

"I don't know. I don't think he'd had much of anything, maybe nothing at all," Kasper said as he took off his seatbelt, "but he was acting so crazy . . ."

Danny looked at the glassy-eyed face hanging over the windshield. That used to be his son. The face didn't even look like Ryan's; it looked like a monster's. He looked at Kasper, red-faced and blubbering like a baby.

"I'm so sorry, Danny. I'm so sorry."

Sorry.

Danny grabbed the collar of Kasper's jacket, wedged his foot into the door pillar for power, and threw Kasper's head through the windshield, next to Ryan's.

The windshield crumpled, leaving a second indentation of a young boy's skull right next to Ryan's.

Danny lifted Kasper's head up next to his and whispered, "You're sorry for killing my son? Sorry? You ought to die right here next to Ryan."

Danny let go of Kasper's and watched him curl into the fetal position on his side. Then, Danny reached through the driver's-side door and pushed Kasper into the passenger seat. Ryan's legs were dangling through the sunroof like a marionette. His heels were pushed grotesquely upwards, and they brushed the top of Kasper's back. Danny was reminded of those Day-of-the-Dead skeletons in black mariachi suits, and he vaguely remembered some legend of having to push through them to get to the afterworld. Now that Kasper was in the passenger seat, he pulled Ryan's body from the sunroof into the driver's seat. But as Danny did so, he slipped on some fluids that had started leaking from the undercarriage and fell backwards out of the car.

Swearing, Danny stood up and dusted himself off. He leaned back into the car and said to Kasper, "Shut up and stay in this car. Don't say a word."

"Danny."

"I said, 'shut up.'"

"But Danny, there are drugs."

"I don't care what you've been taking. It doesn't matter now."

"No. In the duffel bag. There's tons of cocaine in there. We took it away from those guys. That's why they were chasing us."

Danny looked into the back seat and saw the black duffel bags with bricks of cocaine spilling out of them.

"Jesus Christ. That's their stuff? Those dudes in the SUV?" Danny said.

"Yeah. Ryan took it from them. Who knew that guy had that kind of balls?" Kasper looked up at Danny. "Did you know he had that in him?"

Danny started to smile, but then leaned in and hit Kasper in the face.

"Shut up and listen. Are you listening?" Kasper nodded. He looked like he was starting to sober up. "Ryan was always a bad driver. He crashed the car. Got it? Tell them that you told him to slow down. Do you hear me? You say anything else to them and I'll kill you myself."

Kasper nodded, but that wasn't enough for Danny. "I said, 'Do you understand?' If you don't answer me, I'm going to hit you again, and you know I'm gonna like it."

A small smile spread across Kasper's bloodied lips as he said, "Yeah, Danny, I got it. I understand."

Satisfied, Danny picked up the bags and walked over to the SUV. Jesus Christ, he thought, what had those kids been up to?

The fire department had arrived, but they were too busy cutting the three upside-down assholes out of the SUV to hear any of Danny's conversations. "Hey losers," Danny said, "guess what? You just killed a cop's kid."

The three gangbangers glared at him. After a few seconds, one of them spat on the floor. His spit was full of blood. "Screw you, Pig," he said.

"Yeah, good idea. Don't say nothing. You say anything, I guarantee I'll put a case on you so heavy you'll never get out from under it. See these bags? You wanted them so bad, you got 'em. Shut your mouths and take it, otherwise I'll add the drugs to murder and tie you idiots to every slaughtered villager in Mexico. The jury will be falling over themselves to put you in the electric chair. Do you understand me?"

The three thugs were swearing up a storm, dangling upside down like a bunch of fools, (What the hell kind of world was it where the gangbangers were wearing seatbelts, and his own kids weren't) but Danny was pretty sure they got the picture.

When Danny stood up, one of Danny's officers was jogging over. Danny stood up and yelled to him, "Get your partner over here, and when the fire department finally manages to cut these thugs out of their car, they belong to you. And make sure you mirandize them. I want this done proper, 100 percent proper. They aren't saying nothing, but we still have to do our job. Those are coppers' kids over there that they were chasing."

Danny reviewed the scene. The ambulances had arrived, traffic was blocked off, and yellow tape was going up to protect the evidence. It was a textbook crime scene. An absolute textbook crime scene. If Michael didn't know already, he would within minutes. Danny wouldn't have to be the one to tell him, and he sure didn't want to. After a few hours, some higher up would arrive and tell Danny to take a break, but he wanted to make sure things were done the right way until then. Besides, he needed to keep busy because as soon as he stopped, he would have to tell Sara.

Sara.

She would be asleep now anyway. Let her sleep, he thought. The dawn always comes, whether you want it to or not. Plus, Danny knew a couple of bars that opened at seven a.m., and after telling Sara, he was definitely going to need a drink.

PART 2

CHAPTER ONE

Detective Andre Felton was having a bad day. A very bad day. Who did Sergeant Fat Ass think he was, taking him off the homicide team? Outrageous. And now, here he was doing callouts on commercial burglaries? Good Lord. There is no money in responding to commercial burglaries. Absolutely zero. Even the victims don't care if their cases get solved because they'll get an insurance payout either way. And if they do care, it's the kind of corporate care that makes your skin crawl. And anyway, the stores farm out the important cases to private security outfits, so there's no overtime for the police.

No overtime. Felton shuddered just thinking about it. He'd almost tripled his salary in overtime last year. There'd been times he'd worked nearly around the clock seven days a week.

But he'd sensed the move was coming from a mile away after all the nonsense that went down with Reverend-Alderman.

"Hey, Felton!" Sergeant Fat Ass loomed before him, holding a piece of paper in his sweaty little sausage fingers, raising his voice loud enough so everyone in the office could hear.

"Got a big caper for you, Felton. Fortunately, with all your experience being a lazy, suck-ass detective on the homicide team, I know you'll have no problem being a lazy, suck-ass detective here in the burglary unit. You're going to love this one."

Felton didn't respond.

"It's from the old Goldblatt's store. You know it?"

Felton drummed his fingers on the desk.

"Felton. You deaf? I hope not." The sergeant's smile was getting stiff on his face from lack of response. "A deaf person is gonna have a problem in this office."

First day in the unit and Sergeant Fat Ass was already using the supervisor threat, Felton thought. Not a man, whose word was worth something, just a supervisor. But rank won out. He didn't want to give Sergeant Fat Ass an excuse to remember where his discipline pen went, so he briefly flicked his eyes up and down to indicate that he had heard the question.

"What's that, Felton? It seems I'm having a problem hearing you say, 'Yes, sir.'"

Felton grunted out a response that, if you listened real closely, might sound something like, "yes sir," but he made sure his expression indicated to Sergeant Fat Ass that he was really pushing his luck.

Sergeant Fat Ass thought about pushing through, Andre could see that, but he could also see that he wanted to push him down for free, not actually work for it: "Well, hopefully you're smart enough to figure this case out. But seeing as how you're apparently a dumb mute... Apparently, some teenage rent-a-cop wannabe security guard down at Goldblatt's thinks he found something that is relevant to a crime. This kid's great; you'll love him." He said, in an aside to no one. "He originally asked for the 'Cold-Case Unit.' Must be watching too many crime shows." Sergeant Fat Ass swept his hand through the air like a vaudeville emcee from a silent movie.

"Says he found some video from twenty years ago that involves drugs, a burglary, and—get this—disappearing bodies. From twenty years ago! I didn't even know they had video twenty years ago!" The sergeant apparently thought this was the funniest thing he'd ever heard.

He continued, "Don't worry, Felton. I told the kid I'd have my best detective go down and talk to him about it. Sounds like a good case, huh, Felton? There's sure to be lots of witnesses and evidence left from twenty years ago. This case should start your clearance rate out real good. But hey" and the Sgt. pantomimed turning away and remembering something, "just make sure to be back by 1700 hours. The boss told me I have to do face-to-face relief with you at the end of every shift so he can be sure you don't have to do any overtime. Said it like he was real concerned for your well-being and all—like he didn't want you overworking yourself the way you had been—but it was weird because I could swear he had a malicious look in his eye when he said it. What do you think, Felton? You have any idea why the boss might not care about you anymore?" The sergeant looked around the room, beaming at his own comedic genius. "I thought that guy liked you. I wonder what could have changed?"

Felton looked at the torn-up, crumpled piece of paper that Sergeant Fat Ass handed him. It had the words "security guard" and a telephone number written on it. This was his case. This was what that fat piece of lard was giving him. Sergeant Fat Ass walked off laughing.

Sweet Jesus, what had ReverendAlderman done to him?

Felton paused to consider the Honorable Reverend Alderman Jones, and how his fate had brought him to this low state of affairs. You see, ReverendAlderman got himself caught sleeping with a sixteen-year-old from his very own congregation. Ridiculous. Getting caught up in nonsense he could easily have avoided, if only he'd taken the bare minimum of precautions.

Now, in Felton's opinion, ReverendAlderman's actions with that girl were a disrespectful way for a man to live his life, but Felton minded his own business and certainly the personal affairs of people he was beholden to. Certainly, ReverendAlderman not being able to control himself didn't come as a surprise—Felton would be out of a job if men stopped giving into their primal urges—but what did surprise him was that ReverendAlderman had sent the girl inappropriate photos on his work phone. His *work phone*. Now, first of all, no self-respecting fifty-year-old man should be sending photos of any kind—nobody wants to see that—but *sexting?* On his work phone? Unbelievable. In using that phone, ReverendAlderman made his business other people's business, and when it became other people's business, it suddenly became Felton's business.

Everyone knows those phones are company property. Hell, every time you boot the thing up it makes you click on an acknowledgement saying exactly that. Even this embarrassment of a city is eventually going to get around to auditing stuff like that so some enterprising reporters don't get a chance to FOIA the information and do it first. And sure enough, some little snot-nosed twenty-two-year-old accountant barely out of his mother's womb went and did it, and he was too dumb to know that information should have been a rock solid gold mine. If that twenty-two-year-old had been smart, he could have been running any city department he wanted by now.

But he wasn't smart. Instead of playing ball with that information, he went and entered it into the computer. Once it's in the computer, it's over. Discoverable is discoverable once it's been discovered. No doubt when his far smarter superior found out, he gave him a dressing down for his lack of discretion. His superior undoubtedly knew that the dirt on ReverendAlderman was worth a half a million in future salary and all the leverage a man could eat. All flushed down the toilet. For nothing.

Felton had asked ReverendAlderman why he didn't just use his personal phone for that kind of nonsense, but it turns out he didn't even have one. ReverendAlderman didn't even know what a cell phone plan was.

Ridiculousness. But if there isn't a victim, there isn't a crime. And fortunately for ReverendAlderman, the girl denied everything. She said it wasn't her in those pictures. And to be honest, Felton mused, a truly independent observer would have a problem testifying as to the identity of the girl in the photos because let's just say the images weren't exactly focused on her face.

Now the city was hoping they could still get ReverendAlderman on improper use of government property (sadly, Felton thought, sending naked pictures isn't in the proper job description of any city employee, regardless of the age of the recipient), but at the last minute, someone remembered that aldermanic phones were exempt from city rules on cell phone use (to preserve the political independence of their humbly elected selves). If there isn't a rule, no rule can be broken, and the last alleged impropriety vanished in a puff of logical impossibility that impressed even the more cynical observers of the scene.

One would think this kind of behavior might hurt a politician, but ReverendAlderman was no ordinary politician. Sure, sending inappropriate photos of an underage parishioner you'd been diddling for five months was a problem, but it was a . . . manageable problem. That is, so long as the right man was doing the managing.

ReverendAlderman was the right man. While denying everything in public, word is ReverendAlderman simultaneously gave a mea-culpa speech to his congregation where he admitted to being led astray by the devil (in specifically non specific generalities) and begged for the community's forgiveness. With tears and hugs and general adulation from the congregation (Felton was surprised there'd been neither rending of clothing nor gnashing of teeth), the whole thing ended in one massive laying on of hands ceremony at the end of which ReverendAlderman was seen as more real, more worthy, and more loved than ever before. Even the girl's family participated in the ceremony—and a fine city job was waiting for them as a just reward for their Christian forgiveness.

Je. Sus. Christ.

Some guys are so special they actually know it. And ReverendAlderman, he knew it.

But pride goes before the fall (and stupidity lays every brick along the way). Once he got over that little debacle, ReverendAlderman got a little too big for his britches and figured that surely a man of such extraordinary talents would make a better mayor than an alderman.

Now as you can imagine, the current occupant of the mayoral office didn't exactly agree with that assessment, so she sent out word that any dirt on ReverendAlderman would be well received and well rewarded. Suddenly, the feds got a nice tip that on ReverendAlderman's most recent trip to Las Vegas for an ecumenical empowerment zone conference, he had brought along his favorite protégé. Instead of using his own funds to pay for the trip, he had used tax-exempt religious funds. And that was what did it. Felton chuckled: turns out you're welcome to take a sixteen-year-old across state lines to have sex with her, but you sure as hell better not use IRS money to do it.

Felton shook his head. It wasn't like ReverendAlderman didn't have plenty of his own money lying around. Between the six-figure city salary, the committeeman's bumps, the church money, all the real estate he owned (in an unimaginable mixture of profit and for profit), and the government money pouring into the economic development corporation he ran (Felton loved seeing the acronym for ReverendAlderman Jones Empowering, "RAJE," (pronounced, "rage") printed on their little fix-it vans), ReverendAlderman had to be swimming in money. But what was it they said? "You don't get rich spending your own money." Yeah. That was it. And even if that wasn't something people said, those were certainly words ReverendAlderman lived by.

And it was those kind of balls that made Felton respect the man. If ReverendAlderman got a bad hand, he didn't fold, he asked for another. If the dealer refused to give him one, he demanded to see the manager. If the manager didn't apologize and buy him a drink, ReverendAlderman would be down there the next day with a crowd of protesters, cameras rolling, and threats of lawsuits about the percentage of minority workers, the right to unionize, the damn dirt in the break room, about who the hell gives a rat's ass. But you better give a rat's ass about the Absolutely Amazing ReverendAlderman Jones.

Man could that man fight.

Issues did not interest ReverendAlderman. They were malleable and dependent on the situation at hand. But the fight? That he cared about. That he loved.

ReverendAlderman pushed and he fought, and he fought and he won. But he wasn't greedy: he didn't ask for more than you *could* give, he just asked for more than you *wanted* to give. He asked it of everybody; he played no favorites and no one was exempt. If you had a million dollars in the bank, he wanted ten thousand. If you had a hundred dollars in your wallet, ten bucks would do. If you only had one dollar, and even that dollar you stole from your momma—well, ReverendAlderman wasn't a monster—ten cents would do just fine.

But everyone paid because if you didn't, you fought. And nobody wanted to fight ReverendAlderman. Even on those rare occasions when ReverendAlderman lost the fight, the victor would make a mental note that the fight cost too much, and the next time, they'd be better off just to give ReverendAlderman his piece.

Now a man like that makes enemies every day, and those enemies were always looking to put the screw down on the man who was putting the screw on them. So ReverendAlderman needed guys like Felton, and Felton was a man who appreciated the services that a man like Revered Alderman had access to. Plus, Felton and ReverendAlderman had more than just affiliations of political appreciation: they had grown up together. They knew where they had come from and what it took them to get where they were. ReverendAlderman respected the route Felton had followed, and Felton respected all that ReverendAlderman had accomplished. And so, ReverendAlderman didn't ask for much from Felton: he just wanted a heads up about what the police were doing, and Felton didn't ask for much from ReverendAlderman in return. All Felton wanted was a good place in the D-Unit. And as it so happened, the better Felton's place in the D-Unit, the better info he could provide to ReverendAlderman. And so, over the years, one hand washed the other until there was hardly a speck of dirt between them.

Unless you were the IRS. They didn't play fair and they brought in white gloves when they went in looking for dirt. Nobody's that clean. Only way around the IRS was to get a heads up and send a dollar in the right direction so after they ran their white gloves over everything, you could swap in a new pair when they weren't looking. But for some reason, ReverendAlderman had a blind spot for the nerds and didn't appreciate how powerful they were. (In ReverendAlderman's defense, though, he had never even met an accountant until he was thirty.) So while he spent all kinds of time worrying about the G-man and wiretaps, he never thought about pocket protectors and accountants. And it cost him.

ReverendAlderman had been pissed that Felton hadn't

given him a heads up, but Felton told him that was his own damn fault. If he had wanted info about the Feds, Reverend-Alderman should have helped Felton onto that federal task force like Felton had asked him to the year before (a task force that made overtime from the city *and* got all its expenses paid by the US government. Incredible).

But ReverendAlderman didn't listen, so the IRS and the Feds and a deus ex goddamn machina came in and blew the whole thing up. But what was really crazy, and what Felton couldn't possibly understand, was that instead of rolling up his sleeves and getting ready to swing like he always did, Reveren-dAlderman folded. Why didn't he fight? Why would he plead guilty just before the election when, near as Felton (and every poll he saw) could tell, he was still going to win with about 70 percent of the vote? (The community wouldn't let the Feds come in and take their elected official away. They might vote him out *next* election, just to show who was boss, but no out-of-town Fed was going to tell them what to do.)

What had those Fed bastards done to ReverendAlderman? It was incomprehensible. He always fought, and Felton was convinced that, like always, he would have won. But Reveren-dAlderman explained it to him like this: In Chicago, if you get convicted while in office, you lose your seat. And once you're booted, you can't run again. But just *being* a felon doesn't prevent you from running. So if ReverendAlderman had won and been convicted a day later, he'd be out. So he pled guilty and didn't run, but he'd be free to run again next time.

The Feds thought they beat the man, but they were wrong. They never met a man like ReverendAlderman. They were playing the case, but ReverendAlderman was playing the game. It took him fifty years to make himself out of nothing. Meanwhile, those Feds couldn't think farther out than their four-year appointments—which matched the four-year prep school plans their mommas made for them while they were still sucking on their teats. They didn't know nothing. ReverendAlderman was giving them the runaround in the old rope-a-dope strategy, taking punches while the other guy tired himself out. But he'd be back. There were other rounds, and when they least expected it, he'd run on the government-can't-keep-me-down platform and *really* stick it in their eye. They thought his pride wouldn't let him run after he was a convicted felon. They thought they were taking him down a notch. Those poor patent-leather fools ain't never had a prideful day in their lives. ReverendAlderman would be back in business in no time, and next time, ReverendAlderman promised him, Felton would get his federal task force.

Taking punches was one thing. But this thing that Felton was experiencing here in the burglary unit with Sergeant Fat Ass? These weren't punches. This was a beating. Felton wasn't sure he could do it. It didn't appeal to his makeup: he preferred to avoid punches, not absorb them. But he thought about ReverendAlderman, and the later rounds to come, and he resolved that if ReverendAlderman could take a beating, then so could he. But he marked Sergeant Fat Ass in his mind. The fool. Sergeant Fat Ass didn't know that if you are going to beat a man when he's down, you best be sure he won't ever pick himself up again, 'cause if that man picks himself up off the ground, he's going to kill you.

Felton grabbed his keys and walked out of the office. Most of the guys were laughing, and it wasn't the friendly kind. They were the laughs of guys who like to see a man with connections go down because it makes them feel better about their own crap careers. Screw them. Felton didn't want to be there anyway. Felton glanced at his watch. He still had most of the day. He figured he could go visit his mom after going to Goldblatt's. Not that it was on his way. His mom was on the north side at a fancy senior home. And that dumb store for his case was on the south side. But if he was going to be given a fake case without the possibility of any overtime, he would at least take his time finishing it.

Felton sighed. The bill for mom's nursing home had arrived that morning. He hadn't a clue how to pay it. How's a man supposed to take care of his momma without overtime? Felton fingered the keys in his pocket. He'd be thinking about two things while driving to his new case: how to take care of momma, and how to murder Sergeant Fat Ass.

CHAPTER TWO

D anny sighed.

"That was the car."

"What car?" his new recruit replied, somewhat cautiously.

"The truck. The one we're supposed to be looking for, you know, for our *job*?" Danny was exasperated, but it was the kind of patient exasperation exhibited by someone who has gone through this situation plenty of times before. It was the last day of Johnson's first week. "Didn't you hear the dispatcher say, 'older model white pickup truck committing burglaries at 87th and Ashland?'"

"Yeah, I heard." Danny could see the wheels spinning in the kid's tiny brain. The kid had giant football-player shoulders that strained his uniform and a light crew cut. He was constantly blinking, like he was hoping the answers to the test were written on the backs of his eyelids. "That's where I'm going."

"Trucks move, ya know," Danny said.

"Of course they do, but . . ." Danny saw the puzzle pieces finally clicking together in the kid's mind. "So you think that was the truck?"

"You mean that older model white pickup truck that just passed us in the opposite direction with a driver that looked at us like he'd seen a ghost? Coming right from 87th and Ashland? Yeah. That *was* the truck."

"So . . . uh . . . should I try and pull it over?" Johnson offered.

"Ya think?" Danny knew these kids thought he was a wild animal that needed to be treated with extreme caution, but this was ridiculous. "Well, whatever you decide to do, you better decide to do it soon, cause if you haven't noticed, that truck is getting farther and farther away from you."

Danny watched as the kid's eyes bounced from the road in front of him to the rearview mirror to the computer screen displaying the address he was supposed to be heading to. A tiny bead of sweat formed on his forehead. He was probably trying to figure out if Danny was giving him some sort of trick question.

"But don't mind me, Johnson. If catching criminals ain't your thing, that's no problem. All I can say is that you better come up with a damn fine lunch suggestion to compensate me for having to watch you make a mockery of police work."

"No," Johnson said, "I'll turn around."

Danny sighed again as he watched Johnson put on his turn signal and patiently wait for traffic to clear. If Danny had been driving, they would have whipped that U-turn so fast and tight they'd have been behind the truck before the driver even had time to think about peeing his pants.

But this new kid was the same as all the others. First off, he hadn't even seen the truck; second, he'd let six blocks get between them before he turned around; third, he sat in the middle of the intersection signaling with his goddamn signal while waiting for the cars in front of him to turn; and finally, when traffic eventually cleared enough for Miss Prissy Pants to start his U-turn, he didn't do it aggressively enough to complete it in one fell swoop and instead had to back up and make a three-point turn (while Johnson was going backwards, Danny made the beeping sound of a truck backing up, causing the beads of sweat forming on Johnson's forehead to form a river that soaked his uniformed collar. Danny was pretty sure Johnson was about to ask him to adjust the mirrors, (and Danny would have slapped him for it), but the kid thought better of it, and Johnson finally started off in the right direction. Miraculously, Danny was pretty sure he could still see the distinctive tail lights of the pickup a few blocks ahead.

"He's still there. If you hit it, you might actually catch him."

And wouldn't you know he actually *did* hit it! Danny was pleased. As Johnson pushed the pedal to accelerate, Danny eased back into his seat. These streets weren't made for speed, and as soon as you got up to fifty mph, it started to feel scary. Once you got up to sixty, it was downright dangerous, and eighty was definitely considered criminal negligence. When Danny first started, those speeds thrilled him. Now they comforted him, like a baby falling asleep in the back seat of the car, the hum lulling him into a stupor.

They would have caught that pickup in about two minutes, but sadly, Johnson's proper training kicked and he turned on the police lights. As soon as those blue lights flicked on, the pickup quickly turned onto a side street.

"He turned. It's up there! That street. Turn there!" Danny commanded.

"Which one? I thought it was the next one. Are you sure?"

"Yes. I'm sure. Turn. It's that one. Turn. Turn, damn it!" Danny yelled and almost grabbed the steering wheel to do it himself.

But he didn't have to. Johnson finally turned. And it was even a halfway decent turn this time. They could just see the residue of taillights turning two blocks up, and this time, the kid saw it, accelerated, and made the turn without Danny even having to yell at him.

And there they saw the abandoned pickup sitting in the middle of the road. The only indication that there had been passengers in it a few seconds before was the brown blur of puffy jackets fading into the distance as the two criminals ran down the alley as fast as their legs could carry them.

"Go get 'em kid. Get 'em." Danny gestured with his arm like a momma bird showing the baby bird how to leave the nest.

As Johnson lumbered off, Danny looked at the truck. It was great. There was a pallet wrapped up in cellophane in the bed that had to be holding at least forty or fifty brand-new PlayStations. Dudes must have hit up a railroad car up on the tracks and got lucky with this pallet of electronics. Danny wondered how they had moved it onto the truck. Looked heavy. Surely they hadn't figured out a way to get a forklift up there, had they? He couldn't imagine they would be able to assemble those kinds of assets. Or maybe this wasn't random. Maybe they knew this stuff was there because one of their cousins worked for the railroad and it had been more of an inside job. Even people with jobs sometimes get greedy.

Danny looked down the alley and saw his big ox of a partner standing in the alley scratching his head like a comic book character who didn't know what to do. Ordinarily, Danny wouldn't have let a young police officer chase anyone on their own. Danny wasn't as fast as he used to be, but he could still keep up with most of them. But this kid, big and strong as he was, was surely a slow and cautious beast who had about the same chances of catching those two guys as Danny had of winning the Nobel Peace Prize.

Danny felt a little bad; the kid was actually alright. He shouldn't be giving him such a hard time. He was clearly book smart. Sure, he didn't know the streets, but just because you don't know the streets doesn't mean you won't learn them someday, and not knowing something that no one has ever showed you is nothing to be ashamed of anyways. Besides, what good was knowing the streets these days? They don't want you to actually arrest anyone anymore. Arrests just clog up the courts, make paperwork, and if things go wrong, it makes lawsuits which make even more paperwork. And who cares if the criminals get away? It's just a bunch of poor people killing different poor people. Nobody cares about them, so why should the police? The powers that be don't even know what the ghetto looks like. Until, of course, the police shoot someone, in which case they have to get out their GPS just to find the place. Danny didn't need to find the ghetto, the ghetto found him. It always did.

But this kid Johnson, he cared. Said he had played offensive line in college. Scholarship and everything. He even said he got an invitation to the combine for the NFL, but he turned it down, said it wasn't on the day that actually mattered, it was the day they reserved for the B people, and he probably wasn't getting drafted, and he didn't want to walk on to some practice squad, blow his knee out for nothing, and then not be able to walk out.

So he came to Chicago. Became the police. Wanted to make a difference. Didn't even have any family on the job. Just wanted to do something meaningful. Crazy! And funny thing is, he already was making a difference. He and one of the other young guys were "caught" on camera throwing a football around with a bunch of the street urchins. They really liked it. Had fun. They were laughing and smiling. All of them. Made the heart ache to see these little kids smiling. You never saw that. After they hit twelve, they'd learn to wear the neighborhood scowl. And they'd learn to wear it so well they'd barely even know they had it on.

Danny poked his head into the back seat of the pickup. The little bench seat was folded up and there were all kinds of tools and crap back there. Danny was nosy (good cops always were), and he liked to see what he could find out by looking around. On top of the junk, there was a nice little wooden box with a lid that reminded Danny of the box where his dad kept his X-ACTO knives. His dad would go downstairs to the basement and build little World War II planes out of balsa wood and papier-mâché. He even installed little gasoline engines in some of them. He'd attach a string to the plane so it could fly around in tiny circles. Danny loved looking at those planes down in the dimly lit basement that smelled of must and oil and sawdust.

Whatever happened to those X-ACTO knives? He remembered, and regretted, selling the little planes his dad had made. He only got fifty dollars or something for them— he should have held out for more money or just kept the damn things—but what had happened to those knives? He half-expected to see his dad's set when he opened up the box, but instead, he found a pair of another of his father's favorite items. "The Governator!" Danny flinched when he heard his own voice say the words out loud. Since when was he one of those people who talk to themselves? Now Danny really felt like he was ten years old as he remembered his dad coming home from his night security job, popping open a beer can, and plopping his old semi-automatic Colt on top of the fridge where the kids couldn't reach it ("for safety"—ha!) before stretching out on the couch and falling asleep. The proper name of the gun was the Colt Government, but his dad always called it the Governator ("'cause it keeps me as regular as prune juice!") and Danny couldn't remember a time when he left the house without it tucked into his pants.

And here they were, two matching Governators. Danny glanced at the two serial numbers and, sure enough, they were consecutive. These guns had to be seventy-five years old. How had they managed to stay together all this time? A matching pair of his father's favorite gun? It barely seemed possible. No one who cared about these pistols would have kept them in a crappy old wooden box like this. Or maybe that was the point. Maybe nobody had ever cared about them, and that's how they went unnoticed. Sometimes things that look like they go together aren't actually together, they're just next to each other. Coincidentally. For a very long time.

Danny decided. He picked the box up, brought it back to his car, took out his bag, and plopped the wooden box inside. He felt a little bad. He was pretty sure Johnson had never gotten a gun before, let alone two guns. Even without an arrest, two guns was a pretty good day for a rookie cop. Danny looked up to see the kid loping toward him (he had an odd little walk where his head popped up and down with each step, almost like a little boy who could barely resist starting skipping). The kid was barely even breathing hard, he must not have tried too hard to catch those guys. Danny's momentary guilt about the guns left him: if you don't want it, you don't get it.

"What'd you find, Danny? Anything in there?" Johnson asked.

"Yeah," Danny said. "There's fifty PlayStations on a pallet in the back. Brand new. And twenty dollars says the truck is stolen. All the stuff and tools in the back seat doesn't belong to the likes of those two you were chasing. I take it you didn't get them?"

"Naw. They were gone before I was even halfway down the alley. You were right. I should have made that turn quicker," Johnson said.

"Definitely. But it happens. Everyone loses someone eventually. Just don't make a habit of it. Count up those PlayStations. I'm pretty sure there's fifty, but if it turns out there's only forty-eight, don't worry. I promise not to tell anyone." Danny gave Johnson a mischievous little smile.

"Don't worry, Danny. I'll count them up perfectly. I may have lost the guys, but I won't lose any of those PlayStations."

Danny got back into the squad car as the kid walked

around to the back of the truck and gleefully started counting the PlayStations. He looked pleased as punch. The poor kid hadn't even been savvy enough to understand his joke about stealing two of them for themselves. Sad.

Danny picked up his phone and called Mike.

"Yeah," Mike said.

"Remember that thing you asked me about the other day?" Danny said.

"Yeah."

"Well, I got it." Danny said.

"Yeah?"

"Yeah. You wanna meet up?" Danny asked.

"The usual place?" Mike said.

"Yeah. Sure. See you there," Danny said.

"Yeah," Mike agreed.

Danny hung up.

Goddamned Mike. The "usual" place. Like it hadn't been almost a decade. Well, screw him anyway. Screw him for asking for help after so many years, and screw him for expecting that Danny would just give him help without figuring out why, and screw him for undoubtedly getting him in trouble for some nonsense he didn't even understand yet. It didn't add up yet, but Danny'd figure it out.

Danny admired the two handguns, trying to figure out which one he would keep for himself and which one he would give to Mike. They were beautiful. The guard on the handle was wood, not plastic like the one his dad had. And engraved in the wood were these matching swooping S figures with tiny embellishments all over them. He'd never seen anything like them. Anyone who ever saw these guns would instantly know they were a matching pair. Even their serial numbers were consecutive. They were exactly the same except one ended in a 1, and the other ended in a 2. He decided to keep the lower serial number for himself. After all, he was two months older than Mike so he ought to have the first one.

These two guns had stayed together for longer than his dad had stayed alive. He was glad they were going to stay together for one more little adventure. Mike could go screw himself for trying to keep him in the dark. Danny wasn't sure what the hell Mike was doing, but whatever it was, that prick wouldn't be going down by himself.

CHAPTER THREE

F elton had forgotten how huge those neighborhood department stores were back in the day. It stood five stories tall and took up an entire city block, looming over the strip of one- and two-story commercial buildings like a fortress. Back in the day, when old Mr. Goldblatt built this thing, he probably enjoyed building something that was so much bigger than anything that came before it. They might have been able to keep him out of their fancy downtown clubs, but he could make their storefronts look like dollhouses next to his.

Felton could see that the building still had some strength left, but it looked more like an abandoned whale carcass left to rot on the beach than a place you might buy your daughter's Easter dress. The first floor still had some life in it—the current tenant was some cheap furniture place—but the rest of the store was an empty shell, and the exterior wasn't the gleaming white-glazed terracotta that Goldblatt's had envisioned. Instead it was a tired, dirty-clothes gray.

Felton had a hell of a time finding the security office. He was a large man, somewhere between big and fat, and he swept into the store with his long coat and fedora, making sure to mean mug everyone he passed so they'd know he was there on business. It worked a little too well. The little sales people scattered like a bomb had gone off so there was no one left to talk to. They had no idea what to do with a man like him, Felton chuckled. They knew how to deal with the homeless drunks looking for a handout and the beaten-down, working-class people coming in for a cheap sofa and an overpriced TV. They knew which back door to run out of if the Feds showed up to check on immigration. But this well-dressed man's man in a beautiful suit with a handgun on his hip? What in the hell were they supposed to do with him? Felton loved watching them run, but he also knew this job was beneath him. A detective like him didn't belong here, and the fact that these people didn't know what to do with him was even more proof.

After a hurried conference in the back of the store, the salesperson who had evidently been elected to see what Felton wanted scurried toward him. But between the language barrier and the fact that the poor representative started laughing when Felton mentioned that he had been called over by security, it took a while before they figured out the situation together: the store hadn't called the police; it was the land-lords, the owners of the building. They still had a security guard to keep an eye on the rest of the abandoned hulk even if nobody cared enough to protect the one part of the store that was still functioning.

With obvious relief, the employees directed Felton up an old dusty staircase that led to the second floor. The smell of mold and the feeling of asbestos in his lungs caused Felton to take the shallowest breaths he could handle while clambering up the thin, ornate iron stairs.

Once they got to the second floor and entered a room off the landing, Felton saw the chubby little ex-gangbanger secu-rity guard that must have started this aggravation with his call. His uniform was too small, he had a fake plasticky badge, and he was clutching a toy-like CB radio like a security blanket. It was all Felton could do not to spit on the floor in disgust. The little idiot was sitting behind this old-fashioned desk with piles of ancient paper and candy wrappers all over it. His posture was so messed up and the desk so big that he looked like a little kid caught sitting in the principal's chair when the principal was out of the office.

The kid got up right away when Felton walked in: "Oh, hey, good afternoon, Detective. I'm so glad you came by. The sergeant said he was going to send someone. I think I've got something real good here, and I wanted to make sure a fellow lawman got it right away."

"*Lawman?*" Felton's lip curled involuntarily. "What's a *lawman?*"

"Well, you know—"

Felton interrupted him. He'd be establishing who was in control. "Fellow lawman, son? Are you honestly thinking you and I got something in common?"

"Yeah. Yeah, Detective . . . of course. You know . . . we're both involved in law enforcement like . . . we're both officers," the kid said.

"Officers?" Felton had about eight inches on the kid. He leaned into him like he was going to set his chin on his forehead. "Let me explain something to you: I'm a detective with the Chicago Police and you're a little nobody gangbanger who probably gave his cousin's name to the employment office so all the misdemeanors you got as a kid wouldn't prevent you from getting this petty-ass fake security guard job you got going on here." Felton gave him the stink eye. When the little idiot averted his eyes, Felton knew he was on the mark. Actually, the kid almost looked ashamed, and Felton began to think maybe he was being a little too harsh. "Now, I respect what you're doing. I respect your hustle and your work and all it means to try and make yourself a man when no one ever showed you how to do it. But don't get out of your place, son.

Know who you are. Me and you got nothing in common. You understand?"

The kid sniffed petulantly. "You ain't gotta be like that, Detective. I don't mean no disrespect. All I'm saying is that I found something that might interest you, that's all. And I can recognize that it would be of interest to you because I got the same job as you."

Felton fiddled with the lint in his pocket and thought about pounding the kid right here and now, but he decided it was a waste of his time. Besides, something about the little weasel appealed to him. "Alright kid, just show me what you got then. I ain't got all day."

"OK, yeah." He scrambled out from behind the desk and tried to recover his dignity (which was a little hard to do as the uniform he was wearing was about three sizes too big). But it gave Felton a chance to notice him pull down on his shirt sleeves to cover up the bottom of a tattoo on his arm, probably some petty gang nonsense.

Felton filed that info away. It always unnerved people when you knew something about them that they hadn't ever told you.

Felton was good at unnerving people. Getting people off balance meant you could get momentum over them, and if you had momentum, you could roll them.

"Detective, you see all those gray filing cabinets along that wall? They're filled with these old reel tapes, the kind movie projectors use. It's pretty cool stuff. All retro and everything. As it so happens," the kid looked around embarrassedly, "there isn't really a lot for me to do here all day. So I started watching them to see what was on them, and it turns out they contain all this old security footage. It seems they closed down the store in 1997, but they kept running some of the security cameras for a few months after that. See this one here?" he said, holding up one of the reels. "It contains security footage of this big ol' walk-in safe on the fifth floor. They must have kept the camera running because they wanted to know who knew about that safe. You wanna see the safe? It's pretty cool."

"I don't want to see the safe, son." Felton didn't want to extend this trip any longer than he had to. "Just get to the point. There is a point, right? You better not have dragged me down here to give me a lesson on audio-video equipment."

"Naw, naw, that ain't it. Well anyway, it seems from the footage like all these cops started using the safe. Detectives, like you. Or at least, I think they're detectives. They aren't wearing badges or uniforms or anything, but you can just kinda tell by looking at them, ya know?" Felton half-nodded, half-rolled his eyes in response. "Your sergeant said they couldn't be cops—told me that I didn't know crap—but I know what cops look like."

Felton looked the kid up and down, "Yeah, my guess is you've been hiding from cops long enough to know how to recognize them." Plus, Felton thought, Sergeant Fat Ass was dumb as a box of rocks and it gave him pleasure to add this to the list of things he was dumb about.

"Anyway, they start coming in here and having meetings and bringing back criminals who are handcuffed up and stuff. They don't beat 'em or nothing—don't worry." The kid looked at Felton sideways, like he didn't want to piss him off. "But you can tell they're kind of intimidating them, leaving them handcuffed to chairs in the safe and closing the door." The kid shuddered a bit. "I've been in that safe. When the door closes, it's as black as black can be and you feel like you'll suffocate if you stay in there. So when they put those guys handcuffed back there, it must have been to scare them."

"So what's your point, kid? The cops had a second office back in the day. You gotta problem with that?" Felton said.

"Naw, naw." The kid had a curious way of waving his hands back in forth in front of him, like he was attempting to block someone who was about to run into him with a shopping cart. "I think it's cool they used this place like that. It's like a movie where they have this cool old space away from everybody—"

"Right, right, right. Movies, safe, cops. Anything else?" Felton looked at his watch.

"Well, the last tape is from late 1997, like I told you, and on that video there's these two cops, and they put this young dude in the safe and then like, something happens, and they run out of there real quick, and then there's like two hours of tape where nothing happens. The tape ends and then there are no more tapes after that . . ." The kid trailed off, and then looked at Felton expectantly.

"And your point is . . ." Felton said.

"So, don't ya see?" The kid's fending-off-an-oncoming-shopping-cart hands were now clenched like they wanted to say something.

"No. I don't see." Felton couldn't decide whether he was feeling more bored or annoyed with the kid's drawn-out form of storytelling. "And you better stop this nonsense and make me see before I make sure you can't see nothing no more."

"Those cops got set up!" The kid did a little jump he was so excited. "They got set up and maybe even killed, and that's why they never came back and why none of the other cops came back either." The kid lowered his voice, and hunkered closer to Felton. "The place is, like, haunted, Detective. I swear it is. When you're here all alone at night, you think you're going crazy. You'll see, Detective, it really is crazy haunted up there."

"So then what happens to the guy they locked up in there?" Felton said.

"That's exactly it. I don't know. I don't know whether he died in there or what," the kid said.

"How come you don't know?" Felton asked, while picking at his manicured cuticles.

"Like I told you, the video ends," the kid said.

"Well you were just telling me you've been inside the safe, right?" Felton said.

"Yeah, it's really cool. You should see it. I found the key taped up in the back of one of these filing cabinets. I don't think the safe had been opened since those detectives ran out of there—"

"—and what's inside?"

"Well, nothing much. Just dust and a couple of old chairs."

"So you're wrong," Felton said.

"Wrong. Wrong how?" the kid asked.

"Jesus. Think it through, you numbskull. If the guy was in there and it hasn't been opened since the cops ran out, shouldn't there be something in there?" Felton asked.

"No. That's what I'm telling you. There's nothing in there. I've checked it out myself," the kid said.

"For God's sake, kid, would you just stop and think? No skeleton? No little messed up mummy or some other nonsense?" Felton held up his hands, hoping the kid would finally connect the dots, but the blank look on his face indicated that there wasn't a chance. "If there's nothing in there, then he must have gotten out somehow, right?"

The kid pondered this line of logic. "Huh. I don't know. The video ends, so you can't see what happened next. Without the video, you can never really know," the kid said.

Felton shook his head. "That's the problem with you people these days. You think that if something isn't on video, it doesn't exist. But it does. You can know a lot about a thing that's there even if it ain't. It's not magic, it's rationality. Everything doesn't have to be on video." Felton looked at the kid, hoping the lightbulb would finally turn on, but after a few blinks, the kid looked dumber than ever. Felton couldn't stand to look at him any longer. "Look, kid, here's what I see: You don't know nothing and you ain't got nothing. Next time you get a bright idea, call whatever temp company employs you, not the CPD."

The kid just stood there. Sniffed a little. Felton could see the cogs in the kid's tiny brain trying to turn over what he had said and churn out an idea in response. But the cogs seemed to be stuck, and instead of coming up with something novel, he just played back the same thought he'd probably been having since he called: "Can't you please just look at the video, Detective? It's really cool. I think you'll like it."

Felton let out a long sigh. "What's your name, kid?"

"My momma named me Gregory, but all my friends call me Little J."

"Well, Little J, I like to reward a man who asks so politely, so let's see this video of yours. You've wasted so much of my time already, what's a little more?"

Little J smiled dumbly and moved to the other side of the office where he had set up an old-fashioned projector on a table facing a pull-down screen. He carefully examined the set up like he was the scientist who had just discovered electricity and was admiring his own brilliance. Finally, after noticing Felton's increasing exasperation, he turned on the projector. On the screen, in black and white but surprisingly clear, Felton saw two plain-clothes police officers lead a young handcuffed guy in shorts and a t-shirt into a room. There wasn't any sound, but you could tell the two cops were talking, then they walk the guy into the safe. A few moments later, the two cops come out of the safe, talk to each other for a few more minutes, and then suddenly rush out of the room.

To most people, this video would be nothing more than a mild curiosity, a confusing image of tough guys maybe doing something they shouldn't in a world that seems far away.

But Felton wasn't confused. He knew exactly what was going on. In fact, he was pretty sure this was the most interesting video he'd seen in a long time. Little J, it turned out, was correct. Those were officers, and Felton knew them.

"Yeah, Detective, that's where it ends." Little J began stroking his nonexistent beard like he was pondering the complexities of the universe. "That's the last of the videos. It seemed weird that it just ended like that—like something bad had happened—so I thought you should know."

Felton resolved to turn his mind on in the way a man resolves to start an old car on a cold night when he doesn't have anyone to call for help if things go wrong. Felton blinked his mind open, fiddled with the keys, tensed his foot over the gas pedal. He could not mess this up.

When an idiot like Little J has a million dollars and doesn't know it, you want to be sure not to wake his lizard brain. Little J didn't know what he had, but he'd be able to sense an officer's attention being drawn to something in an instant. These dumb gangbangers could smell the police coming for them like a dog smells another dog's piss. Felton had to be careful.

"You said there were other tapes. What's on them?" Felton was all-business now.

"Nothing much. More of the same stuff," Little J said.

"Same officers? Same guys in handcuffs?" Felton asked.

"There's a half dozen officers that go in and out, but these two are the ones you see the most. The guys in hand-cuffs are almost always different, near as I can tell," Little J said.

"Other than the video, is there anything that makes you think anything happened there that shouldn't have?" Felton feigned disinterest by examining his cuticles again. "Because frankly, what you're showing me is absolutely nothing."

"Well, yeah, the drugs. Drug dealers don't mess around. Especially when you're dealing with some weight. They'll kill anybody." Little J nodded sagely.

"Drugs, Little J?" Felton paused, trying to keep the anger out of his voice, his own thumbs pushing into his thighs and causing them pain. "Are you telling me that you have footage of these police officers pulling large quantities of drugs into this room?"

"Naw, naw. There's nothing like that on the videos. You can just tell from the way they're talking that it's about drugs," Little J said.

"Talking?" Felton said, leaning in to physically take up the space that Little J was breathing in. "Have I gone deaf or something? I didn't hear nothing, Little J. You some kind of goddamn lip reader?"

"Naw, naw, Detective. It's in the audio."

Felton seriously considered strangling Little J right then.

"The *audio*, Little J? What *audio*?"

"Well," Little J replied sheepishly, "the audio isn't as cool, so I didn't mention it." Plus, I left the machine that plays it in the trunk of my car and it's kinda hot out and it's a pain in the ass to move it . . ."

Felton's whole body swelled up as he moved in even closer to Little J. "Well, you're going to move that machine, Little J. You're going to move it and you're going to move it right quick. And if you don't, I'm gonna lock you up for wasting my extremely valuable time. Do you hear me, Little J?"

Little J screwed up his lips as though he was about to say something, thought better about it, tried again, sighed, took a long look out the window, and then looked plaintively at Felton. "Can you help me move it? It's really heavy."

"Which car is yours?" Felton asked, looking out the window.

"The red Monte Carlo out there. It's in the back seat."

"Well, how did you get it out there?" Felton asked.

"I carried it, but I nearly fell down the stairs doing it," Little J said.

"Sounds like you need more practice then. I'm going to give you that opportunity right now. Get going."

Little J looked up at him solemnly.

"I said go," Felton yelled. "Now!"

As soon as Little J shuffled out, Felton started looking through the reels. Each reel was labeled with the date. Above the video reels that Little J had shown him, Felton saw another row of tapes that presumably had audio on them. It didn't look like just one system. It looked like two separate systems that ran at the same time. That would be a problem. For the court of law, he'd have to find someone who could vouch for the simultaneous recordings, and that could be tough given that the recordings took place twenty years ago and security guards don't exactly have long professional lifespans. Sure, there was Little J, but Felton sure as hell wasn't going to try and use him to vouch for the tapes. Plus, Little J was just guessing as to how everything worked; he didn't have any actual, professional knowledge. That wouldn't work anymore than Felton's guessing would. Of course, he wouldn't need to get them admitted into the court of law, just the court of public opinion, and luckily, that threshold was much, much lower.

While Felton pondered the situation, Little J huffed and puffed his way back up the stairs carrying something that looked like a full-size suitcase. He set the contraption on the table. "I was actually listening to the relevant (Little J put the stress on the third syllable, rel-e-VANT) tape last night. So it's all cued up to the right place."

He awkwardly put the tape in and pressed play. Two familiar voices rang out from the speakers:

"Man, you better not be messing with us. If you're on some kind of nonsense, I guarantee I'll make this petty-ass case you're looking at right now seem like child's play."

"Office. That ain't me. I can't go to jail right now. I'm telling you, Colfax's got all kinds of drugs and he keeps them at his old man's church in the basement. It's kilos, Office, kilos. And behind all the janitor supplies, there's a bunch of little heaters, about a dozen of them, that got stolen off a railcar last month. It's a huge hit. I ain't gonna lie to you."

"And you expect us to believe that we can find all of these drugs and

guns in the basement of the Great Redeemer Church and that the master-mind is some preacher's kid?"

"Hell yah! That family is a mess. Don't let that religion talk fool you. Preacher surely don't know nothing about it, but every member of that family is either a saint or a sinner, and Colfax, well, he got the sinner part of the apple. He's the one. Check it out. You'll see."

"And you'll swear to all this in front of a judge?"

"On my momma I'll swear it. I've done it before. Look me up. You'll see my info's good."

There was a pause in the tape and some muffled sounds during which the cops were presumably putting the dude back into the safe. After a minute or two, the muffled voices got louder and became intelligible again. This time, it was just the two cops talking to each other.

"I don't know, Danny. Hitting a church ain't nothing to mess around with. Even if the info is good and everything turns out exactly how he says, we're still going to get tons of heat for hitting a church. Those people are highly connected. It's that big church over on 63rd, the one with all the parking lots that fill up every Sunday. That place is an institution. You really want to mess with that?"

"Damn right, I do. These self-righteous assholes think they can hide behind the church? I hate that stuff. And I don't care what that dude says, I bet that preacher is involved with it. All these preachers are the same. Doesn't matter how big their church gets. In the end, all they want is to drive a fancy car on someone else's dime and get the old ladies in the hats to ooh and aah over them. As far as I'm concerned, they're all dirty, and that's even more reason to hit the place."

"But what if he's wrong and the info is bad?"

"For crying out loud. We've seen it with our own eyes. We've seen Colfax loading boxes into his car and then driving them over to the church. He's heavy in dope. What else could it be and where else could he be keeping it?"

"Well, he could also be loading Bibles into those boxes. We don't know."

"We've followed him long enough to know those aren't Bibles. Where

there's an out, there has to be an in—that's just physics. His sales are the out, and the church is the in. It's obvious, and you know it. Besides, I checked up on this dude's background. He's right, he always gives good info, and he gets weight on that info. Weight. He's had four positive hits and no negatives. His info is good."

"But even if his info is good right now, that doesn't mean it will be tomorrow. Plus, he hasn't even been there in a couple of weeks. His info is too old for a warrant, and they could find out that we grabbed old boy back there and decide to move everything out of there to be safe. What if we hit that church and there's nothing there? We'll lose our jobs. It's not worth it.

"Look, I guarantee there will be drugs in that church. And if there's nothing there, I still guarantee it. That church is dirty. We both know it. And besides, old boy will say whatever we need him to in order to get the warrant. He's desperate to get out of here. I bet we can get him to remember that he was actually over at the church more recently. And besides, we don't have to mention that it's a church in the warrant packet. We'll just list the address and no one will be the wiser. Hell, you can barely tell it's a church from the outside anyway. It looks as much like a factory as anything else until you get inside of it."

Felton could hear the crackling of a CB radio but couldn't decipher any of the words.

"We gotta go. They're calling for help."

"What about the dude?"

"Screw him. He ain't going nowhere. He can wait."

Felton heard the radio crackle again, followed by the sound of footsteps receding into the distance. And then silence.

"So what do you think, Detective?" Little J asked. "You think I brought you some good info?"

Felton made a decision. He turned to Little J and said, "You're lucky I don't lock you up for wasting my time. I *know* those guys. They're not officers. Their security guards, like you. I was buying a drill in Sears last week and they were working loss prevention for crying out loud. And they sure as heck aren't dead. Twenty years later and they're still losers working dead-end jobs. Look, I'll do you a favor, though, because I like you. You working tonight?"

"Detective, those ain't no security guards. They're cops," Little J sniffed.

"Little J, I know you heard my question. Answer it."

"My shift ends in a couple of hours, sir."

"Good. Let's load this stuff up into the safe so no one can mess with them, and then we'll come back and look them over tonight. See what we can see. Together. Who knows, maybe there'll be something decent on those tapes even if there's nothing on this one. But you can't tell anybody I'm doing this. The union would be pissed that I was working overtime with a concerned citizen like you on a case without billing the city for time-and-a-half. It's important that we understand each other. So, you understand?"

"Yeah, Detective. Yeah, I understand. Thanks, that's real cool. I'd really like to work with you on this," Little J said.

"Good. Now you're sure you've got the only key to the safe, right? I don't want anybody else to have access to those tapes while we're gone," Felton said.

"No, I'm positive it's the only one. I only randomly found it, and it was covered in dust. There ain't no way anybody else knows how to get into the safe," Little J said.

"Good, good." Felton had to stop himself from rubbing his hands together in glee. "We'll come back tonight around 9:00 p.m. and see what else there is."

"But Detective, the night guy will be here," Little J said.

"Oh damn, you're right!" Felton slapped his forehead with his palm. (He wondered if he was overdoing it a bit.) "I don't want you to get in trouble. How about this: I'll come back here before you. I'll tell the night guy that the boss said there was a law enforcement matter I had to take care of and I'll send him home. Think that would work?"

"I don't know. The night guy is kind of a goody-goody. He'll for sure want to call the boss," Little J said.

"Well then, give me your boss's number. I'll call him first and tell him we need to use the building to watch some dope boys selling out back—building owners love that sort of thing. They think as soon as the police start locking people up, the gentrification dollars will start pouring in. Oh, and give me your keys to the office and the safe. That'll make it pretty clear that I have prior authorization. Then, once I'm rid of the night guy, you can show up at 9:30, and we'll get to work."

Little J nodded and reached into his pocket, but he hesitated. Felton sensed that handing over the keys felt to Little J like handing over his power. And Little J was right. He would be giving up his power.

"You know what, Gregory? I'm not so sure this is the best idea after all." Felton started to stand. "You seem a little hesitant. I'm not working with anybody that doesn't know how to trust. Since you don't need me. You can just tell your boss about those videos, and I'll be on my way."

"No, Detective. Stop. I'm sorry. You can have the keys. I was just thinking about whether I can make it back here by 9:30. I'm supposed to watch my little cousins tonight, but I'll just tell their mom I can't do it. She'll only be a little mad. Let's do this."

Little J handed him the keys and pulled a wrinkled-up business card out of his grubby pocket with his boss's phone number. Little J scratched his own number down on the back.

Felton put on his hat and steeled himself for what was coming next. If he really wanted to win Little J over, he knew he'd have to touch the slimy bastard.

"Great. I'll see you tonight at 9:30." Felton reached out his hand. When Little J grasped it, he pulled him in for a shoulder bump. He dit it twice, to prove to himself he could, only gagging a little.

"Thanks, Detective. I'll see you tonight."

Relief washed over Felton as he left the asbestos-filled office and walked out into the fresh air. Once he was back in his squad car, Felton shook his head. Little J had made a mistake. He never should have let Felton see which car was his. Once you had one of these little pieces of crap's cars, you had them. The only thing better was when you had access to an ex-girlfriend (she'd tell you everything—though he highly doubted that Little J had ever had such a thing). Felton pulled around so he could run Little J's plate on his computer. It came back to some other name, not Gregory. That no-good, lying-ass fool. He started running arrests for the residence listed on the car's registration, and then the former addresses of the people that had been locked up there, and sure enough, two degrees of criminalification later, Little J's photo popped up. He must have used the name of some cousin or uncle that hadn't been arrested in order to get this job. That dumbass had all kinds of gangbanging and reckless conduct arrests. Idiot. Wasn't even smart enough to deal drugs. His only skill was hanging out on the corner and being an asshole. It'd been a couple of years since his last arrest, but Felton knew he was still the same little asshole he'd always been. Getting a job and stopping getting arrested didn't mean nothing. Those guys don't change. Hell, they can't. Their gangbanging friends might leave them, but their gangbanging enemies won't. Felton ran the name through the Secretary of State, and sure enough, Little J's driver's license was suspended. *"Fellow lawman,"* Felton snorted. Piece of crap. The rules are simple: lie to the police, and you go to jail. A man makes his own bed.

Felton had some work to do. He'd have a marked squad car sitting in the parking lot at 9:30. They could yank Little J on the suspended license, which would put him in jail for a few hours. And if Felton was any judge of character, the idiot would lie about his name again, and that would get him an overnight stay too. Once he was in jail, Felton would wait about an hour and then make an anonymous call to Little J's boss to tell him that one of his gangbanging security guards had threatened a poor citizen who was shopping for furniture. He would make sure to mention Little J lying about his name too. About an hour after that, Felton would leave a voicemail for Little J (Felton knew there was no way he would answer since he would be locked up) telling him how disappointed he was that Little J hadn't shown up, that he'd felt almost like he was a son to him (Felton shuddered at the thought), that he wished him the best, and to never contact him again.

The shift schedules were posted on the door, and Felton could see that Little J was supposed to work again tomorrow morning. If Felton could drag his nephew away from his video games, he might even get that lazy ass a job in the same play.

After that, Felton would have all the time he needed to figure out what to do about that tape and to see if there was anything of interest on the other tapes. Most importantly, he'd be the only one in the world with access to them. Beautiful.

Felton sighed with pleasure. The A/C was coming on strong in the car, a good tune was playing on the radio, and the evening sky was looking clearer than it had in years. Felton hadn't felt this much fortune since he was a young man.

It was about time.

He deserved it. All this working and slaving away and simpering up to the right people at the right times. Just a few hours before, Felton had thought that he'd be wandering around in the wilderness until ReverendAlderman was back in the game. But now, he didn't need him. He was good to go all by himself. Felton would bow down to no man.

Felton thought back to the dumb city employee who had found the dirt on ReverendAlderman and was too dumb to know that info was worth a million bucks. Felton wasn't going to make that mistake. He thought of that video locked up in that old safe and patted his side with the only known key in existence with a sense of satisfaction like he'd just finished Thanksgiving dinner.

That video was the best evidence he'd seen in years. It showed two rogue cops locking up wayward youth in their own private prison and then extorting them in order to throw an innocent preacher's kid in jail with drugs that the two cops were going to plant on him. Outrageous.

And I'll be damned, Felton thought, if those two dirty-ass cops weren't his old classmates. He couldn't stand those sanctimonious fools. They thought they were so good, so special. He could picture himself standing at the press conference answering questions. A reporter would say, "When did you first recognize them, Detective Felton?" and he would languidly respond, "Oh I recognized them right away. I've known their type my entire life." Damn right he recognized them, and damn right he knew their type. It was that arrogant son of a bitch Danny and his holier-than-thou partner Michael, the superintendent of the goddamned Chicago Police. He recognized them, he knew them, and he, Detective Andre Felton, would bring them down.

Je.

Sus.

Christ.

CHAPTER FOUR

"Mari," the sergeant said, and then, when there was no response, "Detective Davis? You there?"

The childish, sing-song voice of Detective Mari Davis's boss gradually interrupted her thoughts.

"Oh, hey Sarge, what's up?"

Mari was sitting at her desk in the D-Unit. There was a computer on the desk, surrounded by piles of paper. Half a dozen similar desks were situated around her. The other detectives' desks had different piles of paper, but their office chairs and computers were identical. The entire office gave off the appearance of last being updated—poorly—in 1970, long before many of the detectives working that day had been born.

"What's up?" the sergeant snarled, folding his arms across his chest. "Your job. Remember?"

Mari blinked a couple of times. "Yeah, I remember. What do you need?"

"I need you to quit shopping and pay attention so I can tell you what you need to do," the sergeant said, resting his hand on her desk. Mari noticed that his fat fingers were apparently trying to swallow the rings on his fingers, as she could barely tell which one should have contained his wedding band, what with the flesh congealing around them.

"Shopping?" Mari tried to be polite—especially to her boss—but she couldn't contain the annoyance in her voice. "There's no shopping going on here. I'm working. See all those reports piling up in your queue with my name on them? The ones you haven't approved yet?"

"Yeah, well I don't have time for your nonsense cases right now. They're killing the police out there, ya know." While he was saying this, the sergeant leaned over to see if he could get a better look at her tits.

"Yeah, I know." Mari involuntarily put her hand over her chest, even though she was wearing a high-cut top. "Everyone in this unit is out there allegedly working this case at four in the morning while I'm in here actually working. How much solving you think they're doing out there before dawn in the pouring rain? You think they're interviewing witnesses, busting down doors, sleeping in their cars, what?"

"Yeah." The sergeant didn't bother to disagree with her. "Well, good news. The bosses are coming over here, so you gotta get out of here and pretend to work, just like the rest of the guys you're so impressed with."

"But I *am* working. Actual work. I'm working on all of this paperwork," Mari said.

"Well, then stop," he said.

"Sarge, for crying out loud, some of these are real victims with real court dates this morning. If I don't finish this up, we're going in unprepared. We can't afford another continuance. Some of these witnesses are already getting cold feet about showing up. I have to finish all this up so I can start calling them to make sure they come to court or the judge is going to start tossing cases."

"Mari, I don't care what you do. Just get out of this office."

"Can I at least finish up these two cases?" Mari gestured

toward two particularly convoluted piles of paperwork. It'd taken her half an hour just to get everything in chronological order so she could go over it with the victims. One victim in particular left for work at 5:00 a.m. and she was basically unreachable after that. Mari hated when good people got screwed over for being hardworking. "I've got all my paperwork set up here. It'll only take me about an hour to type everything up so you can approve them. I'll show you which ones they are so you don't have to sort through all the other things you haven't approved, and then I'll get out of here. We both know there's about zero chance that the bosses are actually going to show up here at four in the morning."

"Jesus," Sarge said to no one in particular, "talking to you is like talking to my wife. Pack it up. Now."

"Sarge, I've worked hard on these two. It's two separate incidents: an armed robbery and a rape. It's the same guy, and it looks like he's been doing basically the same thing once or twice a week for at least the last couple of months. He happens to be in custody for some nonsense traffic warrant right now. The judge is going to let him walk on the traffic this morning, but I talked to a county friend of mine and they agreed to let me interview him in the back as long as it doesn't mess up their schedule of appearances before the judge. This guy is going to be relaxed; he's not going to suspect a thing. I'm going to talk to the victim right before, so I'll be totally prepared and I'm sure I'll get him to say something. If I can get even a little on him, I can hold him until I do lineups with all the other victims. I'm sure at least a half dozen of them will pick him out."

"Rapes and robberies? You mean these people are still alive? What the hell is wrong with you, Mari? If they aren't dead, they don't matter. You know that."

"Well they aren't dead yet, and by the time they are, I sure won't be able to do any lineups for them, will I, Sarge?"

"Yeah, screw you, ya smart ass. Rapes and robberies. Jesus

Christ. You think you're so special working these cases like they mean something, but I got news for you. No one cares about your rapes and robberies. I have about three hundred open robberies, most of which are yours because you're still "working" on them while all the other guys have closed theirs out. And as for the rapes, I have about a hundred of those, half of which never should have seen paper in the first place. You think the bosses care about two or three extra offenders you put a case on when a hundred other cases are just sitting there with nothing being done on them at all? And I don't care how pretty you think you are. You can't count on that getting you anywhere with me."

"Pretty? What does that have to do with anything? Sarge, these are good victims. *Good* victims. They've got jobs and everything, decent neighborhoods."

"You're talking to me about good victims? There's a dead cop out there. A dead goddamn cop. *That* is a good victim. I'll tell you what: I'm going to make this easy on you. I don't care what work you do on these cases because I'm not going to approve them anyway. I'm not going to approve *any* of your cases until this one is solved. So pack up your things and get out of here, like I told you to do ten minutes ago."

The sergeant huffed, put two hands on the lapels of his jacket in order to straighten it into a semblance of profession-alism that had lost all possibility 35 pounds ago, and went back to his office. Mari fumed. There wasn't even a point in yelling at the idiot. His twenty-five-year career had made him immune to criticism. Mari angrily gathered up her paperwork and put it into her bag. This annoying and inconvenient obstacle meant that it would take her twice as long to do the same damn thing for no reason whatsoever.

She wished she could just go home, where it was quiet and no one would bother her. But she'd need a department computer in order to finish typing everything in. Now, instead of her reasonably comfortable work desk, with all the things she needed right there, she'd have to go to some other police station and camp out at one of the desk computers. The noise and the lack of comfortable space was one thing, but what was worse was that there was always some jagoff officer in jeans who thought he was Mr. Police because he locked up gang-bangers on petty misdemeanors. It didn't even matter to these idiots that it took them longer to do the paperwork than it took the gangbangers to bond out with nothing more than a signa-ture. They still thought they were doing "real" police work. Yet these loud assholes somehow felt their nonsense arrests gave them the right to give her advice and see what she was working on. As if they had any idea how to actually write up a case. The ballsy ones would ask for her phone number and get turned down. But the really aggravating ones would be too scared to ask her directly. Instead, they'd ask around until they got her number from some friend of a friend, and then she'd have to see their ridiculous and painfully predictable texts an hour later: "What's up? You know who this is?"

Yeah, you idiot, Mari thought, I know who you are, but do you?

Another thing Mari had to admit to herself was that she didn't like to work on this stuff at home by herself. Home was boring. Home had dirty dishes in the sink. Home made it all too obvious that ever since she got this job, none of her old friends bothered to call her anymore. Home was lonely.

At work, stuff happened—people came in and out, had arguments, made up, got killed, and did it all over again (assuming they weren't the ones that got killed). And despite her asshole boss and some of the other losers she worked with, in general, there were lots of good coppers that she could bounce ideas off of, joke around with, and talk to about what she had done the day before and what she might do the next day. The job was still fun. She loved the fact that, because of her, some asshole wasn't going to be able to hurt people anymore.

Dumb idiot sergeant, thinking he could stop her. He was so lazy he had given out his password to half the watch, including her. She would approve her own reports in his name and he wouldn't even know the difference.

Mari pulled into the parking lot of her old district station. She knew people here; it wouldn't be that bad. But before she could get out of the car, her phone rang. The caller ID said, "Cook County Jail Inmate."

Despite her better instincts, she answered the phone.

"This Detective Davis?" said the voice on the other end.

"Who's this?" Mari didn't answer questions; she asked them.

"Cornelius Washington."

"Who gave you this number?" she asked.

"You did. Remember?" The voice on the other end of the line had the quality of a businessman.

"I don't know anyone named 'Cornelius Washington,' and I sure as hell don't need any phone calls from jailbirds. The only reason I picked up was because I was expecting a call from over there. You aren't the person I was expecting, so what exactly is it that you want? I haven't got all day."

"I have some information for you," he said coolly.

"What kind of information?" she asked.

"You alone? Other people shouldn't hear this," he said.

Now Mari was exasperated. "Let me tell you something, Cornelius. You don't need to worry about who I'm with, or anything else about me. What you need to worry about is whatever it is you did to get yourself locked up in Cook County Jail. I'm going to ask you one more time, and this time you're going to answer or I'll hang up: "How did you get my number?"

"I already told you. You gave it to me," Cornelius said, chuckling.

"You're really going to play this game?" she said sharply.

"What game, Detective?" he asked.

"The one where you make me ask a question in order for you to give me any information. I don't like this game. I'm not playing it. You called me. You got my number. Answer the question you know I'm asking," Mari said.

"How about this, Detective: I'll give you a hint. Life ain't interesting when you get everything for free, ya know? Plus, I know you got some smarts on you, and you'll figure it out. You gave me your number back when you were investigating my aunty's burglary. I called the station to say we found a glass bottle that had been moved and might have the robber's prints on it. But then we couldn't get ahold of each other to hand off the bottle, so you gave me your number and we hooked up."

"Hooked up? You wish. You turned some evidence over to me. That's all." Mari had worked a thousand cases by now. Some victims she remembered, but the various random witnesses every case produced . . . there were too many to count, let alone individually remember. But as she listened to his voice, her memory was stirred.

"That's true, Detective. I did wish," Cornelius replied. "A lot of women like when I'm wishing."

"Yeah. I'm sure you're the handsomest guy in the county jail. I hope you like ass, because that's all you're getting. Look, as it so happens, I'm going to give you the only satisfaction you're likely to get until you're out: You're right. I do remember giving you my number. I also remember the 'evidence' you gave me."

Mari remembered it all too well now. Cornelius had called up and said his aunty had found a bottle of Wild Irish Rose that the burglar must have drunk from, because it was empty and on the bedroom floor where it shouldn't have been. Mari was a brand-new detective at the time and was eager to move a case with any evidence she could get. She had not yet learned that sources have motives. The prints she lifted from the bottle turned out to be good not only for that burglary but for about twenty more, and Mari had practically broken her arm patting herself on the back for her fine work.

Mari was excited to tell the aunt that she knew who had done it and it was only a matter of time before they would pick him up on a warrant. But before she could, she found out that the burglar had been shot to death in the alley behind his house. Mari didn't mind. Not the first time one of her offenders got dead before she could get to them.

She'd gone to tell the aunt the good/bad news but while she was sitting there it occurred to her that the aunty lived alone and was one of those born-again religious types who would no more have a bottle of booze in her house than she would take the Lord's name in vain. To Mari's surprise, the aunt asked for the burglar's name and when Mari told her, she muttered "Lord Jesus" and then stole a glance at the empty spot where Cornelius had been sitting the week before.

Mari's interest was peaked so she asked around about why the burglar was killed. Word was, Cornelius had done it, and Mari was livid. He had used Mari to get the fingerprints. It steamed her so much she could hardly sleep at night. He was so brazen about it too. He didn't even bother hiding it. Hell, he wanted the neighborhood to know he did it. All the evidence was circumstantial, so they couldn't put anything on him, but Mari felt like she was an accessory to murder and it made her sick.

So now Mari had the opportunity to confront the man who had tainted one of her first cases: "I asked around about the dude whose fingerprints were found on that 'evidence' you gave me, and the word on the street was, he burglarized some thug's aunty's house. Do you remember that, Cornelius?"

"I do remember that. Strange coincidence, ain't it?" Mari could hear him smiling through the phone. Psychopath. "But Detective, I'm pretty sure you know you're not supposed to use words like 'thug.' It ain't proper, some might even say it's racist."

"You don't know anything about me, and you know even less about what's 'proper.'" Right then, Mari saw a copper she didn't know walk by. Mari didn't like some unknown cop seeing her agitated. He'd assume she was having a domestic. "I'll let you know right now that I don't like being used by pathetic little two-bit thugs, and it isn't going to happen again. Was that guy even an actual burglar, or did you just use me to get prints off some guy who didn't have anything to do with it?"

"That was good info, Detective. The man who touched that bottle burglarized my aunty's house." Cornelius' presence was so physical, Mari thought. Even though he wasn't there, she could feel his body growing and expanding with rage and power. "And maybe that bottle wasn't drunk in that house. And maybe that man who told me who the burglar was had some distaste for saying the man's name out loud, and instead gave me that bottle he drunk from. And maybe I used you to find that man's name, because a man has to use people for power or they will use him in return. But you did a good thing that day, Detective. Rest assured. Don't you worry. Like I told you, everything I say is the truth."

"So what your big dramatic speech is telling me," Mari said, "is that you used my info to give this burglar what he deserved, and shot him in the alley."

Cornelius laughed for a long time, and then said, "This is why I like you, Detective. Here you are, just a few minutes into our conversation and then, boom, you're already trying to pin a murder case on a poor bastard you claim not to even remember."

"You're not as clever as you think, Cornelius. Don't call this number again. My time is way more valuable than yours. Bye."

"It's about that dead cop," Cornelius interrupted.

"Excuse me?" Mari said.

"I'm calling about that dead cop," he repeated.

"Yeah. Congratulations, Cornelius. Every little rat like you is trying to sell someone off for some free time. A jailbird's word isn't worth anything. You can play your ridiculous-dead-cousin-is-the-one-who-did-it story through your lawyer and the state's attorney. There's enough of those nonsense stories running around out there, and I don't feel like hearing yours."

"This ain't a story," Cornelius said. "I got evidence. Or at least I know where the evidence is and I'll tell you where to find it."

Mari snorted. "What kind of 'evidence' you got?"

"The dead cop's blood. The dead cop's missing cuffs. The guy who killed him. All that." Cornelius clicked his tongue, like he was putting a period on the end of a sentence that he knew was too important to ignore.

Mari hated this man. She hated having been used by him all those years ago. She'd been so excited when she got those fingerprints back and solved that burglary. His aunt was a really sweet person. Love just oozed out of every one of her pores. Mari couldn't stand all her religious talk, but that woman's love, wherever it came from, was the real deal.

But what Cornelius was saying now, it was too good. How could she pass this up? The information about the missing handcuffs wasn't anywhere. If Cornelius knew about it, then he had to have some good info. Even Mari shouldn't have known about the missing cuffs. She only knew about them because, while using the lead detectives' passwords to close out some cases, she had taken a moment to look through their notes on this one.

"Cornelius, I'll get the lead detectives on that case to talk to you. They'd love that info. If your info is good, I'm sure they can help you out with whatever trouble you're in right now. But I'm not helping you. Never again."

"Well, I'm not talking to them. I'm talking to you. Besides,

I don't need your help. I'll get out of here my own self. I don't need anything from anybody." He sniffed, his pride and machismo making Mari gag. "I'm calling you because you treated my aunty decently. Better than decently. You walked into her house, treated her with respect, did your job. That means something," he said.

"Yeah. And then you went and murdered my offender. Why are you suddenly becoming an informant if you claim you don't even want a break in exchange? Since when does a person like you care about a dead cop? I smell a lie."

"What I want is my business. This is good info. You're a good cop. This is going to happen," he said.

He was so infuriatingly confident, Mari thought. "It's not going to happen the way you want it to. I'll have those detectives call you."

"I'm not telling them," he said.

"Why not?" Mari replied.

"Cause I ain't," he said.

"Jesus." Mari shook her head.

"Look." Cornelius paused, probably switching the phone to his other ear. "How about I do you a trade: I have my reasons for wanting this info out there, and you have your reasons for not trusting me. Fine. That's fair. That's legit. I'll give you the moral satisfaction of knowing you've been right all along about that old stuff, and then you'll listen to me about this information on who killed that cop. Deal?"

"So your trade is that you'll confess to murder, and in return, I'll use the info you give me? Fine, let's hear it."

"Detective, my mother used to tell me in her best daughter-of-a-preacher-turned-crackhead voice: "There are many tragedies in this world, but I ain't one of them." And I'm telling you, it was no tragedy when that lowlife piece of crap who broke into my aunty's house done got himself killed. You see, he didn't just break in and steal her stuff, that would have been despicable but understandable. No. He was malicious, malevolent, destructive. He threw all her things on the floor, knocked her food on the floor, destroyed those religious figurines she'd collected since childhood. For no reason. Just cause he could, just cause he hated. You can't do that to my family."

"So you killed him for messing with your family?" Mari said.

"No. Because he *disrespected* my family." Mari could feel Cornelius pointing his finger accusatorily in the empty room where he stood. "Killed him, caused him to be killed, let fate take its natural course. It don't matter. The point is, he died."

"How?" Mari asked.

"You got a confession, Detective." Cornelius laughed his infuriating laugh. "You ain't gonna get the book."

"A confession is no good without the details. Details verify. People confess to all kinds of things they didn't do. You're not holding up your end of the bargain," she said.

"Yes I am. I said I'd confess, and I did," Cornelius continued, an edge coming into his voice. "You a liar, Detective? You gonna break our bargain? That's not how I understood you."

"I'm no liar." It was actually a relief that Cornelius was getting angry. On a certain level, Mari was more comfortable with angry people. "I'm just thorough. You don't want any reduced time or anything?"

"Nope. Don't need it. I should be out of here in a few weeks. Weeks ain't nothing," he said.

"Weeks? Hell no. Years. Decades." It was nice to feel confident again, talking to this asshole, Mari thought. "You just confessed to murder. I'd have preferred a better confession, but a recorded confession is still something. How dumb are you? Don't you know all these calls out of county jail are recorded? So yeah. You'd better start talking about what you know about this cop murder. The death penalty is still on the books, even if we haven't used it in a while, and I think you'd be the perfect person to bring it back for."

"This call ain't recorded," Cornelius said.

"God. You think you're so smart. They are all recorded. Every single one of them," she said.

"Nope. They don't record calls between inmates and their attorneys. That'd be contrary to the constitution and all," he said.

"Attorney?" Mari asked. "I'm not your attorney, you idiot."

"Well that's not what it says on the log here. Now you can't see it, being on the phone and all, so I'll read it for you. On the log here, it says I'm talking to Mari Davis, esquire, attorney number 6490392. You're a lawyer, right, Detective? You went to law school, even got good grades I see. That's your attorney number, right, Detective? Ain't it?"

Mari's blood ran cold.

"That's not my attorney number, but good job making up one that sounds about right. I'll give you credit there." Mari found it hard to speak. Her mouth had gone dry.

"Now, Detective, I must say, you are one hell of a liar. If I didn't know you were lying, then I would practically believe you. But you see, I watched those dumbass guards look up your attorney number before my very eyes. It's funny the kind of info they put on the internet, practically criminal, you might say. Anyways, it's no good telling lies when the person you're talking to knows the truth. All the lie does is name the mouth of the sinner that spoke it."

"Why are you calling me?" Mari wanted this conversation to end.

"I told you: I'm returning a favor for a favor. And who knows, maybe I'm getting old. Maybe I'd like to start doing the right thing. Maybe I'd like to see a guy who murdered a cop go to jail. Isn't that something I should be doing, Detective? Isn't that something we're all supposed to do?"

"Shut up." Mari rubbed her face with her palms. She'd

been up all night and she suddenly felt extraordinarily tired. "You don't even know what right is."

" A deal's a deal, detective. You know that. I fulfilled my end, and now you have to fulfill yours."

Mari gritted her teeth, and glared at him through the phone. She'd always promised herself to honor any deal, and this info was a golden ticket anyway. "No promises, but fine, tell me what you want to say."

"You see, Detective, there's this boy named Tron . . ." Cornelius began.

Mari was sure Cornelius was smiling on the other end of the line. She barely remembered what he looked like, but what she did remember was that glinting, confident, evil smile. He thought he was going to use her again, and he would no doubt try, but Mari wasn't a rookie detective anymore. Her fatigue began to wear off as quickly as it had come on. She'd listen to him, she'd use his information, and after she was done, she was going to bury him so deep in Cook County Jail that he would never get out.

CHAPTER FIVE

Rip turned around on them all of a sudden, mean like. Stomped his foot, puffed up his chest, shouted like a mad dog.

But the Corner Boys didn't move.

In fact, they started snickering.

Next, he tried ducking behind a corner so he could catch them off guard. Then, when they walked around the corner, he yelled, straight and strong, like a laser. He imagined them being blown backwards like a cartoon, hair standing on end like they'd put their fingers in an electrical socket. And honestly, they *did* seem surprised. They looked at each other with raised eyebrows, wondering if he'd finally lost it. For a moment, Rip thought it might work, that they'd get scared of him and walk out—but then one of them let out a snort, and they all fell over laughing so hard Rip was afraid the neighbors would complain.

For days now, Rip had been wandering the neighborhood, the Corner Boys trailing behind him like a phantom appendage. Past the jumbled-up houses, past the vacated elementary school where some angry homeless man had set up camp, past the corner store he only dared to go by at night for fear someone would see him. The houses were the same as he remembered: perfect lawn next to an abandoned house, two decrepit homes leaning against each other for support, the occasional burnt-up garage framing a footpath beat through a vacant lot by wanderers like him, the old trees mournfully watching over the neighborhood and remembering how things were when they were young.

Rip kept trying to lose the Corner Boys: running fast (he stumbled now as he ran, but he was still faster than anyone he knew), taking the bus (because surely those loser ghosts didn't have the fare), trying all the things the idiots on the internet said would work (burning sage, scattering salt, asking them politely to go away). Nothing worked.

God, he hated those guys. The only thing that had ever managed to get rid of them was Grandma. One look from Grandma and they would slink away with their tail between their legs and a "yes ma'am, sorry ma'am" on their lips. Where was she? Why hadn't she come back? Why had she abandoned him?

Rip couldn't live like this. He couldn't wander the streets alone, expecting the cops to grab him at any moment for what he'd done while these bumbling idiots pointed and laughed at him. He was breaking. The Corner Boys were taking away his strength and even the ability to control his own body. He stumbled over cracks in the sidewalk, muttered to himself under his breath, waved his hands to God knows who. Terrible. Once it had rained real hard while he was sleeping beneath the stairs in the vacant lot and even though he had rigged a pretty decent tarp over the stairs to keep the outside out, it had still gotten in, soaking through his clothes. Although his clothes eventually dried, they took on a dank smell that seemed to displace all the oxygen from the air. Later, he walked by a gas station and saw some homeless guy reflected in the glass. It took a moment before he realized he was looking at himself.

When he left Tron's house, Rip didn't have a plan. He just left. Didn't even tell Tron. One second, he was going to the bathroom in Tron's basement, and the next, he was zipping up his pants and walking out the front door.

The midday sun had almost blinded him. When had the outside world become so bright? He'd started walking home, but when he got there, he couldn't go in. He just stood there looking at it, acknowledging the invisible force field that surrounded it and shut him out. He thought about going to Vicki's house, but that didn't feel right, either. Besides, how could he talk to her looking like he did and having done what he had done? He had no idea what she would do if she saw him: Would she call the cops on him? Hit him in the head with a lamp? Look through him like he wasn't even there?

Where do you go when you can't go home? Is nowhere anywhere, when home is gone?

In the end, he did nothing. He hovered. He saw the warmth of home from the glow of the hearth. He would stay near that hearth, but he would not enter. He warmed himself with the vision, even though the fire could not burn.

The rear yard of the abandoned house next to his home was the closest he could get. He found the teeth the cop had knocked out laying on the ground and slipped them into his pocket. He'd found that if he didn't smile, no one saw the gap where his teeth used to be, and not smiling, well, that wasn't too hard for him right now. For a few days, he'd slept beneath the porch. But after the rain soaked him, he knew he needed to find a better shelter, so he broke into the empty first-floor apartment and slept in a corner of the living room under a bunch of old newspapers.

Looking out the windows of his vacant house, he thought the world would look different now that everything had changed. But it looked exactly the same as it always had. He could watch his house through the dirty windows where he was squatting. Occasionally, he would see his baby sister come in and out. Sometimes, his uncle would come strutting out, making his ritual rounds to the corner store. His friends, they never came by. The police, not once. Shouldn't there be some kind of action? Shouldn't his family at least report him missing? He thought there'd be some kind of commotion, some *thing* that would happen, that would make his decisions for him, that would decide his fate.

But it didn't. The air got a little colder, the trees started losing their leaves. Nothing more.

It was the smell that brought him around. He'd always prided himself on his neatness: he took care of how he looked, how clean his clothes were. He'd always kept everything about himself neat and square. Now, though, he didn't even have clothes; he had rags, and those rags had stopped smelling anything close to good a long time ago. He had no running water, and although he had become immune to his own smell, he was sure his BO was as powerful as it could be. There was also the problem of not having a toilet. He'd been peeing into a small drain in the floor, and he'd taken a dump in just about every corner of the basement that existed before half-heartedly observing that, after a few days, he no longer felt the urge to make any bowel movements at all. That was probably because he wasn't eating. His hunger had gotten less powerful, and he hardly even noticed it anymore. But the smell—that bothered him, and it was growing. That smell finally pushed him out the door.

He waited until he knew his sister would be out of the house. He'd hoped she and his uncle would both be gone at the same time, but one of them was always there. In the end, he decided he'd rather be forced to see his uncle than his sister. When he let himself in through the front door and poked his head into the living room, he saw his uncle, sitting on a couch he'd never seen before.

His uncle didn't seem surprised to see Rip. "You back?" was all he said.

"Yeah," Rip replied.

His uncle looked him up and down appraisingly. "Your brother called looking for you. I told him you was gone."

"Yeah," Rip said. "That's right."

His uncle waited to see whether Rip would say anything else, and when Rip didn't, he blew air out of his nose like a bull who was figuring out whether it was worth it to charge. "So you got anything to say?"

"Ain't got nothing to say," Rip said.

His uncle took in the tattered clothes, the shrunken body. He was the kind of man who appraised everyone to see whether he'd need to knock them down in the pecking order. "You look like crap," he said. "You smell like crap too."

"Yeah," Rip said. He couldn't afford to fight. He needed his uncle to take him in.

Another measured stare. His uncle tilted his head. Almost a nod. Was it a blessing? His uncle turned back to the television. "Well, you know where the bathroom's at."

"Yeah. I'm going to take a shower," Rip said.

"Yeah. You do that." This time, his uncle definitely nodded.

It was the most glorious shower of his entire life. He cleaned every part of his body, even parts he didn't know he had. Putting on fresh clothes was a dream. They smelled good, like clothes were supposed to smell. The clothes hung off him, so he found a belt. All his stuff was just where he'd left it, as if he had never left at all.

Sitting on the bed, his hair brushed, his body smelling clean, he heard the front door open and someone hopping up the stairs two at a time. Key. Her footsteps stopped at the top of the stairs. She must have sensed that someone was there. She peered at him through the open bedroom door.

She looked older. Rip could see that she was closer to an adult now than she was to a child. Key was only eighteen months younger than him, but it still amazed him how quickly it had happened. High school makes them older, Rip thought. No more games. It occurred to him that she could easily have a baby now, and surely plenty of her classmates already had. Rip saw her taking him in too. Then she shook her head and stalked down the hallway to her own room. Rip heard the door to her room slam shut behind her. Rip got up and followed her.

"Key?" he said through the door.

"Go away," she said.

"Key."

"No one wants to talk to you, little boy."

"Key!"

"Just go away," she screamed. "Now!"

Rip sighed. He couldn't blame her for not wanting to talk to him. He'd only been gone three weeks, but it felt like three years. He'd wanted to reach out to her every day that he'd been gone, send her some sort of message, but he had destroyed his phone on the first day. What would he even say to her, anyway? She undoubtedly knew. You could trust Tron with your soul but not with a rumor. He wouldn't ever say that it was Rip, but he'd be talking about it so much that you'd know that he either knew who did it or had done it himself. Cornelius had known that when he had Rip tell Tron what happened, but Rip tried not to think about that.

Key had been here, in this house, the whole time he was gone. Family always stays. Even if it's the last thing they want to do. Hell, his uncle was still here after forty-five years after he was born there, because he didn't have anywhere else to go. Rip's sister wouldn't have anywhere else to go either.

Rip didn't have to worry about Key. Mad as she might be at him, she was still his sister. Eventually, she'd come around. What he did have to worry about was his girlfriend. She could leave him. She could enter the world and never come back. He'd already lost so much. He couldn't lose her too.

"Key, open the door."

No answer.

"Come on, Key, open the door. Key?"

"No," she said, but Rip could hear in her voice that her anger was dissipating a little.

"Please?" he said, softening his tone.

"Why should I open the door for you?" she said, in a pouty, high-pitched tone.

"So I can talk to you," Rip said.

"I don't want to talk to you," she said. He could hear the outrage in her voice, could imagine her tilting her head to one side on the other side of the door, indicating that she was still mad but maybe wanted convincing.

"Why not?" he asked.

"Why *would* I want to talk to you?" she said.

"Because I'm your brother!"

"Brother? I got so many family members that I can hardly keep track of them all."

"Yeah, well, even if you don't want to talk to me," Rip said, "I need to borrow your phone."

"My phone? What do you need *my* phone for?"

"So I can call someone," Rip said.

"Oh you need to call someone! I wasn't worth calling, but now you need to borrow my phone to *call* someone? *Who* is so important that you need to talk to them on *my* phone?" she demanded.

"Vicki," Rip said.

There was silence on the other side of the door. Key loved Vicki. Probably loved her more than Rip did. Rip eventually heard a book flop onto the bed and Key's feet slapping against the hard floor.

"Alright, fine." The door swung open, and his sister came. Her eyes were wet. She placed the phone against his chest, and pushed it into his heart. "You better use those words of yours good, boy." There was a catch in her voice as she slammed the door in his face, but the door rebounded off the latch—something about it didn't want to close—and as he started to walk away, he could hear her pressing her body against the wall, close to the door.

"I'm going to text her," he hollered, "so no need to try and listen in."

"I ain't listening in on nothing you have to say!" she squawked. "Just don't go reading *my* messages. You better give that phone back as soon as you're done. I'm serious!"

"Girl? Why would I want to read a bunch of messages sent by a child?" He smiled, imagining the look of outrage on her face.

THIS WAS TURNING OUT TO BE EASIER THAN HE'D THOUGHT it'd be. Way easier. Rip had thought that the next time he saw Vicki, she'd put a bullet in his brain or call the cops or stab him through the eyeball, but it wasn't like that at all. When he texted Vicki, their conversation ended with her giving Rip permission to come over and talk. She said that Pastor Harris wasn't home, and Rip was glad of it.

Rip gave the phone back to Key and told her that he was leaving. She asked where he was going, and he told her he was headed to Vicki's. Key smiled, but when Rip smiled back at her, her smile suddenly became fixed and fearful. She must have noticed his missing teeth.

Rip had a lot to think about as he walked to Vicki's house.

What makes a woman love a man? It's easy to love a man who is powerful and has a bright future ahead of him. But what about a man who has nothing to offer? A man who has done wrong and whose pants no longer fit? Why would someone love a man like that? Is pity the same thing as love?

Does absence serve to bind two people together or break them apart? Can a broken window be repaired with the same rock that did the breaking? Rip didn't know. He knew about his own love, but very little about hers.

His love was not something he had created. He didn't choose to love Vicki, he just did. It was something that had always existed. She was the perfect woman for him. Everyone he knew agreed. So even though it seemed random, it couldn't have been. He must have been using good judgment too. But the judgment must have happened in a split second, because his love for her came on him as a thunderclap, a burst of light, an explosion. His love did not grow. It erupted, fully formed, like Eve springing from Adam's rib.

Did God take Rip's rib from him, and give him love in exchange? Did that happen? Did the sudden sharp pain in Rip's side come not from hunger, but from a surgical incision of the Lord?

Rip got to Vicki's house, the truth came out clean and easy. Nothing like the lies; those had come out hard. Rip simply told her what happened. And Vicki, being who she was, immediately leapt into fixing the problem. Well, not immediately. First she berated him for not telling her right away and gave him the side-eye about why the police were chasing him in the first place. (Obviously he left out the part about the drugs; he couldn't tell her *everything*.) Her eyes narrowed as she made him repeat the story, but Rip could sense that she wanted to believe it. Hell, he wanted to believe it. When he was filthy, he could hardly remember whether he was the one who had killed the cop, let alone why he had run. But now that he had showered and was wearing a fresh set of clothes, he could barely remember that he'd had the rocks on him at all. Why would he have had drugs on him? That's not the kind of person he is. Why would he run? That didn't make sense either. And because it didn't make sense, it couldn't be true.

What did make sense was the edited story he told Vicki. In fact, it made so much sense that it sounded truer than the truth. And really, now that he was here with Vicki, that was that truth that had to exist, not that other one. And the other truth? gradually, it faded away. And yeah, sometimes it leaked into his mind when he wasn't paying attention, but Vicki believed him—or at least she said she did—and that was enough. Rip promised himself that he would work harder for this better truth than for anything else.

Vicki's idea, of course, was to tell her father. But Rip wasn't so sure. Telling Vicki was one thing—he loved her and was going to marry her and raise this child with her, but telling Pastor Harris was a step further than he was ready to go. Vicki wasn't thrilled about withholding anything from her father, but she decided that they could take twenty-four hours to decide what they would share with him. Rip liked that compromise. He liked when she gave him deadlines, and he liked the idea of deciding what they would tell Pastor Harris together. "What" meant something other than the version of the truth that he had told her. Telling stories together (Rip thought that "lies" was too strong of a word) means that you are united. She was already separating herself from her family and coming toward him.

Vicki said it would make sense to tell her father about the baby at the same time they told him about Rip's situation. That way, each blow would diminish the other, and her father would want to use all his influence on Rip's behalf—assuming he didn't die of a heart attack first. Vicki said that last part with only the tiniest bit of nervous laughter.

Once they'd smoothed out the logistics, they began talking as they always had—about everything they had missed, about everything that had gone on in their lives since they'd seen each other last, about all the things they had secretly felt but hadn't had the chance to share. Vicki was in the middle of telling him about her morning sickness when she suddenly looked up, alarmed, and said, "Where are all those things you should be hiding?"

"What? Vicki, I told you everything. I swear."

"No, not that, you fool," she said dismissively. "I mean the bloody clothes, the handcuffs, the gun."

"They're . . ."

Rip hated himself.

"They're . . ."

God, why was he so stupid?

"They're . . ."

He had a vague memory of half-heartedly stuffing all that stuff Vicki was talking about up into the rafters in the back of Tron's basement where all those old suitcases were piled up. (What were all those suitcases doing in Tron's basement anyway? Tron's people had never even left the block, let alone traveled.)

All those things he should be hiding. He'd forgotten about them. Blocked them out. Some part of him, he thought, must have wanted to be caught. But then Rip remembered something Cornelius had said about leaving the stuff in Tron's basement. That must have been why he'd done it.

"It's all at Tron's," Rip said.

"Tron's! What is wrong with you?" Vicki's voice was so loud it hurt Rip's ears: "You have to destroy them! Or at least bring them back here so we can protect them,"

"I will," Rip said, but he almost had to cover his ears while he said it, her voice was so strong. But first I want to hear more about our baby, and how you've been feeling." Rip was trying to pull this angry woman back to a place of intimacy. "Like, have you seen a doctor yet?"

"A doctor?!" Do not now concern yourself with me." She stood up, advanced on him. "Go," she commanded. "Go and do what you have to do."

Rip couldn't move. She was glowing now. She was

221

holding a flaming sword in one hand and a decorated shield in the other. A Roman battle helmet was perched on her head.

"Are you listening to me, Richard Washington?" Her voice filled the room like a living entity.

"Vicki, you're so bright I can't see."

"Can't see? What are you even talking about?" The glow momentarily abated, and the quizzical expression on her face made it diminish even more. But then she stood up straight and it was back like he was looking at the sun. "You don't need to see Richard Washington. Just go!" she bellowed. Huge wings were growing from her back now, and dozens of eyes were sprouting from stalks on her body. The light grew ever brighter as she uncoiled herself, and there was an explosion of light and sound as she said, "Find those things and destroy them."

Rip was terrified. He fled. What else could he do in the face of this creature who had replaced his girlfriend?

As he looked behind him, he wished he had an army to bring with him instead of a pack of bickering idiot ghosts. He should have mentioned the Corner Boys to Vicki. If he had, maybe she could have used her power to get rid of them. But he couldn't tell her. She would think that he had truly lost his mind.

Could ghosts snitch? Would they testify against him in court, tell the neighborhood about what he'd done? What he was about to do? Would they tell Grandma?

Rip stopped by his house to grab his favorite hoodie. He needed something to bolster his courage, and although it really annoyed him to be a walking stereotype, he had to admit that he felt a lot tougher wearing it. A good hoodie worked wonders. Anytime you saw a kid with his hood thrown up, it didn't matter how nerdy he was, you thought to yourself, "Man, I best not be messing with him."

Rip looked back at the Corner Boys and snarled at them.

They pantomimed throwing up their own hoodies and then burst out laughing. Jerks.

Rip wondered if Cornelius had the ghost Corner Boys in his pocket like he did actual corner boys. The thought sent a shiver through him. He hadn't done everything Cornelius had told him to do. He'd done some of it. But when he started to tell Tron what happened, it just hadn't seemed right. Tron was already helping him, and it wasn't like he would need Tron's phenomenal powers of deduction, for which Tron would need to know what was going on. Hell, telling Tron might as well be telling it to everyone, and if the source of the info is Tron.... Rip looked at the corner boys. They were looking at him. Hard. Could they read his mind? Seemed like everyone liked Tron, even the ghosts.

"I didn't tell him!" Rip said anxiously. "At least, not everything. I didn't do what my brother asked. I swear!"

The Corner Boys nodded. Was that a hint of respect he saw on their faces? One of them rubbed his fist into his palm. What was that for? Whose side were they on, anyway? When would they count the numbers, realize they already had them, and then go in for the kill?

Rip entered Tron's house through a basement window. It was one of those old metal windows with the lock on top, but the lever was broken and you could spin the window out like a coal chute and fall right in. Most people wouldn't be able to fit through that window. One month ago, Rip could barely fit through it, but now he slid through it easily. The Corner Boys slid through after him, one right after the other like a Super Mario video game. The last one fell to the floor in a heap of ghost dust and they all started laughing. Actually, now that Rip looked at it more closely, he wasn't even sure it was ghost dust. It looked like actual basement dust that had been building up on the floor for fifty years. Rip wondered if the Corner Boys were becoming real. All his other ghosts were family, so who were they, anyway? And why were they following him around?

The house smelled of emptiness.

How was that even possible?

At least twenty people lived at Tron's house at any given time. Where was everyone? Rip looked around. The basement was all torn up. The couch he had slept in was tipped onto its side, the stuffing pulled out. All the boxes of stuff from generations of Tron's family had been opened, and the various knickknacks and photos had been tossed onto the floor like trash. Even the pipes had been unscrewed, and water was dripping out of them onto the concrete floor. What the heck, Rip thought? He turned and looked at the Corner Boys. The police. He heard them whispering amongst themselves. The police had been here. The police had come to this house, and they were looking for something.

Rip ran to the rafters where he had hidden the broken cuffs and the bloody clothing. Gone. What had he been thinking? Was his blood on that stuff, or just the cop's? Rip fell to the floor. He could hear the furnace clicking on, the roar of the gas and then the flame igniting. He'd listened to that noise so often down here. Other than Tron, it had been his only company.

The sound brought a sudden memory of working on the furnace with his dad when Rip was four years old. His father had taken Rip down into the basement of their old house and showed him where the furnace was. Rip remembered the dust and the feeling of doing something important for the family. His father would take him down there once a month because Rip's grandfather didn't trust the filters that were supposed to last ninety days, and Rip's father humored him because why start a fight over a furnace filter? Both men died within weeks of one another, and those memories of working on the furnace when he was four years old was all he had left of either of them.

Rip moved over to the furnace and tried to open up the sheet metal box where the filter was kept, but the latch was stuck, and he cut his forefinger. Rip sucked the blood welling up on his finger as he used his other hand to force the latch open. Inside, the filter was filthy with caked-on dirt and sucked-in hair (apparently, Tron's dad hadn't believed in the thirty-day filter change). It was a miracle the furnace worked at all. When he pulled the filter out, the glowing flames and whoosh of dusty air made him squint his eyes closed. When he opened them again, he saw the glint of black metal reflected in the glowing fire. He immediately recognized the intricately carved wooden handle of the gun that had killed the cop. It was laying there, pointing right at him

How had the gun gotten into the house? And into the furnace, of all places? Rip had no recollection of putting it here, and the furnace looked like it hadn't been opened in years. Yet, here it was, and Rip had somehow known where to look for it.

As Rip went to pick it up, he heard the Three Stooges commotion of the corner boys falling all over themselves to see what he was doing. One of them even managed to knock over a child-sized drum set, and the cymbal rolled around and around in a spiral before crashing to the ground.

Jerks, Rip thought. But how were they making things move now? They'd never been able to affect the real world before.

The Corner Boys looked sheepish but quickly recovered as they crowded around Rip to get a look at the pistol. They were jostling Rip left and right and he nearly dropped the gun, but he was finally able to throw them off by shrugging his shoulders and hunching down in a kneeling position so he could protect the gun while he looked at it. Rip popped out the magazine and looked at the round copper bullets.

Five bullets.

Rip looked at the Corner Boys.

Five ghosts.

Rip stood up. It was time.

Rip mentally measured the distance between himself and

the eager ghosts. He felt calm and confident as he flexed his fingers, and for the first time in a month, his numb hand responded. Rip looked at the ghosts, and he could tell by the change of light in their eyes that they too had counted the number of bullets.

Rip didn't even hear the sound of his first shot. It struck the ghost closest to him, right in the forehead where he'd learned the third eye was supposed to be during a school field trip to an art museum full of Buddha statues. But the second gun shot produced a sharp, ringing sensation like a thin nail being driven into his eardrum. The shot hit the second ghost in the chest, just as he was raising his palms in surrender and backing away. The third ghost turned around and started to run, but then he tripped and fell flat on his face. He started to scramble to his knees, but Rip stepped on his haunches to hold him down and shot him between the shoulder blades.

The fourth ghost was a real piece of work. He was standing proud, sneering, pounding his palm with the back of his hand and silently yelling at Rip. This ghost, Rip shot in the stomach. He wanted to see him suffer, and he did. The ghost crumpled up and started rolling around on the ground, grasping at the blood pouring out of his stomach.

Rip looked around. Seeing the four bodies on the floor, his stomach began to tingle. He had thought that, since they were ghosts, their bodies would just disappear. He thought they would behave like they always did, popping in and out of his life of their own volition, without any thought for Rip and whether he wanted them there. But instead of disappearing into thin air, their bodies lay there, their blood stained the concrete floor, and a sharp acrid smell made Rip cover his mouth with his hand.

A scuttling sound brought Rip's attention back. The last ghost was trying to climb through the same window they'd entered through, but getting out is always harder than getting in. By now, the sweat from Rip's hand and the pain in his finger from the recoil was making it difficult for Rip to hold the gun. All that gunfire resounding in the house was making Rip nervous too. If the ghost had been a little more competent, he probably would have gotten away—Rip's nerve was leaving him—but seeing the incompetent ghost trying to figure out how to open the window enraged Rip. He felt like a eugenics doctor, bludgeoning out the weak parts of his line. He strode over to the last ghost, grabbed him by the hair, pulled his head back, reached around him and fired a shot right into the ghost's chest. Rip felt the bullet entering the Corner Boy's body, the momentum ripping through skin and muscle. He felt it push into his own heart, like a blunt probing spear.

The last ghost fell to the ground. Rip was alone. A strong gust of wind shook the house, and the window the ghost had been struggling with popped open. But Rip no longer had any need for basement windows. He was a front door man now. He looked behind him at the five bodies crumpled on the floor. The blood pooling on the floor gave him pause, and he wondered who else would be able to see it, but he took his gun, saw that it was empty, and stuffed it into his pants. Confidence surged within him. Rip didn't even bother closing the front door. He left it open, swinging in the breeze. Standing on the porch, filling his lungs with air, flexing his shoulders, Rip felt strong. He felt free. He walked home casually. He enjoyed seeing the few people on the sidewalk, locking eyes with them and nodding at them in a way that made them clear the sidewalk for him without a second thought.

Rip came home. With his new eyes, he saw that his house had never looked more run down, but at the same time, never had it made him more proud. He would fix it. Change everything: build it up, buy the lot next door, put a beautiful fence around it, some swings for the baby, everything. The porch steps sagged a little as he went up them, but he would fix those too.

But when he went to turn the handle to the front door, it didn't budge. Locked. The front door was never locked. What the hell? He cupped his hands against the dirty window next to the door to try and see inside, but the curtains were drawn. He heard some shuffling from inside, and the lock turned, haltingly, as it probably hadn't been turned in years. His uncle was there in the doorway, peering out from the darkness. He looked strangely like a butler. Or a soldier. Rip stepped inside and saw why the door was locked and the curtains were drawn.

Cornelius was back.

Cornelius was squatting on the couch like a mountain of ice from which he would hurl his foes. He looked at Rip, baring his massive tusks. Grandma stood on his right side, deferential. Rip felt for his gun, but he knew there were no bullets left.

"Why lookie lookie here," growled Cornelius, "if it ain't the prodigal son." Cornelius's body loomed so large, the house could barely contain him. He looked like he was about to charge. "You think you coming home, boy?" he said. "You think you got a right to come back here?"

CHAPTER SIX

Felton's mother was waddling around her living room in the old folks home with her pants around her ankles.

"Ma!" Felton shouted, while trying to dodge the newspaper she had just hurled at her only living child (he managed to avoid the largest section—Sports—but the Entertainment section hit him squarely in the head). "Ma! You can't walk around naked like this."

"I'm not naked, you fool!" she said, with her hands on her hips and an outraged look on her face (the effect of the outrage somewhat diminished given the fact she was almost entirely naked). "I ought to wash your mouth out with soap for saying something so outrageous."

"Ma, look at yourself!" He gestured at her naked body as she lunged at him, trying to hit him with a black patent-leather church pump, but she tripped on the pants pooled around her ankles and fell instead.

The flappy skin covering his Mother's skinny arms shook around her bones like the opening curtain of the world's most hideous theatrical production. Felton tried to gently catch her, but she was surprisingly heavy for an old woman, and when they made contact, it was much rougher than Felton had intended it to be. He only managed to break her fall slightly before she slumped to the floor.

"Oh Paul, why do you have to hurt me like that? You always hurt me!" she lamented.

The angry recriminating tone, he had expected. What he hadn't was his father's name, particularly called out with such a sense of loathing and betrayal.

"Ma, I'm not your husband. I'm your son, Andre."

"Oh Paul, just *stop it*. Quit your lying and listen to me for once!"

Felton's mother began to cry—big, long, weepy cries that reminded him of the sound of a police siren. Clara came running into the room the moment she heard it.

"Mrs. Felton, what's going on? What is he doing to you?" Clara looked pointedly at Felton and asked, "Why isn't she wearing any clothes?"

Felton threw up his hands. "That's exactly what I was going to ask you!" Felton wanted to stomp out of the room, but he couldn't since his mom was splayed on the floor and clutching his ankles as if he was the last helicopter out of Saigon. "I just walked in here to find my mother naked and talking crazy, and then you run in here and ask *me* what *I've* done? What am I paying you all this money for, anyway?"

"*You* paying *me*? Ain't no dime in my pocket came from you, so don't be talking about anybody's money that isn't your own." She glared up at Felton as she knelt down to comfort his mother. "Mrs. Felton says it's her husband's pension that pays the bill, not you." She spoke soothingly and lovingly to Mrs. Felton.

Clara had worked with Mrs. Felton since the day she had arrived at the facility. Felton had thought she was a cute little thing. That was a mistake. He never should have messed around with someone who was working for him. Now, he had an angry ex-girlfriend-avenging-angel who ignored all his needs, not a staff member he could order around. Clara ran into the bedroom to get a blanket to cover Mrs. Felton. Felton, meanwhile, was gamefully attempting to extract himself from the tangled spider web of arms and legs that had once been his mother. All the while his mother continued kicking, punching, and pushing him. Felton didn't mind the punching. The days of her hurting him were over. But he did mind the smell of feces emanating from her body, which gave him a clue as to why she was naked. Felton knew she had developed the habit of taking off all her clothes before she used the bathroom, and unlike her thoroughness with regard to disrobing, her thoroughness in wiping herself left much to be desired.

"This place charges me $9000 every month!" Felton hoped Clara could hear him over the commotion. "And her pension only covers half that, so don't be telling me where my money goes. And why does she have her church shoes on anyway? It's a Tuesday."

"She has her church shoes on because she wants to go to church! She's been excited about it all morning, and then you show up two hours late. Mrs. Felton says you are supposed to take her to church *every* day." Clara had returned with the blanket and was wrapping it around Mrs. Felton.

"It. Is. *Tuesday*!" Felton exclaimed.

Mrs. Felton was rocking back and forth now, her body gradually relaxing. Felton had managed to disentangle himself. As he brushed off his pants, he spotted the red emergency cord dangling from his mother's bed. He knew what he had to do.

"Don't you dare pull that cord," Clara said sharply, eyeing Felton, eying the cord.

"Paul, what are you doing! Why aren't you helping me?" his mother gasped.

"Andre, do *not* be pulling that cord!" Clara repeated.

Felton looked at his mother. He looked at the angry eyes of Clara.

He pulled the cord.

He could hear the satisfying sound of the alarm blaring in the nurse's station, followed by the pitter-patter of feet on the wall-to-wall carpeting, and he knew his $9000 a month was finally going to get to work. On his way in, he had seen three or four staff members he liked—and who liked him—relaxing at the nurse's station. He knew they would come running the moment he called. The staff at Phoenix Rising Resorts for Seniors loved him. Or at least, most of them did.

When they'd come to tour The Phoenix, his mother had immediately fallen in love with it. It was located in the richer, bougie part of town. A part of town where, twenty years ago, neither of them would have felt comfortable walking around. Mrs. Felton couldn't get enough of the long circular staircase leading from the lobby to the second floor activity room, and she mentioned it day after day (Momma not being able to use these stairs, given her physical condition, and the fact that they ended up costing Andre $9000 a month, particularly galled him). But once she'd seen it, no other place would do.

Finally, after months of Felton begging and pleading for her to move into a more affordable home and his mother insisting that she would not go anywhere unless it was the Phoenix, he had bit the bullet, paid the bill, and moved his mother in. With her Southern manners and odd sense of being better than everybody else, she was the belle of the ball from the moment she arrived. All the staff loved her, and that meant, for the most part, they loved Felton too. But the staff from the neighborhood, people like Clara, they liked his mother but hated Felton. Why, Felton thought, is it always your own people that have it in for you? Why are they always the ones holding you back?

Felton watched with glee as the residential care manager arrived and started yelling at Clara. Felton looked over at Clara and smiled.

But his smile froze as he remembered a very similar smile

aimed at him a few days earlier, back at headquarters. Thinking about the way Mike had smiled at him then almost made him feel sorry for doing the same thing to Clara now. But she had started it, and you've got to give respect to get it in return.

~

FELTON HAD GIVEN RESPECT TO MIKE. HE *HAD*. DESPITE THE fact that Mike was a pompous ass whose already-too-big head had quadrupled in size the moment he became the superintendent, he was the goddamn superintendent, and that meant something to Felton. Felton had been taught to respect the office even if he didn't respect the man. So he had gone up to the fifth floor and done the right thing. But respect had not been given to him in return.

Felton had staked out the lobby to make sure no one else entered Mike's office. He needed him alone. The superintendent's schedule was public, and this two-hour window would be Felton's chance. He should have befriended Mike back in the academy. It would have been easier back then, but who knew how far Mike would rise? The video from Little J was his opening. Felton would generously offer to help Mike out, and Mike would help Felton in return. Nothing wrong with that. Nothing wrong with that at all.

The problem was, Mike thought he had raised himself out of nothing, and because of that, he thought he didn't need help from people like Felton. But Mike was wrong. Felton was the one who had raised himself out of nothing, not Mike. Maybe Mike hadn't been born into it, but he had married into clout, which as far as Felton was concerned, was probably even worse. That poor, soulless bastard didn't even marry someone he loved.

But this video from Little J was going to be tricky. It was definitely good enough to destroy the superintendent, but it might not be good enough to make friends with him. Friends are harder to make than enemies. The video was only valuable to Felton so long as he had it in his possession, but the moment he used it, it would stop belonging to Felton and start belonging to the world, and that would destroy the power and take down Mike right along with it. And if Mike got destroyed, he wouldn't be useful. So Felton needed to thread the needle carefully: He needed to exert his power over Mike without letting on that he was exerting it. And in order to do that, he needed the element of surprise.

There's nothing more surprising than the truth. Throw it fast enough, strong enough, and like a bouncy ball on a concrete wall, it's gonna come right back, hard. The truth would knock Mike onto his ass, and then it would come right back and settle nicely in Felton's lap. And not only would it come back, but it would come back carrying even more truth than it had started with, giving Felton even more power the next time he had to use it. But it had to come as a surprise, come out of nowhere. Give Mike a little time to prepare and that slippery son of a bitch would catch the ball and lob it right back at Felton.

"Can I help you?" the secretary had asked as Felton walked into the office. Felton wondered whether Mike was banging her. Certainly, her personal loyalty, and the way she said, "Can I help you?" indicated that she had no intention whatsoever of helping him.

"Yeah. I'm here to see Mike," Felton said.

"You mean the superintendent?" she corrected. "You're here to see the superintendent, Officer? Do you have an appointment?"

"Detective," Felton said.

"Excuse me?" she barely bothered looking up from her computer.

"I'm a detective, not an officer." Felton wasn't going to let this twit disrespect him.

"Well, *Detective*, the superintendent is waiting on a very important phone call. If you don't have an appointment, I would suggest you go through your chain of command and try to get one."

"Officer," Felton said in his most dominant voice. "I would suggest that you get up off that chair of yours, walk over to Mike's office, and tell him that Andre Felton from class 96-4c needs to see him. He's going to want to see me."

The officer shot lasers at him with her eyes. He shot them right back. She was the first one who blinked. She looked across the office at the other secretary, who shrugged and rolled her eyes.

"Wait here," she commanded.

She walked into the interior office and closed the door behind her so Felton couldn't hear what she was saying to Mike. She reemerged a minute later with a smile on her face. Felton didn't like the look of that smile.

"So *Detective*, the superintendent is unavailable right now but he should have a few minutes to help you out next month. Let me look at his schedule."

"Next month doesn't work," Felton said. "And I don't need his help. I'm here to help *him*."

The staring match recommenced. This time she didn't look away.

"Felton, I'm pretty sure you don't remember me, but I remember you. Third watch? Sixth District? Remember? I watched you fall asleep in the roll-call room every day. Every. Single. Day. And then you'd disappear for eight hours and no one would see you again until it was time to go home. You never helped anyone then, and I doubt you're helping anyone now. The superintendent already told me what to do, and I'll make an appointment for you if you want, but that's all you're going to get."

Felton tried to think of another card to play but came up with nothing.

"*Detective.*" Boy is she cocky now, Felton thought as she continued, "Why don't you go sit on that couch while that little mind of yours goes spinning away. This is a place of business, and you have no business here. But as a courtesy, seeing as how you're 'trying to help' and all, I'll let you sit over there and think. But please try not to fall asleep. I know how hard that is for you."

Felton grimaced. He imagined himself in the boxing ring, bouncing against the ropes. Taking punches and biding his time. Felton decided he would sit down. He knew staying would annoy the crap out of her, and besides, he did need the time she'd foolishly offered. She should have kicked him out. She'd pretended to be nice and now she was stuck with him.

Forty-five minutes later, he was still sitting on the couch. She probably just expected him to get the hint and leave, but he had decided that she would be the one who would need to get the hint. He wasn't leaving. One of the superintendent's muscled-up drivers wandered over, or perhaps he was called in. He exchanged a few private words with the secretary and then sauntered over in a confident, threatening manner. He sat down next to Felton—closer than necessary, just like the idiot jocks from high school used to do—and clapped him on the back, hard, pretending to be friendly even though everyone in the room knew he wasn't.

The oaf leaned in, violating Felton's personal space, "What's going on, buddy?"

Idiot, Felton thought. "I'm waiting to see your boss."

"Why don't you schedule an appointment? He's a chill guy, but his schedule gets filled up real quick. You know how it is," he said.

"No, I don't know how it is," Felton said, "but I do know what kind of a guy he is. You don't need to tell me."

"Oh really, where do you know him from?" the driver asked.

"From the academy. We were classmates," Felton said.

"From the academy! I love it when you guys stop by. I always try and get some embarrassing stories on the boss so I'll have some blackmail to hold over him. Gotta have some way to keep my job, right?" The driver laughed uproariously at his own joke, and pounded Felton on the back.

Felton hated him so much.

"So what kind of stories you got on the Sup?" the driver asked.

Felton despised asking for things from people like this lumbering fool, but he knew small people in these sorts of positions loved it when people asked for their help.

"I've got a story," Felton started out slowly, "but it's one I want to tell the superintendent myself. It's something he's going to want to hear, and I'm trying to tell him in person before he finds out about it in writing, or from the press or something like that. You get me? I've known Mike for over twenty years. I don't know if he pays any attention to his drivers, but it'd help me out a lot—and it would help your boss too —if you got me some time with him. I promise. I'll tell you a good story or two later, and he'll definitely thank you for getting me in there."

Felton watched a shudder pass over the driver's face, and it took a moment for Felton to realize that it was actually a wink. And sure enough, the driver snapped his fingers, ponderously wagged them in Felton's face, and said, "You know what? I like you. I got you." He went over to the superintendent's door and slid in like he was dropping into a submarine. Less than a minute later, he poked his fat, bald head out of the door and waved Felton in.

Felton tried to thank him with a nod as he went by, but his revulsion overcame him and he couldn't even make eye contact with the driver as he passed. Besides, he was too busy basking in the satisfaction of glaring at the secretary as he entered the superintendent's office.

As Felton strolled into the office, Mike looked up at him all kind and confident, as if he hadn't just made Felton cool his heels for an hour.

"Felton! Sorry about that—important phone call! Come in, come in. What can I do for you?"

"I came to talk, Mike."

"What's it been, twenty years?" Mike asked, already glancing over at his computer.

"Something like that."

Felton was about to continue, but Mike cut him off. "If this is about your place on the homicide team, I can't help you. Lt. Johnson chooses his team, not me." Mike tapped sharply on his keyboard. Once. Probably the delete key. Another idea sent perfunctorily to the void.

Felton was annoyed. The fact that Mike knew he'd gotten dumped meant he'd had time to do a little research while Felton had been sitting there waiting for him. He had hoped the superintendent had made him wait because he was busy with other things. Felton didn't like that he'd used the time to prepare. One of the most important things about power was time. Having control over it. It made Felton uneasy knowing that Mike had time on his side.

"My spot is just one thing. I got other things to talk about."

Felton wanted him to ask, to express interest, but Mike just looked at his watch, drummed his fingers. Didn't even have the common courtesy to ask a follow-up question.

"Felton, I've only got a few minutes. And I've seen the overtime reports. It doesn't look like you do anything without getting paid for it. Certainly not solving crime. So I can't help you there. You waited here for an hour. You got something to say, say it."

That pompous son of a bitch, Felton thought. He hated feeling rushed—and he definitely didn't like that wisecrack about his overtime. Felton wanted to get a feel for the room, to understand how people took up space in it. He wanted to listen to the tremors and the cracks in the air so he could sense the moment they shifted. That change in tempo was when you knew that what the thing you were talking about, it mattered.

Time to read the room was even more important with a guy like Mike. Politicians were slick. They knew how to hide things. But Felton could see that Mike wasn't going to give him time. Felton would have to push on without the full picture. So push he did.

"Alright, Mike, since you're so busy, so I'll skip the courtesies and get on with the truth you need to hear. But I'm sorry to say, Mike, that it's bad. Bad for you, that is." Felton was aiming for a friendly tone. It wasn't his preferred tactic, but sometimes your only option is to be nice. "You see, I happened across this video. Of you and that partner of yours. I'm the only person who's seen it, and seeing as we were in the same class and all, I wanted to get over here and talk to you about it right away. See if I could help you before anyone else sees it. Before it hurts you. Before it hurts your family. We're friends, right Mike?"

Felton waited for Mike to say something, to confirm their eternal friendship, but all he did was raise an eyebrow. Felton's heart went a little more rigid, but he continued, "It was over at the old Goldblatt's store on 47th and Ashland. Your old district. You remember it?"

"I remember the ninth district, Felton. But that's a long way back. You haven't got anything more current to talk about than the ninth district? You never worked there that I remember."

"No, I never worked there. But I've always liked it. And besides, it was that video I was talking about that brings me to that district."

"Alright, sure," Mike said, leaning back in his chair with an air of confidence. But Felton could see one of the fingers on Mike's right hand beginning to tap nervously. Good, Felton thought. Mike continued, " The ninth district, sure. I'll play along. I will say one thing, though. You definitely hit the time machine with that one. You might have seen somebody that you thought looked like me, but I don't think they even had video back when I was working the ninth district. You're forgetting how old we are."

"I don't forget nothing, Mike, and I doubt you do either. You remember the place, right?"

"I remember a lot of places, Felton."

"Ha. Admit nothing. I like it, Mike. Don't worry. This ain't a court of law. There's no stenographer recording notes. you can be honest, we're friends, remember? Anyway, very interesting video. All kinds of cops going in, going out. Doesn't make a lot of sense when you first look at it, but I looked at it a few times, and I figured it out."

Felton saw Mike's left cheek twitch a little. Right where a hook would go if he'd been a giant fish. When Felton saw that twitch on the Superintendent's cheek, he felt his own cheeks begin to pull up into a smile in the same place. He was starting to get somewhere.

Felton continued, "I recognized you and Danny as two of those cops going in and out. Bringing people back where you shouldn't be bringing them. I mean, it'd be one thing if it was just Danny. Everyone knows he's a dirty cop. Probably wouldn't even have a job if it wasn't for you. Now that I think about it, why *did* you look out for Danny? That's not your style. Why'd you look out for him when you're normally so eager to make examples out of the people you love?"

"You don't know anything about love, Felton. The police board made those decisions about Danny, not me. I was a nobody back then."

Felton thought he could hear a slight tremor in Mike's voice.

"That's not what I heard. As I recall, you'd just gotten married and your new father-in-law was the head of the police board." Felton waited for a response, but Mike's face remained impassive, so he continued, "If your wife wasn't so pretty, it kind of would have made me wonder."

"Don't talk about my wife."

"You ambitious types marry for all kinds of reasons."

"I told you not to mention my wife."

"I don't criticize, Mike. Love comes in all forms."

"You mention my marriage one more time and I will rip your goddamn tongue out." Mike was sitting on the edge of his chair, fist clenched, voice raised. Felton could almost hear the secretaries' ears perk up outside the door.

"Well, well, well." Felton smiled. He'd been feeling almost bad about messing with Mike—someone who had been decent to him in the past—but turns out, his instincts were right all along. Mike was nothing more than a cheap criminal, just like his lousy partner. In the end, all criminals were the same. This was the way they conducted themselves: with threats and violence.

"Rip my goddamn tongue out?" Felton tsked. "Wow, Mr. Superintendent. Is that the same kind of language you used when you were talking to those poor folks in the videos? Swearing at them? Threatening them? Locking them up in a big old bank safe?" The glimmer of recognition in Mike's eyes when Felton mentioned the safe was indisputable. "I didn't think you'd take to talking like a gangster quite so quick. That's some rookie nonsense. Haven't you ever testified in court? Lawyer's going to have a field day with you if this is how you talk when someone questions you."

Mike sat back in his chair, unclenching the muscles in his jaw, trying to regain his composure. Felton filed away Mike's sensitivity about his wife for later.

"Felton," Mike said, "I don't know what old fools you've been out there talking to, but if you'd spent more time solving crime instead of spending taxpayer money, then you'd know you're out of line. Police work ain't always pretty. It's a shame you don't know that. Confidential informants aren't always comfortable going to a police station, and sometimes you have to take them somewhere private in order to get them to talk. So while it might not be 100 percent kosher for some enterprising officers to use an old building to talk, it isn't exactly a big deal either. Making sausage isn't always pretty, but at the end of the day, people just want to eat their meal in peace. And Felton, you should know better than to bluff about having video of an incident that never happened. You think I don't know what this is about? You think I don't know that you made more in overtime last year than I did in salary? You think I don't know that you've been too lazy to make a decent arrest in ten years, and the only reason you got any of that overtime is because of that sponsor of yours, and now that he's gone you haven't got anything to bank on except for that stupid expression you wear on your face every day?" Mike stood up, leaned over the table, and pointed a finger in Felton's face. "You're making stuff up, and what's worse, you're burning bridges with an old classmate. Stop now, before you say something you're really going to regret."

Now Felton was the one who had to work to control his temper. Who did this son of a bitch think he was? Felton had come here out of friendship, and now, here was being called stupid and having a finger wagged in his face? People always treated Felton like he was stupid.

Mike was getting up and reaching for his coat on the back of his chair. He needed to be put in his place, to know that he was the stupid one, not Felton. "There's audio too, Mike," Felton said quietly.

"Audio of *what*, Felton?"

"You see, Mr. Superintendent, I've found that words explain a lot of things." Felton was pleased to see that Mike had let his coat fall back onto the chair. "Sometimes, young coppers aren't so careful about what they say out loud when they think they're by themselves. That's when they get into trouble."

Mike looked at him darkly.

"So yeah, if it were just putting the screws down on some bust-out criminals, I suppose the public might let that slide, must just consider that was something that happened a long time ago. But I wonder what the public will think about their superintendent talking about putting cases on real families? A goddamned pastor's kid, no less? You think they'll let it slide when they see you, a middling no good copper, flaunting the rules and trying to take down a good family? If you'd do that to a powerful family, then just think what you must have been doing to the regular folks. And what will they think when they learn that, not two weeks later, that same child you were trying to put a case on ends up dead, the police putting more holes in him than the coroner can count?"

"That story was all over the news, Felton. It's a shame that Washington kid got killed, and it's a shame when the streets turn a good kid from a good family into something bad, but I wasn't even working that day, and the ballistics showed that it was his own people who killed him, not the police."

"And that's another thing," Felton said. "Why *weren't* you involved in that case? And why would the feds have let a case like that just fade away? So many questions! And how about this one: How come once nobody remembered anymore, you and Danny jumped the line and got promoted faster than you deserved. Quite the story we got going here, Mike"

"Yup. Just a story, Detective, and an old one at that. I appreciate this trip down memory lane. All those questions of yours are really interesting. Next time, figure them out before you start running your mouth."

"I've got video. You know nothing's true anymore unless it's on tape, but I've got it. And you're right that this story is so old that fools like your son start thinking it's safe to talk about before they've got stories of their own to tell. But he shouldn't be doing that. Him talking about the problem makes him a part of it. Isn't that right, Mike?"

"Don't talk about my family, Felton. There's no video—otherwise you would have showed it to me by now. It never happened."

"Mike. Superintendent. Can't you see that I'm trying to help you out here? If we can work together, if we can be friends, then no one needs to get hurt. I'm not showing it to you because I don't want to hurt you, that's all. Once we're friends again, don't you worry. I'll show it to you."

"You aren't trying to help anybody. And you know what?" Mike went from leaning forward in his office chair to sitting up straight. "I'm sure not going to help you. Get out of my office. You need some attention? Go show it to the media. They're the ones that care about this sort of nonsense. Not me. You think I care about this job? You think anybody does? You must have gotten dumber over the years. My family is going to thank you if you push me out of here." Mike stood up and tried to usher Felton out of the room like he was a child who had stayed too late at school.

That pompous son of a bitch, Felton thought, first calling me dumb, and now pushing me out of his office? "Your *job*? You think we're talking about your *job*?" Felton stood up to meet Mike. "They don't want your job. They want your blood. I'm going to nail you up on the cross like Jesus and they'll be happy to pardon every thief and murderer along the way just so they can get to you." Felton leaned in closer. "Of course you ain't going to have no job. They're going to take your job *and* your pension. Hell, pension? Penitentiary is more like it." Felton was close enough now to shake a finger in Mike's face, just like Mike had done to him. "You ain't got no people. Nobody likes you. No one is going to protect you. Your reputation, your power, it all comes from here, from this job." Felton remembered how Mike had reacted when he'd mentioned his family. He knew he shouldn't let himself get this angry, but it felt so damn good. "Hmmmm . . . let me think. Who could help you understand? How about someone who used to be a federal prosecutor? Oh yeah, that's right. Your *wife*! I'll let *her* explain it to you. I'll show *her* the video. What do you think she's going to think when she sees the man you really are? And then there's your son. Everyone knows about the stories he tells about you when he's drunk. I'm going to love dragging him up onto the stand for corroboration. And you know what the best thing is? He's probably the only guy who actually cares about you, while you just continue to treat him like crap and keep him working in the ghetto for nothing. Pathetic. And you know what he's going to do when I put him on the stand? He's gonna *lie* to protect you." Felton watched a tiny fleck of his spit land on Mike's jacket. "Just like family does, even your family. And then, the only guy in the world that actually loves you is going to get torn down too."

Felton watched as Mike rose from his desk and opened the closet, his face red with rage. Felton wouldn't have been surprised if he'd pulled out a baseball bat and tried to beat him to death with it, but it was just a briefcase. But good as all this felt, Felton had to check himself. He'd pushed too fast. He'd become overly excited about the kill and forgotten that he'd wanted to tame the animal, not eat him. Mike was no good to him in jail.

"Mike, look. I said some harsh things there. Don't leave. I'm just trying to get you to understand. We're on the same team. We can work together and figure this thing out."

"Felton. I don't have time for this, for you. If you've got an ask, ask it."

"That's not what this is about," Felton said.

"The hell it isn't," Mike said.

"Superintendent, I'm a team player, and I want to be on the team. That's all. You're a powerful man, and I've got things I want to get done. There's no reason we can't be friends."

"Friends?" The bitterness in Mike's voice was palpable. "What are those? Does anybody even know what a friend is anymore? Well, I'll tell you one thing: friends share. You want to be friends? Fine. I want to see this so-called video."

"Mike, I didn't even bring it with me. It's on some old equipment, and I'm being respectful by not digitizing it for the whole universe to see. You don't need that."

Felton could see the gears spinning in Mike's head. Evidently, he'd made a decision.

It was the wrong one.

Mike opened his office door. "Jones!" he called out to his driver who'd been eagerly waiting for him on the couch. "I don't need you. I'm driving myself home today. Make sure Detective Felton finds his way out of the same door you let him in."

"Mike . . ." Felton started, but it was too late. The superintendent walked out, glaring so hard that Felton wondered how he managed to avoid running into a wall. The driver looked in at Felton, darkly. Felton was pretty sure the driver didn't want to be friends with him anymore either.

Felton shook his head as he walked out of the office. He'd almost had him. He had seen the fear in Mike's eyes. But something had gone wrong. Hell, he hadn't expected Mike to fold immediately and promptly promote him, but he had at least expected to get put back on the homicide team. For Mike to give him some sort of play. But instead, he'd gotten nothing. Nothing.

Felton knew he could destroy the superintendent with this video. No doubt the superintendent knew that as well. Only a crazy person would sit and wait for the bullet to enter his brain. But destroying Mike wouldn't do anything for Felton. Maybe Mike knew that too. Sure, there would be some long exposé in the newspapers about the brave detective who'd brought the superintendent down, but that would just ensure that no one in the police department would ever trust Felton again, and he'd be stuck on straight jobs for the rest of his career. Can't nobody eat on self-righteousness. Felton needed a man on the inside, not a busted-down fool. He needed Mike.

Felton waited for the superintendent to make his next move. One week went by. Nothing. So Felton was forced to pay Mike another visit. He knew it was a weak play, but what else could he do? The threats hadn't worked, and the wife thing was the nuclear option that would probably hurt everyone, he'd have to try the friend angle again. Giving Mike the video was out of the question. Mike was a slick one. He'd take that video, edit it, talk to whatever citizens and church pastors he could find, line them all up on his side with whatever angles he could find, and then release it in dribs and drabs until it fizzled out. Felton didn't think Mike could survive it, but you never know, and either way, the power would leave Felton's hands. But in order to *show* him the video—not give it to him, just show it—he'd have to see him again.

The reception was chilly when he arrived back at Mike's office.

"Yes, *Detective*?" the same administrative assistant said.

"I'm here to see the superintendent," Felton said.

"Detective, you'll have to go through your chain of command to set up an appointment with the superintendent."

"That's like seven different levels," Felton said.

"Exactly," she said.

"He's going to—"

"Yes, yes, he's going to want to see you. I remember from last time. But the thing is, he doesn't."

Felton stood there for a moment, contemplating his next move.

"Do I need to get my sergeant out here to give you a direct order to leave? I'm happy to do that. In fact, I'd *love* to do that."

"This is for his own—"

"Yes, yes, his own good. I know, Detective."

"He really needs to—"

"Sarge!" the administrative assistant yelled out.

Felton gritted his teeth. The bastard. The goddamned insolent fool. Mike had decided to ignore him, to wait him out and see if he would just go away. Not only had Felton not made it onto the team, he hadn't even made it into the goddamn stadium.

FELTON LOOKED UP FROM REMEMBERING HOW EVERYTHING HAD gone down with Mike to see the manager of the nursing home gently leading his mother into her bedroom. Soon the nurse would give her a few pills and dress her up real nice. Felton liked when that particular nurse was there. She always took the time to get out his mom's jewelry and make her look pretty. Mrs. Felton always held her head a little higher while wearing the pearls she had bought with her own hard-earned money. This place was good, Felton thought. They knew how to treat his mom.

Their hen-like devotion was almost too much to bear. How was he going to continue to afford this place? He'd just gotten his first check without the overtime, and it was half of what he used to make. Half! It would barely cover his own bills, let alone his mother's.

"Mr. Felton?" The nurse addressed him quietly, respectfully. "We're going to give Mrs. Felton some medication to help relax her. She'll feel better soon. Why don't you wait outside while we work? This isn't what you do."

Felton watched them. What exactly did he do? Even for his Mom, he was second fiddle. Felton sighed. With this thing with Mike, he'd tried to be the one pulling the strings, but maybe that just wasn't who he was. A man has to know his place in life. His whole life he'd been in the background, but hell, it had worked. He'd gone places. If he went back there, maybe he'd start winning again.

Sure Mike, he thought. Ignore me. You've got time and power on your side. But I know someone you can't ignore, someone you can't be trifling with. And once I get together with him, you'll be praying for my help. Felton owed ReverendAlderman a call anyway. With Felton in the background and ReverendAlderman in the foreground, Felton was pretty sure he could bring Mike to his knees.

CHAPTER SEVEN

Too easy, Mari thought. Way too easy. Life had never come easy for Mari. Anything this easy had to be wrong.

The last two hours had been a parade of bosses coming by to shake her hand like she was the queen of England. Everyone. The superintendent, the mayor, heck, even a senator. (She was glad the senator's people had alerted her of his arrival ahead of time; otherwise, there was no chance she would have recognized that puffed-up guy in a suit) Even Sarge had come in looking sheepish as he approached her, hat in hand, like a peasant. If he played his cards right, he could probably parlay Mari's arrest into a good spot, or maybe even a promotion— that is, if Mari didn't tell everyone that the only thing he had done was make her job more difficult. But he, like everybody else, suddenly found himself wanting nothing more than to be close to his new favorite detective.

But she'd done it without him, without all of them. She'd broken the case, brought in the cop killer: bloody evidence, a videotaped confession, everything. She had set it all out on a silver platter with a pretty pink bow on top. Beautiful.

Mari was in the station hallway watching Tron sleep in the

processing room. The room was basically a small glass aquarium—anyone who wanted to could look inside. There, they would see a metal bench that was too small for anyone to get comfortable on and a bar that usually had a human being chained to it. Mari hadn't bothered cuffing Tron to the wall. He was a peaceful sort, so it hadn't seemed necessary. But after she had him on murder, she knew she should have. People sometimes change when they realize the cage door will never open again.

"Look at that piece of work," a cop said with disgust as he walked past. "Once they confess, they sleep like babies." The officer looked at Mari, seeking affirmation. "Someone ought to go in there and choke that baby out with a wire sharp enough to cut through every tendon."

What was Mari supposed to say to a thing like that? Why was this guy here, butting in where he wasn't wanted or needed?

"So he confessed?" the officer said. Mari noticed that his uniform was disheveled, like he was too cool or too angry to wear it properly. "On camera and everything?"

Mari wanted to yell at him, tell him to shut up. Maybe even tell him he ought to think about having the tiniest ounce of humanity. But what would be the point? She might as well start talking French to him. Instead, she said, "Yeah. Pretty much."

"Why'd he do that? He stupid or something?" he asked.

"Maybe," Mari said.

"So is this like the easiest arrest you've ever had?" the officer asked.

Easy, Mari thought. Even this blockhead saw it. Mari shook her head as he wandered off.

Truth be told, it hadn't really been that easy. A lot of other detectives would have messed it up. But for Mari, and really for any competent detective, there were lots of solutions, lots of paths—a suspicious number of paths—and hers was just one. She'd made a plan and executed it. Just like she's supposed to.

When speaking on the phone with Cornelius, she'd told him he'd need to swear out a warrant in order to bring in the evidence, but he'd just laughed and said, "If I was going to swear out a warrant, I'd have called my lawyer, not the police. I called you because I know you're smart enough to get this information proper, without me going before a judge like some little snitch."

"Just so you know, Cornelius, you're still a little snitch, talking to me. You're just a snitch who's too scared to go all the way."

Cornelius was silent on the phone for a long time after that. Mari had begun to think he'd hung up on her. She was almost relieved. This whole thing made her skin crawl. But after a few moments, his quiet, lethal voice came back on the line.

"I ain't no snitch, Detective. A snitch talks for money, or to save himself. I ain't saving myself, and I don't need no money. And I'd advise you to never call me that again."

"Hey snitch, you snitching snitch. I'll call you whatever I want, and if you don't like it, you can talk to someone else." Mari's lips curled into a smile. "You're the one who wanted to talk to me, not the other way around."

Mari could feel Cornelius's fury snaking through the phone line. But whatever his reasons for talking to her, they were evidently important enough for him to take getting called more or less the worst thing you can call someone on the street. Finding her own power made Mari's stomach stop churning a little, and her instincts for solving a case kicked in.

"Alright, Cornelius, fine. I won't call you names anymore. You're right, that's not nice. But if you don't want to swear out a warrant, you're going to have to give me some way to talk to this guy outside his home. If I just knock on the door, from the way you're telling it, about half the South Side might show up to answer my knock, and I'm pretty sure they aren't going to invite me in for tea. I'm going to need to talk to him alone."

"I'll give you what you need. But I tell you, you are lucky you are a woman, because I don't care who you are—police, brother, God—any man talks to me like that needs to pay, and if you wasn't a woman, I would reach through this phone line and rip your heart out." Mari rolled her eyes. Gangbangers idly threatening her was nothing new. "But my grandmother taught me to treat a woman with respect, even if she doesn't deserve it."

"I don't need your chivalry, Cornelius. The only thing I need is for you to tell me where to find this dude. I'm not wasting my time hunting him down all over the city."

"All over the city? Naw. Don't worry about that. Dude never gone further than the corner store in his entire life. You'll find him at the gas station on 69th. He works there all day for $40 in cash. He'll be the tall drink of water pushing a broom."

"And is he going to talk to me, or are his people going to be there telling him not to say anything?" Mari asked.

"His people are everywhere, Detective. You'll have to take him somewhere else to get your quality alone time with him."

"Oh yeah, sure, that sounds like a great time. I'm so excited. And Cornelius, I'm going to ask you one more time: Why are you doing this? How do I know you're not lying to me? How do I know this isn't some sort of setup?"

"Detective, I haven't lied since I was twelve years old. When you're strong, you don't need to lie. And if it's a setup, well you can just think it over until it ain't. You're smart enough to figure that out. And no need to worry about getting him to talk. He's been told to expect you. He'll give you exactly what you need."

"Expecting me? What kind of a story is this?" This was a setup alright.

"No story," Cornelius said. "You'll see. I don't do stories."

"Huh." Sometimes the easiest way to see a trap was just to spring it, and she was tired of talking to Cornelius anyway. "The guy pushing a broom. Got it."

"That's right, Detective. The guy pushing a broom. And if that ain't enough or you, here's one more hint: he'll be the one wearing nothing but orange."

AND SURE ENOUGH, THERE HE WAS, WEARING AN ORANGE jumpsuit with broom in hand like he was a backup singer for some German new-wave band. Mari had one of the guys she knew from patrol and his partner come with her. She didn't even trust her own team. Those assholes from the detection division would either treat her like an idiot or try to steal her arrest. None of that was going to happen with Roger. She and Roger had worked together a couple of times when she was just starting out on the job. He'd seemed old back then, even though he was probably in his 40s, and now that he was in his 50s, he no longer struck Mari as that old. Still, he was the closest thing she had to a beat cop mentor, or at least, he wasn't an idiot and had looked out for her and treated her with kindness without trying to get into her pants. Sometimes, that's the best a young female copper could get when she had no time or family on the job, and had only taken the position because she needed a paycheck and didn't know what else to do with her life.

She didn't know his partner, but Roger said he was a good guy, and when he showed up, he didn't say much. That suited Mari just fine. She had the two of them park in the lot next to her unmarked car and get out and lean on their own marked car with their hands folded across their chests. Visible. But not too close. She wanted this Tron guy to know she was the Chicago Police, with all the strength and power that meant, but at the same time, she didn't want to scare him.

Tron was aimlessly pushing some dust around with his

broom, looking like a two-dimensional man who was hoping he could turn ninety degrees and disappear from view.

Sorry buddy, no luck.

As she walked up to him, Tron shyly avoided eye contact and pretended to be absorbed in his broom. But Mari was going to make him acknowledge her. After ten seconds of Mari standing five feet away from him without saying a word, the pressure got to him. He stopped sweeping and leaned on the broom like a sentinel with a rifle, or perhaps like a man in a firing squad who was about to shoot his best friend. His eyes flickered up at her. Behind the fear, Mari could see curiosity and a friendly half-smile covering up his jumbled teeth. The smile put her at ease, but she was going to make him speak first.

"Ma'am?" he finally said, looking at the ground. "You all right, ma'am?"

"You got a right to be here?" She was intentionally authoritative.

"Ma'am?" He took a step backward. The jumpsuit was cinched a little too high on his waist. Mari could see that he was tall and crazy thin, like a scarecrow. His hair had a brown-orange tinge, and he was about four weeks overdue for a haircut.

"I said, you got a right to be here?" Mari wanted to put him on the defensive.

"I . . . I . . ." he had a slight stutter. "I think so, ma'am."

"Why?" she said.

"Well, because I work here?" he said. It was clear that he had never pondered his right to exist before.

"How often?" Mari asked.

"Most every day," Tron said.

"Like, *work* here, work here? With a proper paycheck and all that? Or is it more of a nonsense kind of thing?" Mari liked how Tron actually thought about her questions. Most people just answered without thinking—that is for the easy questions like this, the ones you started on, the ones where they don't need to lie. But Tron actually listened to the questions, thought about them, and tried to answer the actual thing you had asked.

"Well, ma'am, I'd say I don't think it's nonsense. But, I suppose it ain't totally proper either. Like, I don't get no check or anything."

"Cash?" she said.

"Yes, ma'am," he said.

"How much?" she said.

"Well, it ain't right to say," he said, shuffling around.

"Ain't right?" She loved this. She couldn't wait to hear about Trons's morals. "What do you know about what's right?"

"I don't know, ma'am," he said simply, "but I do know."

"So they must treat you alright if you think you shouldn't be telling me how much they pay you."

"Who, them?" He nodded toward the small hut where they sold twenty-five cent bags of chips and candy and off-brand pop and five dollars' worth of gas to the people that actually used it as a gas station and not as a corner store.

"Yeah. The guys, the gas station guys," Mari said.

"Yeah, they treat me OK," Tron said, nodding.

"They don't yell at you? Call you stupid?" she asked.

"They yell a little, ma'am, but not too much." Tron rubbed his sparse goatee. "They're alright."

"Do they charge you for food? Take it out of your pay? If they're alright, they wouldn't do that," she told him.

"No, no, ma'am. They don't charge me. I don't even have to ask. When I'm working, I get whatever I want," he said.

"What do you get?" Mari liked learning about Tron. "Chips? Juice? Stuff like that?"

"Yeah. Yes, ma'am. Stuff like that."

"You ever get stuff but don't eat it? Give it to your friends?" she asked.

"No, ma'am," he replied swiftly.

"Why not?" Mari said, arching an eyebrow.

Tron paused, considering. "I don't know, ma'am."

"Wouldn't be right," Mari said, "would it?"

He looked at her, made eye contact for the first time. "No, ma'am. It sure wouldn't be." He nodded profoundly. "I do believe you're right."

Mari nodded back. It was nice to be in agreement about the moral questions of the world. A small moment.

"This food you take but never give to other people because it wouldn't be right," Mari said, allowing herself a small joke, "what color is it?"

His smile became fully visible now. "Orange, ma'am."

Mari smiled too, but then sighed. It was time. It always became time eventually. They didn't pay her to have fun.

"Tron—they call you Tron, right?" She dropped the smile. She was all-business now. "You got anything illegal on you?"

He shook his head. Straightened up a little. Tightened his muscles like he was a boxer getting ready to accept a blow. "No, ma'am."

"Knives, guns, drugs, anything like that?" she said.

"Well, I got a box cutter, ma'am."

"You got someone that can hold onto that for you?" she asked.

"No, ma'am, I don't. Or, well, I do, but I don't want to have to tell nobody about us talking and all."

"I see," Mari said. "You want me to hold onto it for you?"

"If you'd give it back, ma'am. I'd surely appreciate that."

"Alright, if you can reach into your pocket slowly and give it to me, I'll hold onto it for you. You'll get it back," Mari said. "I promise."

Tron pulled the box cutter out of his back pocket and handed it to Mari. She flicked the blade out. It was rusty and slightly bent.

"Ain't you got any new blades for this knife, Tron?"

"Yeah. I got some, but they're inside the knife, and I lost my screwdriver. I've been using my thumb, but it don't work so well." Tron held up his thumb and showed Mari his mangled thumbnail, split down the middle.

"Tell you what, Tron, I got a screwdriver in my bag. I'll make sure you get a new blade before you get this back, OK?"

"Yeah, ma'am. That'd be real nice. Thank you."

"Anything else? Like something you might have forgotten about or something from yesterday? Something you wouldn't want me to find out about? It's OK," Mari said. "I don't want you to have anything illegal on you. That's not why I'm here."

"No, ma'am. I'm good."

"You see those two police officers over there?" Mari gestured toward Roger and his partner, leaning on their squad car at the other end of the lot, arms folded across their chests, uniforms relatively crisp.

"Yes, ma'am."

"If I ask them to go through you, run your name, you're not going to have any problems?" she asked.

He didn't say anything.

"If you have something illegal on you, just tell me," Mari said. "It's not a big deal. I don't care about that right now."

"No, ma'am. It's not that."

"You think you got a warrant or something?" Mari could see that Tron was worried about something.

"Could be, ma'am. Honestly, I don't know. I get surprised sometimes."

"If it's a warrant you're worried about, don't. I ran you this morning. Unless you got into some nonsense in the last few hours, you should be good. You rob, beat, or kill someone in the last two hours?"

"No, ma'am."

"You sure? You paused a little before you said that." Pauses meant they were thinking things through. Pauses meant lying.

"No, ma'am. I'm sure."

"So I'm going to ask you again: You got anything illegal on you?"

"No, ma'am," he said solidly.

"Then you're good. Go over there," Mari indicated again to where Roger and his partner were standing. "They'll go through you, run your name. We're going to chat."

"Ma'am?"

"What?" Mari was getting tired of this.

"I'd prefer not to," he said.

"You'd prefer not to?" This was standard procedure, Mari thought. Looking like him, growing up in this neighborhood, he must have gone through this at least a hundred times already.

"No, ma'am."

"You don't want to talk to me?" If he wasn't going to talk, Mari thought, then Cornelius was full of crap.

"No, ma'am."

"Well then I can't talk to you. You're not supposed to talk to me unless you want to. I can't just take you away and make you do something you don't want to do." If Cornelius thought he was going to get her on some petty Fifth Amendment violation, he was dumber than she thought.

"But I'm supposed to talk to you!" he said, wringing his hands on his broom.

"Well, do you want to talk to me or not?" she asked.

"No, ma'am, I don't."

"OK, fine." Mari was getting exasperated, but the kid seemed so sweet that she decided to try to humor him for a while. "I'll play: Why don't you want to talk to me?"

"It ain't right," he said, firmly.

"Ain't right! This again!" Mari shook her head. "I had heard you wanted to talk to me. That's why I'm here. That's what somebody told me. You know that's why I'm here."

"Yes, ma'am. That's probably right, ma'am."

"So which is it? You do want to talk to me, or you don't?" she asked.

"I . . . I . . . I don't know, ma'am." His stutter was getting stronger. "You're getting me all confused. I'm *supposed* to be talking to you, but I don't want to. It's not right. Can't I just talk to you here? Why do I have to go over there and talk to those policemen?"

"How are you supposed to give me information in a public parking lot where anyone might see you?" Mari said.

"I don't give information. I don't mess with you all. Don't you see?" Now he was using the broom like a stick shift on an old-fashioned truck where the driver was trying to maintain control on a slippery road. "I'm not about that. I'm not even supposed to be here."

Mari sighed. Her hands were in her pockets. She felt safe talking to him, too safe, maybe. He was supposed to trust her, not the other way around.

"Tron, I can see you got something to say. That's good. You'll feel better after you say it. Those officers over there? I promise they aren't going to hurt you. I give you my word. You're safe."

Mari hated lying to him. They were never safe. That's why she was here. They shouldn't trust her, but it was those damn words of decency and kindness that did it. What little love they must have in their lives that they listened to her. Like sailors dying of thirst, they drank the salty water.

Now Mari didn't even want to talk to him. "Tron, I ain't got all day."

He was struggling, looking over at Roger and his partner and then back at his broom. Mari had noticed that one of the store employees had come out. He was standing outside, watching them. Mari thought she remembered that guy as the manager from back when she worked this neighborhood. He was probably eight hours into his twelve-hour shift. Four more hours before the night manager took over and he could go home to his family. Mari remembered him as generally kind and respectful to the people who came in, and she saw him looking over with the guarded non-kindness kindness that everyone who spends any time in the ghetto has to have. His hands were folded across his chest. Tron looked at the manager, apologetically gesturing toward his broom as if a life preserver. The manager shrugged, tilting his head toward the wall where Tron could put the broom if he wasn't going to use it. Tron's shoulders slumped. He looked at Mari one last time —seeking pity—but she had none to offer him. Tron mournfully leaned his broom against the wall and trudged over to Roger.

Roger went through Tron's pockets. Mari had told him it wasn't necessary, that Tron didn't have even a touch of violence in his background. But Roger had laughed and said that, in his twenty-five years on the job, not one person had gotten into the back of his car without being searched first. He added that if Mari's car broke down and she needed a ride, he would frisk her too before letting her in.

Better safe than sorry, Mari thought. Roger was probably right. You have to have rules. If you don't have rules, you have to think, and it's too hard to get through the day relying on thinking. Mari supposed Tron would have been surprised if he hadn't been searched, so maybe that was better anyway. Ironically, the procedure, once submitted to, would calm him.

Mari had them drive Tron to the back parking lot of the abandoned Save-A-Lot, where the semis were unloaded back when the store still sold groceries. It was wide open and didn't feel weird, but it was out of the way enough that nobody could see them.

As Mari followed the squad car, she could see Tron's head lowered in the back seat. He seemed really torn. Messed up. Coming from his family, it must have been killing him to talk to the police. In his mind, he probably felt like a nazi collaborator, or worse. Cornelius must have told him to talk. But why? It was as confusing to Mari as it probably was to Tron. Cornelius was the man around here. What he said meant something. It obviously meant something to Tron, since he was doing what he'd been told to do even though it seemed to disagree with him to the point of making him physically ill.

Mari realized she was biting her lip, a bad habit. She'd bitten off a tiny strip of flesh. That would probably hurt later, especially if she ate anything salty. It annoyed her that she had done that. A dumb habit leftover from when she was a teenager. She rolled the tiny piece of flesh around on her tongue. It tasted like nothing. She rolled down the window and spit it out.

When they arrived, Roger and his partner got out of the car and shared a smoke a few dozen respectful yards away. Mari sat in the front seat of Roger's car, with Tron in the back. Earlier that day, she'd made sure that Rogers's squad car had a working camera. The video was lousy, but the audio was pretty decent, and that was mainly what mattered. She told Tron about the camera and told him that he wasn't under arrest, but since he was in the back of a squad car and had agreed to talk with her, she'd have to read him his Miranda rights. She wanted him to be aware, to understand completely so there was absolutely no chance that anything he said would be inadmissible in court. Tron nodded. Seemed almost relieved to think he might be under arrest.

She had gotten right into it, no messing around. She asked about the dead cop—what the neighborhood knew and what he knew. It quickly became clear that Tron knew a lot more than he should have. He knew too damn much. All the details of this case had been kept under lock and key from the beginning: the impossibly short range of the shooting, the missing cuffs, the scuffle beneath the porch. Tron shouldn't have known any of this, and the fact that he did showed that he had either killed the cop himself or gotten a firsthand account from the person who did. He knew *exactly* what happened.

Not only did Tron know about the cuffs; he said he actually had them. He said they were in his basement, tucked up in the rafters along with some bloody clothes. Why had he kept them? What kind of dummy would keep stuff like that?

"I don't know why I didn't get rid of them," Tron said, as if he had just read Mari's mind. "We don't throw away a lot of stuff around my house. Stuff just stays. But they ain't mine though," he added quickly. "They ain't got nothing to do with me."

Of course they aren't yours, Mari had thought. You, or the guy you know, took them off the cop after you killed him. But this whole time, as Mari watched the words come out of Tron's mouth, it was as if they were being orchestrated by someone else. She could almost see the puppeteer's muscled arm reaching up through Tron's throat, gagging him, forming words he didn't want to say. But try as the hand might, it couldn't make Tron say everything. Tron never said that *he* killed the cop, just that it had been done. As Tron gradually revealed more about the guy he might have heard had done some of these things, Mari could almost hear the whisper of an unspoken name. Tron wanted to say it. Once, Mari swore she'd even seen syllables forming in his mouth. But he stopped himself before uttering the name out loud.

Mari could sense that the lines Tron had rehearsed were over. The puppeteer was gone, and only Tron remained. This was the time.

"Say the name, Tron. You keep wanting to blame this on someone else, so just go ahead and do it. Say the name."

"I ain't talking about nobody," he said.

"Yes you are. You've been blaming someone else this whole time, you know you're supposed to say it," she said.

"I ain't no snitch, and I ain't blaming no one." He said this matter of factly. Like a truism.

"Again with the snitching!" Mari exclaimed. "Good Lord!

Do you people even know what that means? Of course you are snitching. That's exactly what all these words are!"

"No they ain't." He looked at her out of the corner of his eye. "I didn't tell nothing about nobody else."

"Yes you did. You were going to say a name. You even started to say it, I could see it. It starts with an R." Kindness wasn't working, Mari thought, so he'd have to be pushed. "Do I have to go through your whole family? All your cousins, all your brothers, all your friends, until I find the guy whose name starts with an R and bring him in? Tell him that Tron ratted him out? Is that what you want? You want him to hear it from me that you were talking to the police? Just say the name, Tron. Tell me the thing you know you're supposed to say."

Tron's lips snapped shut. Angry. This was the first time he'd had any emotion other than self-pity during the forty-five minutes they'd been talking.

"'Cause if it ain't someone else, Tron, then it's you. You got that? You understand? There's no two ways about it. You gotta figure out what you want it to be: a capital S for Snitch which puts it all on Mr. R, or are you gonna be a man, understand what you did, and take the consequences you know got coming. What's it gonna be, Tron? Who you got?"

Mari watched Tron transform in front of her. The generations of defiance, the questioning of his manhood, rose up and blotted out his kindness, turning his lips to a snarl and his eyes to fire. He looked Mari squarely in the face, his shoulders taut with tensile fury, and spat on the ground.

"I ain't no snitch, Detective. Shut your mouth. Fine. Alright. Like I said, those aren't my cuffs, but I know whose they are because that son of a bitch put them on me. He didn't have no right. I shot the cop. I'm glad he's dead, and I wish you were too."

That moment should have felt triumphant. The perfect videotaped confession from an angry and hateful murderer. But it wasn't. Instead, Mari was flooded with childhood memories of a storefront church and a well dressed preacher blotting his sweaty forehead: "the lamb must die" he said in his singsong voice, and then the soft chorus of the congregation murmuring the same. "For the glory of God," the preacher said, "and for the meat at the center of the feast" he intoned repeatedly, "The lamb must die.

The feast wasn't worth the death of the lamb, Mari thought. Mari felt sick at the memory of the soft bleating on the sacrificial rock as the blade was raised, the blood desire of history, and the whistling noise the knife made as it arced through the air.

"Tron," she said.

Tron's breathing was fast and empty, almost like he was having an asthma attack. Jesus, was she going to have to call an ambulance?

But then his breathing slowed, his shoulders slumped, and he averted his gaze. "Yeah?" he replied softly, almost sleepily.

"You don't have to say these things if they aren't true. You know that, right?"

Tron was looking down at the floorboard in the rear of the car. He seemed aware of her presence, but like it didn't matter anymore. He was done talking.

SHE HAD CALLED ONE OF HER JUDGE FRIENDS. TOLD HIM about the evidence. He had sworn her in right over the phone and emailed over a signed warrant five minutes later. She didn't even know you could do that. She and Roger had called another car over and put Tron into the back of it—in handcuffs now—before going to Tron's house and knocking on the door.

The door had creaked open when they knocked on it, and there was an older woman standing there in a dirty nightshirt.

"Who you all looking for?" the old lady moaned, vacant

eyed. "Ain't nobody home right now. You'll have to come back later."

"We ain't looking for nobody, ma'am," Mari said. "We just want to take a look around your basement."

"The basement!" The old lady leaned back. Mari wished she would put more clothes on. It was embarrassing to see so much naked flesh on an old woman. "There ain't nobody down there. Them boys is gone."

"We're not looking for boys, ma'am." Mari averted her eyes. "We're looking for things. We got a warrant."

"I told you there ain't no one down there! They're dead! He killed them! Their bodies are disappeared and everything!" The old lady's eyes got a little wider. "Why'd you go get a warrant when there ain't nobody down there?"

"We're going to look around." Mari stepped inside. She didn't need anyone's permission. She had a warrant. "There's nobody here but you?"

"I told you," the woman was almost shrieking, "they're gone. Gone! Nothing but lost things and lost souls down there. Go on down there. You'll see."

And see they did. Found exactly what Tron said they would stuffed into the rafters. The bloody clothes, the banged-up cuffs. Enough corroborating evidence to make any defense attorney talk plea bargain before they'd even had a chance to get comfortable in their chair. Sure, Mari would have preferred to have the gun, but Tron said it was gone. It made sense. A gun was a valuable thing, and it was probably still floating around in Tron's family. Mari was confident that it would turn up eventually. She'd come back later and go over every detail of the house with forensics, but for now, she just couldn't risk the clothes and the cuffs walking away.

After bagging the evidence, she'd left Roger and his partner to secure the house. Then she'd accompanied Tron and the other two police officers back to her office so she could assemble the forensics and have the delicious pleasure of offhandedly mentioning to her pathetic sergeant that the case was done.

Mari was glad she'd taken Tron back to her office instead of the district station. Apparently, some hero plainclothes lieutenant had decided to take matters into his own hands. Without anyone's say-so, he and his team had gone over to Tron's place and torn it up, looking for any shred of evidence they could find, especially that gun.

When the lieutenant's team had shown up, Roger assumed they'd been sent by Mari, so he let them into the house without bothering to let Mari know they were there. Most of Tron's family had returned to the house while they were there, and they were mad as hell that Roger wouldn't let them into their own house. Words were exchanged, fists were swung, and just about the whole family ended up getting dragged back to the station (even the old lady in the dirty nightdress. Mari had heard that the lot of them were creating such a racket in the back of the lockup that the front-desk crew could barely answer the phone.

Tron wouldn't have gotten any sleep with his family banging on every floor and window in existence back at the station, and Mari wouldn't have gotten a chance to see his real self return after his nap.

"MA'AM?" MARI LOOKED UP TO SEE TRON TAPPING SHEEPISHLY on the glass, and looking at her with his mournful eyes. Tron had been sleeping fitfully, twitching like a puppy who was dreaming about chasing rabbits. When Mari entered the room, the angry young man from the interview seemed to have disappeared: "Were those cameras in the car on when I said what I said?"

"Yeah, Tron. I told you they were on. In fact, they're on right now. This room has cameras too."

"Oh." Tron seemed to ponder this news for a while.

"Ma'am?" he said. "So does that mean I can't unsay those things? Those things I said before?"

"You can say more stuff, you can explain things, you can always talk to me, but Tron, what you said is on video. It's all there."

He nodded, biting his lower lip.

"Alright, ma'am. Alright."

Tron lay back down, then abruptly sat back up.

"Ma'am, I'm sorry I said you should die. I didn't mean that. You don't deserve to die."

Mari laughed. "Tron, you definitely aren't the first person to say I ought to die, and I got to tell you, some days, I pretty much say the same thing to myself."

"Ma'am." His eyes blazed at her. "Don't say that. I shouldn't have said it, and you shouldn't believe it either."

He looked at her intently, earnestly. The fire in his eyes went out, and his gaze dropped to the ground.

"Ma'am," he said, "that knife, that boxcutter. I'm not going to be getting that back, am I?"

"No, Tron, probably not."

"Could you get it back to my family? But could you fix the blade first, like you said you would?"

"Yeah, Tron. I'll get it back to your family."

"And you'll fix it first?"

"Yes, Tron. I promise. I'll fix it, and then I'll get it back to them."

He nodded. Firmly. Using his arm as a pillow, he lay back down and turned away from her. He stared softly at the wall.

"Too damn easy," Mari thought. She turned away from Tron and tried to stretch her shoulders. They were tight, tense, involuntarily clenched as if to absorb the blow that would surely be coming her way.

CHAPTER EIGHT

"There he is!" Kasper exclaimed as Danny walked in. "The watch hero, the man, the myth, the legend." Kasper looked around the roll-call room, grinning broadly at the dozen uniformed officers sitting sleepily on mismatched folding chairs under dull overhead lighting, waiting for their shift to start. "You ready to bring it today, Danny? You got your gym shoes on? 'Cause I was born ready, and for some reason, they got us working together again."

"Yeah, kid," Danny said. "I saw that. What's the matter, you need some retraining or something?"

"Aw, hell no," Kasper said. "I think management must have made a mistake. Forgot you hit mandatory retirement age a few years back and shouldn't even be on the streets anymore, let alone working with the real police like me."

Kasper seemed to be directing half of his speech at his father's old partner and the other half at the rest of the room, particularly the two pretty coppers, fresh from the academy, sitting on a bench on the other side of the room. Kasper liked the way they giggled when he talked. It made him feel good, lifted some of the heaviness from his eyes.

Him poking the old bear, Danny, was just an excellent side benefit of the speech.

But Danny didn't take kindly to young officers trying to show him up in roll call.

"Kid, my jock strap has more time on the job than you do. And if you're talking about foot chases, I'll have already caught the guy before you can tie those shoelaces."

Kasper reflexively looked down at his shoelaces. Of course they were tied (he wasn't three years old). Danny was just messing with him. But the cute girls had laughed when he glanced down at his feet. Kasper felt his temper rising.

"So you're saying you *did* bring your running shoes? Alright, old man, we'll see."

"My work shoes don't even come off," Danny said. "I wear them to bed. Besides, even if you did win, it'd only be because you have an unfair advantage when it comes to aero-dynamics since your balls haven't descended yet.

"Well, Pops, with that belly of yours, I'm definitely at an aerodynamic advantage."

Kasper saw Danny wince a little. His cut had been double-sided. Danny had confided in Kasper that he had been feeling a little old and fat and tired lately, and he hated being called Pops. Kasper knew that, so he tried not to say it. But it annoyed him that the name bothered Danny so much. He had started calling Danny "Pops" right after Ryan died. Kasper thought it should have meant something to Danny, but apparently it didn't.

But sometimes, wanting to respect him and hurt him at the same time, it came out. Like today. Why had they put him with Danny again? He hadn't minded training with Danny back when he was brand-new to the job. Danny was one heck of a cop, and there was no one better to learn from if you really wanted to learn how to be the police (But Jesus, Kasper had gotten tired of hearing that. He could hardly walk down the hallway without someone stopping him to say how lucky he was to get to learn from a guy like Danny). And then there was the fact that Danny was practically family. And that Kasper more or less owed him his life.

But working with him now, when he knew more and was trying to make a name for himself, felt a little like being in your twenties and having to move back in with your folks. Waking up in your twin bed every morning to the Bears poster that you loved when you were ten but now just looked faded, ripped, and too small for the wall. You can't go back. You just can't.

The first few times they'd put them back together this week, Kasper had been excited. He looked forward to showing Danny the cop he had become, the new tricks he'd been learning. Maybe even work with him as an equal and get some good arrests. But it hadn't worked out that way. Danny couldn't stop treating him like a child who didn't know what he was doing, even though Kasper had three years on the job and was one of the best producers on the watch, which Danny knew. Kasper wanted to try new things, not listen to some guy who thought he knew the answer before Kasper even thought of the question.

It was already a pain in the ass being the superintendent's son. Fricking annoying. He wanted his own name. Everyone figured that, as the superintendent's kid, Kasper had it made, that he could do whatever he wanted, go wherever he wanted. He hated the weight of his father, having to do everything twice as good as anyone else so no one could say that his father had gotten him there. He was a better copper than any of them. He neither needed nor wanted his father.

But now, for the last three days, they had put him back with his dad's old partner. Like he was some retread who needed more training.

"Kid," Danny said, "it's my job to make sure young coppers know how to do this job. And if someone out there thinks it's a good idea for you to work with me, you should probably just accept it. Don't worry, I'll make sure you're smarter by the end of today than you are right now."

"Whatever, Old Man. I already went and got the squad car keys. I'm not going to have you drive me around like you've done the last two days. If you want to sit in the passenger seat and see how it's actually done, that's fine by me," Kasper said.

Danny looked at him sharply: senior-man-on-the-car decides who's. But Danny decided he'd been a little hard on Kasper and let it go. "Ha! I like it, kid. You've earned it. Let's see what you can do."

ONCE THEY'D GOTTEN THEIR COFFEE, KASPER STARTED cruising the side streets where he knew he could find trouble. Seeing which of the assholes in the neighborhood were out and about.

"Look, Kasper, I'm sorry about the last few days. I've been wanting to talk to you, so I asked if we could work together. I know it's not what you want. You should be working with some of the younger, more aggressive guys instead of me. You're right, I'm done with the kind of police work you should be doing. Sometimes I think it'd be fun to work with you like I used to work with your dad, but for some reason, I just can't. The motivation isn't there. But for some reason, I still like talking to you."

"Sheesh, Danny. I like working with you. It ain't like that at all. And what the heck—if you want to talk, just call me. I mean, I'm pretty sure you gave me my first cell phone."

"Ha! No. Not quite. Ryan's mother was the one who got you guys those phones. She was always worried about Ryan, him being all sensitive and all, like her. She didn't want you two to be jealous of each other, so she made sure you boys both got phones at the same time."

Kasper noticed that Danny got all soft when he talked about Ryan. Didn't seem right for a man like Danny to get soft about anything.

"Huh. No kidding," Kasper said.

"But anyway, I thought about calling, but none of us is as close as we used to be, and we're all busy with other stuff anyway. Life just keeps coming. Plus, it's personal stuff. Not the kind of stuff you talk about on the phone," Danny said.

"Personal? What, you can't get it up anymore? They got pills for that stuff, man. You gotta talk to a doctor, not me." Kasper had no desire to talk about personal things with Danny.

"Shut up, Danny. I'm wide like a Coke can down there. You got any doubts, just ask your girlfriend. Besides, I'm serious. I wanted to ask you about your dad. How's he doing?"

"Dad?" Kasper scoffed. "He's the same as always. Still thinks he's better than everybody else. Nothing's changed."

"No, how is he, like really? You guys talk?" Danny asked.

Kasper was annoyed. Danny was looking at him. He wasn't supposed to be looking at him. He was supposed to be looking at the streets. "Yeah, we talk," Kasper said. "He calls me once a week or so to tell me about something I'm doing wrong, and then every Sunday I see him when I pick up the kids from his house."

"How come you don't stay for dinner?" Danny asked.

"'Cause I'm busy. I've got my side job," Kasper said.

"The movie detail?" Danny asked.

"Yeah, that one," Kasper said.

"Every week?" Danny said.

"Yeah," Kasper replied, an edge creeping into his voice, " every week."

"*Every* week?" Now the edge was creeping into Danny's voice.

"*Most* weeks. Jesus!" Kasper banged the steering wheel with his hand. "And besides, I've got a family and responsibilities. When am I supposed to get anything done if I spend three hours on Sunday at my dad's perfect house kissing the ring while being told about all the things I need to do to be as cool and special and amazing as him?"

"Family's family, Kasper. It's important," Danny said, with an uncharacteristic softness.

"Sheesh, you should talk. You haven't spoken to that asshole in what, five years? Don't tell me I have to talk to him when you're not willing to do it yourself," Kasper said.

"You have a point there. Your dad and I, we've had our hard times, but some things you have to do even when you don't want to."

"Yeah, whatever. He likes the photo op of his multigenerational family. That's all he cares about. But I'm tired of him trying to control my life. He tried to put me in that yuppie district. I'm sure he was afraid I'd get into trouble in the hood and embarrass him. Well screw that, I'm no softie. I'll go where I want. I'm probably the only copper in the city that had to use his union rights to bid *in* to the ghetto. He needs to stay out of my life," Kasper said.

"You're right. He shouldn't have done that without asking you. But he's just trying to protect you, to give you a safer career than we had. For your family, for his grandkids. We do things for our kids that we shouldn't, things we would never do for ourselves . . ." Danny trailed off.

Kasper wasn't sure what the hell that last sentence was referring to, but he didn't like it. "Screw that. I'm not going to do that to my kids. They're going to choose their own lives."

"Yeah. We'll see," Danny said. "Wait until they get older and then we'll talk. Plus, by then you'll know that this neighborhood, this ghetto, might be fun, but it's a beast. It don't care and it never will. Every second here is another chance of getting hurt. The cops, the teachers, the citizens, dude working on a telephone poll, heck, even good old Ray Ray on the corner—they're all at risk. Sure, getting robbed, getting killed, everyone knows about that, but then there's the risk to your bank account, to your heart, to your very soul."

"Soul? Jesus. Don't tell me you're getting religious now, Danny."

"Shut up. I don't need that foolishness. Never did." Kasper was still whipping the squad car around corners, looking for trouble, as Danny continued, "I'm telling you, man, it really doesn't matter. In the end, the ghetto gets everyone. Even when you think you're done, and it's over. You think you made it out safe with the same number of holes in your body that you started with. Well one day, you come home and your dog ate the food you left out on the table, and you beat that dog, you scream at him, you hurt him so much his ears go flat and he yelps and runs away and then your kid looks at you from the couch and you can see he's scared of you, but instead of comforting him, you slam your hand down on the table and yell at him for not taking the dog out even though you know he's too young for that." Kasper could see Danny's hands clenched in anger. "And that's when you know that you didn't make it out. The ghetto got you. The ghetto got you like it gets everyone, like it always will."

"Sheesh, Danny. Do I need to stage an intervention for your dog?"

Danny continued, ignoring Kasper, "Your dad just wants to take that away from you. Protect you. That's all."

"Don't you guys have cats anyway?" Kasper looked over at Danny with crinkled eyes.

"Kasper. Shut. Up. Are you listening? I'm talking to you. I'm really talking. For crying out loud, the cats are fine. Are you hearing me?"

"Yeah, yeah, I hear you." Kasper tried to be serious for a minute. "But are you hearing yourself? Aren't we *supposed* to be out here in the hood? Isn't this where we're most needed? Aren't we *paid* to protect these people? Why the hell are you and Dad trying to protect me when I'm the one who's supposed to be out here protecting *other* people? That way, this ghetto might actually get a little nicer."

"Kasper, you're not listening."

"Oh, I'm listening. I just know you ain't right." Kasper's eyes never stopped scanning the streets. "If the ghetto got you, well then, fine. I'm sorry. But it ain't got me, and unless it kills me, it ain't gonna. You hear me?"

"Yeah. I hear you," Danny said.

"Do you really?" Kasper asked.

"Yeah, Kasper, I hear you. Maybe you're right."

"I'm not so sure you and Dad do hear. You want to take away my opportunity to have a little fun and maybe help some people along the way because you're scared? Turn me into one of those 'welfare coppers' Dad used to talk about? You remember that? Because I can still hear him down in the basement playing cards with you guys and preaching like the obnoxious know-it-all he is: 'They're nothing more than a bunch of welfare cops. They take a government check and don't do nothing. At least the welfare queens are honest about it.' And anyway, what the heck? If you think all that's true, then why are you here? You've got kids, a family, a bank account. You don't need to be here. You're the one who should leave."

"Ha!" Danny exclaimed. "Well that's one thing you got right. I should leave. But it's too late for me. The ghetto took my soul a long time ago. I wish I were a welfare queen; at least then I'd have my family around. Instead, I'm more like a crackhead: I know the ghetto ain't good for me, but I come back to it every time. I don't know. Me and this neighborhood, we like each other, we're comfortable. We like hanging out and partying, and then, by the time the anger and abuse starts up, we're too messed up to remember it the next day." Danny settled back into his seat. Kasper was still whipping around corners. Danny figured he should probably put his seatbelt on, but he didn't feel like it. "Besides, those idiots up in management ain't in charge out here. I am. I'm the captain of this ship. And you know what? I guess I am old school. If the ship goes down, I'm gonna go down with it."

"Now you're talking," Kasper said. "I'll drink to that."

They rode in silence for a while. Listened to the police radio. It was a quiet day. Not much going on.

"Your dad," Danny broke into the quietness, "me and him spoke. About a month ago."

"Jesus, I didn't think you two would ever speak again," Kasper said.

"Oh, I knew we'd speak. I just didn't know when," Danny said.

"What the heck, he need something from you?" Kasper curled his lip.

"Man, you really got it in for him, don't you?" Danny said. "But as it turns out, yes."

"What a jerk," Kasper said.

"No, that's not it." Danny draped his arm out the open window and looked at the neighborhood going by. "Something's wrong."

"Course something's wrong," Kasper said. "He's an asshole."

"No. Something's really wrong. Would you shut up and stop acting like a baby for one second? Can you can it for just a minute?" Danny turned and looked at Kasper. They were so close together. Two large men dominating the front seat of the squad car. "That's why I wanted to talk to you. To see what's wrong with Mike, with your dad. Just shut up and think for a second. Is he sick or anything?"

"No." Kasper was stung by being called a baby. "He seems OK. Honestly, he's the same as he's always been. Or, well, I suppose he and Gloria might not be getting along too great. Nothing big, but I hear some arguments from time to time. Probably about money. Either they haven't got enough and she doesn't want to go back to work, or they don't have enough and she wants to go back to work but he won't let her. He's a controlling dude and he likes having a little wifey at home to show off."

"What are you talking about? Gloria doesn't work anymore? What happened to that fancy law firm job? I see the two of them on the news with their fancy crowd. There's no way they can afford that lifestyle without her salary." Danny knew what it was like to live higher than you can afford.

"Yeah, but no, she quit that a couple of years ago. Wanted to spend more time with the kids because they were having some problems," Kasper said.

"Problems? What kind of problems? Mike didn't mention anything about that," Danny said.

"Sheesh, Danny, you don't know about that? You really are out of touch. Evelyn tried to kill herself, not real hard, but she did try. Pills or something like that. They pulled her out of school and put her in some special school for troubled kids or some nonsense like that, and then Christine OD'd at some rich-kid party. Her grades are OK, but they're nothing like they used to be. Little Mikey's still a superstar and everything, but I don't know, that kid don't seem happy either. Last I heard, he doesn't even want to go to that fancy college Dad was so proud he got into. Dad about blew a gasket when he mentioned that."

"He or Gloria messing around?" Danny asked.

"Messing around?" This was getting crazy, Kasper thought. "Sheesh, how would I know? I don't care who either of them are sleeping with."

"Well, are they still living together? Sleeping in the same room?" Danny asked.

"Yo, dude, if you want to know who they are sleeping with, just ask them." Kasper chuckled. "I ain't into that kinky stuff like you are."

"Stop it!" Danny raised his voice for the first time. "Stop

messing around. This is serious. I'm trying to figure out what's going on. They're still in the same house, right?"

"Yeah, man," Kasper said, unchastened. "They're there. They haven't got anywhere else to go as far as I know, and every time I go over, they're there. That's all I know."

"Well, damn it, that house is big enough that they could be living apart even if they're in the same house." Danny rubbed his chin. "They got that big master suite they added on upstairs with that huge closet, so I know she ain't moving. But your dad, does he seem to be going upstairs with her, or is all his stuff down in the man cave?"

"Dude! I *don't know.*" Kasper squeezed the steering wheel with each syllable. "How many times I gotta tell you that? I suppose he does seem to be coming up from there most of the time, so that might be it."

"That might be it," Danny said. "You're sure he's not sick?"

"I'm not sure. Jesus. You care about him so much, why don't you ask him? Everyone thinks he's a natural leader and diplomat here at work, but I'll tell you, all the fancy words and self-control he shows to everyone out here, just hides the powderkeg of anger that he's stuffing down to explode when he gets home. No wonder his family is messed up. I told you, I'm through with him. *I don't care.* And ya know what? Neither should you. You think he'd notice if *you* had a problem?"

The police radio jumped to life. It had been silent for fifteen minutes, an eternity.

"Is there a tactical car available for a selling narcotics on 722's beat?" the dispatcher asked.

That was their beat, and Danny didn't like anyone else getting involved with his business.

"The Washingtons," Danny muttered as he looked at the job on his computer.

"What?" Kasper grunted.

"The Washingtons. They're a fake preacher's family that

sells drugs. Your dad and I put half of them in jail twenty years ago. Someone's calling on them. Says a 'Rip' is on the corner selling drugs."

"I know that street," Kasper said. "There's heavy traffic there. Let's go."

"Yeah. Let's do it. Why not?" Danny flexed his shoulders. "The next generation of that family deserves getting the business too."

Danny keyed up his radio: "Squad, put that job on our box. That's my beat and I don't like anyone else messing with it. My partner and I, we'll take care of it."

Kasper put his foot on the gas pedal. The engine growled smoothly, powerfully. He felt the wheel wanting to bounce in his hands as he accelerated over the rough pavement. Danny seemed calm and relaxed next to him, like a little dopamine had just hit his bloodstream. He'd finally stopped asking those annoying questions about his dad. Kasper punched the gas pedal further and the car grew even more wild. The sun was shining, and Kasper's heart was beating faster. He started to feel better. He started to feel much better.

CHAPTER NINE

The gun Danny had given him felt cold in Mike's hand. Heavier than he'd expected, too. The coldness was from last night. He'd been leaving the gun in the trunk while he did his research and, if he was being honest with himself, worked up his courage. The heaviness, well, sometimes things just feel heavy. The shades were drawn on Felton's house. Mike sat in the car and watched. Darkness lay inside.

Mike wondered, briefly, how long it took the average man to work his mind up to murder. Did it come on fast and sudden for most of them? Or were they like him, gradually steeling themselves? Letting their heart clench up slowly until it became hard and unfeeling, the blood pressurized and constricted, a river dammed.

For a while, he felt like he wouldn't need the gun. Stupid Felton. Trying to come up to *his* office and blackmail him, treat him like he was someone who could be pushed around. Felton thought he had something on Mike, and he was right. He did. But Mike had tamped down his fears and insecurities so Felton couldn't see what he actually had. Because Mike knew that if you give a man nothing, he can't really hurt you.

Still, Felton's words scared him. Of course he remembered that case, that bank vault. Most of those memories made him smile. Those were good years. The most fun he ever had on the job. It had been like something out of a movie, bringing dudes back there to Spy Camp for interviews, hanging out, talking, messing around. And that's all it was, just a game. It was just boys having fun in a tree house they built themselves and kept secret from the grown-ups. Spy Camp didn't have anything the district didn't have. In fact, it had less, so there was no real reason for them to be there. But like a secret tree house with an electrical cord running up the trunk and the sound of the breeze rustling the branches, everything up there was just more fun.

From his car, Mike saw the lights in Felton's living room snap on and off. Felton did this every night. Mike guessed that he was looking for his keys, swearing at his forgetfulness.

FELTON HADN'T NEEDED TO REMIND MIKE ABOUT THE Washingtons. He'd never forget that family of saints and sinners. For some reason, Danny absolutely hated them, couldn't get enough of messing with them. Anytime he had an opportunity to stop one of them, he did. It was like their very existence bothered him. The fact that they were half good/half bad offended his vision of the universe. For Danny, a spoiled apple is a spoiled apple, no half and half about it. Mike disagreed. You could enjoy the good part of the apple and throw away the bad part, no reason to make it personal. Maybe it was the percentage that bothered Danny. "But this ain't just one spot you can cut out, it's half the apple. If half the apple is rotting, then you know the other half is bad too, even if it looks OK. You know it's still gonna taste mealy and ain't nobody's gonna enjoy that apple unless they're starving, and even then, it would probably make them sick."

For about five months, they locked up members of that family practically every day: cousins, siblings, uncles, play cousins… everyone. He and Danny hit those blocks, and if a Washington, or someone they knew, was doing something wrong, they got handcuffs placed on them. Some of those handcuffs came off within hours, while others stayed on for years. And once people start looking at years, well, they start wondering why they're the ones going to jail instead of being the ones who are calling the shots. That's when they start talking. One guy even started talking about the very top, the church itself, where the real weight was held. When Danny found out about that, he was so damn excited he practically pissed himself.

"See! I told you," Danny had said. "I told you that whole family's dirty."

"Jesus, man," Mike had said, "it's a church. What are we doing? This is messed up. Nothing good is going to come of this. Even if we're right, they'll figure out some way to make it look like we're wrong. And man, if we're wrong, I don't even know, man. We'll be lucky to have a job."

"So what, we just let them get away with it because we're scared? No way, man," Danny said. "Screw that. They're wrong, and they're going down. That's it."

And Danny could push. Man could he push. Eventually, Mike was convinced that if he continued to refuse, Danny'd just wait until Mike took a few days off of work and do it without him. Mike didn't want that. Because sometimes Danny was too sure, and that surety made it too easy to get sloppy, cut corners. When you know you're right, it becomes harder to see the things that might make you look wrong. And in this case, they couldn't afford that. They'd need perfect paperwork. Perfect, ironclad paperwork to make sure they'd survive. And even then, who knew what would happen?

So while Mike didn't remember a specific conversation in which they talked about putting drugs in the church if they didn't find any, he could certainly imagine saying something like that, especially back at Spy Camp where they felt so empowered. And Felton had to be telling the truth about the video, because otherwise, how would he have found out about any of it? What he was describing was too accurate, down to the very words they would have used. It couldn't be a bluff. Nobody would try to do that sort of thing to the superintendent of the police. Certainly not Felton. He wasn't that reckless. He'd only bluff if he could afford the loss, and Mike knew he couldn't. He had to have a video. He had to.

What was so frustrating was that it was just talk. They were just kids playing in a tree house, telling big fish stories, talking about how great they were and bragging about stuff they would never actually do. Danny just said that stuff because he heard the old timers say it, and everyone wants to be as tough as their father was. They didn't put cases on people—who would even bother? There was crime everywhere, no need to create it. And even if they were going to do it, Mike liked to think he could put a better case on someone than the way it actually turned out.

He should have stopped the warrant. Their first mistake was trusting Wallace and Heine, those idiots from their team, to watch the building overnight and make sure the drugs didn't go anywhere. Everyone knew those idiots couldn't stay awake. They said they saw a big truck parked in the alley for two hours, and they saw Colfax come in and out of it, but they swore up and down that nobody had loaded anything into it. Well then, why was it parked there for two hours in the middle of the night, with their target driving the thing? They had obviously loaded it up and driven everything away.

And that was it. Mike and Danny had done perfect paperwork, and then those two sleepy idiots let the evidence drive itself away.

Did anyone honestly believe that if police officers were putting cases on people they would come up empty on such an important search warrant? Hell no. There were so many drugs and guns floating around that neighborhood that they could have put any reasonable amount in the church if they'd wanted to. But they didn't need to. They knew where the drugs went. They went into that truck. They'd just missed it. And they had to find it.

Sure enough, not two weeks later, when the truck was found, it was filled with almost ten kilos of heroin. Hell, two weeks later, it probably wasn't even the same stuff. Those guys were moving so many drugs they might as well have owned a pizza delivery service. He and Danny had been off work when the truck was found. They'd been told that they could either take time off or it would be taken from them in the form of a suspension. All the bosses were furious at the way they'd written up the paperwork to hide the fact that they were trying to put a warrant on a church run by one of the most popular preachers on the South Side.

When the rest of their team found the truck, it saved their jobs, even if it cost the preacher's son his life. What an idiot. Driving a truck full of heroin. He must have thought they were stopping him for a regular traffic infraction and he could bluff his way out of it, but when four coppers hopped out with their guns drawn and then the rest of the team pinned him in from the front, he must have realized it was over. He was able to let off six rounds before the police put thirty holes in his body that hadn't been there before.

Why had Colfax done that? It was dumb. He had no chance of winning that gun battle. Must have been the embarrassment of driving a church van full of heroin. He didn't want to live to see the shame it would bring on his father.

But his life saved Danny and Mike's jobs.

Only, the paperwork had disappeared.

The supplemental report neatly linking the truck and the target and the drugs and the warrant, the report that made the church family a bunch of criminals and the cops a bunch of heroes, it disappeared.

Back then, the reports were on paper, and if someone came and took something out of a file, there was nothing to say it had ever existed at all. Mike and Danny hadn't even known the paperwork was gone until they got to court and were discussing the case with their lawyer. The lawyer had said, "Why the hell didn't you guys write this down on paper? You got a search warrant on a church, and then you killed the pastor's son, and you're too dumb to write it down that you had seen the truck pulling away from your original warrant?" Danny and Mike and the guys, sitting in that meeting room in the back of the courthouse, couldn't even understand what the lawyer was saying. He continued, "I mean, *I* believe you, but any independent observer is going to think you're just making this stuff up to cover your tracks. I'm sorry, officers, but Judge Francis is not going to let you testify about this alleged truck being on scene at the warrant without any corroborating evidence, so the drugs are going to get thrown out and now you've got a negative warrant followed by an unlawful traffic stop followed by the son of one of the most influential preachers in the city getting killed. It's bad, guys. Bad."

Who took that report out of the file? It could have been any number of people. Those files weren't protected. Practically any officer who knew what cabinet the file was kept in could have walked in and done whatever they wanted with it. Sure, they were supposed to be under lock and key, but most offices were too lazy to do that. Any number of coppers could have been bribed, or just been sympathetic to the plight of the pastor, and gotten rid of it. Mike had thought to protect the paperwork from everyone outside the department, but it had never occurred to him that it would be so easy for someone to bring them down from the inside.

Mike had looked everywhere for that paperwork. For the last two decades, as he rose up through the ranks, any time he got a chance to look through old files, or copies of files, or copies of copies of files, he looked for it. Because it had to be there somewhere. Otherwise, there was no reasonable explanation for why the Feds suddenly showed up and made the whole thing disappear.

Mike and Danny were going down. The outraged church, the dead son, the missing paperwork. Their lawyer was advising them to quit the department so they wouldn't be subject to any discipline-related interviews and could save their fire for the inevitable criminal probe.

But then poof, as quickly as their own paperwork disappeared, so too did the whole case. One day, the Feds came and told them the family didn't want to move forward with pressing charges. As long as Mike and Danny agreed to sign a confidentiality agreement, the whole thing would go away. Mike had been so relieved. He'd just started dating Gloria. Even at that early stage in their relationship, her family's connections were making it easier for him to move up the ranks and get a job in administration. He could finally slow down a little. Somehow, he'd managed to hide all this Washington nonsense from Gloria, but if it had hit the press, it would have been over. He couldn't wait to sign the confidentiality agreement and make the whole thing disappear, but Danny had other plans. Danny *knew* they'd been right the whole time. He figured the Feds found their paperwork, saw how messed up the situation was, and started backpedaling real fast. Once Danny saw their fear, he pounced: "So you just want all this to go away? You suspended us, ruined our careers, and all this time we were right? Hell no. If you want this to go away, *they* need to sign a confidentiality agreement too, and we deserve a promotion. If this is going away, we deserve to be compensated for what they did to us." And to Mike's amazement, they did it. Danny took a nine-high hand and bluffed them both to the biggest pots of their entire career.

~

MIKE'S MEMORIES WERE INTERRUPTED WHEN HE SAW ALL THE lights go out in Felton's house. He knew Felton would be taking the car out now. He'd visit his mother for at least an hour and then head to work. What kind of single guy visits his mom every night? On one level, it was admirable, but on another level, it was pathetic. On one of those evenings, Mike had broken into the house after Felton left. He needed to know if there were any cameras in there. He'd checked out the exterior of every house in the neighborhood, and he knew that none of them had anything relevant, but Felton was the sort of pervert who might have hidden cameras. Once he was inside the house, he saw why Felton visited his mom every day: Felton was living in his mom's house. It was the most old lady house he had ever been in. No doubt Felton was born and raised in this house, and now he had packed his mom off to the nursing home so he could live here for free. Pathetic.

And this momma's boy thought he could push Mike around? Mike had been kind to Felton. He'd helped him out a couple of times, or at least not stood in his way. Mike had asked around, and nobody had anything positive to say about Felton. Mike wasn't going to let a person like that destroy all the good he had done. Sometimes the greater good trumps the lesser evil.

Mike didn't want to do this, but Felton was making him. If Felton had been a little more patient, had given him a little more time, it could have worked out. Mike had waited three weeks—just to show Felton that he couldn't be pushed around—and then his plan was to give Felton a spot in the superintendent's office. He'd let him make as much lazy, worthless overtime as he wanted, but Felton would always know that Mike had his eye on him, and the minute any nonsense got leaked about Mike, forcing him to leave, Felton would be forced out too.

But that goddamn idiot was impatient, and before Mike could make it happen, Felton went and paraded out in front of headquarters with that disgrace of an alderman. Felton had the gall to be out there—on company time, no less—holding a hand-painted sign saying "justice" with a crowd of two hundred people marching behind him. It was a warning to Mike. Felton was telling him that he had allies too, and while Mike was pretty sure that Felton didn't have the guts to reveal that video, the alderman was a different story.

That alderman had hated Mike from the moment he'd been appointed superintendent. Mike didn't play the nonsense patronage game he wanted, and the alderman's people had never worked a minute in their lives, so Mike had gradually squeezed them out of most of the police contracts. That alderman would take that video and destroy Mike in a heartbeat. If he was able to bring in two-hundred people without a video, he'd surely be able to bring in twenty thousand with it. And he had the connections to bring whatever criminal investigation he wanted against Mike too.

Felton was right about one thing: It wouldn't be an investigation, it would be a crucifixion. Worse still, he'd be all alone on the cross. He and Gloria had pretty much stopped relating the moment the kids were born. The diapers, the crying, the disagreements—no matter what he did, no matter how hard he tried, everything always seemed to be his fault. No way their marriage would survive this. Most of her family had already moved down south, so she would surely take this opportunity to move down there too, and take the kids with her. And then there was the job. The real police, all the guys he'd known since they were young, hadn't liked him in years. They hated him, literally turned their backs on him at that copper's funeral. All because he had fired a cop who had gone bad. They should have been thanking him. The work he'd been doing had at least gained him some new friends—real friends, like the old ladies at the church and the people from the neighborhood. He'd been working so damn hard for them. If this video were to get out and Mike had to see the expression on their faces? And then to have the media dredge up every imaginary wrong he had ever done and trot it around like it was God's honest truth? What the hell would he do?

And even Kasper? Jesus. What had he been saying? Mike doubted Felton was bluffing about that either. Kasper was a loudmouth, and Mike could only imagine what he might have said—and who he might have said it to—when he was drunk. Mike should have been paying more attention to Kasper. He didn't understand how it had gotten so bad between them. Kasper, Danny, the guys, his wife, his children. The only thing he had left was his work.

And because of Felton, that would be destroyed too. For nothing. For absolutely nothing. All so that good-for-nothing momma's boy could get a few more dollars in overtime.

Mike saw the light go on in Felton's garage. The gun Danny had given him still felt cold through his gloves. Mike had test-fired it. It fired well, not any kick at all. The bullets had come with the gun, and Danny assured him that he'd never touched them. Mike had wiped the gun down and then let it sit in the oven for a few hours until there wasn't a speck of either one of them left on it. Polished the bullets until they shined. This gun had come from the neighborhood, and back to the neighborhood it would go. Mike was wearing a dark coat over his uniform. His license plate was obscured.

Mike knew exactly what was going to happen next. He'd seen it a dozen times. Felton would start the car. Back it out to the driveway. Close the garage door. Leave the car running while he reentered the house through the front door. A few minutes later, Felton would open the garage from within. By then, Mike would be standing just outside the garage. Then when Felton half-heartedly shuffled out, Mike would empty all the bullets from the gun into Felton's heart.

That would be it.

The garage door opened and Felton's car eased out. With the headlights on, only the silhouette of Felton's body was visible against the darkness. Mike fiddled in his seat as he waited. After it was done, he would drive around the block and then come back in uniform to "discover" the body of the man he brought to the grave.

He would do it. He had to. Sometimes the right thing is just the right thing to do.

BUT SOMETIMES A MAN'S LIFE GETS SAVED.

It doesn't even matter whether that man deserves it. Sometimes, a voice speaks out from the darkness, molecules tremble, and that voice, those molecules, they save the man. For Mike, that voice, that savior, was his son.

"HE'S RUNNING WEST, THROUGH THE YARD!" MIKE HEARD Kasper's voice crackling through the radio. It had been about three weeks since they'd last spoken. They'd been missing each other, intentionally or unintentionally. Mike felt the hate from his son acutely. He'd been able to hug his younger kids, talk to them, feel their love—all the things he'd never done with Kasper when he was young. But when he finally started trying with Kasper, Kasper just pushed him away. He'd tried, he'd really tried. But sometimes, you can't let the bad bring down the good. Mike couldn't let Kasper tear his family apart, so he had to let him—and his hate—go.

But now, when he'd finally worked up the courage to kill Felton and save his family, here Kasper was, calling for help. And every cop who heard that call through the radio—they were coming. Revving their engines, flying to the scene, ready to do whatever was necessary to help a fellow cop, for no reason or for any reason or every reason, but mainly, just because he asked. Mike was a cop, and even more than that, he was a dad.

Mike knew Felton hadn't told anyone about the video, and certainly not the alderman. If that alderman knew about the video, he would have exposed it by now. Felton had to be hiding it in order to keep his power over Mike. But that wouldn't last. Mike should have done this weeks ago. Every moment he wasted was a moment in which Felton could destroy everything Mike had built. This was Felton's last day before vacation. He wouldn't come back to work for another three weeks. This was Mike's chance to do what he had to do.

Felton parked the car in the driveway and went back into the house. He'd be in there for his usual three minutes. Plenty of time for Mike to get out of the car, position himself, and get the job done. On the radio, cops everywhere were saying they were on their way to help Kasper. There were plenty of cops coming. Kasper didn't need him. Mike's wife and kids needed him, this old family didn't even want him. And yet, he was only two blocks away. What were the chances they were so close? Even with the minute he'd already wasted, if Mike were to leave right now, he would likely be the first one there.

Felton was in the house now. This would only take one minute. All Mike had to do was cross the street, fifty feet at most. He could still help Kasper after that. Mike got out of the car. The solid thunk of the car door almost drowned out the last transmission from the radio: "Just go, officers. No need to identify yourselves. We all know who you are. Just let us know when you get there, and tell us when he's safe."

"Goddamn Felton," Mike said out loud, grimacing as he pictured Felton's lumpy body falling back into the garage, arms spread wide, the bullets entering his chest, all his problems flowing away with the river of blood. "And goddamn you too, Kasper."

The pistol in Mike's hand wasn't cold anymore, it was burning hot. He stuffed it into his pocket.

Felton would have to wait.

Mike got back into the car and accelerated into the night, to chase down the bad guy, to help his son. He's done it a million times before. What was one more?

CHAPTER TEN

E ven from a block away, Danny could see that the dude Kasper was talking about was a Washington. But at the same time, he seemed different somehow, kinder and less dangerous than Colfax and his crew used to be. But then Danny caught himself: There was no such thing as not dangerous. Whenever you started thinking something around here wasn't dangerous, people got killed.

Still, the kid was just standing in front of his house, minding his own business, looking at his phone absentmindedly. Danny wondered who had it in for him that they'd called on him. Danny's own son, Ryan, had looked like that every day of his life. An ache and a hardness formed in his chest as he stared at the boy on the corner and remembered his dead son.

Why in the hell was he thinking about him now? Ryan had never been like that, being out on nonsense and getting the police called on him. He didn't deserve to be here, in Danny's imagination. Erase my mind, Danny thought, but the image of Ryan remained.

Danny looked at the boy. Even if he wasn't like Ryan, he wasn't one of the regulars, either. Those guys would never have their hands in their pockets. They'd be out there, heads on a swivel, getting ready to deliver a blow, or take one. Those kids had dead eyes. He used to see their soulless faces in his nightmares.

This kid though, his eyes lived.

DANNY THOUGHT OF THE THOUSANDS OF KIDS HE'D SEEN moping around these corners. By now, they were the second generation, sometimes even the third, of the original assholes he'd stopped back in the day when he was barely older than they were.

When he and Mike first started, Mike had always wanted to smile and wave at them. It annoyed Danny. He thought it made them look weak. The really little kids were a different story—it was almost impossible not to wave at them as they ran and jumped and chased after the squad car like the circus had just come to town. Even Danny had to admit there were few things more charming than standard grade ghetto kids running around like free-range puppies. Their laughter and vibrancy was so different from the scared, sheltered kids Danny somehow raised himself.

But Mike wasn't satisfied with just waving at the little kids. He insisted on waving at the bigger kids too. That was the problem. Little kids grow, and eventually, they'll take your kindness and use it to play you for a fool. Somewhere along the line, cuteness goes and assholeness comes waltzing in to take its place. Maybe it happened the first time their mommas chewed them out for talking to the police. Or maybe it was the first time some copper told them to get the hell off the corner. Or maybe, if none of that ever happened, it was when eventually, inevitably, some car drove down their block and unloaded a full clip full into the heart of a kid they'd known since they were babies. Once you see a friend bleed out on the corner, it's hard to smile.

Everybody has to learn that the ghetto ain't a place, it's a monster. If you keep looking at it, eventually it'll look back at you. The kids' dead eyes helped them block out the ghetto's stares, like Inuit snow goggles. Without them, even just wandering around in the snow, you'll go blind.

But Mike somehow just kept trying to smile his way past those dead-eyed children. For most guys, all it took was one innocent-looking eleven-year-old scoffing at you when you raised your hand to wave. They wouldn't risk getting punked by a kid whose voice hadn't even changed yet.... Gotta say, it kinda stung when it happened.

And yeah, no doubt, it sometimes went the other way too. You see a kid who looks hard, but then the kid gives you a big smile and a wave. But by the time you realize your mistake, you've already looked at him like he's the usual killer, and then you see the smile harden. You know you ought to turn around and give him a big hug, tell him you're sorry, you thought he was someone else, it's going to be OK.

But you don't.

Because it'd be a lie. It's not going to be OK, and it never will be OK. After all, the kid's out there in the ghetto, hanging out with the monster. And you know it's only a matter of time before it gets him. Better to just rip off the bandaid. Smiling only makes it hurt more in the end.

As they got closer, Danny could see that the Washington kid wasn't actually as head-in-the-clouds as he first appeared. He looked nervous—pacing a bit, jumpy—like he had things on his mind that he shouldn't. The caller had been right. He was up to no good. He was still a part of the Washington clan. In that family, you had to do something mean just to get seconds at Thanksgiving. Didn't matter who that boy reminded Danny of. He was who he was.

DANNY THOUGHT OF THE CAUTIOUS NODS HE GAVE TO THE men on the corner. It was different from what Mike did, but it was something. He'd see these grown men standing there, and not knowing who they were, he'd look at them, not all hard like, like he already knew they were criminals, but not kind either. Level. If they sneered back at him or spat on the ground, he'd know who they were and respond in kind. If they looked away, he'd wonder what they were hiding. But if they returned his gaze, if they looked at him like he looked at them. Maybe he'd take the risk. If he thought they deserved it, he might give them a slight, almost imperceptible nod. If you weren't looking for it, you wouldn't even be sure you'd seen it. But a lot of them were looking for it, and they would see it, and maybe they'd take their own risk and give him a little nod back. And in those two tiny nods, they gave each other something that every man needs in order to keep his heart from hardening: respect.

Two men. Acknowledgment. That was something the ghetto couldn't take away.

KASPER STOPPED THE CAR RIGHT IN FRONT OF THE Washington kid, blocking Danny's view. There would be no nod.

That wasn't how Danny had taught Kasper. Stopping so close was dumb. They can unload on you before you even get out of the car. On the other hand, if you stop too far away, it gives them a chance to run. Still, catching a criminal isn't worth dying. Let them get away. They'll be back on the corner the next day. Danny supposed that when you're young, tomorrow seems pretty far away. He remembered stopping pretty close when he was young too.

Kasper was basically right next to the kid when he stepped out of the driver's side door. Danny opened his own door and leaned against the roof of the car, curious to see what the kid would do when he finally noticed they were there.

The kid looked up. Blinked. He didn't utter a word. Silently, like a little mime, he began dance-shuffling backwards, subtly pivoting his body and then accelerating like a madman. It took him a second, but once that kid got going, he got. Flying through the air. What he was doing didn't even look like running. It was more like floating, and only once in a while would one of his feet would coincidentally touch the ground.

Danny grinned as he saw Kasper launch off after him like a heat-seeking missile. Now that was how it was supposed to be done! Not too long ago, Danny remembered, Kasper would have given him a sidelong glance as he chased, asking for permission, making sure he was doing the right thing. But not now. He saw the kid and he went. No questions asked.

Danny pictured all the extra weight that Kasper carried on his body: the gun, the body armor, the radio. Probably twenty pounds of weight there. He could also see how much muscle Kasper had built up over the last few years—where did these young guys find the time to work out? If you were single and childless, you had all the time in the world. But Kasper wasn't either of those things. He had as many responsibilities as anyone, and yet he still managed to hit the gym seven days a week, and judging by the results, he hit it hard. Danny sure didn't do that anymore. The only extra weight he found on himself these days was in his belly. He sighed. Kasper was just young, that was all. He didn't need time, intelligence, none of that. Youth trumped it all. At least here, in this moment.

But all that extra equipment Kasper carried annoyed

Danny. He shook his head. All these young guys liked that stuff. The tactical stuff. The fancy vests and radios and knives. Danny didn't like it. It made them look like the military, not the police. Danny hadn't needed that stuff when he was young, and he sure didn't need it now. All he needed was a gun, a set of handcuffs, and maybe a pen to write it out after.

Danny looked at Kasper, sprinting down the yard. If Kasper was a young kid, a new officer, Danny would have had to sprint after him, or at least keep him in view to make sure he didn't get into trouble. But despite what Danny called him, Kasper wasn't a kid anymore. He knew what he was doing. Danny could already picture the explosion that would occur if Kasper collided with that string bean of a kid. The kid wouldn't stand a chance.

The squad card was sitting there idling, just like Danny. Fortunately, Kasper had left the keys in the car and that was all the excuse Danny needed to take a well-deserved break. He hopped into the driver's seat, reversed the car around the corner, then threw it into drive, the momentum closing the passenger door that he had neglected to shut.

Danny saw the kid running south. He parallelled him, figuring he could cut him off at the end of the alley. But when he got there, the kid was still running, with Kasper no more than sixty feet behind him. When the kid saw Danny at the end of the alley, he broke off to the right and cut into the yards again. No problem. If he didn't cut him off at this street, he'd get him at the next, and by then the kid would be starting to tire and Danny figured he'd be able to hop out fresh and catch him. Except some pedestrian-friendly cul-de-sac was in the way. Danny hated that yuppie nonsense. These streets were his, and no stupid sidewalks could hold him back. The way to get around them was to hop the car up onto the sidewalk and sneak through the metal barriers. But that took time, and by the time he got over, there was nobody there but an old lady watering her garden. No Kasper, no kid. Nothing.

Danny zipped up to the next alley. Still nothing. Then the next street. Nothing again. Damn it.

"Squad," Danny spoke into the radio, "Where's my partner at? He still talking? I lost sight of him. Where is he?"

"Beat 722's partner," the ghostly dispatcher's voice rang out, "you still chasing this guy?"

Silence.

"Beat 722's other half," the dispatcher tried again, "are you still there? What's going on? Talk to us."

The neighborhood was quiet. Peaceful. Danny could hear the birds chirping, even over the sound of his heart pounding.

"Squad, I don't know where my partner is. He might have doubled back. I don't think he got further than two blocks, but I'm not sure. Kasper, where are you?"

"Beat 722, are you there?" the dispatcher tried again. "Talk to us 722. Are you out there?"

Danny thought of all the things that could go wrong. He thought of Kasper wrestling with this kid, maybe losing his gun. Or maybe rounding the corner to find a whole group of them. Maybe they'd decide that a lone cop, left behind by his partner, was worth trying to take advantage of. Danny wished he had stayed with Kasper. Why hadn't he followed after him? Had he really been that tired? What would he tell Mike if the worst happened?

But then, there he was.

With relief, and with no shortage of comic ridiculousness, Danny saw Kasper coming out of the alley, swinging his baton through the high weeds, looking like a cross between an absent-minded gardener and a kid who'd lost his backpack at school.

"Squad!" Danny heard Kasper yell exasperatedly into the radio, "He vanished! He's gone. I have no idea where my offender went."

Danny pulled into the alley in front of Kasper. He was covered in sweat and breathing hard. "What the heck?"

Danny was enjoying a tremendous chuckle as he leaned casually out the car window to mock Kasper. "I would have thought the real police like you would have caught that guy? What, was he a ghost or something, and he just vanished into thin air?"

"Damn it. Shut up." There were grass stains on Kasper's pants from chasing the kid through the weeds. "I don't know what happened. You could have at least gotten out of the car."

"You're telling this *old man* to get out of the car? That wasn't the way you were talking earlier. I'm the only reason he didn't dust you in the first place. I cut him off and forced him back toward you. What happened? Did he double back on us, or do you think he got away?" Danny said.

"I honestly have no idea. I thought I had him. He couldn't have had more than twenty feet on me in one of those gangways, and then when I popped out, he was just gone. Like a ghost. I don't think he could have crossed the street on me, but honestly, I don't think he could have gone anywhere without me having seen him. And yet, obviously he did. I've been looking through all these weeds. Even if I lost him, I figured he might have tossed something in here. I couldn't possibly have lost everything."

"Sorry, brother. I would have seen where he went, but the mayor's beautification project back there slowed me down. Before you become a full-time gardener in these weeds, you might want to consider giving a better description of this dude on the radio. Maybe some of the other coppers can catch him even if you can't."

Kasper glared at Danny, but he got on the radio and said, "Squad, he was wearing—"

The transmission was interrupted by the sharp, hollow sound of a single gunshot.

"Was that—"

"Yeah, kid, it was—"

"Squad, I got one shot fired immediately east of here."

Kasper started running to the gunfire. He figured it had to have come from almost exactly where the chase started. Stupid Danny. Didn't even get out of the car, and now he was blaming Kasper for losing the kid. Dad always said that Danny was the one who caught most of their guys, so he was particularly annoyed about somehow losing this kid while working with Danny. He knew he wouldn't hear the end of this.

And geez, that kid sure did vanish. He'd seen him running straight down the gangway and hopping over one of those wooden gates. Kasper had gone to hop over it too, but then the damn gate just fell down, collapsing beneath him like it had been hit by a car. (Kasper could swear he had seen some asshole gangbanger pulling a pin out of the gate and then laughing at him as he fell, but when he turned around, the gangbanger was gone, so Kasper figured he must have imagined it.) Kasper hit the concrete face-first. By the time he got up, slightly disoriented, and gasping from having the wind knocked out of him, dude was gone. Gone. Danny had been joking, but he really did seem like a ghost.

Kasper scanned to the limit of his vision, looking for anything that could hurt him. He held his gun with both hands with the barrel pointed toward the ground so he didn't let one off accidentally, but at the ready. If there was going to be shooting, he'd be shooting back. Kasper arrived back at the alley, approaching the house where the chase had started. He made a mental note of a clean-looking Ford, the sort of car bosses drove, in his peripheral vision. Kasper couldn't remember exactly which yard they had originally run through —everything looked different coming from the opposite direction—but the unfenced weed-strewn yard looked familiar.

And then he saw something in the yard.

A body.

Black shoes, blue pants. A simple uniform. Every police

officer in the city recognized those pants. They were the uniform of the Chicago police. Guys wore them to work, and home from work, taking off their light blue shirts—what most people looked for in the uniform—but keeping on those dark blue pants. It was too much trouble to change them. You took off the job's easiest and most obvious things: the shirt, the badge. But all the other stuff—the pants, the white t-shirt, the gun around your waist—they were too hard to remove so you kept them on. Sure, you made some half-hearted effort to cover it up with a sports jersey or a jacket, but it was still there.

The average Joe Blow might sense there was something odd about what you were wearing and subconsciously wonder what was wrong, but that was it. They wouldn't see a cop. But the criminal on the street, he saw you and stayed away. And your fellow coppers, they saw you and immediately knew that another cop was walking the streets with them, even if you were off duty.

But the blue pants that Kasper saw were silent. They had nothing to say. No internal movement, and only an occasional ripple in the cool breeze.

Kasper's blood ran cold.

Just like he'd been taught, Kasper slowly circled the opening in the fence, bringing more and more of the scene into view while protecting himself from harm. The body in front of him grew larger, the image coming into focus. The police radio crackled, the sun sparkled. Kasper saw the polished mirror of the black shoes. Stiff. Awkward. Fixed. The shoes were pointing upward to the sky, where Kasper as a child, had always been taught God was supposed to lay.

MIKE'S CHEST HAD LOOSENED ONCE HE HAD DECIDED TO GO TO Kasper, but when he heard that they couldn't find him, it tightened once more. When he finally heard Kasper's voice on the radio, and then Danny's a second later, his heart relaxed like a broken dam.

Idiots.

Stupid Kasper. From the way he had sounded on the radio, he must have been right on top of that guy. How could he have let him get away? Mike and Danny sure wouldn't have. Well, really, he shouldn't be too confident. They definitely caught most guys, but they hadn't caught them all. No one did, unless you only chased the fat ones. But still. If Kasper wasn't such a know-it-all and had listened to him, maybe he wouldn't have missed this one.

Kasper was doing OK on the job, maybe even better than OK, but he ought to be doing better still. Kasper was smart. He could have had more than this job. It was a shame he was so damn stubborn.

Mike never even got to the chase. By the time he was close, there were cop cars everywhere. (Mike made a mental note to meet the lieutenant in charge of the watch after this. Backup had been great. Guys going hard to jobs was a tribute to management, and Mike wanted them to know that he noticed.) There was no need for the superintendent to show up at the end of a foot chase like some dumb glory seeker pretending he was still out there pounding the pavement with the troops. Mike hated bosses like that and had always vowed not to be one. Besides, he didn't need someone else's glory. He still had a few tricks up his sleeve. If they lost the kid, he had almost certainly doubled back on them. So while everyone else was going where the radio told them the cops were, Mike was going back to where his brain was telling him the criminal might be.

If there was one thing the last two decades had taught him, it was that these people never went far. The old ghettos had walls and guards to keep people in. The new ghetto didn't need them. They kept themselves in. He remembered the car chases when he was young, and how he had always been confused about why they'd just drive around in circles. Why didn't they hit the highway? Head on out? Leave, for crying out loud? Instead they drove around and around, thinking they were getting away, as hundreds of coppers arrived to tighten the noose. It was only later that he figured it out. They didn't leave because they never had.

They couldn't run from the police because they had nowhere to go. Their whole lives took place in a six-block radius, like a medieval canvas map. Outside the tiny world they knew, there was nothing but a blank map, maybe a hand-drawn picture of a dragon with the words *"here there be monsters"* written above it in fancy script.

They would live and die in this tiny, godforsaken patch of earth. No money but what they had in their pockets. No property except what the government gave them. Nothing to sustain them other than their pride. No wonder they killed when someone called them outside their name. Their name was the only thing of value that they owned.

Mike sighed to himself. He genuinely tried to expand horizons for these people. Tried to find them a job, teach them about a life where kids actually respected their fathers. He wanted to help them figure out a way to bring the wider world in, or at least keep them out of jail. But they didn't care. Spit in his face, told him he was the problem. A hundred people a day raping and robbing and murdering and pillaging, and he was the problem?

All that time he gave them. Endless meetings. Phone call after phone call. Twenty hours a day, seven days a week. Standing up from an anniversary dinner with the wife—staring icily at him as he walks away from the half drunk bottle of wine—all to hear the news about three boys slaughtered where no one can even remember their name. Fatigue. Endless, overwhelming, core-of-the-earth fatigue.

In one meeting, people yelling at him for not doing enough, and in the next, yelling at him for doing too much.

His wife drifting away, his kids looking at him in surprise whenever he walked through the door. All that to try and widen the world and bring a sense of peace to these neighborhoods, these people. All for nothing. The same people who called him "Superintendent" to his face to try when they were trying to get something out of him, called him a racist the moment he left the room, and half the time, they didn't even wait for the door to close behind him. What did they know about the world? What did they know about him? Ignorant.

Because Mike had spent his whole career studying their ignorance, he knew to go back to where the chase had started. When he arrived, he recognized the house immediately. Of course it would belong to the Washington family.

Mike personally knew three generations of the family. He remembered meeting the patriarch, the last of the real family, before he died. Running that big church and making speeches downtown. Such a respectable man. Huge heart.

His children were nothing compared to him. A few of them tried to run the church after he was gone. It limped along for a while, but it was a shadow of itself. The next generation was nothing but trouble. Colfax was just a small-time drug addict who enjoyed the trappings of power with no understanding of how to use it. He used what was left of his father's legacy to try to enrich himself, and when that didn't work, he turned to selling drugs until Mike and Danny brought him down. But that wasn't anything special. Colfax was going to bring himself down eventually. If it hadn't been them, it would have been someone else.

Mike had learned about the third generation from the intelligence briefing for this neighborhood. Cornelius was the guy's name. He seemed to be formed in the image of his grandfather, but the image was twisted. Cornelius had the power to motivate people, but only for the worse. He was murderous and surprisingly efficient. Mike had taken the time to stop him once, and the hatred radiating off him was so strong Mike had wondered if he should be wearing sunscreen.

Mike could think of at least half a dozen murders that had been attributed to Cornelius, but Cornelius had always intimidated them out of existence, or really, maybe the neighborhood didn't care anymore. Who cared who murdered whom when the victims and the killers were one and the same?

The Washington home was an old Victorian mansion. It had to have at least a half a dozen bedrooms. The grandfather had bought it back when owning the biggest house in the neighborhood meant you had made something of your life. But Colfax had let it all deteriorate, and Mike got the feeling that Cornelius didn't need the attention of a good-looking house and let it molder away too. Most of the family was gone now anyway. They were dying, or fleeing. The patriarch had nine kids and who knows how many grandkids. The ones that hadn't fled or died of the usual sorts of diseases that killed off poor people had turned to drugs and violence. A couple of the girls were still active in the church, but they didn't have the old man's power. They ran it, but that was it. All the other grandchildren had scattered like seeds in the wind. Cornelius seemed to be the remaining one in power, but even he seemed to be spending more time in jail than out of it these days. Was he back out? Had he fallen so low he was out running away from the police like some kid on the corner?

Mike parked his car in the alley and got out to see if he could hear anything. He stood a little behind one of the neighbors' yards and kept watch. If whoever was running circled back, he likely wouldn't see Mike, but Mike would be able to see him.

He'd only just gotten out of the car when he heard a cell phone ringing under the vacant porch. It rang once before Mike heard someone struggle to turn it off.

Mike walked into the yard slowly. A quick scan revealed

two little eyes looking at him from beneath the shadows of the porch.

"Yo!" Mike called out in a strong voice. "I see you. Yeah, that's right. Come out here slowly." The glowing eyes blinked. "You got anything illegal on you? That's it. Easy, kid."

The kid was cautious. He had to crawl out on all fours because the ceiling of the dugout was so low. The kid entered the sunlight and sat down on his haunches. He was looking up at Mike, squinting through the sun in his eyes. He looked familiar. The kid had the strength and beauty of the old preacher man, but he was sitting down in the mud looking up at the police in a way his grandfather wouldn't have dreamed of. Sad. Mike wondered why he'd been running. Must have pitched whatever it was though. Suddenly the kid's hands flashed, and Mike saw him go for a gun. The kid's head went down low and Mike took two quick steps forward and caught him right in the face like he was kicking a field goal.

The kid slumped down almost immediately, moaning a little in pain. Jesus, Mike thought. He was barely out of his car and he's already ended up kicking some kid who looks like a choir boy. Mike briefly patted the kid down, looking for the gun. Nothing. Jesus. Were there any cameras here? Had anyone seen? His wife talking about leaving him. The mayor wondering why crime was spinning out of control. Every day, two homicides, a dozen shootings. His damn company phone buzzing every hour with another death, another failure, another crisis that needed to run itself out. The phone calls from the aldermen, from the chief of internal affairs, from goddamn Felton. Another protest, another scandal, another cop killing himself, a line out the door of people who wanted to give him a problem he hadn't caused and that no one could solve.

Mike looked at the boy. Definitely a Washington. It was possible he wasn't even the one Kasper had been chasing. You never knew what might turn up in the ghetto. Maybe he'd just been the kid next to the kid who ran, gotten scared, and then hidden under the porch. Just a child who needed protection, and here Mike had booted him in the face. This would look great when Felton went to the press. Mike shook his head. If a guy like Felton looked at the paperwork and saw that he was messing with another Washington kid, he would laugh and laugh. The perfect fool, that's who I am, Mike thought. I might as well hand in my badge right now.

Felton laughing. Goddamn Felton laughing.

So be it.

It was over. Mike would man up and take it. He was still a man. He didn't have it in him to kill Felton, and he was too tired to do anything else. The job would be as good as gone. The pension, who knows? But he probably wouldn't go to jail. If he led from the front, got his warts out before Felton did it for him, he could manage it. His kids would eventually forgive him. That's what matters. Kids will forgive parents for just about anything. Habitually, he cuffed the kid, but he did it in front so he wouldn't hurt him anymore and he pulled his moaning body into the light to make sure there was nothing else wrong with him.

That was when he saw the rocks. About a dozen of them strewn across the boy's chest as he lay there in the sun.

Well, there you go. Mike shook his head. Drugs or guns. It's always one or the other. These fools don't have anything else.

The kid was no good. Mike had been wrong when he'd imagined he could ever be anything else. He could handle this Washington like he'd handled all the rest. If there were ever any good Washingtons, any good stories coming from this godforsaken city, they wouldn't be coming from here. As the boy drowsily opened his eyes, Mike's own eyes began to droop.

God, he needed rest. It had been at least a month since he'd slept even adequately, and years since he slept good. He could hardly remember a day when he could hold his head up without a struggle.

Mike thought of his children and all the money he wouldn't be able to give to them. He thought of Kasper, the embarrassment of first having to follow his father's good name, and now having to follow his bad name.

He thought of the gun Danny had given him.

Fine, he said to himself.

It was easy. So easy. So much easier than it ought to have been: Knee on the boy's chest. He was a thin one, easy to hold down. Put the gun in the boy's hand, his uncomprehending face looking up at Mike. Why should they have to suffer? Why should Mike's family have to lose so much? Why shouldn't Mike, for once, get the sleep he deserved?

Ain't no point crucifying a dead man.

Mike raised the boy's hand and placed the gun against his own skull. He had a momentary pang of guilt seeing the fear in the boy's eyes, but it didn't last long. Mike figured he'd probably be able to get away. It was just a story that some copper would have to write down and summarize in a report.

Make the boy put it where the brain is, Mike said to himself. That's where the thoughts are. It's the thinking that makes you care.

Mike was surprised not to hear the bang.

CHAPTER ELEVEN

D anny admired the smooth line of Mari's thigh under the sheets, particularly where it ended, at the delicious swell of her ass. He watched her roll over sleepily. She hadn't bothered to put her clothes back on.

What was he doing here? A cool room, clean sheets, the light smell of perfume, a woman who was not his wife. He didn't do this nonsense anymore. Falling asleep in bed like a little boy being rocked asleep in his cradle? Jesus. He should have been in his own bed hours ago, at home with his family, not here.

IT WAS THAT DAMN PARTY LAST NIGHT. THAT WAS WHAT HAD done it. It seemed to have made everyone do crazy things. Who'd have thought that Mike getting killed would make everyone feel so free? It definitely wasn't because Mike's spirit had inspired it. No doubt Mike's ghost would be just as stiff and boring as Mike was in life. In his mind's eye, Danny pictured an Irish wake, with Mike's body laid out on the kitchen table. At some point, Mike's body would rise from the dead, check his watch, and declare he had an early meeting with St. Peter, so apologies to everyone, but they would have to go.

Somewhere along the line, a somber gathering for a murdered officer had turned into an old-style cop party the likes of which Danny hadn't seen in over a decade.

Back in the old days, people didn't much care if a hard-working copper wanted to blow off some steam and have a good time. So long as you didn't hurt anybody, or do something truly stupid, you could count on being protected, with very little fear of ending up on the cover of the newspaper the next day. So sure, yeah, fire off your gun in the parking lot, wrestle a homeless guy for money, sleep with a coworker in the back of a squad car. No harm, no foul. And besides, it gave you something to talk about in roll call the next day. It was nothing like now, where if you use one wrong word or accidentally sneeze in the wrong direction your whole career goes down the tube.

The fundraiser had started out like it should, with the Good Widow Gloria looking like a Hollywood version of a hot wife attending a fundraiser for her murdered husband. The hero's children appropriately dressed in somber clothing, an occasional sniffle and a muffled cry from the youngest orphan. The proper stage was set too: tables full of flowers, envelopes full of donations, bigwigs complimenting each other left and right on what beautiful and important bigwigs they all were.

But then the rumor started. Needless to say, like all the best rumors, it started at the bar. The bar was in the middle of the restaurant, and then behind that, you had the banquet hall where the actual event was supposed to be held. But the old guard never made it past the bar. They were the old-fashioned sort who got information by talking to people. And what they were saying was that the little gangbanger who had killed Mike had gone and plead guilty. Most people didn't believe it. Guilty? Already? Nah. This was the sort of case that ran for

years, even though the outcome was pretty much already
known. But someone flipped the TV on, and after the
nincompoop college grad bartender was finally able to find
the remote, they managed to turn it to the local news to see
what was up.

And it was up. The self serving, pompous state's attorney
was holding a press conference. From the smug look on her
face, it was obvious she was enjoying the room full of cameras
on her. Danny immediately heard grumbles from the other
coppers, "Yeah, he probably plead guilty because that whore
gave him probation." But no, according to the state's attorney,
not only had the guilty plea been entered with no strings
attached, but it was her intention to seek the highest penalty
possible, including, for the first time in seven years, the death
penalty.

They sat in stunned silence. A flip got switched. A roar
went up from the bar.

Visceral.

It was like your team was down 47–0, and just as you were
leaving to get ahead of the traffic, they scored three touch-
downs. Then you were suddenly clamoring to get back into
the same seat that, just a few minutes before, you were hoping
to never see again. Danny felt chills go down his spine.

The room crackled with energy. Energy fed and forged by
the anger and resentment that had been bubbling in the stomachs and livers of these broken, bitter coppers for thirty years.
It finally erupted, their anger transforming into bloodlust and
joy as it exploded into the open air. Danny had never seen
anything like it: strangers jumping up and hugging each other;
bosses wiping tears from their eyes; people pounding each
other so hard on the back it seemed like someone had spiked
the Heimlich convention punch bowl with steroids. Danny
saw one guy jump onto the bar, scream, and flex his muscles
like he was a three-hundred-pound defensive lineman who
had just sacked the quarterback. The relief, the anger, the

disrespect, they all floated away like they had never existed at all.

The wake was over. The party had begun.

The room decided: Mike was dead, and it was sad, but good men die, it happens. That's part of the job they all signed up for—even if the wife didn't know it (though she ought to, that's what those twenty years of city checks were for). And even though nobody wants to get killed, when it happens, and it's for something noble, the sacrifice is worth it. Seeing a fellow officer sacrifice his life for the greater good makes your own life feel more special than it otherwise ever would have been—particularly as you're not the dumb idiot that got himself killed, you're the one drinking a beer and shaking your head with your buddies.

But telling yourself that you're special isn't enough; you need other people to say it too. To tell you that, if worse comes to worse, and you have to do what you have to do, then society is going to have your back and respect the sacrifice that you and your family made. And goddamnit, everybody ought to know that if you shoot a cop, you're gonna die. That's it. You're going to die for what you did, and the sun is going to rise tomorrow. That's all you need to know.

That's the way the world is supposed to be, and when the state's attorney said those words, the coppers started believing that the world was just again. All the things they thought about when they were alone at night, wondering if any of it had been worth it—yeah, it was worth it.

Some young guys went behind the bar and figured out how to turn the music up. A bunch of older coppers then started dancing—holding their cheap bottles of beer over their heads and shuffling to the music like they were drunk college girls (ignoring the fact that they were fifty years old and their guts were spilling over their pants like a waterfall and their hairlines hadn't seen their foreheads in over a decade). And that's how a solemn memorial dinner at a down-

town restaurant suddenly transformed into a drunken cele-
bration.

Gloria had been standing by the table with all the flowers
and gifts and notes, her we-are-the-world children lined up
next to her like faithful toy soldiers. They'd been there about
twenty minutes when the news hit. As the news spread and the
volume got turned up, Danny saw the anger and annoyance
building on Gloria's face. She was nobody's fool. She knew
how these things worked. After a brief conversation with some
political guy he had never seen before, Gloria gathered up her
things and hustled the kids out the door.

Danny was embarrassed. I mean, he definitely loved
where this thing was going, but drunk cops chasing a grieving
widow and her children out of their father's own memorial
was a little much, even for Danny. He ran out the door after
Gloria.

"Gloria, I'm sorry." She turned around to face him as
Danny continued, "I'll get them to turn it down. They don't
mean anything by it. They just got excited. That's all. No one
expected a guilty plea this soon."

"Yeah. Whatever. He's barely dead and you people are
already over it." Gloria had too many bags in her hands, but
she was handing them off to the children, one by one, unbur-
dening herself.

"Gloria, I'm—"

"No, I get it. You people are just doing your cop thing.
You're like poorly potty-trained children peeing on the floor.
Who can blame you? You don't know any better. But all of
this," she said, waving an arm toward the restaurant, "it
wasn't him." Her gaze softened then, and Danny could see
newly formed wrinkles around her eyes. "You of all people
know that. I hate him being reduced to all this stuff. You, the
newspapers, even Mike himself, they jammed him into this job
and made him into a stereotype, but that wasn't actually him."
The kids were standing by their mother, forming a soft,

protective cocoon around her. "And now they're claiming him as their own and he can't argue with them because he's dead. But I know they hated him. All those asshole cops talked crap about him every time he left the room. I saw him come home most nights looking defeated, not because he couldn't do the job, but because he couldn't do the job without you people hating him." The older kid (what was his name again?) was gently pulling on Gloria's shoulders. "And now, for the rest of my life, I'm going to have to get trotted out for memorials, funerals, picnics . . . God those fricking bagpipes!" Two officers had started wailing away on their bagpipes at the bar. "Can somebody please tell them to shut those damn things up?"

"Gloria," Danny interjected. "It'll mean something to the kids, even if it doesn't mean anything to you."

"Goddamn it, Danny, you think I would be here if it weren't for the kids? You think I don't know that if I didn't bring them here, you and your people would somehow turn them against me, make them blame me? And then somehow I'm the bad guy for my husband being murdered?"

She looked around helplessly. Her shoulders were shaking, almost imperceptibly, but her voice was still clear. "Mike . . . these last few years, I don't even know who he was. I'm not sure *he even* knew who he was. He got lost in this role he wanted so badly, and he couldn't stop acting the part. He lost his sense of where the stage ended and he began. I don't even know how I felt about him, or at least, what was left of him. But whatever I thought of him, whatever he was, he wasn't this. He wasn't this thing you people are going to use him for."

"Hey, look," Danny said. He was getting a little tired of hearing about who he was supposed to be using. "Mike chose this job. He wanted it. And whatever you might think now, I know he would have been glad to see his killer going to jail. You and the kids ought to be glad too. Come back inside."

"Jesus, Danny. Some kid in jail? Who cares? Mike's dead,

Danny. What does any of this matter? Sure, I know, you people are going to be happy for the body you've claimed. You can't hold back the ocean, I know that, but I swear there's nothing to celebrate today."

"Gloria, come on—" Danny reached for her hand to try to lead her back in.

"Enough, Danny." She yanked her hand away. "You people do your thing. Just go. You don't really want us here. You'll have more fun without us reminding you of everything he left behind. It's fine. We're going home."

"Gloria, we're not going to forget about you. I'll be there, we'll all be there, for every birthday, every Christmas—"

"Oh stop it. For God's sake, stop it. I told you, I don't want that. Pathetic photo gifts on Christmas of all of you dressed up in uniform? Escorts to the daddy-daughter dance in fancy police cars? I know all about that, Danny. Mike went to every one of those family-of-the-dead-cop worship sessions. I know exactly what they mean to everyone, and they mean a hell of a lot more to you people than they do to the families you're supposedly helping. Thanks, but no thanks. Just leave me alone."

Gloria got into the car, and the kids followed her. Except the oldest. (Damn it, Danny thought, why can't I think of his name?) He stepped up and extended his hand to Danny. "Thanks, Danny. Our family appreciates everything the department is doing for us, and for our father." Danny looked at him appraisingly. The adolescent was gone and a young man was standing before him. The political nonsense didn't fall far from the tree with this family. Kasper must have been wrong. Those kids were going to be OK. The oldest kid got into the car and motioned to the driver, an immaculately dressed policeman, that they were ready to go.

Of course it was the department that was driving them, probably in a department car. Even as Gloria was yelling at him that she wanted nothing to do with the police, it was the police that were taking her home. Danny wanted to help too, but what could he do? As the car drove away, he saw the eyes of the youngest, strong but glistening. Maybe this child was someone Danny could help. He'd definitely have to remember their names. Danny shook his head and turned back toward the restaurant as they drove away.

The music had been turned down and everyone in the room was looking at the floor like they'd been scolded by their favorite kindergarten teacher. Danny shrugged to everyone, held up his arms in helplessness, and then motioned for the bartender to turn the music back on. It was still early, only 5:00, so the crowd wasn't too big yet. But within thirty minutes, more people started arriving, people who had no idea that they'd just chased off the widow and her children, so they had no reason to feel bad about their obnoxious behavior.

Soon, there were hundreds of people, maybe a thousand. Cops, prosecutors, aldermen, hangers-oners. Acting however the hell they wanted. The state's attorney arrived to more cheers from more coppers than she'd ever received in her life. The room was full to bursting and everyone was joking that if the fire marshal wasn't blind drunk on the stage, he would be shutting this down. They were all there. Anyone who cared about the old beating heart of the city, the men and women in blue who had protected these streets for generations, the Streets and Sanitation workers, the people who knew how to take a punch, they all came.

Even if Danny had been able to convince Gloria and the family to stay, the crowd had grown so huge and out of control that no one would have been able to find them even if they wanted to. Because Gloria had been right, who wanted them? Widows and dead fathers' children? Nobody needs that at a party. Hell, if you liked tragedy and death, you should have just stayed at work.

Kasper. Danny's lip twitched. Kasper had stayed at work.

Selfish bastard.

But he must have heard that Gloria and the kids got chased off, because after they left, Kasper had shown up already three sheets to the wind, none of his own kids with him, and some big-titted woman in a tight fitting dress who definitely wasn't his wife dripping off his arm. Over his head, he held a big silver trophy. He staggered through the room like the heavyweight champion of the world, bobbing the trophy up and down to the beat of the music while shouting, "Daddy's here, everybody! Daddy's here!" It was hard to figure out exactly what he was raving about, but eventually he yelled, "They might be able to kill a man, but they will never keep him down!" And then Danny figured it out.

Danny let out a low, admiring whistle. That wasn't a trophy Kasper was carrying. That was an urn. That lunatic had brought his father's ashes to the party.

DANNY WAS PAINFULLY DRAGGED BACK TO THE PRESENT WHEN he banged his knee on Mari's bedroom wall and practically fell over—one pant leg dragging on the floor and the other one halfway up his knee. He swore a little under his breath and glanced at his watch. It was 5:00 in the morning and his tongue was thick with drink.

"So you're running away now?" came Mari's voice from behind him. The pain in his knee was nothing compared to the aggravation he felt at having woken her up.

Danny turned around. Mari was sitting up in bed. Danny was impressed that she didn't make any effort to cover her nakedness.

"Running away?" Danny scoffed as he continued to gather his things. "I'm not running anywhere. I'm trying to get my pants on."

"Looks like you need some practice." Mari arched her eyebrows.

"Well, it's a little hard when you're trying to be nice and do it quietly," he said.

"Nice?" she laughed at him. "You weren't trying to be nice. You were trying to get out of here without me noticing."

"Great, Detective. Thanks for your observations." Danny looked around. Where the hell was his shirt? "What do you want me to do? Wake you up, give you a peck on the cheek, and tell you I love you before I go? I'm trying to get home to my wife for crying out loud."

"Oh Danny," she swooned, "no wonder all the girls want to get with you. You're such a mess that they can be damn sure there's not even the slightest chance they'll be tempted to fall in love with you."

"Oh they fall, Baby. They fall hard. I've just gotten more experienced at keeping them off of me." Danny saw his shirt dangling from the ceiling fan. "I'll tell you one thing, I'm surprised I ended up here with you last night. I got the impression you were into women."

"Your instincts are sound, Officer," she said, continuing to laugh at him as Danny jumped to reclaim his shirt. "But every once in a while, I make an exception. And like I said, I knew if I brought you home, I wouldn't have to worry about you bothering me again."

"I'll be bothering you in your dreams, that's what's going to happen." Danny successfully grabbed his shirt on his fourth jump. "But you're right. No need to worry. I'm going home."

Danny's mood lightened. This whole thing was going well. This girl was cool. He tried to remember why he had given up on messing around since he had married Jasmine. After all, as long as you don't get caught, there really isn't a problem. Maybe his issue was that he had always messed around with the wrong kind of women. Maybe lesbians were his thing?

The happy, goofy expression on his face froze when he

turned around. Mari was standing there, still completely naked, with her gun pointed directly at his chest.

Jesus, Danny thought, maybe lesbians weren't his thing.

"Where did you get my gun?" she said, keeping her tone cool and measured.

"Your gun?" he opened his arms to show there was nothing in his hands. He had just tucked the Governator into his waistband. "What are you talking about? The only gun I see is the one you're pointing at my chest."

"Not this gun," Mari said. "I'm pointing this gun at you so I can make sure you don't destroy my case like you destroyed your own career." Mari gestured her gun toward the ornate wooden handle poking out of Danny's waistband. "I'm talking about that gun."

"Hey, my career's just fine." Danny tried to stand up a little straighter without making any sudden movements. "So if that's what you're worried about, ain't no need to point that thing at me."

"I will stop pointing it at you once you've removed the gun from my case from your pants." Mari was taking a shooter's stance, with one foot behind her and the other aggressively weighted toward Danny, finger on the trigger.

"That's *my* personal gun—very personal. It hasn't got anything to do with you, or any case of yours," Danny said.

"Stop being an asshole. I don't know how you got it, or where you got it, but that's the gun from my case. I'd recognize it anywhere. I'm not letting you ruin my case just so you can take home some stupid personal memento from your dead partner," Mari said.

"That's my gun, goddamn it. Not anybody else's." Danny's voice was rising as he fought the urge to try to lunge and grab the gun from her hand. "Now stop pointing that thing at me."

"Where did you get my gun?" she said, taking a half step

back in case Danny took a run at her. "Did you steal it out of evidence? What the hell is wrong with you?"

"What. Are. You. Talking. About?" Each syllable was like the bang of a drum.

"The gun from my case!" she repeated. "The one you just stuffed in your pants. The one that killed your partner."

She saw him blink. For once, he was silent.

"Now take it out of your pants slowly." Mari regretted not putting her clothes on. She felt the inconvenience of being naked while trying to be taken seriously. "I'll get the gun back to where it's supposed to be, and no one needs to know anything, OK?"

"Wait. Do you think I killed my partner or something?" Danny still wasn't moving.

"No." Mari's tone softened. "Tron killed your partner. He just plead guilty, remember? But that's the gun he used to kill him."

"Tron?" Danny exclaimed. "Who is Tron? I thought some kid called Wilson did it."

"Yes. That's his real name, but nobody calls him that. Everyone calls him Tron," Mari said.

"Oh great, so you two are close friends now?" Danny said.

"Shut up. You know that doesn't matter. I worked the case. That's my job. Now give me back Tron's gun," she said.

"This ain't Tron's gun," Danny said, shaking his head slowly. "And I guarantee that he didn't kill Mike with this."

"Yes he did, you psychotic delusional liar." Mari felt her teeth clench and remembered her dentist's scoldings the last time she went in. "This is my case and I know what happened."

"What the hell? Why is everyone calling me a liar tonight? I'm telling you, this gun didn't kill Mike. This is my gun," Danny said.

"Well, what, that gun's identical twin did it?" Mari said sarcastically.

"The gun that killed Mike looked like this?" Danny said.

"Quit blowing smoke." The games these people play, Mari thought. "Just take it out—slowly—and set it down."

"You're sure it looked like this?" Danny said.

"Goddamn it!" Mari was done playing. "Anyone with eyes can see that's the same gun. Don't make me do something you'll regret."

Danny's body remained frozen, but he started talking again, slowly. His voice had a fake, soothing quality to it that Mari didn't like. It was dangerous. It was better when he was yelling. She knew how to put down a raving dog if she had to. "OK," he said. "I'm going to take this gun out, and put it down, just like you asked. In fact, I'm going to show it to you while I do it. Is that OK? But can you please stop pointing your gun at me?"

"That's fine." Mari nodded. "Just do it slowly." She watched as Danny began to reach for the gun. He had probably cashed in a favor for someone to let him into evidence and look the other direction so he'd be able to pull the gun. They should really be more careful. Especially in important cases like this. Cops needed rules to protect themselves from themselves. The warehouse was a big mess and it wouldn't be that hard for someone to come in and pull a memento. Danny was the type who probably had the bullet from some kid he shot made into a necklace.

"Now I'm guessing this gun looks like whatever gun you found on Mike, but it ain't—"

"Slowly," Mari interrupted.

"I hear you, don't worry." Danny looked awkward as he held his half-buckled belt in place with one hand while pulling the gun out of his waistband with the other.

"How do you know what the murder weapon looks like, anyway?" Mari said.

"I don't know," Danny said. "Or at least I didn't until you told me. But I do know one thing: this is my gun." He paused and tried to capture her with his eyes. "You were right, though. It does have a twin." Danny grasped the gun, holding it carefully between his thumb and forefinger so she wouldn't think he was going to use it.

"Just give it back to me." Mari was barely listening to him now. Once he got talking, he was so cocky she could hardly stand it. She was so close to getting her evidence back, and that was all she cared about.

"Are you hearing what I'm saying?" Danny said. "There is another gun that looks exactly like this one. It does have a twin."

"Jesus, Danny. What kind of an idiot do you think I am? You expect me to believe that there are two guns that look exactly the same, and you two morons each coincidentally have one? Or *had* one," she corrected.

"Ain't no such thing as coincidences when it comes to me and Mike. We have the exact same gun because I gave it to him" Danny slowly laid the pistol on the bed so she could see the grip. "You got a good memory? Take a look at the serial number on this pistol. If you can remember Mike's, you'll see that it's off by one."

Why was this man still talking? Mari thought, as she cautiously looked at the pistol on the bed. She kept her own gun trained on Danny as he continued to talk. "Ever since Mike died, I've been carrying this one around with me. Stupid, I know. I'm like a fourteen-year-old girl wearing her boyfriend's sweater to bed. But it makes me feel better. Mari, I'm on your side here. I ain't lying to you. You can lower the gun now."

Mari begrudgingly lowered her gun. You have to give them something every now and then if you want to keep them talking. It was an essential part of the interrogation dance. She took a look at the gun Danny had placed in front of her. It looked exactly like the gun they had found behind Tron's place. And now Danny was saying there were two of them?

Things were starting to click into place in Mari's mind, and those things made her nervous.

SHE HAD NEVER LIKED HOW SHE'D FOUND THAT GUN. IT wasn't when they found all the other evidence, but the next morning. An anonymous phone call came in about a gun in a garbage can behind the house. It had seemed pretty much impossible that they hadn't found it the night before. Their search had been so thorough. In her dreams, she heard Cornelius's voice on the tip line saying where to find it, but when she checked the tapes, it wasn't his voice. But the gun popping up the next day had continued to unsettle her.

She had told herself that maybe they were just entering the next phase of the case: the part where the evidence stops making sense, and starts making trouble. It always seemed to happen that way. People think that the more you look at something, the clearer it's going to get, that with every new bit of information, you get closer to the truth, like a puzzle where every piece makes the picture clearer.

"The truth will come out!" they think. But that's not how it works. Sure, at first it does. At least in a normal case, you start out not knowing anything, and then as you learn more, it starts to make sense, and then once you've got enough evidence, you convict the bastard and you move on to the next one.

But with these heater cases, you can't stop just because you know who did it, the bosses and the brass insist that you dot every i and cross every t and follow every lead you can possibly think of until you've found "everything." Because everything is what people think they want.

But it's not.

It's not even possible. "Everything" surpasses what anyone can know and "everything" never ends, and instead of "everything" making the truth clearer, the opposite happens, the puzzle pieces stop fitting. Worse yet, "everything" suddenly includes stuff that makes no sense at all, like you accidentally grabbed some pieces from a different puzzle. Sure most of the wrong puzzle pieces don't fit, and they're just annoying, but sometimes, inexplicably, they do fit, and then not only is the picture getting all messed with weird unrelated pictures of another scene fitting into yours, but, you're event taking away spots where the right puzzle pieces are supposed to be.

Yet no one will let you throw the obviously wrong stuff out, because then you're a dirty cop 'throwing away evidence.' But you're not, you're just sorting things out, and throwing away what doesn't fit. But they won't let you, so you're stuck with these screwed up puzzle pieces, and the need to fit them somewhere where somewhere doesn't exist.

People want everything to line up nice and neat, and for all the loose ends to get pulled into the fabric. They want the world to look nice and pretty so they can say they understand it and sleep well in their beds at night. But if they're sleeping well at night, it's not because of the truth, it's because some cop figured out a good story in spite of the impossibilities.

So, like always, they were there again.

This damn double gun, appearing out of nowhere. You look hard enough, you try too much, and eventually, all the pieces that used to click right into place become scrambled. But prosecutors can't do anything with evidence that doesn't fit. It confuses juries. Of course, defense attorneys love it. But cops, they just learn to accept them as part of the job. Things don't make sense, and the more you know, the less you know, and those same gut instincts that were so essential to follow at the beginning of the case in order to figure out which of the thousands of leads to follow become just as important at the end of the case, as you need to figure out how to put it all together, bluff past the impossibilities, and turn a white lie into pure truth. In sum, you need to put a guilty man in jail because that is your goddamn job.

MARI LOOKED AT THE WEAPON DANNY HAD GINGERLY PLACED before her. As it so happened, she did remember the last three digits of the serial number. Not because she had a great memory, but because they were the same as her home telephone number growing up. (God, Mari hated all these coincidences.) Sure enough, the numbers were off by one.

"YOU gave this gun to Tron?" she said, barely believing it.

"Tron? I wouldn't give a gangbanger a gun, especially a beautiful gun like this one. I've never given this gun to anyone. It's mine. But I did give the matching one to Mike." Danny turned on her suddenly, like an animal that smelled blood. "How do you even claim to know it was Tron's gun, since I know for a fact it was Mike's? Sure is convenient for a detective to find the weapon in the back alley of the person they think did the crime."

So this was where he was going to take it. "Go screw yourself, Danny. I don't think Tron did it. I know he did it. Because he told me. He confessed on video, there's gunshot residue and blood on the clothes found in his house, and the blood has already come back as belonging to the superintendent. The case is over. It was over the night I brought it in. Not only did I not need that gun, but I wish it had never been found."

"Then why did you go back to the house the next day?" Danny demanded.

"An informant," she said.

"An informant?" Danny said. "Who?"

"None of your damn business," she said.

"It was that Washington kid." Danny had started pacing around, rubbing his fist into his palm. "I knew it. I knew it had something to do with my foot chase."

"Washington? You weren't chasing Cornelius, you idiot. Cornelius was in jail that whole time," she said.

"Cornelius? Who's talking about Cornelius? I'm talking about a young kid, I don't even know which part of the family he was from." As Danny was talking, the pieces were clicking together in his brain. "Cornelius was your informant?" She didn't confirm it, but she didn't deny it either. "Jesus. Ain't nothing good ever come from that family."

"I got the guy who did it. It was good info. That's something good." Mari wasn't sure who she was trying to convince.

"There's no way Mike would have lost that gun. He wanted it, asked for it." Danny was rubbing the stubble on his face now. "And that kid never mentioned wrestling the gun away from Mike?"

"No. He said it was his gun." Mari couldn't seem to stop herself from answering Danny's questions.

"Maybe someone else killed Mike and planted the gun at Tron's house?" Danny said.

"Why are you messing with my case?" Mari closed her eyes.

"Maybe Mike gave him the gun?" he said.

"Oh yeah," Mari replied sarcastically, "you don't think Tron would have mentioned that to me? That the cop was the one who gave him the weapon?"

"Maybe no one took the gun from him at all."

"So what," Mari glared at him in exasperation, "he just killed himself with it then?"

Danny thought about Mike saying he wanted an untraceable gun. He thought about how Kasper was always telling him his dad was such a phony.

"Danny?" Mari said. He could hear the annoyance in her voice.

He thought about Mike's family problems, the money, the haggard look on his face.

"Hey!" Mari said sharply. "Danny!"

He thought of the last five years and wondered whether, in all that time, Mike had even one friend that wasn't trying to get something out of him. Not once had Danny thought to pick up the phone and call him.

"Hey, asshole! Danny! You deaf? Why do you suddenly have so little to say?"

"I need a minute," he said.

"A minute?" she asked. "For what?"

"To think. I just need a minute to think," Danny said.

"Sure, great. Afterall, we're just hanging out here threatening each other with guns, no big deal, sweetie, take your time. But as long as you're thinking," she flopped down on the bed. "Why in the world were you fighting with that detective at the party last night?"

Danny's hand involuntarily went to his jaw, and he rubbed the spot that was still sore from wrestling with Felton the night before.

Felton. Some people couldn't help being assholes. It's like being tall or bald. It's just the way you are.

THE PARTY HAD BEEN GETTING LOUDER AND LOUDER. KASPER had been running around with his dad's urn, posing for pictures like it was the Stanley Cup. Really messed up, honestly. Danny half expected to see people doing shots out of the thing and drinking Mike's ashes as if they were the salt rim on a tequila glass.

Danny saw Kasper looking for him, but it wasn't hard to avoid him with the big crowd. Mike would have been horrified by the way Kasper was acting, and Danny could see the instability leaking out of Kasper's eyes. Danny had seen those eyes in the mirror for too many years to be seeing them now with Kasper. Danny pulled himself toward the outside of the crowd, nursing his drink.

And then Danny had heard someone behind him say, "Kid's a piece of work. I wouldn't want to go near him either."

Danny had turned around to see Felton following his gaze. Felton was leering drunk. Danny hadn't remembered him being so big. At least six foot three, and fat. He hadn't been that fat in the academy. Must be over three hundred pounds now.

"Mind your own business, Felton," Danny had said.

"Just like his father, that one." Felton was still dressed like a detective, but his brown suit was rumpled like he'd slept in it and there was a food stain on his left jacket pocket. "At least his son has the excuse of being drunk. But his dad never drank. He was just naturally a selfish prick. A criminal since the moment he got on the job—but you know that already."

"Shut your mouth, Felton. I'm pretty sure the only drunk asshole in this room is you."

"Oh, you wish I was drunk. You wish *you* were drunk. Yeah, that's right, I see your alcoholic ass crying into your drink 'cause your partner's dead and you're a little baby who can't handle his liquor."

"Felton, I'm not going to tell you again. Shut your mouth or I will shut it for you, right here in front of all these people."

Felton shook his head stupidly. "You and that dead partner of yours think you're so much better than everyone else. But he's lucky he's dead. These people only think he's a hero because I didn't get a chance to show them who he really was."

"You can't even spell *hero*, Felton."

"Yeah, whatever." Danny could smell Felton's breath and feel the spittle hitting his ear as Felton leaned in closer. "I got video on you. Both of you. I could bring you down just as easily as I was going to bring him down, only you're not even worth it. You're so broken down it'd be like getting a freebie from the neighborhood prostitute. I'd be afraid of getting some disease."

"You better step away from me, Felton. Your breath stinks."

"You wouldn't be tired of me after I put handcuffs on you and brought you to prison. After I took your pension."

"You ain't got nothing on me. And if you did, I'm sure you would have used it already," Danny said.

"Yeah, Mike talked tough too. But he realized what I could do and now he's dead. Coward," Felton said.

"A man's dead, and you're still jealous?" Danny said. "Pathetic."

"You're pathetic," Felton said. "I wish you had something worth taking. But you can't even take care of your family. I got no respect for someone who can't protect their kid so he gets killed on the street like some gangbanging piece of trash."

Danny remembered rearing back and hitting Felton. He meant to hit him right in the jaw. Break it. Shut his fat face up. But he missed. It ended up being a glancing blow that fell harmlessly into his shoulder. Felton had stepped back and dropped his drink. Everyone turned around and stared.

"That all you got?" Felton said, brushing some of the liquid from his jacket. "You really aren't a man anymore. And you don't know who I am. Try another."

Danny strode into him, throwing haymakers left and right, but Felton was like a mountain. He just absorbed everything. Danny tried grasping him in a bear hug, sweeping his right leg through the back of Felton's to throw him on the ground and start pummeling him. But Felton didn't move. Danny used all the strength in his body, but he might as well have been trying to flip over a house. Jesus that guy was strong. Finally, all Danny had left in him was to bring them both down. He leapt up, grabbed Felton around the neck, and hung onto his back like a squirrel on a giant. Screw this guy. He'd bring him down or die trying.

Felton had spun left, then right, until he stumbled backward and both of them fell onto a big table, breaking it in two. There was an enormous whooshing sound followed by a huge crack when they hit the floor. Danny meant to leap up then and get on top of Felton, but Felton was too quick. By the time Danny was up, Felton was up too, rubbing at his eyes. This was Danny's moment, his chance to hurl himself against Felton and stuff every word down his fat face.

But the thought of trying to bring Felton down a second time was too much for him. He was too tired to beat away the past.

By now, the crowd was pulling them apart. Danny offered token resistance, but really, he was glad to be saved from the humiliation of giving up. If only all the shouting had been able to drown out the memory of Felton's words.

"JESUS, DANNY, YOU GONE MUTE?" MARI WAS LIGHTLY shaking her head and shrugging her shoulders. "I never thought I'd have to pry any words out of you."

"Mari, it's time for me to go home. I shouldn't be here."

"Oh no. We're figuring this out," she said.

Danny was done. The truth had never done him any good. "Are you satisfied that this isn't your gun?" he said, gesturing toward the gun on the bed.

"No, I'm not. How am I to know that you didn't change the serial numbers? This twin guns thing is going to mess my case up royally. If I'm not sure who did it, how the hell am I supposed to convince a jury?" Mari had stood up and was putting on her shirt and pants.

"Mari, you know I didn't change the serial numbers. You know this is a different gun. I've told you what I know."

"Well, does that guy you were fighting with know too?" she asked.

Good question, Danny thought. "No. He doesn't know anything about this gun."

"But he knows about something, right?" she said. "That's why you were fighting."

"He was talking crap, Mari. At a memorial. That's why we were fighting."

"Memorial? Some memorial," she said.

"Yeah," Danny said.

There was a hum in the air from Mari's air conditioner. "No one knows about that gun, Mari."

"So you say," she said.

"We wouldn't have even known about it if you hadn't spotted it tonight," Danny said.

"True," she said.

"We shouldn't know about this gun," he said with finality.

"I wish we didn't," Mari said.

Danny looked at the gun. It was resting in the same spot where they'd made love only a few hours before. He thought about Mike. He thought about Mike's kids.

"I'll take care of it," he said.

"Take care of it?" Mari's heart froze.

"Yeah," Danny said, almost absentmindedly. "I'll take care of it." And with a clean quick economy of movement, Danny pocketed the gun.

"What do you think you're doing?" Mari ran around to his side of the bed. "This isn't your decision to make."

"I know." Danny was two hundred pounds. Not all muscle anymore, but still plenty strong enough to take care of this.

"You can't do this. This is my case," Mari said.

"I'm going home." Danny put on his jacket. "This gun ain't evidence, it's coincidence." He slipped on his shoes. He looked at Mari standing in front of the door. She seemed small. "But go ahead. You still got that gun in your hand." Mari looked at the gun in her hand, like it surprised her with its presence. "You think I'm escaping with important evidence? Go ahead and pull the trigger. You'll get away with it."

"Danny, we need to plan." she pleaded. "It can't just appear out of nowhere. We have to figure out where it fits."

"It doesn't fit anywhere," Danny said.

"It does. We can fit it in. We can figure it out," she said.

"I'm tired of trying to make things fit that don't." Mari had placed herself as if she was going to physically stop him from leaving, but he could see her heart wasn't in it. He slipped by easily. "I'm going home," Danny said, "to my family. That's where I'm supposed to be. This figuring stuff out . . . it doesn't really matter."

"Danny, *Mike* is your family. We need to set things right. You can't just leave."

Danny was in the hallway, his hand on the door, ready to slam it shut.

"Is he my family? Is he?"

CHAPTER TWELVE

R ip was walking down the same streets he'd walked down his entire life, only this time, they looked different. It was like the first time he'd worn glasses. He remembered putting them on, taking them off, looking at the world and then looking at it again. Marveling at the magic of sight and how the world looked crisper and cleaner than it ever had before.

He and Vicki had talked it over. They'd figured it out. It had taken them a long time, including a whole lot of yelling and crying and hugging (and then a whole lot more crying and yelling and hugging). But they'd decided that they couldn't let Tron rot in jail. The cop had killed himself, not Rip, and definitely not Tron.

At first, he and Vicki had gently probed each other to see if they could just do the simple thing: leave Tron where he was. Why should Rip throw himself into the flames for something that wasn't his fault? Leaving Tron in jail would allow them to live the lives they were supposed to live: college, jobs, money. Tron was never going to do any of those things anyway. And besides, Rip had never asked him to take the fall for him. And if Rip hadn't asked for it, could he really refuse it?

Plus, Cornelius would make it right by Tron's family. The simple fact of the matter was that Tron ending up in jail wouldn't come as a surprise to anybody, and it might end up being the best thing Tron had ever done for his family.

But the thing all those meditations left out was the baby. Their baby. It still put a soft hole in Rip's chest every time he thought about that. Rip knew it was one thing to imagine the two of them going off to college together without a baby. But with a baby? There wasn't any way they were going to raise a baby in some college town with a bunch of rich people looking at them like the welfare office just sprung a leak. Their baby (*their* baby!) needed his family. And their family was the neighborhood, and the neighborhood was their family. The only way they could do right by one was to do right by the other.

Vicki looked at the man she thought of as her husband: "Are you sure about this? Are *we* sure about this?"

"I think so," Rip said, cautiously, "We can't just wait around for the other shoe to drop. We have to drop it ourselves. Plus, like Grandma always said, 'The truth will set you free.'"

"That wasn't Grandma, Rip. That was Jesus."

"Really?" he asked, smiling goofily. It was so easy to smile now that he and Vicki were on the same team again.

"Oh for crying out loud, Rip. The Gospel of John."

"Jesus, John, Grandma . . . they all sound like the same thing to me!" Rip laughed.

"Well they aren't, Richard Washington." Vicki's hands were on her small hips, but she was laughing too. "And I'm pretty sure Grandma would prefer you cite the original."

"Maybe," Rip pondered, "but honestly, humility wasn't one of Grandma's most godly attributes. I think she'd be happy I learned it, regardless of who got credit."

Vicki shook her head and smiled. Rip's grandma was the best part of him, her father always said that. But still, some of Rip's stories about his grandma worried her.

"Rip, you used to say that your grandmother's . . . spirit . . . was with you. Is that still true?"

"I don't want to talk about it," Rip said, looking away.

"Why not?" she asked.

"Because I don't." Rip turned away from her completely.

Vicki looked at the back of him. When would it end? He was still shutting her out. Still keeping her separate from his family.

"Why won't you tell me what happened?" she asked.

"I did!" Rip replied, clenching his fists.

"No. You leave things out. Important things. Things I ought to know. If we're going to trust each other, we have to *actually* trust each other. We don't have to tell my father everything. He'll help us even if he thinks we're only telling him four-fifths of the truth. But we have to trust each other," she said.

"Vicki, I've told you the truth," Rip lied. "There's nothing left to tell. The only people I've got to talk to now is my family. They're the ones I haven't told anything to."

"You say your family, but what you really mean is that man, your brother," she said. "Why do you have to talk to Cornelius? I don't understand. My family can help you. My father will give you resources, counsel, a lawyer. Your brother will give you nothing but hatred and a sword. He will call you a fool and try to talk you out of everything you know is right. Talk you out of what we've already agreed to."

"But that's exactly why I have to talk to him. If I can't stand up to him now, when am I ever going to?" he asked.

"Has it not occurred to you that he's probably the one who put Tron in jail in the first place? That he will lie, cheat, and kill for his benefit, and he might do the same to you once he learns you're going to start speaking the truth?" she asked.

"I have thought of that. But I also talked to Tron. People think he's dumb, but he's not. He knows what he's doing. Tron might have done what Cornelius wanted him to do, but he did it voluntarily. He's not a sucker," Rip said.

"If he's not the sucker here, then who is?" Vicki looked at him pointedly.

"Vicki, I am not the fool here. I have to do what I have to do, and I have to know that I can do it myself. In spite of my family. Don't you see? I have to challenge him in order to win. If I can't do that now, I will never be able to stand tall in this neighborhood."

Vicki remembered the long-ago warnings of her mother: to fear this boy and his family. She remembered the long-ago prayers of her father: to love this boy *and* his family. All these years later, the warnings, the temptations, the redemptions— they would all have to occur in order to make her family, and Rip, whole.

Oh how Vicki longed to speak to her mother. To learn anew the things Momma had told her, to hear the things Momma had never said. Vicki missed her so much. Her father was a beautiful man, but in some ways, the strength of his hope canceled out his ability to understand anything else. Can a man who only sees hope be expected to understand darkness, let alone defeat it? But Momma was gone. Taken. The world is what the Lord has wrought, and we must understand the riddles he has left for us, in order to learn his will. Vicki would have to make her own decisions, with nothing but the foolish thoughts of her husband to guide her.

"Fine. I am going to trust you and I am going to let you go to your family. But just this one, last time. Promise? Do you promise me, Richard Washington?"

"I promise, Victoria. With all my heart, with everything I've got. Right after I tell my family, I will come home to you. Then we'll go to your father and I will never leave your side again."

Vicki watched as he stood up, smiled, and kissed her. She smiled too. She couldn't help it. Why did she have to smile at Rip even when she wanted nothing more than to push him down to the ground and talk some sense into him? She watched Rip walk out the door, smiling and happy. She hated that her mind flitted back to the image of the last time she had sent him back to his family, in a blood-stained shirt and with shame in his eyes. She wondered what he would look like the next time she saw him.

RIP FELT CALM WALKING BACK TO THE HOUSE. CHILL, EVEN. Eerily chill for a man who was about to confront his brother and then confess to the police that they had the wrong guy, that he was the one who had held the gun when the cop died.

But he had done nothing wrong. Doing the right thing had to be right. The truth would set him free. Reflexively, he looked for Grandma. She had always been there to give him counsel or nod sagely, to let him know that what he was doing was the right thing. But Grandma wasn't there. She was with Cornelius. Now that Rip was doing the right thing and walking the narrow path, shouldn't she return to him?

Of course he was lying to Vicki: he was only partly going back to confront Cornelius. Really, he was going home to tell Grandma. She would be the one he'd be looking to for approval. Only now, the only way to tell Grandma anything was to also tell Cornelius.

The other little lie he'd told Vicki, the one Rip knew she probably knew about, was that he had learned more about why the police had stopped him in the first place. When he'd last gone back to the house to get some stuff, he'd seen police reports lying around. Cornelius must have gotten them some-how. The police hadn't stopped him by accident. Someone had called them. Someone snitched. Who would do that to him?

Rip looked up to see one of Tron's brothers, Simeon, watching him. Rip had been avoiding Tron's family. Avoiding the whole block. Coming from the other direction just so he wouldn't see them. Not answering any of their messages. But now, just when he had figured everything out, just when he was going to make everything right, he had lost his head and was walking right by the very place he'd been avoiding.

"I've been watching for you, Rip," Simeon said, coming down from the porch and taking long strides to catch up to him.

Rip kept his head low. Quickened his pace. Tron's brother sped up too.

"I said," Simeon repeated, "I've been watching for you."

Rip looked at him. He could see the tendons in Simeon's hands flexing and releasing.

"I'm just going home," Rip said.

"Yeah. That's right," Simeon said, looking down at Rip. He was the tallest in his family, and he had at least six inches on Rip. "Running home."

"I'm not running. I'm just going home," Rip said.

"You think Tron's coming home?" Simeon said. "You think Tron gets to go home?"

Rip closed his eyes, hunkered down. He wished he had his hoodie on. He'd be tougher then. He wished he was Cornelius. Nobody dared mess with Cornelius. But really, more than anything, he just wished he knew what to do. The plan had seemed so clear when he was discussing it with Vicki. For some reason, they had forgotten to factor in Tron's family.

Should he turn around, punch Simeon in the face? Should he run? Should he apologize? Rip quickened his pace, praying it would all just go away.

"I'm going to make it right," Rip said to Simeon. "I'm going home to make it right."

"What do you think you can make right?" Simeon grunted.

Cornelius's advice rang in Rip's ears: show no fear; never blink; remember that you own this place and you own these people. But Rip couldn't follow that advice.

"Ain't nothing you can make right, Rip," Simeon said. "Not when you're the one who done wrong."

"I didn't do anything wrong," Rip said.

Rip was only three houses from home. He looked toward his house to see whether he could see anyone. Cornelius, Grandma, anyone. Was anyone there to help him?

"You did do wrong, Rip," Simeon said, "and you ain't going home."

Simeon grabbed at Rip's arm. Rip yanked it away and watched as Simeon reached into his pocket. Rip didn't need to see the gun to know it was there. Rip turned, hunched over, covered his face.

He ran.

~

RIP YEARNED FOR THE YELLS OF HIS FAMILY. HE CRIED FOR THE ghosts of his ancestors. Even the cackling of the Corner Boys, this too he longed to hear. But there was nothing, only silence.

The silence was broken by the slow, methodical crack of gunfire, each like a church bell.

Rip felt each precise punch to his body: twice to his leg, once to his lower back, twice to his shoulder blades, once to his hand as he reached out to stop the pain.

The last thing he saw was the cold gray concrete as his face met the ground, his eyelashes unblinking against the grime. He mourned, very much, the bright limitless sky above him that he would never see again.

EPILOGUE

Victoria addressed her congregation. The subject did not matter. To be loved was to be loved fully. They would love her even if she spoke to them in pig latin. What mattered to her people, she thought, was herself. She had planned to stay away for one year. She thought it would be too painful to be here. But she hadn't even lasted one semester. This church was where she was supposed to be, and it called to her. First, she came back once a month. Then, once a week. After that, it was every day she didn't have classes. Finally, she had given up and transferred to a college closer to home. Now she found herself in church almost every day. Most evenings too.

Although the subject of her speech didn't matter, other things did—the cadence, the energy, the emotion—people needed those. But the words? Hardly at all. Victoria wondered if she'd been disrespectful in thinking about pig latin. But was that really any different than speaking in tongues? And cannot tongues say a thing when even words fail?

Her father was behind her, resplendent in his robes yet shrunken like a dried husk of corn. His brokenness annoyed her. Rip wasn't even his son. He was just a boy who had got himself killed like so many other boys before him. Yet her father had allowed Rip's death to diminish him, while his own flesh and blood stood before him, leading the church that he was failing to pastor.

She looked at her son in Mo-ma's lap, in the bosom of the church she loved. It had surprised everyone when Rip's family's church had joined her own congregation. The two Christian bodies had stood in righteous rivalry for fifty years, and Victoria would have thought that even the last dying member of one church would have opted to worship alone rather than join the other. But Mo-ma had said it was time, and so it had happened. The people had come. Rip's death and the birth of their child had formed a medieval marriage, bringing two warring countries together where documents and treaties never could.

It was to this new, united church that Victoria gave herself. She had managed to bring back—in a single summer—the energy, courage, and hope that had been dying for two generations. And in return, this church gave Victoria back the life she was meant to lead. As Richard Jr.—beautiful, kind, happy—was passed from mother to mother and lap to lap like a puppy, Victoria wanted, with every fiber of her being, to gather her son up in her arms and swallow him whole. But she knew that if she let that happen, it would stifle her drive, and the work she had to do would be left undone. She had chosen the church. And the church would therefore have to raise her child.

So she left her boy with Mo-ma and Mo-ma's sisters and Mo-ma's nieces and Mo-ma's friends and Mo-ma's family and Mo-ma's church. And everyone raised her boy in his father's house and his mother's church, and no boy in the history of the world had received more gifts, time, and love than this boy received from the congregants around him.

But sometimes it pained her that she didn't know her baby. In moments of weakness, she would give in and hold him, and his body would shake, and his eyes would flicker away from her, and thank God, because if he looked at her she would surely melt.

But he clearly feared her, especially when she held him. Instead of looking at her, he would look to the half dozen other women who surrounded him. Victoria knew that it was better this way.

She knew she wasn't the first woman in this neighborhood to lose a son, and that this was about the softest way possible for it to have happened, but her loss was to save other mothers from their own losses, and that comforted her. If fewer mothers could avoid losing their sons because of what she was doing, her sacrifice would be worth it. She could still look at him and know that the world she was creating would be his to inherit.

But it was not for him that she was creating it. She would not be one of those women—those centuries of women—who had laid down their own lives for a man's improvement. She did not live for this boy, and knowing the church was here to care for him was what allowed her to live for this church, this people, and this neighborhood—the soil that must nourish them all.

For her people were leaving the soil. Her flock was in diaspora. They were born here, but they no longer lived here. She had to gather them back. If not the elders, who were too far gone and tired and weak, then at least the youth. She could not allow them to flee the neighborhood every day except Sunday. Sunday was the day of rest, but that meant they must work the other six. The city on the hill must have a hill.

Victoria would gather the sheep, she would gather the wolves, and then she would bring them in and raise them up and give birth to the garden her father had always dreamed of. But unlike her father, she would not just dream it—she would live it.

Her eyes landed on Cornelius. Why was he here, amongst

her flock? She stared at him. Hate was a sin, but she felt it flow through her blood like alcohol. She could not welcome this man who had killed her husband—his own brother. Even if he hadn't been the one to pull the trigger, everyone knew it. Every week he came here and sat down and looked at his nephew. He had no right.

The congregation had tried to welcome him, but his mere presence was radioactive. Anyone who tried to sit close to him was driven off. He was like a cancer, a dead zone in the ocean. She hated him as she had never hated anyone. Still he came. He came with his presence and her hatred grew.

How could she fulfill her calling with this man here? How could she build a city when a barbarian lies within its gates? She sighed. Rip had always been haunted by the ghosts of his family, and now his brother haunted the lives of those who remained. Victoria looked at her flock: loving, growing, singing. This man, though he was made of flesh and blood, was just another ghost. He was not real. She would overcome.

CORNELIUS SAW THE FLASH IN VICTORIA'S EYES WHEN THEY met his own. He admired the hatred. Even more so because she didn't make even the slightest attempt to hide it. Damn, he thought. Good for her. He'd probably hate himself too, if he was in her shoes. But he wasn't. He had his own shoes to fill.

And what fine-looking shoes they were. Cornelius leaned back in the pew. Stretched his arm across the top of the bench like he was putting his arm around the hottest girl in the club.

Only, there wasn't any girl. It was just him.

At least as far as anyone else could see. But in fact, he was never alone anymore. He was surrounded by the ghosts of uncles and aunts and grandmas and grandpas and great-grandpas and great-grandmas and who-the-hell-else-knows-what-kind-of-first-and-second-twice-removed-cousins   that surrounded him. It was like a never-ending family reunion picnic. Jesus, he thought, the whole clan? The whole family, rooting about in his business and covering him with mud?

But no, he checked himself, it wasn't the whole family. It was just the proper ones, the church people, the ones Cornelius remembered filling the house when he was a boy. The other ones, the rest of the family, Cornelius was pretty sure he knew where they were, and he was pretty sure none of them were going to be allowed to visit. No doubt Cornelius would end up there too.

Just as well. It was hard for him to respect these church people. It didn't matter whether he was supposed to or not.

He looked at them. A big, noisy, cackling flock of geese sporting hats and suits like they were in some old movie from a hundred years ago, one of those black-and-white things where there wasn't any sound. Instead of sound, there was the occasional insert of a screen with text about what they were supposed to be saying. And what those aggravating fools were constantly saying to him was this:

Stop being so rude.

Be nice to that lady.

Sit up straight in church.

Sit up straight in church!

Grandma had been nagging at him to go to church ever since Rip died. Needless to say, he didn't pay her no mind. But after a few weeks of being ignored, Grandma got tired of it and decided she needed reinforcements. And boy did she bring them. First, an occasional cousin he vaguely remembered from back in the day, then a great-aunt he'd only seen in photos. Finally, at least once a day she started dragging out ghosts that she had probably never even met. They had to be family, though, seeing as how they looked like Cornelius. But based on their old-fashioned dress, they must have been kin from a few generations prior.

By now, there had to be at least forty of them. And they

never left him alone. Each and every one of them spent the whole day stomping about and silently yelling and holy rolling around on the floor until Cornelius didn't know what to do with himself.

In the end, Grandma won, like she always did. Screw it, he figured. He'd go to church just to make them shut up. And besides, he wanted to lay eyes on that woman who had gone and stolen his family's church.

Victoria. What was a nineteen-year-old kid doing leading a thousand-person congregation anyway? And what gave her the ability to lure Mo-ma from the church she was born into and had surely intended to be buried in? He'd been sitting there watching Victoria, figured he'd intimidate her, but it didn't take. And every week, there were more and more people filling up the pews.

At least there was one good thing about the ghosts: they gave him space. The forty of them crowded around him so tightly that they didn't leave any room for the living.

But oh how the living tried. They'd cozy up next to him, not realizing that they were sitting right on top of the ghost of Great-Aunt Gertrude. And Great-Aunt Gertrude did not appreciate it.

Turns out all the ghosts seemed to be able to give any living creatures that touched them a jolt of electricity, and if you violated their church pew, which was now Cornelius's church pew by reason of abdication, they didn't hesitate to give a little shock to whoever was trying to sit there until the person got the message and moved on.

So at least he had his space.

He liked the privacy. And even though he knew that the power didn't come from him, nobody else knew that, and Cornelius believed the attribution of power is almost as good as the thing itself.

Rip's ghost looked at him, and Cornelius nodded back.

Screw you, Rip, he thought to himself.

If Rip had been smart enough to listen, he wouldn't be dead. Then he'd be the one dealing with these goddamn ghosts instead of Cornelius. Rip should be the one living in Grandma's house and raising his own child.

Not that Cornelius still lived there. Goddamn Reverend Victoria thought she had kicked him out, but she hadn't. He had decided to leave as a gift to his nephew. It was right that the boy should be raised in the house of his ancestors.

Rip's ghost looked at him a little more loosely now, head tilted to the side, questioning, suspicioning, or reckoning— Cornelius wasn't sure which.

Yeah, that's right, baby ghost brother, Cornelius thought. I could have stayed and fought and won, and then I'd be sleeping in your house with your cute little wife thinking about me every night. But turns out I'm a chivalrous son of a bitch. Who knew? And I was tired of the place anyway. There's plenty of females happy to put me up for as long as I want.

But don't kid yourself, Rip, Cornelius thought. I've still got it. Anytime I want. I'll come back home. I'll take control. This world is mine. Never forget.

Cornelius watched as Rip's ghost eyes narrowed in anger. "Fine, fine. Don't you worry, little brother. I won't. I promise." Cornelius had already made a promise to Grandma, and now he made the same one to Rip: That boy will be protected, just like you were protected, but better. Maybe I've even learned a few tricks from you and I'll lay back and let that prissy little girlfriend of yours think she's running the show. But mark my words, ghost. I am here. I ain't going away, and if I want, I will take back what is mine.

Cornelius heard a peel of laughter coming from the front of the church. The fricking nephew. He was the one who ruled this roost. Mo-ma was trying to hush him, but Richard Jr. was jumping up and down, opening a hymnal and then slamming it closed, enjoying the banging sound it made with every shut. That spoiled little brat: a prince at home and a pope at church. Lucky little bastard. But happy. Cornelius liked that. He'd never seen a happy baby before.

RICHARD JR. SENSED UNCLE CORNELIUS LOOKING AT HIM AND he looked up. Their eyes met. Richard Jr. quickly looked away, like he was supposed to. Richard Jr. wasn't allowed to talk to Uncle Cornelius, and even if he were, Uncle Cornelius scared him.

Richard Jr. wondered why Uncle Cornelius always sat alone. He never saw him speak with anyone else either.

But today, there was a new man standing next to Uncle Cornelius. He shimmered in the air, almost like he wasn't really there. Richard Jr. could see right through him. He looked at him a little closer and saw that he looked a lot like Uncle Cornelius, but even more so, like himself.

Richard Jr. looked into the man's eyes and saw that they were kind, sparkling, full of intelligence, laughter, and hope. There was a slight downturn of his eyes that showed he was sad too, but only a little. Richard Jr. looked at this man and knew he would be with him for the rest of his life. His mother, his church, his family, his neighborhood... this man. they would never leave him.

Richard Jr. looked into the eyes of his father, and he smiled.

ACKNOWLEDGMENTS

The classic phrase is: if I have seen so further it is by standing on the shoulders of giants. But with apologies to Isaac Newton, one sees further standing on the shoulders of very tiny persons as well. I have been assisted by giants, small persons, occasional strangers, and so many more that have lent me a helping hand or a sympathetic ear.

I would particularly like to thank my mother and father who raised me. My sisters, Karen and Lynn who have always been there for me. My children, Will and Mathilda and Nicola who have been everything I ever wanted (and are definitely inspiring editors). The writing professionals who lent me their skill, Hadley and Abby and Lisa. Idilia who lent me her artistry, Clancy who helped me to record, and to all the people who read my drafts and shared their thoughts: Aaron, Amy, Angela, Jon, Missy, Patrick, Rita, Tom, and a bunch of other people I've forgotten about.

And of course, most of all, best of all, to Family.

ABOUT THE AUTHOR

Carl Wasielewski is the father of the three most glorious children in the entire world. He lives in Chicago and has been a cop for twenty years. This is his first novel.